Rio takes a long look at Strand. How odd that she feels she can study him more closely now than before. There is something so unguarded about him now. He's vulnerable, Rio realizes, and there is a rush of sympathy, but along with the sympathy comes a less creditable emotion.

He looks weak.

Rio stands up. Everyone, the two other flyers and her own squad, even Greer, are looking at her. No . . . looking *to* her. She's in charge, even with Strand here, even with his crew, both of whom are senior NCOs.

The moment is heady and disturbing. It's exciting, thrilling even, and yet drops a ton of weight on her shoulders. She almost feels her boots sinking deeper into the dirt.

SILVER STARS

A FRONT LINES NOVEL #2

MICHAEL GRANT

 KATHERINE TEGEN BOOKS
An Imprint of HarperCollins Publishers

Photo credits for glossary: C-47, DUKW—Duck,
Focke-Wulf 190, Betty Grable, Supermarine Spitfire: public domain;
German half-track: ShareAlike 3.0 (CC BY-SA 3.0 DE)

Katherine Tegen Books is an imprint of HarperCollins Publishers.

Silver Stars

www.epicreads.com

Library of Congress Control Number: 2016938948
ISBN 978-0-06-234219-5

Typography by Joel Tippie
17 18 19 20 21 PC/LSCH 10 9 8 7 6 5 4 3 2 1
❖
First paperback edition, 2018

*Dedicated to 1st Lt. Shaye Haver
and Capt. Kristen Griest.*

DATE DUE

They are saying, "The generals learned their lesson in the last war. There are going to be no wholesale slaughters." I ask, how is victory possible except by wholesale slaughters?

—Evelyn Waugh, 1939

1943

Three great Axis powers: Germany, Italy, and Japan. Italy's Benito Mussolini began as Hitler's mentor, but after failure upon failure it has become clear that Mussolini's Italy lacks the resources and the will to fight effectively. The war in Europe will be fought between the Allies and Germany, with Mussolini more a hindrance than a help.

For too long Britain stood alone while the Soviet Union's paranoid dictator, Stalin, purged his own army and worked backroom deals with the Nazis to seize Finland and divide Poland. But in one of the great mistakes of history, Hitler attacked Stalin. The Soviet Union's vast size, terrible winter, and the astonishing courage and endurance of its people have proven too much, even for the Wehrmacht.

And now, thanks to the Japanese bombing of Pearl Harbor, the United States of America is in the fight, bringing staggering industrial might and a military that will, in just a few short years, go from being a negligible force of 334,000 to a 12-million-strong juggernaut.

In the Pacific, the US Marines have survived a protracted living nightmare on Guadalcanal. Japanese expansion is halted. Australia and New Zealand are safe, but China, the Philippines, and Southeast Asia still bleed under brutal Japanese occupation.

In Europe, the Soviet Red Army has fought the German Wehrmacht to a halt at Stalingrad. Hitler's mad order allowing no retreat will lead to the death of a third of a million Germans and Romanians and the surrender of 91,000 more. The greatest tank battle in history will be fought at a place called Kursk, and by dint of sheer numbers and steely determination, the Soviet T-34 tanks will beat the German panzers back.

London is still struggling to recover from the Blitz, and now German cities cringe beneath falling bombs. In Poland, the Jews who had been herded into the ghetto to be starved to death rise up against their Nazi oppressors and, despite great heroism, are exterminated.

The Americans, British, British Commonwealth, and Free French forces have pushed the Nazis out of North Africa. Benito Mussolini is weakened and discredited but not yet destroyed.

No one is certain about the next objective, including Allied leadership.

The Germans have been bloodied, but Nazi Germany is very far from beaten. And in places called Dachau, Bergen-Belsen, Buchenwald, and Auschwitz, the killing gas still flows and the ovens still burn hot.

Prologue

107TH EVAC HOSPITAL, WÜRZBURG, GERMANY—APRIL 1945

Welcome back, Gentle Reader, welcome back to the war.

I've got quite a pile of typed pages now, quite a pile, and I'm not even a third of the way through. But I've already got some readers, some of the people here in this hospital with me, and, well, they've stopped complaining about me being up typing at all hours. So I guess I'll keep at it.

I'm still not quite ready to tell you who I am. I'm not being coy or cute, I just find it easier to write about all of it, even my own part, as if it happened to someone else. And if I put myself forward, you might start thinking of me as the hero of the story. I can't allow that because I know better. I know who the heroes are and who the heroes were, and I am neither. I'm just a shot-up GI sitting here typing and trying not to scratch the wound on my chest, which, dammit, feels like I've got a whole colony of ants in there. I suppose this means I'll never be able to wear a bathing suit or a plunging neckline. That will bother me someday, but right now, looking around this ward at my fellow soldier girls, and at the soldier boys across the hall, I'm not feeling the urge to complain.

I hear civilians saying we're all heroes, heard someone . . . was it Arthur Godfrey on Armed Forces Radio? I can't recall, but it's nonsense anyway. If everyone is a hero, then no one is. Others say everyone below ground is a hero, but a lot of those were just green kids who spent an hour or a day on the battlefield before standing up when they shouldn't have, or stepping where they shouldn't have stepped. If there's something heroic about standing up to scratch your ass and having some Kraut sniper ventilate your head, I guess I don't see it.

If by "hero," you mean one of those soldiers who will follow an order to rush a Kraut machine gun or stuff a grenade in a tank hatch, well, that's closer to meaning something. But the picture in your imagination, Gentle Reader, may not bear much similarity to reality. I knew a guy who did just that—jumped up on a Tiger tank and dropped a grenade (or was it two?) down the hatch. Blew the hell out of it too. But he'd just gotten a Dear John letter from his fiancée in the same batch of mail that informed him his brother had been killed. So I guess it was right on the line between heroism and suicide.

Don't take me for a cynic, though; I am not cynical

about bravery. There are some real heroes, some gold-plated heroes, here on this ward with me. There are still more lined up in rows beneath white crosses and Stars of David in Italy and France, Belgium, Holland . . . And some of them were friends of mine.

Oh boy, it's hard to type once I get teary. Goddammit, I'll just take a minute here. . . .

Anyway, my feeling bad doesn't raise any of those people from the grave.

They brought some wounded Krauts in today, four of them. They're in a separate ward of course, but I saw them through the window, saw the ambulance, dusty olive green with a big red cross on its roof. It wasn't easy to tell that they were Germans at first—they were more bandage than uniform—but even through the dingy window glass I could make out that one still had some medals pinned to his tunic. Not our medals. So I guess he was a hero too, just on the wrong side.

I hope the medals give that Kraut some comfort because he was missing both legs above the knee and his right hand was gone as well. I saw his face. He was a handsome fellow, movie star handsome, I thought, with a wide mouth and perfectly straight Aryan nose and dark, sunken eyes. I knew the eyes. I didn't know the Kraut, but yeah, I sure knew that look. I see it when I look in the mirror, even now. If you stay too long in the war, it's like your eyes try to get away, like they're sinking down, trying to hide, wary little animals crawling into the cave of your eye sockets.

No, not like animals, like GIs. There's nothing a soldier knows better than squatting in the bottom of a hole. Cat Preeling wrote a poem about it, which I'll probably mangle, but here's what I recall:

Dig it deep and in you creep,
While all around there's the boom-boom sound.
Mud to your knees while your buddy pees.
Another hole, like the hole before . . .

Yeah, that's all I remember. It goes on for a couple dozen verses.

Anyway, I still type away at this battered old typewriter, and some of the girls come by and take a few pages to read when they're tired of the magazines the USO gets us. They seldom talk to me about it; mostly they just read, and after a while they bring the pages back and maybe give me a nod. That's my proof that I'm writing the truth because sure as hell I'd hear about it if I started writing nonsense. We soldier girls—sorry, I mean Warrior Women or American Amazons or whatever the hell the newspapers are calling us now—we've had about enough of people lying about us. The folks who hate the idea of women soldiers tell one set of lies, the people who like the notion of women at war tell a different set of lies. If you believe the one side, we're nothing but a drag on the men, and the other side acts like we won the war all by ourselves.

We could probably get a pretty good debate going here on the women's ward over the question of which set of lies we hate more—the one denies what we've done; the other belittles what our brothers have done.

We won't have either.

We women are a red flag to the traditionalists—which is to say 90 percent of the military. But as much as we don't want to be, the truth is we're a symbol to people who think it's about time for women and coloreds too to stand equal. Woody Guthrie wrote that song about us. Count yourself lucky you can't hear me singing it under my breath as I type.

> Our boys are all a-fightin' on land, sea, and air,
> But say, some of them boys ain't boys at all,
> Why, some of those boys got pretty long hair.
> It may surprise, but I can tell you all,
> When it comes to killin' Nazis, our girls stand tall,
> And Fascist supermen die every bit as fast,
> From bullets fired by a tough little lass.

For our part, we sure as hell did not want to be a symbol of anything, though we did sort of like Woody's song. We wanted exactly what every soldier who has ever fought a war in foreign lands wants: we wanted to go home. And if we couldn't go home, then by God we wanted hot food, hot showers, cold beer, and to sleep in an actual bed for about a week solid.

But we're just GIs, and no one gives a damn what a GI wants, male or female.

Tunisia, Sicily, Italy, France, Belgium, Germany. Vicious little firefights you've never heard of and great battles whose names will echo down through history: Kasserine. Salerno. Monte Cassino. Anzio. D-Day. The Bulge. About all I missed was Anzio, and thank whatever mad god rules the lives of soldiers for keeping us out of that particular hell. There's a woman here, a patient on the ward, who was a nurse at Anzio. All she ever does is stare at her hands and cry. Though the funny thing is, she can still play a pretty good game of gin rummy. Go figure.

Whatever the newspapers tell you, we women are neither weak sisters nor invincible Amazons. We're just GIs doing our job, which after Kasserine we'd begun to figure out meant a single thing: killing Germans.

So, Gentle Reader, we come now to a period of time after Kasserine, when those truths were percolating inside us. We were coming to grips with what we were meant to do, what we were meant to be, what we had no choice but to become. We were girls, you see, not even women, just girls, most of us when we started. And the boys were just boys, not men, most of them. We'd only just begun to live life, we knew little and understood less. We were unformed, incomplete. It's funny how easy it is to see that now. If you'd called me a child three years ago when this started I'd have been furious. But looking back? We were children just getting ready to figure out what adulthood was all about.

It's a hell of a thing when a person in that wonderful, trembling moment of readiness is suddenly yanked sharply away from everything they've ever known and is handed over to drill sergeants and platoon sergeants and officers.

"Ah, good, the youngster is learning that her purpose is to kill."

Yeah, we figured that out, and we knew by then how to be good army privates. We could dig nice deep holes; we could follow orders. We knew how to unjam an M1, we knew to take care of our feet, we knew how to walk point on patrol. Mostly we knew what smart privates always figure out: stick close to your sergeant, because that's your mama, your daddy, and your big brother all rolled into one.

But here's one of the nasty little twists that come in war: if you don't manage to get wounded or die, they'll promote you. And then, before you're even close to ready, you are the sergeant. You're the one the green kids are sticking to, and you're the only thing keeping those fools alive. Right when you start to get good at following, they want you to lead.

Some of us made that leap, some didn't. Not every good private makes a good sergeant.

But enough of all that; what about the war itself? Shall I remind you where we were in the narrative, Gentle Reader?

After Kasserine, the army in its wisdom got General Frendendall the hell away from the shooting war, and it turned the mess over to General George Patton, "Old Blood-and-Guts." He and his British counterpart, General Montgomery, finished off the exhausted remains of the German Afrika Korps and their Italian buddies and sent General Rommel back to Hitler to explain his failure.

Everyone knew North Africa had just been the first round; we knew we were moving on, but we didn't know where to. Back to Britain to prepare for the final invasion? To Sardinia? Greece? The South of France? Being soldiers, we lived on scuttlebutt, none of it accurate.

Turned out the first answer was Sicily.

Sicily is a big, hot, dusty, stony, hard-hearted island that's been conquered by just about every empire in the history of the Mediterranean: Athenians, Carthaginians, Phoenicians, Romans, Normans, you name it, and now it was our turn to conquer it. And damned if we didn't just do it.

This is the story of three young women who fought in the greatest war in human history: Frangie Marr, an undersized colored girl from Tulsa, Oklahoma, who loved animals; time after time she ran into the thick of the fight, not to kill but to save lives. Rainy Schulterman, a Jewish girl from New York City with a gift for languages and a ruthless determination to destroy Nazis. And Rio Richlin, an underage white farm girl from Northern California who could not manage her love life and never was quite sure why she was in this war, not until we reached the camps anyway, but she could sure kill the hell out of Krauts.

They didn't win the war alone, those three, nor did the rest of us, but we all did our part and we didn't disgrace ourselves or let our brothers and sisters down, which is all any soldier can aspire to.

That and getting home alive.

PART I

1

"What was it like?" Jenou asks. "That first time? What did you feel?"

Rio Richlin sighs wearily.

Rio and Jenou Castain, best friends for almost their entire lives, lie faceup on a moth-eaten green blanket spread over the hood of a burned-out German half-track, heads propped up against the slit windows, legs dangling down in front of the armor-covered radiator. The track is sleeker than the American version, lower in profile, normally a very useful vehicle. But this particular German half-track had been hit by a passing Spitfire some weeks earlier, so it is riddled with holes you could stick a thumb into. The bogie wheels driving the track are splayed out, and both tracks have been dragged off and are now in use as a relatively clean "sidewalk" leading to the HQ administrative tent.

The road might once have been indifferently paved

3

but has now been chewed to gravel by passing tanks, the ubiquitous deuce-and-a-half trucks, jeeps, half-tracks, bulldozers, and tanker trucks. It runs beside a vast field of reddish sand and loose gravel that now seems to have become something like a farm field with olive drab tents as its crop. The tents extend in long, neat rows made untidy by the way the tent sides have all been rolled up, revealing cots and sprawled GIs in sweat-soaked T-shirts and boxer shorts. Here and there are extinguished camp-fires, oil drums filled with debris, other oil drums shot full of holes and mounted on rickety platforms to make field showers, stacks of jerry cans, wooden crates, and pallets—some broken up to feed the fires.

The air smells of sweat, oil, smoke, cordite, and cig-arettes, with just a hint of fried Spam. There are the constant rumbles and coughing roars of passing vehicles, and the multitude of sounds made by any large group of people, plus the outraged shouts of NCOs, curses and blasphemies, and more laughter than one might expect.

At the edge of the camp some men and one or two women are playing softball with bats, balls, and gloves assembled from family care packages. It's possible that the rules of this game are not quite those of games played at Yankee Stadium, since there is some tripping and tack-ling going on.

Both Rio and Jenou wear their uniform trousers rolled

up to above the knee, and sleeveless olive drab T-shirts. Cat Preeling, fifty feet away and playing a game of horseshoes with Tilo Suarez, is the only female GI with the nerve to strip down to bra and boxers. She's a beefy girl with a cigarette hanging from her downturned mouth. Tilo, like many of the off-duty men, wears only his boxers and boots, showing off a taut, olive-complected body that Jenou would be watching much more closely if only Tilo were six inches taller.

The bra and boxers look is a bit too daring for Rio and Jenou, but Cat seems to have a way of deflecting unwanted male attention, like she's wearing a sign that reads: Don't bother. Even the ever-amorous Tilo is content to toss horseshoes with her, though the shoes in question are actually brass rings roughly cut from discarded 155 brass and the peg is a bayonet.

Rio and Jenou both have brown-tanned faces, necks, and forearms, but the rest of them blazes a lurid white with just a tinge of pink where the skin is beginning to burn.

"What was what like?" Rio repeats the question slowly. She has a wet sock laid over her eyes to afford some shade. There is a half-empty bottle of Coca-Cola beside her. It was almost cold once and now is the temperature of hot tea. Jenou has a book held up to block the sun, *The Heart Is a Lonely Hunter*, in a paperback edition.

It is the summer of 1943 in Tunisia, and it is hot. Desert hot. Completely immobile—except when they swat at a fly—both young women are still sweating.

"You know," Jenou insists. "The first time. I'm just trying to get an idea."

"What are you, writing a book?" Rio says sharply. "Suddenly you're reading books and now you're trying to plumb the depths of my soul?"

"My usual appetite for fashion and Hollywood gossip isn't being satisfied," Jenou says, adopting a light, bantering lilt before restating her question in a more serious tone.

Rio sighs. "I don't know, Jen." She pronounces the name with a soft *j*, like *zh*. Jenou's name is inspired by the word *ingenue*, a perfectly inappropriate reference point for Jenou, who is far from being the innocent the name suggests.

Jenou is blond, with hair cut short to just below the ear. General Patton has decreed that all female soldiers will have hair cut to above the bottom of their earlobe. The general is improvising—army regulations have not quite caught up with the realities of female soldiers. In addition to being blond, Jenou is quite pretty, just shy of beautiful, and has a pinup's body.

Jenou remains silent, knowing the pressure will build on Rio to say something. And of course she's right.

"It was . . ." Rio searches for a word picture, a metaphor, something that will convey enough meaning that Jenou will not feel the need to ask any more. Thinking about it takes her back to that moment. To the sound of Sergeant Cole's voice yelling, *Shoot!*

Richlin! Suarez! Lay down some fugging fire!

Rio remembers it in detail. It had been as cold then as it is hot now. Her breathing had become irregular: a panicky burst followed by a leaden *thud-thud-thud.*

She remembers lining up the sights of her M1 Garand. She remembers the Italian soldier. And the pressure of her finger on the trigger. And the way she slowed her breathing, the way she shut out everything, every extraneous sound, every irrelevant emotion. The way she saw the target, a man in a tan uniform lined up perfectly on the sights.

The way her lungs and heart seemed to freeze along with time itself.

The moment when her right index finger applied the necessary seven-point-five pounds of pressure and the stock kicked back against her shoulder.

Bang.

The way she had first thought that he had just tripped. The way the Italian had seemed to be frozen in time, on his knees, maybe just tripped, maybe just caught his toe on a rock and . . . And then the way the man fell back.

Dead.

"Like it wasn't me," Rio says at last. "Like someone else was moving me. Like I was a puppet, Jen. Like I was a puppet."

This is the third time, not the first, that Jenou has asked about that first killing. Rio is vaguely aware that it has become important to Jenou that Rio remain Rio. She understands that Jenou does not have the sort of home you get sentimental over, and that as a result Rio *is* home to Jenou. Sometimes she intercepts a look from Jenou, a passing betrayal of inner doubts. Jenou, who Rio would never have thought capable of any sort of reflection, has developed a sidelong, contemplative gaze. A judging gaze tinged with worry. And sometimes Rio looks for ways to reassure Jenou, but at this particular moment it is just too damned hot.

"Doing my job," Rio says with a hint of wry humor. "Rio Richlin, Private, US Army, sir! Shootin' Krauts, sir!" She executes a lazy salute.

A truck rattles by, and a dozen male GIs whistle and yell encouragement along the lines of "Hey, sweetheart!" and "Oh baby!" and "Bring those tatas here to papa!"

Rio and Jenou ignore the catcalls as just another bit of background noise, like the coughing engine of a Sherman tank lurching toward the motor pool, or the insect buzz of the army spotter plane overhead.

"Hey, I got a letter from Strand," Rio says, wanting to change the subject and dispel her own lingering resentment.

A dozen soldiers, mostly men, march wearily past, coming in from a patrol. "Which of you broads want me between your legs?"

Jenou raises a middle finger without bothering to look and hears a chorus of shouts and laughs, some angry, most amused.

"Well, dish, sweetie. How is tall, dark, and handsome doing?" Jenou asks.

"He says he's fine. And he's looking for a way to get here."

"From Algiers? Kind of a long walk."

"I think he was hoping for a train. Or a truck. Or a plane."

"He'd fly his own plane over here if he really loved you."

Does he? Does he still? Am I still the girl he fell for?

Rio reaches blindly to give Jenou a shove. "I don't think the army just lets you borrow a B-17 whenever you want one."

"He could offer to pay for the gas."

"Let's roll over. This side's parboiled."

They roll over, Rio recoiling as bare flesh touches the metal skin of the vehicle.

Suddenly a siren begins its windup and both girls sit up fast, shield their eyes, and scan the horizon.

"Aw, hell," Jenou says, pointing at two black dots rushing toward them from the direction of the sea.

The cry goes up from a dozen voices. "Plane! Plane! Take cover!"

They climb down quickly—much more quickly than they climbed up.

"Under the track?" Rio wonders aloud, looking toward the nearest ditch, which is already filling up with scrambling GIs.

"The Kraut will aim for the track!" Jenou yells.

"He'll see it's one of his own and burned out besides," Rio counters in a calmer tone. They crawl madly for the shelter of all that steel and lie facedown, breathing dust, almost grateful for the shade. Antiaircraft guns at the four corners of the camp open up, firing tracer rounds at the dots, which have now assumed the shape of Me 109 fighters with single bomb racks.

Bap-bap-bap-bap-bap! The antiaircraft guns blaze, joined by small arms fire from various soldiers firing futilely with rifles and Thompsons.

The Messerschmitts come in fast and low, and starbursts twinkle on their wings and cowling. Machine gun bullets and cannon shells rip lines across the road and into the tents. A voice yells, "Goddamn Kraut shot my goddamn coffee!"

The planes release one bomb each, one a dud that plows into the dirt between two tents and sticks up like a fireplug, smoking a little. The second bomb is not a dud.

Ka-BOOM!

The front end of a deuce-and-a-half truck, clear at the far end of the camp, explodes upward, rises clear off the ground on a jet of flame before falling to earth, a smoking steel skeleton. The engine block, knocked free by the power of the bomb, twirls through the air, rising twenty feet before falling like an anvil out of a Bugs Bunny cartoon as GIs scurry out of the way. Rio does not see where it lands.

The planes take a tight turn and come roaring back overhead, machine guns stitching the ground like some mad sewing machine.

And then they head off, unscathed, racing away to the relative safety of their base in Sicily.

Rio and Jenou crawl out from beneath the half-track and gaze, disgusted, at the caked-on dirt that covers their fronts from toes to knees to face.

"They could have waited till we toweled off," Jenou says.

"We best go tell Sarge we're still alive," Rio says.

The air raids are fewer lately, as the Royal Air Force planes with some help from the Americans have claimed control of the North African skies. But now Rio hears a distant shriek of pain and thinks what every soldier thinks: *Thank God it isn't me*, followed by, *At least some poor bastard is going home*.

A term has become common: *million-dollar wound*. The million-dollar wound is the one that doesn't kill or completely cripple you but is enough to send you home to cold beer and cool sheets and hot showers.

A team of medics, three of them, rush past, with only one taking the time to turn and run backward while yelling, "I have some training in gynecology; I am happy to do an examination!" as he grabs his crotch.

He trips and falls on his back, and Rio and Jenou share a satisfied nod.

The US Army, Tunisia, in the summer of 1943.

2

FRANGIE MARR—CAMP MEMPHIS, TUNISIA, NORTH AFRICA

Several miles away there is a different scream. This scream comes and goes, rises, falls, lapses into silence, then starts up again.

It's a battlefield sound, but they are not on the battlefield, they are in a camp very much like Rio's. Tents stretch away toward the west in long green lines across the dried mud and gravel. Austere, lifeless hills rise in the far distance, like red waves rushing toward a shore, but frozen in time. The only immediately noticeable difference between this encampment and the one where Rio and Jenou sunbathe is that here all the soldiers—except for the officers—are black. It is a colored artillery battalion, its 105mm and 155mm howitzers parked in a well-spaced, random arrangement so as to make air attack a bit more difficult for the Krauts.

There is a Sherman tank ahead. It weighs 72,750 pounds.

Corporal Frangie Marr, army medic, does not know this fact, but it doesn't matter much because she's spent some time in close proximity to tanks and she does not need to be convinced that they are large and terrifying and very, very substantial.

The Sherman, the 72,750-pound Sherman, is oddly perched with its nose pointed up at about a seventy-degree angle, which aims its 75-millimeter main gun almost straight up in the air, as if someone has decided to use the tank to shoot at airplanes.

"Gotta help him, Doc, get him some happy juice. Poor bastard, he's in a bad way!" The staff sergeant takes Frangie's arm—not bullying, just urgent—as he pulls her along, practically lifting her off her feet as they leap over a half-dug latrine ditch.

"What happened?" Frangie asks, panting a little. She is mentally inventorying the medical supplies she has in her bag and the extras stuffed into the ammo pouches in a belt hastily slung over her shoulder.

"Green kid sacked out in a bomb crater beside the road, and the Sherman pulled off to check something, a bad bearing, or maybe the driver just needed a piss." The sergeant takes a beat and says, "Sorry, I meant maybe he had to answer nature's call. Anyway, side of the crater collapses, tank slips, and that's all she wrote."

As they hustle along the scream grows louder and the

tank larger. Several dozen men are gathered around, including the tankers, distinguished by their leather helmets and white faces. The tankers stand a little apart and smoke and ignore the angry muttering of the gathered troops, who naturally blame them for crashing their tank.

"Make a hole, make a hole," the sergeant says. He releases Frangie's arm and uses both hands to pry men apart. At last Frangie—far and away the smallest person of either race—sees the tank up close and has the distinct impression that it is in a very precarious, certainly temporary, position. All 72,750 pounds of it is held in place only by the bite of the treads into soft, crumbling earth. With a good firm push it could even topple onto its back like an upended turtle. But the more likely scenario is that it will slide down onto the still-unseen screaming man.

Frangie squats beneath the shade of the tank's sky-tilted prow and tilts her head sideways, but she cannot see the man trapped beneath. She goes counterclockwise around the tank to the back, and the once-muffled moans of pain are now more clearly audible. She has to lower herself onto her belly and stick her head over the lip of the crater to see a man's helmeted head a few feet away. He is facedown with his head and shoulders free but is pinned at the bottom of his shoulder blades by some—but surely not all—of that massive weight.

The sergeant squats beside her and says, "Hang on,

Williams, Doc's here." Then more quietly he says to Frangie, "We were going to dig him out, but we're worried the damned thing could slip back farther. We called for a tractor but that could take a while, nearest engineers are twenty miles away."

"He could go into shock," Frangie says through gritted teeth. "Hey, Williams, are you bleeding?"

The answer is a scream of pain that rises, rises, and then stops. Followed by a twisted, barely comprehensible voice saying, "I don't know. Give me a shot, Doc. I can't . . . Oh, Jesus!"

"I'm going to help you," Frangie says, and twists her head sideways to see the sergeant looking at her skeptically. She understands his skepticism. In fact, she is pretty sure she has just told a lie.

"Can't you run chains or rope to the front of the tank and pull it forward?"

"That could make it settle deeper."

"What am I supposed to do, crawl down there?" It's a rhetorical question that the sergeant answers with a blank look.

Why am I doing this? I could be killed.

Several curses come to Frangie's mind, but as the words form she sees her mother's face, and worse still, Pastor M'Dale's disappointed look, and she swallows the curses. She tosses the belt with the medicine-stuffed cartridge pockets aside. Then she buttons her uniform to the top button, hoping to avoid pushing ten pounds of Tunisian red dirt down her front. She pulls a morphine ampule from her breast pocket and clutches it in her left hand.

There are many ways Frangie does not want to die, and being crushed face-first in the dirt by a tank rates high on her list. But it's too late now to say, "This is not my problem."

Keep me strong, Lord.

"Grab my ankles," Frangie says.

The sergeant summons two beefy soldiers and each takes a leg.

Using her elbows, Frangie moves like a half-crippled insect down the slope of the crater. The tank blocks the sun, and she can feel its mass poised above her, inch-thick steel plates, mud-clogged treads to left and right. The rear of the tank is a louvered grille that radiates the stifling heat of the engine, which, added to the hundred-degree air temperature, makes the crater a place where you could bake a biscuit.

Frangie imagines her body being squeezed through those louvers, like so much meat in a sausage grinder, cooking even as she . . .

Fear. It's been creeping in, little by little, tingling and twisting her stomach, but now it is beginning to seem that she is actually going to do this, and at that point the fear sets aside all subtlety and comes rushing up within her.

Lord, help me to help this man.

And don't let that tank slip!

She should add a prudent and humble "Thy will be done," but if God's will is to crush her with a tank, she doesn't want to make it any easier on Him.

Frangie has known fear in her life. Fear of destitution when her father was injured and lost his job. Fear of hostile whites, a fear made very real by the history of her home state and city. Just twenty-two years have passed since white rioters burned down all of the Greenwood district, once known as the black Wall Street, blocks from her home in Tulsa, Oklahoma.

And since enlisting she has felt fear (mixed with anger) as she endured various threats by white men who hated the very idea of a black soldier. Then, too, there were the dark mutterings of many of her fellow colored soldiers, who equally despised the idea of a woman in uniform.

But right now her fear is focused on the fact that her head and now shoulders too are right in line to be crushed if the tank slips.

I'm a roach beneath a shoe.

She is far enough down that Williams can look at her and she can see his face, though it is so transformed by pain and terror that she doubts his own mother would recognize him.

Don't cry, don't cry or it will scare him.

But I want to cry.

"I think we best get him out of here," Frangie calls back to the men holding her ankles. She tries to keep panic out of her voice—Williams doesn't need to be reminded that he's in danger—but fear raises her tone an octave and she sounds like a child. A scared child.

"Just give me the shot, Doc! Oh God!"

"Just hang on, Williams, hang on."

The problem is clear. If she can dig out enough dirt beneath Williams she may be able to pull him free, or at least do so with some help. But with every spadeful she will increase the odds of the tank sliding.

"The tractor will get here sooner or later," the sergeant says.

"It's the later that's a problem," Frangie says. Her voice is strained, she is very nearly talking upside down, and grit has already found its way to her mouth, sucked in with each breath. She tries to spit, but her mouth is as dry as the dust she inhales. "I can scoop the dirt that's just right under him."

There's a moment's pause as the sergeant confers in low tones with someone else, perhaps an officer.

"Give it a try, Doc," comes the verdict.

"Pass me an entrenching tool," she says. She is fully, blazingly aware of the possibilities. She's always had a good imagination, and imagination is not a help at times like this. She can imagine the sounds. She can imagine the cries of warning from the men watching her. She can imagine them yanking her back, but too slowly, too slowly to stop that hot louvered grille from turning her head into thick, sizzling slices of salami.

An entrenching tool—a foldable shovel—is passed down to her, blade open and locked in place by its adjustable nut. She is head down, hardly the best position for digging.

Williams lets loose another scream.

"Listen, Williams, I can't have you unconscious or flaking out. So you can either die in a morphine haze or maybe get out of here. Hang on. Just hang on."

She draws the shovel to her, turns it awkwardly, and stabs it weakly into the dirt beneath Williams's face. It is immediately apparent that this will never do because she has nowhere to put the dirt she digs out. It will pile up but then tumble right back down.

The sergeant, looking down from what feels like a very distant height, sees the problem and says, "Get me a poncho. Now!"

In less than a minute the sergeant has flapped the poncho down, like a housewife making a bed, to cover the ground to Frangie's left.

Frangie digs out another spadeful, and Williams screams.

Another spadeful, and another, and Williams screams as the sergeant carefully draws the poncho and the dirt up the slope. He empties it and returns the poncho.

This process is repeated a dozen times. The blood is rushing to Frangie's head and hands, making her eyes tear up and her nose run and causing her legs to go numb. The heat is appalling, and she can smell her own hair singeing. After twenty minutes Frangie has herself pulled back up just long enough to clear her head.

"Water," she gasps. She upends a proffered canteen and some sensible fellow drains a second canteen over her head. Then she slithers back down and the slow, slow digging proceeds anew.

Finally she notices that Williams is screaming less. She asks for and is passed a flashlight. In the light she can peer ahead and see that a small gap has opened between Williams's back and the bottom of the tank. His shirt is soaked red.

With infinite care despite the trembling in her fingers she walks her fingers down his back until she finds the place where a shattered rib sticks out. She feels around the hole; there shouldn't be an artery there, but she has to be sure. Has he lost so much blood he'll go into shock?

"Pass me a rope. Put a loop in it!" Frangie calls, spitting dirt. "All right, Williams, I'm giving you the shot now." She stabs down into his shoulder and squeezes the blessed pain relief into him. "Before you flake out, try to raise your hands together."

This brings a fresh cry of agony, but Williams can sense the possibility of life now, and he does it. He has big hands, the calloused hands of a man who has picked cotton since the age of five. Frangie passes the rope over them and tugs to tighten the knot.

"Okay, Sarge, pull me up first," she yells.

She is yanked up like a cork popping from a bottle of champagne.

The sergeant takes over. "Okay, boys, on the rope and pull, but slow and easy."

They pull and Williams slides up the side of the ditch and is dragged several feet away to cries of relief from his comrades, followed quickly by relieved insults and hectoring. Frangie leaps to kneel beside him. She tries not to think about the fact that within five seconds the tank slips with a muffled but earth-rumbling sound to crush the narrow gap beneath its thirty-three tons of steel.

Thank you, Lord.

She uses scissors to cut Williams's shirt from tail to collar and examines his broad back. The rib is a mess and the exit wound is gruesome, but that alone won't kill him. But that says nothing about internal bleeding and possibly fatal damage to internal organs. And she counts at least three other broken ribs, though not extruding.

"Turn him over, gently," she instructs the attentive soldiers around her.

This time Williams's scream of agony is cut off abruptly as he faints. Morphine only does so much.

She pulls away the cut uniform and sees that a piece of root or perhaps a branch has been shoved into his belly. The wood is still in place, a bung in a barrel, limiting the bleeding.

"We have to get him to a field hospital right now," Frangie snaps.

"Shouldn't you pull out that stick?" the sergeant asks, much more deferential than he had been earlier.

"No. It may be acting as a plug, in which case we'd need whole blood and plasma and an operating theater."

"Right," the sergeant admits.

"And a surgeon," Frangie adds. "Move him to a jeep while he's out—he's better off not feeling it."

In less than five minutes Williams is on a stretcher tied to the hood of a jeep.

"That was good work, Doc," the sergeant says. "You okay?"

"I'm going to throw up."

The sergeant grins. "You go right ahead, honey, you deserve a good puke. Hell, you deserve a damn Silver Star, although they aren't handing those out to colored soldiers much."

Frangie vomits into a shallow depression, and a soldier solicitously shovels dirt over the mess as the sergeant hands her a hip flask.

"It's some French brandy we liberated from an A-rab shop."

Frangie has never before tasted any form of alcohol. Her church does not approve, not at all, and she has sat through many of Pastor M'Dale's sermons on the subject of demon rum. But it would be rude not to accept, and she wants something more than water to wash away the vile taste of her own bile. Maybe it will stop the trembling in her hands. She takes a careful swig and gasps.

The brandy burns its way down her throat to form a small ball of liquid fire in her stomach. She's a small person and inexperienced at drinking, so even this small draft is enough to spread a strange but comforting warmth out through her limbs.

"Thanks," she says.

"You saved that boy's life."

She has no answer to that. She's broken the prohibition against alcohol, but she's not ready to abandon the humility she's been taught. "It's my job, I suppose," Frangie says.

She walks away on legs shaking from the aftereffects of adrenaline and notices that the alcohol has done its job of pushing fear back just a little.

Just a little, but enough for now.

RAINY SCHULTERMAN—NEW YORK CITY, NEW YORK, USA

"Sergeant Schulterman, sir."

"At ease. Please take a seat, Sergeant; we are not very big on formality around here."

Rainy removes her cover—her cap—and sits in a well-worn wooden chair, the kind with arms that come around and are too high for her to prop her elbows on comfortably. She places her hands flat, palms down, on her neatly ironed olive drab uniform slacks, keeps her mirror-polished shoes flat on the linoleum floor, and trains her eyes on the lieutenant colonel. Rainy is on leave in New York, having returned from a successful mission in North Africa.

Colonel Corelli is middle-aged, with steel-gray hair cut a bit too long, a pale face, and thoughtful brown eyes sunk deep beneath bushy brows. The brass on his uniform says colonel, but his look, his demeanor, says professor.

No sooner is she seated than there is a brief knock and

they are joined by a very different sort of creature. He is a civilian in a passable dark-gray suit, starched white shirt, conservative tie, and expensive and properly shined—but not military-polished—shoes.

The colonel performs the introductions. "Sergeant Schulterman, Special Agent Bayswater, FBI."

Rainy's heart sinks. She knows immediately what this is about. The end of her career in the US Army may be only minutes away. Her expression turns from curious to deliberately blank.

"Agent Bayswater."

"Sergeant Schulterman."

They do not shake hands, and she does not rise from her seat.

She doesn't like him. It's a snap judgment, in part a reaction to what she expects he will be saying next. But beyond that, there's something smug and condescending in the way he looks her up and down, like he's trying to decide whether she's a crook or a piece of meat. He has a bent nose, broken while boxing perhaps, and that prominent twist in his nose has given his mouth a permanent sneer.

"I don't suppose you know why you're here, Sergeant," Colonel Corelli says.

"No, sir."

"Oh, I bet she's got some idea," the FBI man says. "Don't you, honey?"

Colonel Corelli winces, the way refined people do when they hear someone being rude or unpleasant.

Rainy turns slightly toward Bayswater. "*Sergeant*. It's Sergeant Schulterman."

"Is that so? Well, *Sergeant*, you're supposed to be a very bright girl, so I'm betting you have a pretty clear notion of why the FBI is here. Am I right? Or have I been misled and you're not so bright after all?"

"When my superior officer informs me as to *his reasons* for bringing me here, then I will know," Rainy says frostily. She places the emphasis on *his reasons*. She is a soldier, not a civilian, and she does not take orders from the FBI.

The colonel takes the opportunity to lean forward, his body language favoring Rainy. "There may be a mission. A mission you may be able to carry out better than anyone else."

Rainy is intrigued and ready to feel relieved, but she keeps her face guarded and neutral. Rainy Schulterman is of medium height and medium weight with frizzled, black hair that has been pinned down to stop its tendency to spring up and out. Her eyes are brown and distinctly skeptical, even judgmental. She gives the impression of being closed up tight, self-contained; not quite hostile, but not one to suffer fools gladly either. For a person of the female sex, neither large nor powerful, possessing

27

neither rank nor title, and young besides, she is unsettlingly intimidating.

"Yes, sir," Rainy says.

"Your old man's a crook," Agent Bayswater says.

Rainy shoots to her feet. "Colonel, do I have permission to return to my duties?"

The colonel smothers a grin and waves her down. "Sit, sit. You don't *have* any duties, Sergeant, you're on leave." He pulls a slim manila folder from atop a pile of folders, opens it, and reads. "In fact, you are on thirty days' leave in recognition of your actions in Tunisia, where you parachuted—and with only the most minimal training— into the middle of a retreat, joined a lost platoon, and managed by the end of it to come away with a Waffen SS colonel in your custody. I understand you've been recommended for a Silver Star."

"I have that honor, sir, though it was the GIs in that platoon who did the real work."

"Well, it was a hell of a thing," Colonel Corelli says, shaking his head in admiration. "I've read the reports from your colonel and from a Sergeant Garaman who was in command of the patrol after both the officers were killed."

Bayswater isn't having it. "Which doesn't change the fact that your father, Shmuel Schulterman, is a numbers runner for Abe Vidor, who works in turn for the

Genovese crime family. And that could mean hard time in Dannemora prison for your old man."

Rainy turns a cold glare on the FBI man. "Agent Bayswater, you want something from me. Threatening me is not the way to get it." There are times, she reflects, when her own chutzpah amazes her.

"On the contrary, honey, I don't want a damn thing. It's your people, Army Intelligence, who want something from us. I'm just making sure you understand who's in charge, and it ain't you."

The colonel sighs and raises pacifying hands. He has no patience for this posturing, but neither does he have the force to end it. "Maybe we should get to the point. Schulterman, the US Army is planning an action—I won't say where or when—but there is a person in the . . . let's say, target area . . . who may be of some use to Army Intelligence. Agent Bayswater, perhaps you'd like to explain your end of it."

Bayswater stares at Rainy. It is a hard, aggressive stare, an intimidating stare, no doubt a stare he has used to cow many a criminal suspect. Rainy is worried, but she is not intimidated by Agent Bayswater, and she lets him know it by returning his gaze with a blank, emotionless expression.

Finally, the FBI man sighs, shrugs his shoulders, and mutters, "Broads in the army. You can keep 'em. It'll

29

never happen in the FBI; I can promise you that."

"A woman might have gotten to the point by now, rather than playing games," Rainy snaps.

Bayswater snorts a derisive laugh. "A real woman would still be gossiping; I don't know what *you* are, honey. But okay, I've got things to do, and maybe you do too. So here it is. We've tried working out deals to get help from the crime bosses. A lot of 'em have connections overseas, and in addition to that they could help with labor troubles on the docks. But all any of them wants is for Lucky to be let out of jail, and that ain't gonna happen."

"He means Lucky Luciano," Corelli explains unnecessarily. Charles "Lucky" Luciano is the boss of all bosses in New York crime. He is in prison for "pandering," which is a polite way of saying he ran a prostitution ring, along with gambling, protection rackets, union rackets, and assorted other profitable enterprises.

"Luciano is in a hole in Dannemora and he ain't getting out, but that's all the mob wants, all it says it wants anyway. Give us Luciano and we'll be good, patriotic Americans and help out the war effort. That's their demand, and they won't budge."

Corelli picks up the narrative. "The target area is a place where certain members of New York criminal gangs have useful contacts. Contacts who may provide us with intelligence on German positions."

"I see," Rainy says, and she does. Obviously the target is Italy or perhaps one of its islands, Sicily or Sardinia. It was not hard to look at a map and see that the next move for US and Allied forces in Tunisia might be some portion of Italy. Knocking Italy out of the war would be very helpful.

"I doubt very much that you do see, honey," Bayswater says.

Rainy's pride flares and she very nearly becomes indiscreet, but she reins it in. Barely. "You believe my father has connections to organized crime. You believe he can introduce me to someone in the organization who wants something *other* than freedom for Lucky Luciano. You believe this person has connections in Sicily or Sardinia or wherever in Italy that would be helpful. You want my father to make a connection and for me to approach this person with a suggestion or at least pave the way for someone more senior to have that conversation."

This leaves the FBI man openmouthed and temporarily flummoxed. His mouth closes with an audible click. But he recovers quickly. "We don't want a damned thing, the army wants it, and we are just making sure you don't say or do something you shouldn't. And we want a full report on whatever goes on."

"I don't take orders from the FBI."

"You damn well will take orders from me, sister."

31

He's moved from *honey* to *sister*. Progress, of a sort. "No. And I will not be threatened either."

"How about if I arrange to put your old man in the clink?"

"Then you'll report back to your superiors that you jailed a small-time numbers runner and blew the assignment, which I would guess was to render support to Colonel Corelli."

"Jesus!" the FBI agent explodes in disgust. He can no longer remain seated but jumps up, nearly knocking his chair over. "Who the hell do you think you are?"

Rainy is about to tell him when Corelli intervenes. "She's a soldier and under military law, not civilian law, so how about we all calm down? What do you say?" He shakes his head in irritation mixed with amusement. "Sergeant, I am not going to order you to take this on. But as I understand it, there's a lesser boss, there's a term for it—"

"A capo," Agent Bayswater says, still glaring at Rainy. "Or underboss."

"Underboss. *Le mot juste.* An underboss named Vito Camporeale. He's got family connections in . . . the target area. And he has a son named Francisco—Cisco they call him—right here in New York. Cisco has gotten himself into a heap of trouble."

Bayswater says, "Racketeering, pandering, pornography, and loan-sharking. Only, Cisco screwed up and got overly ambitious. He tried to take over a block that belongs to a colored gang up in Harlem. But see, there's a peace deal between the Wops and the coons, and the Five Families don't want a war with the coons right now, what with making money hand over fist on the docks and off drunk soldiers. Cisco shot a colored boy who was connected, see, and now it's blood for blood."

The full truth begins to dawn on Rainy. "You're going to offer to get Cisco to . . . to a safe place. And you want me to get my father to introduce me to Camporeale and—"

"Vito the Sack, they call him." Bayswater now comes close. He puts his hands on the back of Rainy's chair, leans down so she can feel his breath on the side of her neck. "Because when a fellow displeases him, see, he likes to take a razor and swipe, swipe, the man's not a man anymore, if you take my meaning."

Without turning to face him, Rainy repeats, "You want me to get my father to introduce me to Vito the Sack and get him to help us in . . . the target area. In exchange, we'll save his son."

Bayswater is taken aback by her calm. She feels him release his grip on her seat back. Of course her calm is mostly an act because Rainy's mind is screaming with complications and personal fears, the foremost of which is confronting her father with this. She wrote to him months earlier to let him know that she knows about his other activities. But since coming home on leave she and her father have never mentioned it. Forcing him to face it? To face the fact that his activities have now ensnared his daughter? That feels very, very hard to Rainy.

On the other hand, part of Rainy is excited. The part of her that wants to contribute something to destroying the monster Hitler. She is a mere buck sergeant, one of hundreds of thousands of such in the US Army, but she's being offered an assignment that could really amount to something. She could help to save the lives of GIs like those she met in Tunisia. She has fond memories of solid, reliable Dain Sticklin and charming Jack Stafford, and she was amazed—and just a little scared—by Rio Richlin.

Since the desperate combat in the desert, that young woman, Rio, has insinuated herself into Rainy's mind. The mix of freckle-faced naiveté and savage Amazon brutality has affected Rainy's worldview, has shown her a glimpse of a future in which ideas of masculinity and femininity could be utterly transformed. There is a revolution in Rio Richlin (who would no doubt snort derisively at such a notion). All over the country women are going into factories and doing jobs previously reserved for men only. All over the world clever women—and Rainy knows herself to be in this category—are contributing their intelligence and insight to the war effort. But women have always worked, if not as shipfitters and aircraft mechanics, then as maids and nurses and teachers. And there are examples going back to the time of the Romans of women bright and determined enough to wield real power, though often it was from behind the scenes.

But Rio, and women like her, are intruding in an area that has always been reserved to men: Rio is a warrior. She and others like her have shown that girls—women— could do more than work; women could be brave and aggressive. Women could kill. And Rainy is sure that reality will change the world.

She's sure it will have no effect on the minds of men like Agent Bayswater, but for Rainy it feels like a challenge.

Colonel Corelli takes charge again as the FBI man seems to have run out of steam. "You will be required to give us a full report of the contact. You must attempt to convince them to speak with me directly, but if you find yourself dealing directly with Vito Camporeale, you will prepare a full report on him and on anyone else associated with him."

"Of course," Rainy says.

"And on your father," Bayswater adds.

"No," Rainy says without hesitation.

"That's not a request, that's an order," Bayswater snaps.

Rainy turns in her chair to look the agent in the face. There's a confident sneer on his thin lips. His head is cocked to one side, a parody of some movie tough guy. "Agent Bayswater, I'm not an informer. I will not betray my father."

"Well, you uppity little skirt," Bayswater snaps. He seems to think insults will move her. Or . . .

Or he's deliberately trying to goad her. Is he testing her? Or is he just a deeply unpleasant man?

"You'll report to me, *Sergeant* Schulterman," Corelli says with strained calm, glaring at Bayswater. "And I have no interest in your conversation with your father. You'll find a connection. You may even meet with Camporeale yourself. But you will only report back, you will make no commitments. Is that understood?"

"Perfectly, sir."

"I'll have your orders cut," Corelli says. "You are dismissed."

She is out on the crowded sidewalk and heading toward the subway station when Special Agent Bayswater catches up to her.

"A moment, Sergeant," he says.

"Yes?"

They are in the middle of the sidewalk, and Bayswater draws her into the relative calm of a department store doorway. The FBI man's arrogance is undiminished, but the smug offensiveness is toned down now.

"You don't like me much," Bayswater says.

Several answers pass through Rainy's quick mind. *I don't like you at all.* And, *Don't be so modest, I actively despise you.* But Rainy is a tightly controlled person when in performance of her duty. So she says nothing.

"You're a smart broad," Bayswater says. "And I don't want to have to bring your old man in to identify your body. So a word to the wise: we got Naval Intelligence, we got this new OSS spy service, and we got us, the FBI. Everybody and their aunt Tilly is playing spy all of a sudden. Bunch of amateurs mostly."

"I freely confess I am an amateur," Rainy says, impatient now, not interested in another futile go-round with the annoying agent.

"Not talking about you, sister." He jerks his thumb back toward the door through which they have both just emerged. "You know what Corelli did before the war?"

"Colonel Corelli?" She pointedly emphasizes his rank.

"Professor of Oriental Languages at some college up in Vermont."

He lets that sink in, and it does. Rainy's guard comes down just a little.

Bayswater continues. "We have professors too, all kinds of professors working for the Bureau. Very helpful, some of them. But we don't let them plan or run operations.

37

Guy like that is way smarter than me, but he's never done this work before. His whole outfit—*your* outfit—you're supposed to be counting tanks and deciding where some bunch of Krauts will be. This is not your bailiwick."

That sinks in as well.

"Word to the wise," Bayswater says. "Do this, this meet, but no more. Amateurs get people hurt. And your colonel is the textbook definition of an amateur. I know you don't want to hear it, but that man is going to get you killed." He touches the brim of his fedora, nods, and walks briskly away.

4

RIO RICHLIN—CAMP ZIGZAG, TUNISIA, NORTH AFRICA

"You know what I want to do today?" Luther Geer says, stifling a yawn and using the heel of his hand to grind the sleep from his eyes. "I want to go sit in a damn LC and invade that same damn beach all over again. At least I get cool and clean wading through the waves."

His kitten, the former Miss Pat, now renamed Miss Lion of the Sahara, blinks owlishly from her position on his chest.

Rio Richlin has not warmed up to Luther Geer. She thinks he is a bully and not very bright to boot, but she nevertheless agrees.

Since the fighting wound down in Tunisia, the 119th Division has trained and practiced and trained some more. There has been renewed effort to improve soldiers' effectiveness with the bazooka. There have been lectures on the necessity of actually firing one's rifle and not just carrying it around like some family heirloom. There have been the inevitable marches around the desert—marches that had started off unpleasantly cold and then moved without seeming transition to being fiercely hot. And there have been amphibious assaults.

They have assaulted the same beach three times already, and the weary consensus among the deeply bored GIs of Second Squad, Fifth Platoon, Company A of the 119th, was that today heralded yet another phony invasion.

Jenou rolls upright in her canvas cot and upends her boots before putting them on. There are scorpions and snakes and things that have no name in the Tunisian desert, and many of them like to find shelter in a shady boot. Jenou is already partly in uniform and has in fact slept in it, there being no such thing as army-issue pajamas or nightgowns. And anyway, with zero privacy she'd have had no way to change without being stared at by the men of the squad, especially Tilo Suarez, who reacts to boredom by becoming even more irritatingly amorous.

Jenou stands up and says, "I'm grabbing chow before the coffee gets cold."

"I'm with you," Rio says. "I like to get the powdered eggs before they start separating."

"This is the life, man," Dain Sticklin says, scratching his chest through his OD undershirt. "A thousand tents surrounded by a million square miles of sand with a million sand fleas per man—or woman."

"Are those sand fleas or lice?" Cat Preeling teases. "Because if it's lice, we're going to have to barbecue you, Stick. It's the only way. Death by fire."

"I think mine are sand fleas." Stick picks up his uniform blouse, shakes it, and begins peering closely at the fabric, searching for tiny crawling things.

Dain Sticklin, inevitably called "Stick," is the closest thing to a real soldier in the squad. Smart, educated, disciplined, with a prominent widow's peak that somehow makes him look the part of the mature GI, he's been in only as long as Rio herself and in fact went through basic training with her.

"We're not going to know until we put them side by side whether it's fleas or lice," Geer opines. Geer is a big ginger hick, the least open to the idea of women in the unit. But in battle he's performed well, and that has become more meaningful to Rio than his daily obnoxiousness.

"We ought to take a louse and a flea and put 'em together, see who wins." This from Tilo, who seems vaguely excited by the idea, or as excited as a bored, doe-eyed young lothario in a deathly hot tent can get.

"Jesus, let me out of here," Jenou mutters. She and Rio head for the flap and throw it open onto a blindingly bright day.

There, just arriving, is Sergeant Cole and some male private neither Rio nor Jenou recognizes.

41

"Where you headed?" Cole asks.

"The latrine followed by the chow line," Rio answers.

"Then the latrine again," Jenou says darkly. There is some dysentery in the camp, and the food is the prime suspect.

"Hold up a second," Cole says, and the two young women back into the tent.

Sergeant Cole is the oldest member of the squad, in his midtwenties but with the air of an older man. He has wide-set eyes in an open face, thinning sandy hair, a gap-toothed grin, and the stub of an unlit cigar in the corner of his mouth.

The young man with him is a mystery, so for the moment no one bothers to acknowledge his existence.

"I got good news, and I got kinda good news," Cole announces.

"Oh, I do hope it's a five-mile hike in full gear," Jack Stafford suggests. He's just about Rio's height, with sparkling eyes, reddish-blond hair, and a grin that practically defines the word *devilish*. Jack is a displaced British boy with the luck (either good or bad) to have ended up in the American army.

"First, the not-so-good news," Cole says. "We got a replacement for Cassel."

A replacement? For Cassel?

"This is . . . Who are you?" There's something antici-patory in Cole's voice.

"Private Ben Bassingthwaite," the young man says.

"Tell 'em where you're from." Cole hides a smile by taking a sudden interest in the ground.

The private suppresses a sigh. "I'm from Beaverton, Oregon."

"The hell?" Geer demands rudely.

"That's right," Cole says, struggling to keep a straight face. "He's Private Benjamin Barry Bassingthwaite from Beaverton." And then he waits as his squad runs through various possibilities.

"Call him Beaver?" Cat suggests.

"But that's what I call Castain," Tilo says, grinning at his own wit and batting his admittedly gorgeous eyelashes at Jenou.

"Not before I get my coffee, huh, Suarez?" Jenou says. "Coffee before bullshit: it's in the manual."

"Triple B?" Cat offers.

"Beebee," the newcomer says. "That's what it always comes down to. Beebee." His tone is resigned. Not happy, but not unduly upset either.

"I still like Beaver," Tilo mutters. "Not that I'm getting any in this dump."

Jillion Magraff and Hansu Pang do not join in the banter. Magraff is either shy or sullen, Rio still isn't sure which. And Hansu Pang is a Japanese American, and despite his good soldiering he remains deeply suspect.

"Beebee it is," Stick says. "Seen any action, Beebee?"

Beebee is short, painfully thin, scrawny even, nothing at all like Cassel. He has the slightly nauseated look Rio would expect from a new guy suddenly pushed into a room . . . well, tent . . . full of new people all giving him the stink eye. For the moment at least, Beebee embodies the gap that opens up between those who have been under fire and those who have not. He is an unknown quantity, and just like the new kid in high school, people size him up, looking for vulnerability.

Cat's begun rolling up the side of the tent nearest her. The tent sides go up during the heat of the day and down for the chilly desert night. "Okay, that's the bad news," Cat says. "So what's the good news?"

Cole displays his uneven teeth. "Children, I got you a twenty-four-hour—"

The word *pass* is lost in an eruption of cheering followed immediately by a whirlwind of GIs grabbing whatever money they've stashed away and pounding for the exit with such enthusiasm that Cole might well be trampled.

"If only I could get you all to move that fast for inspection," Cole says. "Now hold on! *Hold on!*"

They freeze, forming a comical tableau, like a freeze-frame in a cartoon.

"Do not, I repeat, *do not* make damn fools of yourselves. I don't want anyone in the hospital because of some drunk bar fight, and I don't want anyone falling out because they've caught the clap, and Richlin? You and Castain have custody of the new man."

Cassel's replacement.

Rio wipes her right hand down the side of her pants, unconsciously wiping Cassel's blood from her hand. Cassel, the first to die. His final word, "Oh."

Oh. And two minutes later he had bled out into wet sand.

"Aw, jeez, Sarge," Jenou complains theatrically. "If I've got to babysit, at least get me someone with some shoulders on him. Dammit." She sighs. "Okay, Booboo or whatever your name is, you got thirty seconds to drop your gear and grab your cash because we are heading for town."

"Wait a minute," Rio says. "I thought being a private meant I didn't have to babysit. I mean, that's sergeant work, isn't it?"

Cole says, "Yes it is, Richlin, just like it's my job to delegate, and hey, guess what? I just did."

Rio is not specifically excited to see Tunis, but she is bored to the point of unconsciousness and welcomes anything at all that breaks the routine. Tunis, Paris, or the Gates of Hell, she's up for anything that is not this tent. She shoulders her rifle.

"Nuh-uh-uh," Cole says. "No weapons. Drunk GIs

and weapons are not a good mix. Do you all comprehend me? I am dead damn serious: I sure as hell better not be hearing about you from the MPs."

Rio and Jenou, with Beebee in tow, join the others climbing aboard an open deuce-and-a-half truck whose driver has been persuaded to drive into town in exchange for half a carton of Luckies.

It's a dusty, bouncing, behind-pounding, spine-crunching, noisy, two-hour drive down roads choked with military vehicles. A sort of hierarchy governs the roads: at the lowest end are civilians, Arabs and Berbers with huge loads on their backs or smacking heavily laden donkeys; next, soldiers on foot; then the trucks. Jeeps carrying officers are next, and at the top of the precedence, tanks, because no one wants to get in the way of a Sherman.

Speaking of which, there is a very odd sight by the side of the road, a Sherman pointing vertically out of a crater. A bulldozer idles beside it, and colored troops are running a thick chain from the tractor to the front of the tank.

Beebee says, "So I guess some of you fellows have seen action?"

Luther Geer seizes the opportunity to impress and terrify the new guy. "We have been into the jaws of death, youngster. Jaws of death! Krauts everywhere, bullets flying, blood up to our knees!"

"And how about you girls?" Beebee asks, unconsciously drawing closer to them.

"Well," Jenou drawls, "we mostly just follow behind the men and bring them tea and cookies when they get tired of killing Krauts."

Jack emits a guffaw. Then, as if it's the most serious matter in the world, he leans toward Beebee and says, "Of course you Yanks call them cookies, but the proper term is biscuits."

"I like Castain's biscuits." Tilo smirks. "Richlin's biscuits haven't quite risen, if you see what I mean."

"Stick, you've read the manual cover to cover," Jenou says. "Is it okay if I shoot Suarez?"

"Gonna get me some A-rab tail," Tilo says, undeterred. "Gonna see for myself what they've got underneath those scarves and outfits they wear. I hear an A-rab woman will go with a GI for a dollar."

"I'm getting me some hooch first," Geer says. "Then tail. What about you, Jappo?"

Hansu Pang jerks in surprise. He is rarely spoken to directly.

Before Pang can decide on a reply, Geer continues. "I know you Japs like pussy, what with all the raping and such your people did in China."

"Knock it off, Geer," Stick says.

"I am one-quarter Japanese," Pang says with all the dignity he can muster as the truck rattles noisily over ground torn up by tank treads. "Half Korean and one-quarter white."

"Well, goody for you," Geer says. "So you're a half-breed who's only one-quarter traitor."

No one comes to Pang's defense, though the silence that follows is distinctly uncomfortable. It nags at Rio's conscience, this baiting of Pang. There were Japanese (or Jappo-American, whatever, she isn't sure what to call them) farmers around Gedwell Falls. They were just regular, hardworking farmers, no different than the various English, Scots, Italians, French, and so on in the area. She has heard about them being rounded up and sent to camps, many of them being forced to sell their farms for far less than they were worth.

She thinks someday she might get annoyed enough by Geer to say something. But not now. Not yet. She tells herself she has enough trouble being a woman in the army, she doesn't need to pick fights on behalf of Japs.

Anyway, they have a twenty-four-hour pass. Time for fun, not for picking fights.

Tunis is a city, not a town—a vast, sprawling maze of sun-bleached one- and two-story stucco homes, narrow crooked streets, and narrow, even more crooked alleys. Their progress is slowed by donkeys piled high with bushels of dates, big pottery jars of honey, bushels of wheat, and colorful rugs; by men with dark, suspicious faces glowering from the shade of hoods; dirty, excited, nearly naked children racing alongside yelling their few words of English, "Hey, Joe, gimme cigarette?" and "My sister love you long time—one dollar!"

Jillion Magraff digs in her pocket, comes up with a chocolate bar—or what passes for chocolate in army rations—and tosses the bar into the gaggle of children, who instantly start fighting over it.

Finally the truck lurches to a halt outside an intersection choked with foot traffic milling past awning-shielded stalls selling olives, grapes, dates, chickpeas, bright orange spices, and war souvenirs that run from German medals and helmets to British tea and cans of bully beef to American cigarettes.

"Far as I go," the driver yells, leaning out of his window.

The squad piles out, eyes wide, voices high, various uncreditable appetites honed to desperation.

"So what do we do now?" Rio asks Jenou. Rio is still a small-town, rural girl, intimidated by cities, especially strange cities full of people who do not look at all happy to see her.

"We look around, I suppose, see what there is to see." Jenou has always been the worldly-wise balance to Rio's naiveté, though in truth Jenou is a bit overwhelmed too.

"What, no whorehouse?" Cat asks, joining them. Jillion Magraff hovers at the edge of their little group.

"Where are you ladies going?" Jack asks Rio.

Rio shrugs. "I'll follow Castain; she's my guide to the seamy side of life. I suppose you're off to have a different kind of fun."

Jack grins. It is an irresistible thing, his grin, full of mischief and fun. "I'm not much for bordellos, I'm afraid; I'm saving myself for the future Mrs. Stafford. But I guess I'll see if I can keep Suarez and Geer out of the guardhouse."

Beebee shows every sign of wanting to go with the men but says, "Well, I suppose the ladies will need an escort. Anyway, Sergeant Cole said . . ."

"Yeah, you protect us," Cat says, rolling her eyes, but not unkindly. Cat Preeling is approximately twice Beebee's size, and Cat once strangled a Kraut with the strap of her M1.

The five of them, Rio, Jenou, Cat, Jillion, and Beebee, spend the next several hours wandering alien alleyways, buying snacks of unfamiliar food from women squatting beside open charcoal braziers, and picking out trinkets to send home to little brothers and sisters, moms and dads. Rio buys a small silver necklace for her mother and tucks it into her pocket.

At a stand whose rickety table looks ready to collapse under the weight of bronze cookware, brass filigreed boxes, and, incongruously, a ragged and scorched chunk of steel bearing most of a German cross, Rio spots something.

She points at it and says, "Show me that."

The shopkeeper, a very old man with a face like leather that's been boiled then left out in the sun to shrivel, ignores her.

"That!" Rio says, pointing insistently.

The shopkeeper shakes his head and adds a wagging finger.

"Can't you understand plain English?" Cat demands, self-mocking. "We've come to save you from the Hun, you ungrateful—"

"It's on account of you being a woman, I expect," Beebee says. "The men, most of them, have a blade of some kind, not the women."

Rio stares at him. Clever boy. "Okay, you ask him."

Beebee steps past Rio and points at the object, and the shopkeeper reluctantly hands it to him. It is a dagger, a curved knife with a silver butt on the dark, hardwood hilt and a silver scabbard covered in a repeating pattern of curlicues.

Beebee hands it to Rio, who draws the blade slowly. The scabbard is curved, the blade, almost a foot of lightly corroded steel, slightly less so. Rio tests the edge.

"A little dull, but I could sharpen it up."

"You sending it home?" Jenou asks skeptically. "For who, your dad?"

"Maybe," Rio says with a shrug and hands it back to Beebee, much to the shopkeeper's relief. "Tell him you'll give him a dollar."

Beebee and the shopkeeper haggle for ten minutes before arriving on a price of six dollars. Beebee takes the prize and hands it to Rio, who slips it into her belt.

"I think he was saying how it's called a *koummya*," Beebee offers.

"*Koummya* and I'll stabbya," Cat quips.

"My birthday present to myself," Rio says with some satisfaction.

"Your . . . ," Jenou says, and then stares at her, mouth hanging open. "Oh my God, honey! It's your birthday! I cannot believe I forgot your birthday!"

"Eighteen," Rio says, then, noticing the surprised looks from everyone but Jenou, adds, "Um . . . nineteen?"

"They're not going to kick you out now," Jenou says, and gives her friend a hug before holding her out at arm's length to look her up and down. "Well, there you go, honey. You are a legal adult."

"Clearly we need a beer to celebrate," Cat says. "How the hell do we find it, that's the question."

"Down that alley over on the right," Beebee says, which earns him curious looks from his companions. He shrugs. "I noticed some GIs coming out. They looked like they'd been drinking."

Cat slaps him on his narrow shoulder, earning a wince, and says, "We may have use for you after all, young Bassingthwaite. Lead on!"

The tavern is a low-ceilinged, dimly lit place with a short and narrow door providing the only light. Had there been artificial light it likely would not have penetrated the thick blue cigarette smoke that swirls and hovers and is parted by the squad's entry into the room. At least twenty GIs are crammed in so tightly that the two small round tables have become de facto stools.

Rio has been in British pubs, and those could be raucous at times—she has sidestepped more than one drunken brawl between American GIs and British Tommies. Or between American GIs and American sailors. Or between white GIs and black GIs. Or . . . Well, fit, energetic young men far from their families had a tendency to get into trouble, especially when drunk. But the tone of this place is subtly different. Here there is more weariness on the one hand and on the other hand a more desperate edge to the braying laughter. There are silent, sullen drinkers and loud, lit-up, electrified drinkers who are all raw nerve.

Rio checks shoulder patches and the condition of uniforms and the look in men's eyes and knows these are not rear-echelon soldiers but men who had been in the fight.

There are a number of long looks plus the inevitable catcalls and lewd propositions as Rio, Jenou, Jillion, and Cat, with their male escort Beebee, walk in. The more civilized men offer to buy them drinks; others offer to give them a baby so they can muster out and go home.

The four women have very different ways of dealing with this. Jenou smiles and in a loud, welcoming voice says, "I'll decide who buys me a drink, and it ain't you, short stuff. I want handsome and I want rich. If you're rich enough, I'll give a pass on the handsome."

This confuses most of the men and leaves them temporarily stalled, unsure how to proceed. They might be veterans, these men, but few are over twenty-five and none of them are suave or sophisticated with women.

Cat Preeling has a different approach. When a rowdy, red-faced buck sergeant comes up demanding a dance—despite the absence of music or room to dance—Cat says, "Aw, fug that. Pull up and tell me a war story, Sarge." In five minutes Cat has a gaggle of men around her, all competing to come up with the best story, or failing that then the most extravagant complaint about the army. And of course Cat is giving back as good as she gets.

Jillion is the lost lamb, clinging nervously beside Rio, glancing toward every new sound. Rio manages to push her way up to the bar—actually a section of perforated steel resting at a noticeable angle on a sawhorse and a chest of drawers. The man behind the bar glares at her with naked hostility as she says, "A beer, please, and one for my buddy here."

The barman ignores her. So Rio pulls the knife and scabbard from her belt and lays it on the bar, examining her recent purchase. She draws the blade, holds it up to the smoky light, and runs her finger carefully along both sharpened edges.

The beers appear, and the knife is put away.

"I wish I could do that," Jillion says ruefully.

"It's all bluff," Rio says. "But don't tell anyone." She avoids smiling because she knows her grin, which is slow to arrive but dazzling when it does appear, makes her look even younger than her current just-barely eighteen years.

"I've only ever tasted beer once," Jillion says. "I didn't like it then. But now I like anything wet." She offers Rio a cigarette, which Rio declines, then lights one for herself.

She's a fussy person, Jillion, with quick, small movements and an air of alertness that makes Rio think of a squirrel hiding its nuts. She has none of the physical robustness that Rio, Jenou, and Cat all share, and Rio wonders, not for the first time, how Jillion made it through basic training. She can't picture this nervous squirrel running five miles in full gear, though to be fair she's always kept up with the rest of the squad. Not much of a fighter, maybe, and a bit of a goldbrick, but there are others in the platoon as useless. Or almost as useless.

"So, what's your story, Magraff?" Rio asks, partly from curiosity, more just to have an excuse to shut out the noise around her.

"Me?" It comes out almost as a squeak. "Well . . ." She has to think about it while hunching her shoulders around her drink as if afraid it will be snatched out of her hands. "I'm from a place called Chapel Hill in North Carolina. It's where the university is."

"Uh-huh."

"Small town really, I guess. My father works in a print shop. I was figuring to go to work there maybe someday."

"What does he print?"

"Oh, you know, flyers and church bulletins and diner menus and such. But they do some artwork sometimes and well, I kind of, uh . . ."

"You like art?"

Jillion nods and looks away as if admitting something shameful.

"I see you drawing sometimes in that notebook you have."

"It passes the time."

"What do you draw?" Rio asks, and now she's actually interested. The closest she's come to knowing anyone with artistic interests is Strand, who enjoys taking pictures. Her hand moves involuntarily to the inner pocket where she keeps her photographs and letters.

"The squad, mostly. Folks from the rest of the platoon too, whoever is sitting still long enough but won't notice me. It makes people nervous, but it keeps me from getting nervous."

Rio half turns to favor her with a skeptical look. If this

is Jillion Magraff *not* being nervous she'd hate to see her nervous.

"Would you like to see?" Jillion asks.

"Sure."

Jillion draws her bent, sweat-stained sketch pad from under her blouse. She opens it to a page and shyly holds it for Rio to see.

"That's Castain! Hey, Jenou, come here." But Jenou is busy flirting with a drunk but darkly attractive staff sergeant. "You got one of me?"

Jillion pales. "Um . . . I have a few of you."

"Well, let's see."

"Okay, but, you know, I'm just an amateur," Jillion says deprecatingly. "This is the first one I did of you."

The sketch is of a girl, in partial profile, looking off to one side and smiling. The girl is in uniform, but without a helmet, and she looks just ready to start laughing.

"Oh man, my freckles," Rio says. Jillion starts to put it away, but Rio puts her hand on the page, stopping her. "Who was I looking at when you drew this?"

"I don't remember," Jillion says.

But Jillion blushes, and it's pretty clear she's lying. Why, though? Who would she smile at that way? Not Stick. One of the other girls? Certainly not Pang or Tilo. She hopes it wasn't Cassel, but then the answer slowly dawns: Jack. Of course. She was looking at Jack, ready to laugh.

"Okay," Rio says, confused as to how exactly she should be reacting. She wants to compliment Jillion: it's a very good likeness, but it's also, maybe . . . revealing. Rio swallows and forces a laugh. "Any others?"

Jillion, perhaps reading Rio's uncertainty, shakes her head.

"Come on, Magraff, you said there were others." Rio dreads seeing something equally revealing, but dreads more *not* seeing it.

Jillion turns through the pages, past a frightened-looking Tilo, past Geer strangely tender in a face-to-face with his kitten, past Sergeant Cole's gap-toothed grin in an obviously posed picture with his Thompson on his hip. And then, at last, reveals a somber picture of a GI. The GI's face is partly shaded by the brim of a helmet, so only the mouth is visible. It's a partly open mouth, showing a hint of upper teeth. It's a wolfish half-smile, nothing like the laugh-ready grin of the first picture. There's something predatory in that expression that matches the tension of the body. In the picture she has her M1 leveled, and a wisp of smoke curls from the barrel.

For a moment Rio can only stare. For some reason she feels the collar of her blouse chafing her neck, distracting, annoying, spreading irritation through her. She searches for something to say, because again, it's a very good drawing, but she doesn't like it. It seems connected to the scrape of collar on her neck and connected as well to the vague nakedness she feels not having the weight of her rifle on her shoulder. In the sketch her right hand melts into the trigger housing of the rifle.

"That's—" she begins, but suddenly two male hands appear, reaching around Rio to cover and squeeze her breasts. Rio says, "Can I borrow your cigarette?" and without waiting for a reply takes Jillion's cigarette from her mouth and stabs the lit end into one of the hands.

"Goddammit!" the man shrieks. "You burned me! You fugging bitch!"

"Sorry," Rio says mildly. "I must have slipped." There's an angry red-and-black circle on the back of the man's hand, and he alternately shakes it and massages it.

"If you weren't a woman, I'd punch you in the face!"

This is loud enough and angry enough to cause Jenou and Cat to close in, standing shoulder to shoulder with Rio. Beebee dithers uncertainly before finally deciding that loyalty to his new platoon mates is more important than loyalty to a fellow male.

"How about I buy you a beer to show there are no hard feelings?" Rio says, breaking out a tight, false, predatory smile which, it occurs to her, she has just seen in the sketch. That very smile. No smile at all, really.

"How about you—" the man begins in a belligerent tone, but taking a second look at determined faces, he backs away muttering curses under his breath.

They order another round of beers and then move on to a different establishment, where the Arab barman, and his whole family who help serve and clean up, is happier to serve them. There they run into Jack, Stick, and Tilo, all somewhat impaired and clearly intent on getting still more impaired.

Suddenly self-conscious, Rio whispers, "Don't mention my knife. Or the masher back there."

Jenou rolls her eyes but just says, "Oooookay," with a drawn-out vowel. But she can't stop herself, so in a whisper adds, "We wouldn't want you frightening your backup boyfriend."

This leaves Rio in the impossible position of either denying or asking who Jenou means by "backup boyfriend," both of which seem likely to cause Jenou to say still more. She limits herself to shooting Jenou a furious look—not the look from the sketch, an angrier but less dangerous look—which Jenou laughs off, saying, "Save it for the Krauts and the mashers. You don't scare me, Rio."

"The ladies are here, thank God!" Jack says with a big and somewhat misaligned grin. "I'm stuck with these two." He waves vaguely at Stick and Tilo. Tilo has the look of an unfocused owl trying to see in daylight. Stick is less tipsy but not quite his usual solid, steady self.

"Why, you boys have been drinking," Jenou drawls.

"Why, yesh, yesh we have," Jack confesses without shame. He bows from the waist, almost falling over, takes Jenou's hand, and kisses it.

"Well, la-di-da, aren't we fancy?" Jenou says.

Jack moves to take Rio's hand, but she deftly sidesteps and he winks knowingly at her. On a previous occasion where too much drink had been consumed, Rio and Jack shared a drunken kiss. Rio has tried since then to put it entirely out of her mind, to file it away under "irrelevant distractions," but the memory is too strong and seems oddly to be growing stronger and more specific over time. And now it takes the form of that first sketch, the happy one, the one where she isn't holding a smoking rifle.

Wet, freezing cold, and suddenly so warm, warm all the way through, when we kissed.

Her hand reaches for the photograph of Strand Braxton but thinks better of it. It would be too obvious that she was using it as a talisman to ward off thoughts of Jack.

Inevitably the comparisons come floating up through Rio's somewhat addled thoughts. Strand is taller, better looking, a pilot, a dashing figure, an officer, not to mention being a hometown boy who will no doubt get married when the war is over, presumably to Rio.

Maybe.

If that's what I want.

Which it must be.

Surely.

Jack is tall enough without being striking, has reddish hair, faint freckles like her own, and he's funny. And charming. Strand is also charming, but he lacks Jack's quick and easy wit.

I've kissed them both, and . . .

Jillion and her damned pictures.

Strand, unlike Jack, is not here. Strand is on an air base three hundred miles away on the coast of Algeria. She's had letters from him, all censored of course, but it is clear that he is not flying the fighters he'd hoped to pilot but rather is flying bombers. Where he's bombing and who he's bombing, she does not know.

What she does know is that there are women with the Air Corps, as well as nurses and local women, all of whom would presumably find Strand as attractive as she does herself.

Strand isn't that kind of fellow.

But really, is there a male who isn't that sort of fellow? Really?

Suddenly Rio wants a drink or several. Or else to hide away somewhere, all alone, and think. Or better still, not think.

Jillion and her damned pictures.

Tilo says, "Heard we're shipping out. For real, this time." He speaks with the exaggerated care of an inebriate.

Rio nods. Everyone knows they aren't staying in North Africa. Everyone knows they're going somewhere, and probably soon since summer is coming on and up north the Soviets are crying endlessly for the Allies to open a second front by invading Europe proper.

"France," Tilo says in what he mistakenly believes is a confidential whisper.

"Not France," Stick says. "It's either Sardinia or Sicily."

"What's the difference?" Cat asks and drinks half her beer in a single long pull that leaves her with a foam mustache.

"Damned if I know," Jack says, but he's not really paying attention, he's watching Rio, head cocked, grin hovering.

Stick sighs and says, "Okay, here it is." He dips his finger in his beer and begins tracing squiggly lines on the countertop. "That's the Mediterranean Sea. That big boot sticking down? That's Italy. And here's Sicily and Sardinia, which the Eye-Ties control. If we set out for southern France, see, we'd pass right under Kraut and Eye-Tie planes and get shot to hell."

Rio looks on, partly out of actual interest and partly because it allows her to form a blank expression. *Is Jillion recording this too?* Like most frontline soldiers, Rio has no real idea where she is, let alone why. The geography is a mystery to her. "That one," she says, stabbing a finger at the larger of the two islands.

"Why?" Stick asks, curious.

"Because it's bigger?"

Stick laughs. "That'd probably be enough of a reason for the generals," he admits.

"We'll know when we know," Jillion offers in a soft, almost-inaudible voice.

"But when?" Tilo cries in exaggerated despair, arms thrown wide and nearly sweeping an overflowing tin can ashtray onto the floor.

"You in a hurry?" Cat asks him.

"I don't like not knowing. It gets on my nerves. Back and forth, scuttlebutt and more scuttlebutt. Let's just get this war over with!"

"I'm happy to let someone else win it," Rio says. "I'm happy just to sit here in the desert. I can have my folks send me some magazines. Maybe I'll take up knitting."

"Right," Jack says. "Knitting."

He can't even imagine me as I am back home. He's never even met that Rio. He doesn't know me. Not me.

And that's when a half dozen exceedingly drunk Goums come bursting in, loud and aggressive.

The Goums are Berbers, French colonial troops now supporting the Allies. They are Muslim, so they are not allowed to drink, but like the many Baptists equally forbidden to drink, they have suspended some rules temporarily. They are dark-skinned, fantastically bearded, dressed in loosely belted, open-front robes of sorts, like bathrobes, with wide vertical stripes of tan and sun-bleached burgundy. They wear last-war French helmets or white cloth head wrappings and carry what appear to be daggers very much like the one Rio purchased.

"I thought towel-heads didn't drink," Tilo says. It is unlikely that any of the Goums speak enough English to understand his words, but they see the challenge in his eyes and then see that he is in company with women.

One of the Goums shoves Tilo, knocking him back against Rio. Stick moves quickly in front of Tilo, holding up his hands, palms out, and speaking in a soothing voice.

The Goum laughs, takes a step back, grins, and launches himself forward.

And the bar fight begins.

The *first* bar fight of the night.

RAINY SCHULTERMAN—NEW YORK CITY, NEW YORK, USA

Rainy Schulterman is wearing a dress in the bathroom. It is a perfectly nice dress, a young woman's dress, a navy-blue dress with a white collar. She puts it on, twists the collar into place, and performs the necessary gymnastics to raise the zipper from her lower back to her neck. Then she resets the collar, runs smoothing hands down the front of the garment, and stares at her reflection in the bathroom mirror. She moves this way and that, trying to see it from as many angles as possible, a little dance that causes her to brush against her mother's brassieres, hanging from the shower curtain pole.

She last wore this dress to attend her cousin's bar mitzvah. It is her good dress, the only thing she can wear to a place like the Stork Club.

"No," Rainy says.

She considers, face solemn, and decides to try the look with her hair down. She pulls a few strategic hairpins and her black hair explodes out into its natural bristle brush.

"No."

Her uniform hangs neatly from the hook on the back of the door, and in five minutes she is in her Class-A's, complete with shiny men's shoes and bright brass buttons. Three gold chevrons adorn each shoulder.

She sighs with resignation and begins pinning her mad tumbleweed of hair back into place. Finally she settles her service cap, steadying it with a hairpin as well.

Rainy steps out of the bathroom. Her mother is waiting.

Her mother says nothing—nothing in actual words— but with sighs, rolled eyes, a mouth opened as if in shock, and with gestures of shoulders and hands, manages to convey her weary disappointment.

"I was in uniform when he met me," Rainy says defensively.

"Oy."

"Mother."

"Is it so wrong I should miss my daughter, my little baby girl?"

"Your daughter is right here," Rainy says with teeth-gritting impatience.

"My daughter wears a dress when she goes out, especially to the Stork Club. What if Walter Winchell is there and he sees you dressed like a man? And who is this boy you're seeing? Is he a good boy?"

"I don't know yet."

"You go out dancing till all hours with a boy you don't know?"

Rainy's father sticks his head around the corner. "What boy?"

"He's a nice Jewish boy," Rainy says.

"At least there's that," her mother says. Her shoulders slump. Her entire body is one big, middle-aged advertisement of disappointment and desolation. This disappointment at least is not really about Rainy, but rather her brother, Aryeh, a Marine, who married his pregnant *shiksa* girlfriend, Jane, before heading off to the Pacific. Their baby is expected momentarily.

"You look beautiful, even in uniform," Rainy's father says, "and I don't want you looking too beautiful in a dress with legs and arms and legs, giving this boy ideas." He puts a hand over his heart. "I speak as a man when I say never trust any man."

Rainy is not worried about Halev Leventhal getting too familiar. What does worry her is speaking to her father. She's put it off and put it off, each time looking for some perfect moment.

She glances at the wall clock. She has time.

"Get it over with," she mutters. If she doesn't get it over with, the anxiety of it will ruin her night with Halev.

Her *date* with Halev. That's right, it is a date. Definitely a date.

She waits until her mother decides the living room rug needs a quick vacuuming and pulls her father aside in the hallway outside her bedroom.

"What, you need cab fare to come home if he gets fresh?" He starts to dig in his pants for his wallet.

"Dad. I . . ."

And now he knows this is not about producing a five-dollar bill for cab fare.

"What is it, sweetheart?"

"Dad, I love you and nothing will ever change that."

"Of course nothing will ever change that, what could change that?"

"Vito Camporeale," Rainy says.

She watches in fascination as various options play out across her father's face. Should he play dumb? Should he say it's none of her business?

"Dad, the people I work for want me to talk to the people you . . . someone you may know."

"Oh, Rainy," he says, and sags back against the wall, head down on his chest. *"Oy vey iz mir."*

"Dad, listen to me. Daddy." She waits until he raises a face she has never seen before, weary and defeated and ashamed. "Dad, you know the FBI found out and told Army Intelligence. I admit I was shocked, but do you

69

think I really care if you run numbers? Everyone in the neighborhood plays a number."

He moans and scrubs his face with his palms.

"The army wants something, and they think they can get it from this Vito Camporeale."

"It didn't start out like this. I was working for one of our people, a Jewish businessman, but there was some deal and he gave the territory to the dagos. So . . . there is still rent to pay each month." He shrugs.

Rainy takes a moment to note that most of her father's shame over running numbers stems from the fact that he's no longer doing it for a *Jewish* mobster.

"Listen, Dad, we need to talk about this now while Mother is vacuuming. I don't want—"

Her father waves his hand. "Oh, she knows. She's my wife! Of course she knows."

This keeps getting stranger.

"Okay, but we don't want anyone to know who doesn't have a need to know," Rainy says. It takes her father a moment to figure out that by "we" she does not mean the family, but the army.

"Of course," he says, straightening up and sending a glance in the direction of his wife.

"You just need to pass the word that we'd like one of our people to meet with him. No cops—this is not about the law."

That sounds strange coming out of her mouth, but she will have time to consider the moral question later.

Her father nods. "I can tell someone who will tell someone . . ." He shrugs in a way that signals that after that it will be out of his hands. "But you, you don't talk to Don Vito, you understand me? Some of those people, they're animals, these dagos."

Rainy gives him a kiss on the cheek and the doorbell rings. "I'm just passing along a message," she says, sure that she's telling the truth. No one with any sense would strike a bargain with a three-striper. "Please do make the call as soon as possible. My colo—my superior officer is in a hurry."

Halev arrives looking perfectly respectable, wearing a dark suit and a yarmulke, shoes shined, hair combed, face scrubbed, fingernails trimmed, manner a bit intimidated and nervous. After enduring a thorough grilling from Rainy's mother and father—an interrogation that is only slightly more gentle than what Rainy's SS colonel endured—Rainy and Halev escape into the stairwell and finally into the glowing Manhattan night.

"Sorry about all that," Rainy says. She breathes a long exhalation of relief. She's bearded her father in his den, and Halev has not been frightened off by her mother, so now she can let herself relax, at least a little.

"Oh, it was nothing," Halev says. "Just help me get

71

these bamboo shoots out from under my fingernails."

Rainy laughs. Then says, "Sorry about the uniform too. My good dress needed mending."

"I wouldn't have recognized you any other way," he says, and adds with awkward gallantry, "Besides, you look better in a uniform than any other girl in a ball gown."

The eternally logical part of her brain considers counterarguments to that obviously false statement. The rest of her brain tells her to shut up and accept the compliment.

They walk side by side, but not arm in arm, and descend into the subway before emerging on Fifth Avenue, just blocks from the club on East Fifty-Third Street. They race, laughing, to avoid a sudden shower.

The Stork Club is *the* place to see and be seen, and Rainy half expects to be denied entry. This is, after all, the epicenter of New York's low society—actors and actresses, impresarios, promoters, theater owners, and writers—all presided over and reported on by the powerful columnist Walter Winchell.

The Stork Club's owner, Sherman Billingsley, a garrulous, table-hopping force of nature and former bootlegger, greets them as they squeeze through the door just ahead of a woman in evening wear with gloves up to her biceps and décolletage down to . . . well, much farther than

Rainy would ever have dared.

"So, you're Saul's boy?" Billingsley says, shaking Halev's hand before bowing slightly to Rainy, raising her hand and not quite touching it to his lips. "And with a charming sergeant on your arm!"

They are not given the best table in the house. In fact they are shown to a small table far from the dance floor and far too near the banging kitchen door, but it is impossible to resent this in any way as the best tables are occupied by the rich and the famous.

"Is that Orson Welles?" Rainy blurts. "And . . . and . . . is that . . . is that really Frank Sinatra? He's not very tall, is he?"

The room is all swank leather booths, crisp linen on the tables, glittering crystal, and rushing waiters. The band is just filing out onto the stage.

"This may not be a discreet question, but how did you get reservations here?" Rainy asks.

Halev smiles, leans across the table, and says, "My father is rather successful in the garment trade, and my uncle Max is tailor to probably a quarter of the men in the room."

"Do tell me you're rich," Rainy jokes. "It will make my parents so happy. The only thing better would be if you were a doctor."

"I am not in any way rich," Halev says. "My father?

My uncle?" He shrugs. "They make a living."

They make a living. So, yes: rich, or close to it.

They sip cocktails and sneak discreet glances at the famous folk. They each order a shrimp cocktail to be followed by a steak with asparagus and potatoes au gratin. A very tall man trailing a small gaggle of men and women passes by and tosses a casual salute and a wink at Rainy. It's not until the big man is past that Rainy recognizes him and very nearly stabs her fork into her tongue.

"Was that John Wayne?"

"Elisheva Schulterman," Halev says, leaning back in his chair with an expression of great satisfaction. "You have just been saluted by the Duke."

"And winked at, let's not leave that out of the story."

"Wait until you hear the band. You won't see them very well unless we go up to dance, but that's Benny Goodman's band."

Rainy frowns. "This is mad! I shouldn't be in a place with these people! And . . . I don't think I dance."

"You don't think you do?"

"Well, I am certainly not dancing at the Stork Club in front of Frank Sinatra."

But she does dance after a few more cocktails and fortified by a massive steak of the sort regular folks aren't supposed to be getting, what with there being a war on.

It is a glittering, wonderful evening, but Rainy has to work at enjoying it. This is not her place, not her people. Her people wear green uniforms, curse frequently, smell usually, and complain constantly. But within Rainy's limited ability to relax and enjoy life, it is an enjoyable, even somewhat enchanting, evening.

Be honest, she scolds herself, *it's better than somewhat enchanting.*

Emerging into the fresh air afterward they find the rain has stopped, leaving the streets wet and shining. The washing that often hangs from balconies and fire escapes is gone, the sidewalk vendors have all fled, and the streets feel empty and clean. There's a metallic smell that is at once chemical and sanitary, as if the city has just been mopped with ammonia.

An aging Hasid, his beaver hat sparkling with raindrops, casts a disapproving look at them, and only then does Rainy realize that Halev has taken her hand. Ultra-Orthodox Jews do not like men and women walking together, let alone holding hands, let alone a man holding hands with a woman wearing a uniform.

Rainy feels Halev's hand shrinking in hers, and she tightens her grip in defiance. Let the *alter cocker* sneer, she will not be shamed by those people. She will not be shamed by anyone.

And if he wants to kiss me?

Halev insists on walking her home, despite acknowledging that she was the one who at their first meeting rescued him from a street fight and not the other way around. Still, a gentleman does not let his date roam the streets of the city alone at night.

They are a block from Rainy's home when she notices that a long, black Plymouth sedan is creeping along the wet street behind them. Halev notices it too. "Let's walk a little faster, shall we?"

"Actually, Halev, I have a feeling that may be my ride."

"What?"

She stops and turns back to face the car, which now accelerates gently to come even with her. A burly man in a heavy overcoat and wearing a homburg hat rolls down the window and says, "You the Jew's girl . . . uh, what's her name?"

A second man, smaller but with the dead eyes of a porcelain doll, says, "Schulterman."

"That's me," Rainy says.

The car brakes and both men get out. Both wear loose-fitting overcoats to conceal the bulge of shoulder holsters. That they are gangsters is not in question, they practically have the word *gangster* hung on a sandwich board around their necks.

"Come on, Rainy," Halev says nervously.

"I'm so sorry, Halev, but I have to say good night."

"But—"

"It's something . . ." She searches for the word and only comes up with, "Official."

"I see."

"I had a great time."

"So did I. But these gentlemen are definitely putting an end to my schemes for a good night kiss."

Rainy smiles. "Next time?"

"Promise?" he asks with a crooked smile that reveals a sweet mix of desire and bashfulness.

Feeling an overwhelming swirl of mismatched feelings, including the giddiness of attraction to Halev, nervousness, and fear—but mostly fear of screwing something up—she shakes Halev's hand chastely and self-consciously, and slides into the backseat of the Plymouth.

RIO RICHLIN—CAMP ZIGZAG, TUNISIA, NORTH AFRICA

"You Cole?"

It is four o'clock in the morning, and the man speaking is an MP corporal. He is behind the wheel of a jeep pulling a wooden cart on bald automobile tires. It's a makeshift arrangement that has never appeared in an army field manual. But then the army manual does not contemplate this particular sort of cargo.

Sergeant Cole rubs sleep from his eyes and looks at the MP, then at the bodies piled and intertwined in the cart. Eight of his soldiers—the new guy Beebee, plus Suarez, Stick, Stafford, Castain, Preeling, Magraff, and Richlin—are in various states of consciousness. They are bleeding, bruised, groaning, and trying unsuccessfully, in the case of the marginally conscious ones, to climb out.

"I'm Cole," he admits, with disgust in both syllables.

"I think these belong to you." The driver jerks a thumb over his shoulder.

"You can drive 'em right on back to the stockade," Cole snaps.

The corporal laughs. "No can do, Sarge, stockade is full. So's the city jail. And anyway, the dark-haired one there slipped me a fiver to get them here. There's been some roughhousing. Your bunch were in a fight with some Frog colonials. Then, best as we can tell, they went on to get into a second round with a Texas outfit."

"Dammit," Cole says, which is about as extreme as his language gets unless there's shooting going on.

Rio rolls off of Cat, tumbles, and slams hard into the dirt. She lies there, facedown, for quite a while, arms and hands flattened on the ground. She might just as well have fallen out of a passing plane.

How did I get here?

The ground does not feel quite solid to Rio, in fact it is spinning, spinning, and sort of falling away, like one of those boards they use to ride the waves at Stinson Beach. Oh, she wishes she were there right now, wishes she were far away, lying on some beach. And also really wishing hard that she had not started drinking that ouzo they got . . . somewhere.

Her tongue is a dead rat coated in tar; her muscles are both limp and sore; her stomach . . . oh, she doesn't even want to think about that because she's got nothing left to puke up unless she's going to start puking up her liver.

Also, her face hurts. She almost remembers the punch that connected with her right cheek. And she can vaguely trace the soreness in her throat muscles to an armlock, possibly from an MP, that part is not at all clear. The one thing she does remember with a certain satisfaction is that the sprain in her right ankle is from the impact of her boot tip on a sensitive area of a male Texan's person.

"All right, you useless bunch of clowns, crawl off and shower. Who knows what bugs you picked up, and I won't have them in my tents. And, Suarez, for God's sake pull up your pants!"

Cat says, "Hey, I lost a tooth."

By reveille they have showered and caught ninety minutes of sleep. Rio returns only very reluctantly to consciousness because consciousness is pain. Her head. Oh God, her head. And her eyes! Oh no, that's even worse.

Like a zombie she dresses and runs a comb across a head that has become a big bass drum pounding, pounding.

"You okay?" Rio says to Jenou through gritted teeth.

"Unh," Jenou answers.

"You have a black eye," Rio points out.

"Unh," Jenou agrees.

The squad shuffles miserably toward the assembly area. They feel that their misery must be obvious to all, but as Rio blinks in the painful sunlight she notices that the same misery afflicts at least two-thirds of the forty-seven—now forty-eight—men and women who make up Fifth Platoon.

Sergeant Cole lines up with them, no one too concerned with spit and polish given that this is now a veteran platoon with a number of experiences in combat.

Phil O'Malley, the new platoon sergeant who has replaced Garaman, is an ancient forty-five-year-old veteran of the last war. He's a man who gives an impression of being almost as wide as he is tall, but the width is in the shape of solid muscle and gristle. He has a salt-and-pepper buzz cut, a tan face, and slitted brown eyes that could be amused or cruel, depending. O'Malley stands a little ahead of the formation.

Rio assumes this is the usual morning ritual, with the usual pro forma assurances that all are present and accounted for. But it's already gone on too long and the thought that maybe she should force herself to pay attention begins to form in the woolly depths of her hungover brain.

Or I could just sit down right here in the dirt. That would be nice.

There are two lieutenants up there now in the eye-searing light. One Rio recognizes as the headquarters company lieutenant who has been filling in until a new lieutenant can arrive to replace the deceased-but-not-mourned Lieutenant Liefer.

This would explain the second lieutenant who is shaking hands now with the acting lieutenant, who salutes pleasantly and ambles off.

"Better put them at ease, Sergeant O'Malley, some of them look about ready to keel over," the new lieutenant says.

He's young—they always are—twenty-three or twenty-four years old. His uniform is perfection, creases all crisp and ruler straight, lapels starched and ironed to a knife's edge, cap set to the correct angle with just a bit extra for a hint of swagger. He has a patrician face with high cheekbones, smooth peaches-and-cream complexion, and eyes the color of a calm sea on a sunny day.

"Now we're getting somewhere," Jenou says voicelessly.

The lieutenant is gorgeous.

"I'm Lieutenant Mike Vanderpool, I'm your new platoon commander."

Despite the dandy's uniform, he stands easy, a slight tilt to his head, and neither his voice nor his expression marks him as any kind of martinet.

"I'm a West Pointer, I'll just confess that right from the start."

There is a rustle of low laughs, quickly quashed.

"Yes, I am one of *them*. And this is my first time in the actual war. So I am relieved to find that I have under me some of the finest NCOs in the army. Sergeant O'Malley, Sergeant Shields, Sergeant Cole, and Sergeant Alvarez, I will rely on your experience as we work together."

Rio almost smiles to see Cole standing a bit taller before self-consciously relapsing to an unimpressed slouch.

"You men—and women—I will come to know each of you in time. Give me a chance, and I'll return the favor. Sergeant O'Malley? Anything you or your NCOs would like to say?"

Jack suddenly collapses, but he picks himself up and is diplomatically ignored by the new lieutenant.

Cole speaks up. "Sir, I don't know if this is the right time, but I'm down a corporal and I'd like to replace him out of my squad."

"You have someone in mind?"

"I've got a man who's been filling the role temporarily. Stick. I mean, um, what the hell is your actual name, Stick?"

"Dain Sticklin, sir." He winces noticeably, perhaps because his jaw is bruised a yellowish blue and may not be quite centered. But he looks better than Jack, who may well have died, been buried, and only recently been dis-interred.

Lieutenant Vanderpool steps over, hands behind his back, interested. "You seem to have been injured, Private Sticklin."

"Sir, we had a pass and . . . well, those back streets get pretty dark, with stairs and all, so I tripped."

"Ah."

"Landed on my face, sir."

"Well. Maybe we could issue more flashlights. This tripping problem seems to be something of an epidemic in the platoon."

"Yes, sir," Stick says, his expression that of a man straining not to throw up.

"I will also require more attention to your uniforms in the future. The general is a stickler for proper uniform, including ties and shined boots. I would rather not be chewed out by General Patton. I saw it happen to a bird colonel once, and it was not a show I care to see twice."

O'Malley, standing beside Lieutenant Vanderpool, says, "Yes, sir. Understood, sir."

Vanderpool flashes a grin that gradually becomes a thoughtful frown. "It seems this platoon is afflicted with an unusual degree of clumsiness. At least half of you seem to have . . . tripped and fallen on your faces. But we'll fix that right up. Sticklin, do you know what's good for the aftereffects of tripping?"

"Oh . . ." Stick says, sensing where this line of questioning is going.

"A nice five-mile run, out to the wadi and back. I need

to confer with my sergeants, so *Corporal* Sticklin? Lead the men out."

Jenou raises a trembling hand, and Vanderpool says, "Yes, the women too."

Rio has made many five-mile runs. But a five-mile run with a crashing headache and a mouth full of wool is a whole new level of agony.

"Is it okay, do you think, if I marry the lieutenant?" Jenou asks as they slog through the camp toward the distant cluster of trees they've taken to calling the wadi.

"Unh," Rio answers.

7

RAINY SCHULTERMAN—NEW YORK CITY, NEW YORK, USA

The smaller gangster slides in beside Rainy. Something about him reminds her of the SS colonel. There's something not fully human about him, as if one parent had been a lizard or a snake.

"You have a number for me?" Rainy asks, keeping her voice level on a sea of rising and falling waves of emotion.

"Number? You trying to be funny?"

"I assumed you were here to give me a way to contact Mr. Camporeale."

"Way to contact? *You're* the contact, girly."

"It's sergeant, not girly," she says, and the instant the words are out of her mouth she thinks it's a mistake. The little man's reptilian expression turns feral for a moment, the look of an animal ready to pounce. But he leans back, reins in his hostility, and says, "All right then, *Sergeant.* We're all good Americans, aren't we, Louie?"

"I bought a war bond for my kid," Louie offers over his shoulder. "Twenty dollars!"

"Don Vito don't want to talk to some FBI or some army officer either, don't trust 'em. He'll talk to you."

"Then I would be pleased to talk to him," Rainy says stiffly, feeling very uncomfortable, as if she's disobeying an order. She isn't exactly, her orders had contemplated the possibility of a face-to-face meeting, but she's already thinking ahead to having to report all this to Colonel Corelli.

Professor of Oriental Languages Corelli.

Amateur.

They drive far longer than is strictly necessary, sometimes creeping at walking speed around a block only to go racing away up Broadway at full speed. Louie keeps a close eye on his rearview mirrors.

"We're clean," Louie says at last, and moments later they pull to a stop in the oily darkness beneath an elevated train track. They are in the Bowery, an elongated rectangle of streets around Delancey and Forsyth in Lower Manhattan, just north of Chinatown. It is a neighborhood of secondhand shops, employment agencies, cheap hotels, and narrow all-hours diners catering to the crowds of sailors and soldiers who wander unsteadily from tavern to tavern.

The nearest lit-up establishment is a second-story pool hall above a closed-for-the-night grocer.

Louie climbs out and opens Rainy's door. Then he glances in the direction of a loud shout floating down from the pool hall and says, "This may not be the most suitable place for a young lady of quality."

"She's a kike, she ain't quality," the smaller one says.

"I've been in worse places," Rainy says, images of the Tunisian desert appearing in her memory. She ignores the casual anti-Semitism.

They walk up a long, steep, narrow flight of stairs, at one point having to turn sideways to let a trio of Marines come down. Before she sees the pool hall she hears it, a rich concerto played by cues hitting balls, and balls snapping into others, and glasses tinkling with ice, and shouts of frustration and triumph, loud guffaws, and somewhat more distant the musical *ding-ding-ding!* of pinball machines. All of that, and someone is spinning records, because Rainy hears the risqué Andrews Sisters song "Strip Polka" playing.

> *There's a burlesque theater where the gang loves to go*
> *To see Queenie, the cutie of the burlesque show.*

There's no door at the top of the stairs, so they emerge directly onto the gaming floor, onto wood stained almost black by generations of benign neglect, and wallpaper that fairly drips with congealed smoke. There are a dozen tables in three rows of four, green felt bright beneath bare bulbs, and three pinball machines against the far wall, *ding-ding-ding*ing away. There's a bar at the back and a record player perched on one end of the bar along with a tall stack of 78s.

A lanky, sad-looking sailor in a stained white uniform sits at a stool thumbing through the records. All the pool tables are in use, sailors, soldiers, working men in dungarees or overalls, and interspersed here and there like flowers in a sea of weeds are women—women of the type one would expect to find in a pool hall late at night. They aren't all beautiful, but they are all young, or pass for young, and they are all dressed down to the very lowest limits of propriety.

"Like I was sayin'," Louie says with an abashed half-grin, "maybe not the place for a young lady such as yourself, miss. Sergeant, I mean."

"I promise not to faint," Rainy says, which tickles the gangster's fancy and he gives up a huge guffaw.

"Take it off, take it off," cries a voice from the rear.
"Take it off, take it off," soon it's all you can hear.
But she's always a lady even in pantomime,
So she stops and always just in time.

They cross the length of the room toward the bar, and there is something in Louie's size, and in the eyes and manner of the other thug, that causes even inebriated longshoremen and ladies of the night to step gingerly out of the way.

There's a door beside the bar. The driver knocks once, hears a single gruff syllable, and opens the door wide for Rainy to step in.

It's an office, a square room with a curtained window that probably leads to a fire escape. There's an impressive oak desk with a vacant swing office chair behind it. One wall is covered in thumbtacked travel posters with curled edges: Naples, Sicily, Rome, but also Miami and New Orleans.

The wall to Rainy's right is fitted with shelves, mostly empty, but some bearing stacks of newspapers and magazines. There are three books, one of which, Rainy is sure, must be the Christian Bible. An impressive engraved silver crucifix hangs from the leading edge of the top shelf.

There are two men already in the room, one small and old and gray, with a face that looks like a piece of driftwood, improbably craggy with a sagging mouth, and wearing no expression.

The other is a large, portly man in a decent brown suit. He has a round, cheerful face and the red nose of a dedicated drinker. He steps forward smiling, hand out.

"So you're Schulterman's kid. Well, glad to meet you, honey, your old man must be proud as hell—excuse my French—proud as a peacock."

"Thank you, and it's good to meet you, Mr. . . . ."

"Camporeale," he says. "It's hard for folks to pronounce unless they grew up speaking Italian. We go with Campo, mostly, but you can call me Don Vito. That's easier, right?"

Instinctively, Rainy lies. "Don Vito it is, then, because I don't speak any Italian. I have no head for languages."

She's hoping her father has not bragged too often about his multilingual daughter. But almost certainly he would not have brought her name into his work, and in any case he works only indirectly for Camporeale.

"And what do they call you, aside from sergeant, I mean?"

"Rainy will do fine," she says, forcing a smile. Time to be friendly: she is surrounded by gunsels.

"Rainy. I like that. Must be a story there, huh?"

"No doubt, but my parents have not shared the details."

He laughs knowingly. "Come, sit, what are you drinking?"

"I'll have a club soda," she says.

"Ah, a killjoy," Don Vito says in mock irritation. "Get her a soda. Put a straw in it. Plenty of ice. Throw in a cherry, it'll be like a, what do they call 'em? A Shirley Temple. She's just a kid, after all. What are you, eighteen, nineteen?"

Rainy sits in a hastily supplied wooden chair, and Don Vito settles in behind his desk. He leans forward, forearms on his desk blotter. "So. What can a humble immigrant do for the United States Army?"

"Well, sir . . . Don Vito . . . I'm only a lowly sergeant, and this is a conversation you should have with someone who has some rank."

He winks, a move which, owing to his chubby cheeks, closes both eyes for a second. When his eyes open again the cheerfulness is gone, replaced by shrewd appraisal. A second earlier and Rainy might have mistaken him for a door-to-door salesman. But a much different animal is looking at her now from dark, porcine eyes.

"I'm allergic to people with rank. Regular beat cop? That's no problem, I buy 'em free drinks and let 'em play some pinball. Cops with rank? You never know if they'll be reasonable or not. Same thing in the army, I'm guessing."

He lets the silence stretch and at last Rainy speaks. "I have no opinion on my superior officers."

Don Vito and Louie, now leaning against the door, both erupt in loud laughter. The gray man does not laugh.

"That was funny, Tony, you should laugh," Don Vito says to the gray man, who still does not laugh. Then he says something in Italian—although in a dialect that to Rainy's ear is subtly different from the standard Roman Italian she's learned.

Still, she can translate it. Don Vito has said, "The Jew bitch thinks she's smart."

This, finally, earns a dusty wheeze that might be a laugh from gray Tony.

"Listen, Rainy, right? Rainy. Yeah. Okay, Rainy, for obvious reasons I'd rather talk to people I know. People I trust. And I trust you because I know you love your father and would never want to do anything that could hurt him."

The threat is clear, and Rainy nods in acknowledgment. It occurs to her that playing word games with NCOs and officers, who are, after all, generally reasonable and constrained by the uniform code of military justice, is very different from sparring with a man who earned his nickname by castrating the men he kills. The threat is not empty, and this is not a friendly chat.

"Here's the thing," Don Vito says. "I got a son, little older than you, a good boy but headstrong. You know? Impulsive. He's smart but he's young." He shrugs.

Rainy sips at her drink and takes a moment to realize that what Don Vito means by "headstrong" and "impulsive" is probably violent, predatory—the gangster son of a gangster father.

Don Vito, speaking that same odd Italian to Tony, says, "Ten bucks says Cisco's in her pants inside of twenty-four hours." Then to Rainy he says, "I'm translating for Tony, his English isn't so good. He's my counselor. Like my law-yer, but *Napolitano*."

Napolitano? As in Naples? That's *mainland* Italy, not Sicily. Rainy nods, blank, giving nothing away.

"So my boy, Cisco, Francisco, but hey, he's born Amer-ican, right, so Cisco. Anyway, Cisco has a little problem with some people up in Harlem. They want an eye for an eye, but we ain't giving 'em Cisco, so that could be war—our own kinda war—and that's bad for everyone. So it would be convenient if Cisco could spend some time in the Old Country, with my uncle. My uncle is a very wise man; he'll get Cisco straightened out."

"You want the army to get your son to Italy?"

"You're very quick, you know that?"

"The army would want something in exchange."

Don Vito made a comical face that translated meant, *Of course they do. How could they not?*

"I'll need to talk to my superiors. I don't have a list of their requests."

He waves that off. "I know what they want. There's a city called Salerno in Italy. It's at the north end of a beau-tiful long beach, beautiful, you should see it. Just the kind of beach an army might want to land on."

Rainy freezes and is too slow to stop the reaction from showing. Don Vito grins like a barracuda.

"I hear things," he says. "Sicily first. Then Salerno.

You want to know the dates?"

"No," she says quickly. "The less I know, the less I can reveal." She feels safest speaking stiffly, formally.

Vito the Sack nods with sincere approval. Of course he *would* favor closed mouths. "Here's the deal. I'll give you chapter and verse on Fascist and Kraut positions around Salerno. My family runs most of Salerno, not all, but enough that nothing moves there we don't know about."

"I don't have the power to make a commitment," Rainy says.

"Fair enough. You go talk to your colonel or captain or whatever. You know where I am. Just one thing: you." He points a thick finger at her. From Rainy's angle it seems to come at her from just beneath dark and dangerous eyes. "You come back. Just you. And you personally, *and your father*, will guarantee my boy's safety until he gets to my uncle's house."

"I'll do my—"

"Uh-uh!" He interrupts sharply, wagging a finger for emphasis. "I don't care about your best. Simple yes or no: is my boy with my uncle, that's it. You got that? You get him there. Clear?"

"Signore Camporeale," Rainy says, pronouncing his full name in a very credible Italian accent, "I follow orders. If my orders say to get your son to Italy, then I will get your son to Italy. But I don't work for you, I work for the army."

"Is that so?"

"Yes, sir, it is. And your son will not be getting into my pants, not in twenty-four hours or twenty-four days or twenty-four years."

It takes a few beats before Don Vito realizes what's happened.

"*Lei parla Italiano?*"

"*Si, Don Vito, un poco.*"

"You deceived me."

"I gained an advantage."

"And now you give up that advantage?"

Rainy shakes her head. "No, Don Vito, because now you're going to have me checked out, and you'll soon find out that I'm often used as a translator."

"I've always said Hebes were the smartest race . . . next to *partenopeos*. That's people from Naples, see."

Rainy stands up and discovers that her knees have gone a bit wobbly and her breathing is ragged. Yes, there is something about these people that is similar to what she'd felt coming from the SS colonel. It was like trying to hold a calm discussion with a hungry tiger.

Don Vito stands and comes around the desk. He takes Rainy's hand in two of his and holds hers firmly but not harshly.

"You'll do this?"

"If my commanding officer orders me to, yes."

Rainy disentangles herself and leaves, by way of the pool hall. There's a new song playing, the bleary, slow-tempo tune with lyrics sung over a mellow sax.

What's the use of getting sober
When you're gonna get drunk again?

Rainy is trembling as she reaches fresh air, and the stress catches up with her. Down the street she finds an all-hours diner with a pay phone in one corner. She fumbles in her purse for a nickel and makes a call to Colonel Corelli.

Ten minutes later an unmarked army staff car picks her up a block away.

RAINY SCHULTERMAN—LAGUARDIA FIELD, NEW YORK, USA

Amateur.

That's what Bayswater said of Corelli and his organization. *Amateur. He's going to get you killed.* And it eats at Rainy. From her first days in the army she's been taught that her first duty is to obey orders. She has latched onto that thought, relied on it, let it shape her thinking about the army and her job in that army.

It is comforting to be able to shift responsibility, to be able to shrug and say, *I'm following orders.* But what if the person giving the orders doesn't know what he's doing?

Rainy saw the colonel again, was congratulated, thoroughly debriefed, and sent home for two days. Then she was summoned to see Corelli a third time and given a sealed packet of orders along with instructions not to open it until she is airborne out of New York. She pats it through her overcoat as her car and its driver come to a halt on the bleak tarmac.

The C-47 is a twin-engine tail-dragger, meaning that it lands on the wheels beneath its wings and lets the tail settle down onto a third, smaller wheel. It is the workhorse of American air forces with variant versions used to haul supplies, to haul men, to haul VIPs, and to carry airborne troops to drop zones. Its civilian version is known as a DC-3.

This plane sits tail down, with both engines running, round nose pointed optimistically toward the eastern sky. A light, early morning rain falls, slicking the concrete runway and turning the green-painted fuselage almost black. The props are kicking up a horizontal tornado of mist that plucks at Rainy's cap, so she has to hold it with one hand while hefting her light pack on one shoulder.

At least she won't be jumping out of this plane. Hopefully.

Ground crew lead her from the colonel's thoughtfully provided car to the doorway abaft the wings, which means passing right through that gale of backwash. She shouts a "thank you" that the ground crewmen cannot possibly hear.

She is helped up the steps by a sergeant, who grabs her bag and with quick, practiced movements whips it into one of the seats and ties it down with a series of cords. The seats run down both sides, facing toward what would be the center aisle on a DC-3. Inside the plane are some crates, one quite large, lashed down with thick straps.

There is only one other passenger, a civilian, obviously Cisco Camporeale. At first glance he doesn't look like a gangster, though there is something flashy and cheap about him. He's dark of hair, eye, and complexion, of medium height, solidly built. He's dressed in an expensive overcoat with an equally expensive and fashionable dark suit beneath. His tie is silk, somewhat flamboyant, and carefully knotted.

Rainy is shown to a seat beside him and has her seat belt fastened for her. A second, more careful inspection takes in the way the young gangster looks at her. His eyes are large and moist, framed by girlish lashes. His lips are thin and rest in an ironic smile. It is a handsome face, a very handsome face, but his expression, at first predatory, softens into dismissal.

Apparently, Rainy is not his type.

She breathes a sigh of relief at that. She's been worried he might, over the course of a long mission, get ideas that would make Rainy's job harder.

"I'd stand up, you know. I am a gentleman, but I'm strapped in," Cisco says, and extends his hand with a languid superiority that almost suggests he expects it to be kissed rather than shaken. "Cisco Camporeale."

His palm is damp, either with nerves or perhaps just a result of the steam rising from wet clothing.

"Sergeant Schulterman," she says.

"What do I call you?"

"Sergeant Schulterman." She wants to set the tone of their relationship at the start.

"Okay, Sarge, have it your way," he says, smirking and then dismissing her.

It amazes Rainy that the uniform she wears and the stripes on her shoulder do such a very good job of transforming her from a teenaged young woman into someone who can shut down a mobster. For the very first time she has the fleeting thought that military life might be something to extend even after the war is over. For all its incessant hostility toward women soldiers, the army is one place that a bright but uneducated young woman can do important work.

But as soon as that thought pops into her head she quashes it. Good grief, become a career soldier? She'd thought of becoming a lawyer or a teacher or starting a business. None of those careers involve risking life and limb.

To which another part of her mind, using a very different tone, answers, *Exactly: none of those careers involve risking life and limb*. And damned if she doesn't sort of enjoy the danger. She's jumped out of a plane and survived a firefight without turning tail. Having walked so close to danger, some part of her wants to return, to see whether she has the courage to take it further still.

Within minutes the plane is trundling down the runway, tail rising to level, and the noise from the wheels rushing down the pavement gives way to the whine of electric motors raising the wheels into the underbelly of the plane.

The sergeant, who explains that he is the "loadmaster," a term Rainy has not heard before, shouts the itinerary and the rules.

"Okay, folks, here's the deal. First stop is St. John's, Newfoundland. That's 1,130 miles. We'll be cruising at about 180 miles an hour, so figure six, six hours and change, depending on tailwinds. We top off the fuel tanks—our range is just 1,600 miles, so we top off in Newfoundland and then head to Lajes base in the Azores, which is 1,420 miles. It's within range, but there's some weather up north, so we'll assess things when we approach the point of no return."

"The point of no return?" Cisco says, skeptical.

"Halfway. It's the place where it takes the same amount of fuel to get back as it does to continue," the loadmaster replies seriously. "Our motto is, 'Don't get cocky.' The Atlantic is a big ocean, and I'm not that good a swimmer."

"Point of no return," Cisco repeats in a more serious tone. "That's good. I'll have to remember that."

"We've rigged a chemical toilet behind that draw

curtain back there. It's awkward, but at least you get a little privacy. I'll bring you a thermos of coffee and some sandwiches in a while, and once we're at cruising altitude you can unbuckle and sack out on the floor if you want, but it'll be plenty cold."

"Thanks," Rainy says.

The vibration and engine noise make it necessary to concentrate in order to make out what's being said, but Rainy has taken note of the flight times and the mention of coffee. She pulls her orders from her pocket. Three typewritten pages, though the last page is only a paragraph.

She reads it quickly. Reaches the end. Frowns.

She goes back and reads it more carefully, certain that she has missed something. Missed more than a few things, actually.

By the time she's done with her second reading, her hands are trembling and her breath is short. This can't possibly be all there is. She checks the envelope again in case she's overlooked a sheet. Nothing.

She is ordered to appear at the airfield, to take the flight to the Azores, there to rendezvous with a Royal Navy submarine, which is to take her to Italy. She is to deliver Cisco to his uncle and receive in return a map of enemy emplacements around Salerno. She is to deliver the packet to a certain person working at the Swedish Embassy in Rome.

And then?

Her orders are silent about *then*.

She swallows past a rising lump in her throat and barely stops herself reading through one more time. Nothing about *then*. Nothing about where she is to go, what she is to do, how she is to escape.

She wants to throw up. Her face feels like it's burning. Surely this can't be it. Surely even an *amateur* would have a plan? But of course there is a plan for getting what Corelli wants, just no plan for keeping her alive and out of the hands of the Gestapo or Italian counterintelligence.

The Swede. He must have the next set of instructions, the ones explaining how she is not simply being forgotten in the middle of enemy territory.

The Swede. Sure. That's it. He'll help her.

But try as she might, she cannot make herself believe it, not all the way.

There's a difference between taking risks and committing suicide.

The six hours and twenty minutes pass in relative silence. Cisco leans back and dozes, eyes half-shut. Rainy's mind races in circles. This isn't a plan, this is a sketch. This is espionage through rose-colored lenses. It is impossible to avoid the conclusion that if she were an officer more attention would have been paid to her survival.

I'm a nobody, a buck sergeant, a GI. Expendable, like any other GI.

The Newfoundland base is a bare, scraped place beside dark water. There are rows of Nissen huts, the British version of a Quonset hut, a scattering of tin-sided administrative buildings, and a hangar. A bulldozer with a snow blade attached lies parked between two huts, but while it is chilly for summer, there is no snow.

A jeep fetches the two passengers and hustles them away to thaw out around an iron stove in a Nissen hut equipped with the usual military lack of comfort.

"Can a man get a drink at least?" Cisco asks a Canadian airman, who looks him up and down before walking away without a word. Cisco intertwines his fingers and cracks his knuckles and says, "That fellow needs a good punch in the neck."

Rainy feels sleepiness steal over her and spends the hour's break savoring the warmth of the stove. Then it's back aboard the plane, another takeoff, and a rapid ascent into low clouds. They burst through into hazy, declining sunlight beneath a higher, thinner layer of cover, and take a big, sloping, rightward turn to the south. This leg of the trip is to take eight hours, a very long time to sit on what amounts to a hard bench contemplating the line between duty to the mission and the duty to stay alive.

Gestapo. That is the word that keeps pushing its way

into her thoughts. *Geheime Staatspolizei*, the secret state police, Hitler's enforcers, his torturers. Beatings. Beatings at the very least. The breaking of bones, the crushing of fingers, the gouging of eyes, rape, and . . .

She sucks air, feeling panic add volatile fuel to her misgivings, panic that seems to crush the air from her lungs. She licks her lips and glances at Cisco to make sure he isn't watching her, isn't seeing the sick fear she has not yet suppressed.

Rainy slips off her seat belt and stands, urgently needing to move. She explores the bare cylinder of the plane's fuselage, locating the chemical toilet and . . . and nothing else. She uses the facility, sitting perched on the tiny seat, bent forward, face in her hands.

Soldiers die every day. Soldiers are sacrificed every day. She is a soldier.

She heads forward to the open cockpit door and looks inside at a confusing array of dials and switches. The pilot is head-back and mouth open, fast asleep, while the copilot keeps his hands on the yoke. Peering through the windshield, Rainy sees taller, darker clouds ahead.

"Boomers. Thunderstorm," the copilot says over his shoulder, indicating the clouds with a jerk of his chin.

The piles of cloud are red in the light of the plunging sun. Darkness looms in the east beyond. Rainy returns to her seat and straps in.

Thunderstorm it is, and the C-47 is not able to rise above it and has no slack in its fuel supply to try an end around.

A flash, like the world's biggest camera flashbulb going off and . . .

Craaaack!

Boom!

A massive fist punches the C-47 in its aluminum spine and drives it down a stomach-churning five hundred feet.

"Shit!" Rainy yelps as she is thrown against her seat belt.

Cisco looks at her, amused, and yells, "Nice language coming from a lady."

Boom-bum-bum-bum-BOOM!

The thunderclap is louder than anything Rainy has ever even imagined hearing. The physical blow that follows shivers the thin skin of the fuselage. She's amazed the small porthole hasn't blown out.

The cockpit door is still open, and Rainy can see the pilots are both awake, engaged, and tense, but not so tense that one doesn't take a moment to glance back and grin at what must be a look of terror on Rainy's face. His face is illuminated by the sickly glow of instruments and then in blazing white as a bolt of lightning flashes and fractures and crawls across the cloud face ahead.

Wind buffets the plane, sends it slipping sideways and

off-center, like a car sliding on an icy road. Thunder batters them again and again, each clap more violent than the one before. The lightning is so close and so wild it seems to pass right through the plane, turning every last rivet blazing white and leaving behind an afterimage on her retinas. Static electricity raises the hair on the back of her neck and arms.

Hour after hour. Rainy has never been one to get seasick or airsick, but she clutches the paper vomit bag close, just in case, because the lunatic elevator ride they are on kneads and shoves and twists her stomach as if determined to reduce her to shivering, puking helplessness.

But eventually the lightning comes from farther astern and the thunder falls away to a distant, disgruntled rumble. The wind, however, intensifies, and the plane is a very small piece of flotsam on a continent-wide river of turbulent air. Up . . . down . . . up . . . down, like riding the Cyclone at Coney Island.

The loadmaster comes walking back, moving easily with the lurch, and carrying a small cooler and a thermos.

"Want to try to eat something?"

Rainy glares hatred at him and his sandwiches, but Cisco says, "Sure, whatcha got?"

"I got ham and cheese on rye, and I got tuna salad on white."

The mention of tuna salad almost does it, almost has

Rainy puking, and she would have but for the fact that her stomach is empty.

"Grab me a ham and cheese," Cisco says. "And some coffee. Black."

"Black it is, since we got no sugar and no milk," the loadmaster says. "We'll be landing in an hour. Might be a bit hairy."

"Hairy?" Rainy asks.

The loadmaster holds his hand out flat, palm down, and simulates a plane trying to land in heavy wind. It is not reassuring.

And in fact the landing is not pretty. There is an unusual amount of bouncing and tail-skewing involved, but eventually the plane comes to a stop, the door opens, and Rainy piles out just as quickly as she is able. The ground is hard and it is wet and the sky is dark, but she barely restrains herself from falling to her knees and kissing it.

Cisco? Unaffected. "Now what?"

A jeep with its canvas cover up tears across the tarmac from the direction of a squat, unimpressive control tower, bearing a woman lieutenant and a male sergeant. Rainy remembers belatedly to salute.

"I trust you had a pleasant flight?" the lieutenant asks with the gleefully malicious grin common to airmen and sailors when dealing with earthbound folk. She's wearing

109

a black armband that reads OD—officer of the day. Or night, in this case.

Only then does Rainy realize she's still clutching the unused vomit bag. She crumples it and shoves it into her pocket.

They are driven to a white plaster building full of unoccupied desks. Someone has thoughtfully laid out Azorean bread rolls, roast beef, a local cheese, giant cans of mustard and mayonnaise, and a dozen Cokes in a bucket of ice. The Coke settles Rainy's stomach enough for her to recognize and feed a ravenous hunger.

"Where the hell are we, anyway?" Cisco asks.

The lieutenant answers. "Lajes Field, Azores. The island is called Terceira. It means third. There are nine islands all together. We're about two thousand miles from New York and just under a thousand from Portugal, and no distance at all from the U-boats, although they've had their horns trimmed a bit. Soon as you've finished, we'll drive you down to the harbor, Angra, the biggest city they got here."

"Any action in Anger?" Cisco asks.

"*Angra. Angra do Heroísmo.*" Rainy recognizes a fellow linguist. The lieutenant has worked on her pronunciation, not a normal thing for American troops overseas. "It means Bay of Heroism. And to answer your question, no, no action unless you mean two bars serving bad beer, worse wine, and no whiskey."

Cisco nods thoughtfully. "Sounds like an opportunity. You got horny GIs and . . . pardon my, uh, choice of words . . ."

"Oh, there's a cathouse," the lieutenant assures him, showing no sign of feminine embarrassment. "Like you said: horny GIs will find a way."

They drive through slackening rain down a road paved with cobbles made of black lava. The road is lined with hydrangea bushes, blue and pink. The fields are small, extravagantly green rectangles marked off by low, volcanic-stone fences. The road winds and curves upward before beginning to descend into Angra. They pass a donkey cart and a small civilian truck, but that's all for the half-hour drive.

The harbor is a small, neat bowl surrounded by two-story whitewashed buildings with red tile roofs. The only prominent building is a church with twin square towers topped by neat white domes. The Americans have erected an antiaircraft tower, but no German plane has the range or the inclination to fly this far. There are two naval vessels tied up on the ocean-facing side of the protectively curved pier. One is a small destroyer or corvette, Rainy doesn't know ships well enough to know quite what to call it. But she recognizes the long, narrow, gray dagger of a submarine.

The sub is a Royal Navy T-class, a sullen-looking beast with a strange bulge at the front where external torpedo tubes look like the nostrils of a dragon's flared head. She's 275 feet, about four railroad cars long, or just shy of a football field, but just a tenth as wide in the beam. There's a superstructure divided in two bits, the higher rear portion festooned with antennae and what can only be the retracted tops of two periscopes. The lower, forward part of the superstructure is taken up by a four-inch gun that seems oversized for its environment.

Fishing boats are heading out from the shelter of the pier, chugging slowly, one after another into choppy seas gray in the faint light of dawn. The night has been shortened by their eastward progress.

"There's your ride," the lieutenant says. The sergeant shows his face to a bored Portuguese sailor on sentry duty, and they drive out onto the mole, coming to a stop beside the sub.

"Hey," Cisco says. "That's not ours, is it?"

"His Majesty's boat, *Topaz*," the lieutenant says. "They're your ride."

"The hell they are," Cisco says. "There is no goddamn way I am going down underwater. No way in hell."

"You'll have to," Rainy says.

"No. No." Cisco shakes his head violently. He looks like a man ready to crawl out of his skin. Fearless through the battering airborne thunderstorm, he is transformed now. "No way. No way, no how. The hell with this! Uh-uh, no way."

But in the end there is a way, involving quite a bit of Azorean *vinho de cheiro*, a red wine that smells of strawberries. And just two hours behind schedule an exceedingly drunk and raving mobster is manhandled down the hatch and lashed into a canvas hammock by wonderfully amused British submariners.

RIO RICHLIN—CAMP ZIGZAG, TUNISIA, NORTH AFRICA

"Richlin! Someone here to see you." Sergeant Cole holds the tent flap back, and a tall young man bows his head to enter.

"Everyone decent?" Strand Braxton asks, grinning. He's in an Air Corps uniform: khaki slacks and a sheep's-wool-trimmed leather jacket that looks very dashing and is completely wrong for the heat.

Rio at that moment is carefully cleaning and oiling her M1. The pieces are laid out on her cot atop a spread-out towel. She has removed the strap. She has pulled the trigger guard forward and pulled the trigger assembly all the way out. She has separated the stock and has even disassembled the gas cylinder, laying the parts out in a neat, familiar pattern.

With clean rags, brushes, and solvent she has cleaned each and every part. She is now busy using a second clean rag to cover all moving parts with a thin coat of oil.

Her hands are greasy, and she smells of sewing machine oil and kerosene. She is dressed in dungaree trousers and a sweat-stained T-shirt. The army has spent approximately zero time considering the fact that army bras—a device with as many straps and as little sex appeal as a parachute—is only indifferently covered by the T-shirt.

The fact that she is in a shocking state of undress flashes through Rio's mind, but that does not stop her from yelling, "Strand!"

She sets the traveler (a small, curiously shaped metal piece) down, glances furtively around to see if Jack is there. Then she runs to Strand, throwing her arms around him.

They kiss, but discreetly, a kiss that is more passionate than brother-sister, but more self-conscious than would be the case if Geer, Stick, and Cat were not watching with undisguised interest.

"Huh," Geer says. "So Richlin is still a girl. I'll be damned."

"Strand, this is Stick, the one with the clean new corporal's stripes, that's Preeling there, and the asshole is Geer."

The word *asshole* is out of Rio's mouth before she can think it through. She sees Strand wince, then cover it up. Geer doesn't even pretend to be offended.

"Sorry," Rio says, genuinely embarrassed. "My language

has gone to . . . I mean, well, you know . . ."

"It's good to meet you all," Strand says. Then he looks more closely at Rio. "Is that a bruise?"

"What, this?" Rio waves it off. "Just, um . . . I accidentally ran into a pole last week." She avoids eye contact with her squad members, all of whom maintain what might be called a patently false silence, including Cat, who ostentatiously makes a turning key motion over her mouth.

Just then Jenou enters, spots Strand, and gives him a peck on the cheek. "Well, if it isn't Mr. Tall, Dark, and Handsome. What are you doing, *Lieutenant* Braxton, slumming with lowly enlisted types? Did you remember to salute him, Rio?"

"She gave me a different kind of salute, and I liked it a whole lot better," Strand says.

"What are you doing here?" Rio asks. She's holding him by the biceps, keeping him close, enjoying the feel of him. He's a solid reminder of a different life, and a different Rio. And she quite likes the feel of his lean muscles.

"I volunteered to fly a bird colonel over here. He and his staff were in some big hurry, and we're stood down for a couple days. So I gassed up my plane, grabbed my copilot and flight engineer, and here I am, at least until tomorrow morning. I don't suppose you can wrangle a twenty-four-hour pass?"

Jenou laughs, and Rio shoots her a warning look, but of course Jenou ignores that and says, "Well, we had some passes last week, and you see the results." She aims an accusing finger at Rio's bruise. Mock-serious she says, "I'm afraid Rio can't handle her drink."

"Knock it off, Jen," Rio says, not quite playfully.

"Why, Rio told me she ran into a pole," Strand says with a wink. "And I am honor-bound to believe her."

"You should have been there when that big old Texan boy, the one with the bandaged ear, came after her, thinking she was easy prey, and she pulls out that big knife of hers—"

"Jen!"

"Knife?"

"It's a keepsake," Rio says quickly. "You know, a souvenir. I think it's something the A-rabs carry just for show."

"'I will stick this in your guts and push it till the point comes out of your mouth.' That's what you said, wasn't it, Rio?"

Jenou bats her eyes at Rio, who is not interested in being teased, not right then, not when she's hoping Strand doesn't notice that she stinks of solvent and oil, not to mention just stinking from the lack of a shower after a sweaty morning spent unloading a truck.

"Let's get out of here," Rio says. "Let me just reassemble my rifle."

She sits back down and looks at the pieces laid out. It's a complex job, but one she can do blindfolded by now. But having Strand watch with a show of interest makes her self-conscious. Her best time is four minutes and six seconds. If she does it that fast won't she look like . . . well, like a soldier? But if she slows down the others will spot it immediately and the reaction will not be kind.

"Who's got a watch with a second hand?" Cat asks, batting her eyes at Rio, obviously perfectly aware of Rio's dilemma. And that settles it. Rio can only do her best.

Slide bolt into receiver. This is always tricky and usually involves some wiggling of the piece, but Rio has it down to a single, smooth insertion. Then slot the operating rod back into the housing, slide it back to make sure it catches the rod. Then the follower assembly—drop and slide. Bullet guide, follower arm, operating rod catch, holding pin, check the movement, slide in the long spring, lever the assembly into the stock, pop in the trigger guard, lock it down, check the bolt, squeeze the trigger to earn a pleasantly layered metallic click and . . .

"Five minutes, thirty-eight seconds," Geer says. "Hell, I can beat that, Richlin."

"Not my best," she mutters, and when she looks up, Strand's expression is not congratulatory but serious. His forehead wrinkles, his brows lower over his eyes, shadowing them. His mouth is set in a stern, pressed line, and it takes him longer than she would like for him to ease it into a pleasant smile.

"Okay," Rio says with false cheer to conceal her unease, "let's see if Sarge is feeling generous."

She takes Strand's arm, actually clamps a hand on his bicep—and draws him outside into the light and heat and dust. She looks around for someplace private, any place, but she is surrounded by a half a square mile of tents, temporary huts, cooking fires, male soldiers naked to the waist, piles of discarded crates that once held canned food, the cans that came from those crates, parked jeeps, and deuce-and-a-halfs rumbling by in clouds of dust.

One of the parked jeeps apparently belongs to Strand, at least for now, and he has a corporal dozing in the driver's seat, helmet tilted forward to shield his eyes, feet up on the dashboard.

Sergeant Cole is sitting on a camp chair drinking coffee with O'Malley and another sergeant. Rio says, "Come on," and hauls Strand over.

"Sarge, meet Lieutenant Braxton, a friend of mine from back home. Strand, Sergeants Cole, O'Malley, and Alvarez."

Cole stands, pivots, salutes, then shakes Strand's outstretched hand. "Good to meet you, Lieutenant."

"And you, Sergeant, I've heard a bit about you through Rio's letters." He raises a finger, forestalling a response, and reaches into his inner pocket to pull out a small parcel wrapped in newspaper. "Rio happened to mention that you enjoy an occasional cigar. I don't know if these are any good, I picked them up in a little shop in Casablanca . . ."

Strand unwraps the parcel, revealing six fat brown cigars. Cole swallows hard. "Those are Cubans. Those are the real thing!"

"Well, they're yours," Strand says.

"Thanks, Lieutenant. I take that very kindly. So, just what is it I can do for you in response to this very, very, *very* welcome bribe?"

"Well, I'm only here for twenty-four hours, and I was wondering . . ." He shrugs.

"I see." Cole pretends to consider this carefully. "Sergeant O'Malley, I wonder if we might be able to rustle up a twenty-four-hour pass for Private Richlin."

"Wait," Strand says. He darts over to his jeep, feels around inside a canvas carryall, and produces a bottle of rye whiskey, which he carries back to O'Malley. "I don't suppose you're a drinking man?"

"I'd have thought an officer would have more sense than to even ask that question." O'Malley hefts the bottle and says, "I do believe you're correct that we're being bribed, Jedron. And a damned fine bit of bribery it is too. Make it a case next time, Lieutenant, and you can have

Richlin for the whole rest of the war."

The pass appears with record speed—it's possible the rye will be shared with the captain. Strand dismisses his corporal to the mess tent and settles behind the wheel with Rio beside him. They drive off, and then Rio sees Jack. Jack is shirtless, stripped down to his boxer shorts and boots, wielding a shovel and digging a new latrine trench. He is bathed in sweat that rolls intriguingly down his smooth, tanned chest. He spots Rio, then does a double take, eyes narrowing as he realizes who is driving.

It is the moment Rio had hoped to avoid. Strand is oblivious, Jack being just one more soldier with a shovel. Jack nods at Rio, tries and fails to smile, and ends up seeming to grimace in disgust. Rio raises her hand in a guilty, halfhearted wave and the jeep roars on by, its dust-cloud swirling over Jack.

It doesn't matter. Strand is Strand, while Jack is just Jack.

"Where are we going?" Rio asks, raising her voice to be heard over the rush of wind in her face.

"I, uh . . . I arranged a little privacy."

"How much privacy?" Rio asks archly.

"It's a room in a hotel, but we can leave the door open. And I'm told there's a shower."

"Uh-huh." A slow, skeptical drawl.

Strand grins at her. "You know, being in the army has made you cynical."

"Being around men all day and night will do that to a girl."

"I imagine that's true. Say, how are you, Rio?" It's a serious question, more serious than it would have been back home, more serious than it would have been on the *Queen Mary*. As she feared, the sight of her in an OD T-shirt reassembling her weapon like an automaton has left an impression.

She shrugs. "Fine as anyone, I guess. Sick of living in the dirt. Sick of the same three things to eat every day. Sick of hearing the same old stories from the same old people day in, day out. I swear if Suarez starts in again on the time he caught a fly ball at Yankee Stadium . . . But I'm okay." She smiles and reaches out to touch his hand on the gearshift. "Let's make a deal."

"What deal?"

"No more war talk."

He reaches awkwardly with his right hand and she shakes it, softening the grip of her muscles, wishing the pads of her fingers and palm weren't hard with calluses earned wielding shovels and hauling supplies. The morning had been spent hauling food supplies into the mess tent with Beebee and pretending not to notice as Beebee stole roughly 10 percent of what they unloaded for use as "trade goods."

The hotel is a relic of French colonial influence, even flying a faded and tattered French tricolor over the door. A new sign has been nailed beside the front door that reads: *Amis et Alliés Well Coming.*

Friends and allies welcome. Given that Vichy French forces were firing on Americans just months earlier, it elicits a skeptical grunt from Rio. But inside there's a desk and a manager and a bellman, and overstuffed leather chairs arranged around low tables topped with beer bottles and glasses and overflowing ashtrays.

The bellman, a surly young Arab, shows them to a third-floor room that is clean enough and furnished with a dresser with peeling veneer . . . and an iron bed.

"Get us a bottle of Champagne," Strand orders the bellman.

"No have," the bellman says, but with something in his eyes that suggests the answer may be only temporary. Sure enough, when Strand hands him a ten-dollar bill, it turns out the hotel does indeed have a bottle of Champagne.

"You can close the door," Rio says. "I'm not worried about my reputation."

"But what about *my* reputation?" Strand asks with a wink. He closes the door.

Rio notes her own lack of concern for propriety and reputation. She would never for a moment have considered being in a closed hotel room with a man back home.

The very idea was outrageous. She'd have slapped the face of any man who suggested such a thing.

They kiss, a tentative first peck, and then a longer kiss, and then a kiss that threatens to end with both of them on the bed. Rio pulls back and says, "I'm going to find the shower."

The shower is down the corridor. It is none too clean but wildly luxurious by army standards, with actual tile on the walls. Rio strips down and turns on the cold water, which, as she expects, is plenty warm, and in any event there is no hot water. She uses a bar of fragrant soap to shampoo her hair and carefully clean every square inch of grime from the rest of her.

"Wow," Strand says, as she lets herself back into the room.

Rio hesitates a moment then closes the door behind her. Is she sending him a signal she doesn't mean to send?

Or do I mean to send that exact signal?

"Should we taste that bubbly?" she says, striving to find a voice that sounds less like Rio the GI and more like Rio the girl from Gedwell Falls. This new-old voice sounds false to her, but Strand is not here to see her as she is now.

Is he?

"It would be a waste of a generous tip not to," Strand agrees. He pops the cork and pours. Strand and Rio both drain their glasses and take the refill more slowly.

Strand sits in the only chair and pulls it close to the bed, where Rio perches on the edge of the mattress.

There's nowhere to sit but the bed, Rio assures herself, but the shower and the distinct memory of Strand's bicep have set off some turmoil within.

I can sit on a bed without it meaning anything.

A bed. With a man. In a hotel room.

With the door closed!

"I can't believe you're actually here," Rio says, trying in vain to ignore the bickering voices in her head.

"I'm amazed at my own resourcefulness," Strand says.

They fall silent, looking awkwardly in the direction of each other's feet.

"So, really," Strand says at last. "How has it been? Have you seen action?"

"I thought we weren't talking about the war," Rio teases, then relents. "Some."

"Some?" He draws a packet from his pocket and carefully unfolds a piece of newspaper. "Do you know about this?"

She takes the paper from his hand, impatient, and is confronted with a grainy photo of a woman soldier holding what looks like a six-shooter straight out of a cowboy movie.

"Oh. That." She reads quickly through the accompanying text. It's the story of a small action, just a minor vignette in the war really, but one that stars Rio Richlin.

"Gosh, I hope my folks haven't seen this."

"It went out on the wires and may have been picked up by the *Gedwell Falls Democrat-Press*, I don't know. A buddy saw this in the *New York Herald Tribune* when he was home on leave. I talk about you a lot, so . . . I guess he recognized the name. There aren't a lot of girls named Rio, let alone one who can handle a six-shooter."

Rio sags back onto the bed and lets it bounce her back up to a seated position. "I'm . . . sorry."

"Sorry?" He is genuinely puzzled. "Sorry for what? Sounds like you single-handedly wiped out a Kraut mortar team."

Rio snorts. "Single-handed? Any time you read 'single-handedly' it's bullsh—it's an exaggeration. I was just the one that climbed down the rope. And the gun wasn't even mine, I borrowed it off the reporter who . . ." She realizes that makes no difference to the story, but she is mortified to have the story out in the wider world, and annoyed to have Strand showing it to her.

They drink some more Champagne. Conversation rises and falls, with each silence more awkward and pregnant with meaning than the preceding one. Rio is looking more and more frequently at his lips, which are, according to that great expert Jenou, eminently kissable. And in doing so the memories of every kiss they have shared comes welling up, bringing a wave of feeling, a wave of . . .

She leans forward just as he leans forward and their lips meet. It's an awkward stance, both leaning, so Rio takes his quite wonderful bicep and draws him to sit beside her on the bed. They kiss some more, quite a bit more, and Rio's heart is pounding, but Strand does not press for anything more intimate. Rio is certain—almost certain, nearly certain, kind of certain—that she would rebuff him if he did.

After a while they move to a more comfortable position, side by side on the bed with their backs against thin pillows that barely soften the brass tubes of the headboard. Rio unlaces her relatively mud-free but far-from-clean boots and kicks them off. When they land they sound like they weigh ten pounds each. Strand leans down and carefully unlaces his polished shoes and places them next to each other on the floor.

"Tell me about flying, Strand. Bombers, right?"

"Turns out I couldn't take the G-force for a fighter. You get into a dogfight, take those tight turns, and it presses all the blood down out of your head. They say it's worse in big guys, tall guys like me. Fighter pilots tend to be more compact." He sounds abashed and seems almost to be gritting his teeth. It's a story he's had to tell before, Rio guesses. Everyone wants to fly fighters—the Battle of Britain and the romance of the Spitfire pilots have settled that.

"I like you less compact," she says, and kisses him again. It is a tender kiss, a gentle kiss, one with less animal need and more affection. Love? Maybe. She isn't sure how she'll know if it's love.

Maybe when you stop thinking about Jack Stafford.

She kisses him again, this time putting more heat into it, as if trying to push the thought of Jack out of her thoughts. But Strand has cooled now. In fact he seems distracted.

"Tell me about it," Rio says again, feeling like a hypocrite since she herself dislikes being asked about her actions.

He shrugs. "Mostly we sit around the bar—the officers' club—or else lounge in the briefing room being lectured by captains and majors and such. There's a lot of big maps on the wall and all sorts of exceedingly dull talk of course adjustments and radio direction finding."

He's striving for nonchalance and failing.

"Don't you ever fly?"

"Occasionally." His tone is transparently false. "Sure, there are missions. Sometimes, though, we don't even find the target and have to dump our loads in the water."

"And other times?" she presses.

He rolls away from her then, ostensibly to fetch the half-empty bottle and refill their glasses. But he does not return to his place beside her. Instead, he paces the ten linear feet available to him.

"Sometimes we reach the target and deliver the package." He smiles and adds, "Bombs away!" He has a hand motion to go with it, wiggling fingers emulating the bombs as they fall from the bomb bay.

"Is it rough?"

He shrugs. "The flak isn't so bad, but we do run into the occasional 109 or Focke-Wulf."

She sees something in his eyes, though he looks away. "Have you lost anyone?"

Strand shoves his fingers back through his hair and paces to the window. "I, uh . . . my tail gunner. This Indian kid, Sioux from North Dakota, we called him Poke, on account of calling him Pocahontas at first when he was still green, and then that got to be Poke."

"What happened?"

"A 109. Nobody spotted him, Kraut just dropped down out of the sun. Ground crew says we only took one round. We've come in all shot up, two hundred holes, and everyone safe, and then one lousy round . . ." Then, after a stretched and painful silence, he adds, "Just last Thursday. So it's . . . um . . . kind of raw, I guess." He smiles as if it's something he should apologize for.

There's nothing to say, so Rio nods.

"I haven't lost anyone before. Buddies, sure, you remember Bandito? You met him on the *Queen*? Well, his crate went down, we saw some chutes, so maybe he's sitting in a POW camp, but see, it's different when it's your own crew."

"Nothing you could have done," Rio says.

This causes Strand to bang the meaty part of his fist against the wall. "I know that," he snaps. "Doesn't change anything, because you still have to go over and over it in your head. It sounds crazy, I know, me being the youngest pilot and well, you know me and I'm not . . . But the guys—see, to them I'm the skipper. It's my fault because who else is there to blame?"

She goes to him as he gazes idly out of the window, stands behind him, and slips her arms around his chest. He puts his hands over hers. She brushes his ear with her lips, and he twists in her grip to face her. He kisses her, soft at first, gentle and almost melancholy. But she opens her mouth and touches his tongue with hers, and it is as if someone has attached them both to electric wires.

They kiss madly, almost violently. Rio pulls his tie off and throws it toward the bed and goes to work on the buttons of his uniform. She is disappointed to find the OD T-shirt beneath, more OD is not what she craves. Having never before formed the thought, she suddenly now knows that she wants very badly to see and touch and taste bare flesh.

What am I doing?

She pushes his shirt down and off impatiently, then forces him to bend forward so she can draw the offending T-shirt from his body.

Whatever I'm doing, I don't seem to be stopping.

She has always imagined this moment as a type of surrender. That's certainly been Jenou's notion: you surrender at long last to the man and he . . . But that is not what is happening right here, right now. She is not surrendering, she is pushing the pace, she is practically forcing herself on him.

One more step and it will be too late . . .

Okay, then: one more step.

Finally Strand begins to undress her, so much more carefully, slowly, uncertainly than she had done to him, and hesitation again and again. He stops, breathing hard, when she is down to her bra.

"I . . . uh . . . how is this thing attached?" His voice is octaves lower than normal.

Rio laughs shakily. "It's an army bra, so it makes no sense." She reaches the snaps at the sides, pulls them free, and shrugs the bra to the floor.

For a moment she has forgotten to be self-conscious about her body, which has always been described unhelpfully by Jenou as "boyish." But all of that, all of that shyness, all of that modesty, all the lessons incessantly drilled into her head by her mother, seem very far away and unimportant now. Because now she's a teapot coming to full boil, not entirely right in the head, not at that moment, not when he stops breathing, not when he starts again but with a ragged, desperate urgency.

My God, it's happening. It's happening right now.

Her mouth is as dry, her heart as fast, her breath as shallow as when she stood blazing away at the Krauts. In fact, some distant part of her observes, she was calmer then. This is like some mad race inside her head, with animal desire and indifference to consequence pushing to overwhelm modesty and chastity and even the vague notion that she is meant to be passive, resisting, saying no.

"Do you . . . ," she says, but finds her voice breaking. In a lower octave she says, "Do you have a French letter?" using one of a dozen common euphemisms for a condom.

Strand strains to raise his head. His expression is comical, a battle between shocked disapproval and urgent longing. "Are you? Do you? Should we . . . ," he babbles before ending lamely, "You could get pregnant."

"That's why I'm asking about the . . . the thing," she says, irritated by this conversational delay.

"No, I mean . . . I mean, if you *were* in a family way they'd send you home."

It's like a dash of cold water in her face. Does Strand actually believe she would do that? Use pregnancy to escape the war?

But that dash of cold water is a mere dribble of spit to the fire inside her. "Find it. Put it on," she says, and watches with bold attention as the job is carried out.

The deed is done with a great deal more wild thrusting than Rio expects. The springs of the bed squeak loudly in telltale rhythm.

There is some pain, but nothing to compare with the punch she took from the Texan's fist. It takes much longer than it takes a bull, she notes, and it is more fascinating than it is pleasurable.

They lie side by side then, talking for a long time, not about the war or even the army, but about home. Rio talks about her parents, acutely aware that there is something transgressive about discussing parents while naked beside a man to whom she is not even engaged, let alone married.

A line has been drawn in the sand of her life. Before and after. Some part of her mind dreads the inevitable confession to Jenou. If Jenou has become annoying in asking about killing Krauts she will become an absolute Sherlock Holmes in ferreting out every last detail of this *first*.

I am no longer a virgin.

Am I a woman now?

They make love again, more slowly this time, cautiously, learning about each other's bodies.

Two hours later, as Rio lies in bed beside a dozing Strand, staring up at a bug on the flaking ceiling and wondering whether she has just done something very stupid, a siren wails.

Air raid?

But no, not an air raid, because moments after it stops—without being punctuated by explosions—she hears a loudspeaker. She goes to the window and looks out onto the street. There's a jeep driven by an MP coming slowly up the street. A passenger is speaking into a microphone with the loudspeaker mounted on the windshield.

"All US military personnel are ordered to return to their assigned posts immediately."

The time for romance, sex, and possibly love is over.

The war is starting again.

She retrieves her *koummya* from the nightstand.

And is . . . relieved.

PART II

OPERATION HUSKY
THE INVASION OF SICILY

This is our war, and we will carry it with us as we go from one battleground to another until it is all over, leaving some of us behind on every beach, in every field. We are just beginning with the ones who lie back of us here in Tunisia. I don't know if it was their good fortune or their misfortune to get out of it so early in the game. I guess it doesn't make any difference once a man is gone. Medals and speeches and victories are nothing anymore. They died and the others lived and no one knows why it is so. When we leave here for the next shore, there is nothing we can do for the ones underneath the wooden crosses here, except perhaps pause and murmur, "Thanks, pal."
—Ernie Pyle, war correspondent

JOURNALS AND LETTERS SENT

JENOU'S JOURNAL

Looks like they're getting the war started up again. Sitting here at the dock, GIs cheek by jowl, thousands of us waiting to stand in line to board our ship, which is who knows where. The usual madhouse. I feel I could walk dry-footed from ship to ship from the dock out to the far end of the harbor.

Rio's been mum since coming back from her time with Strand. Something clearly happened— that girl thinks she's got a poker face, but Auntie Jen sees all. Something happened between them. Did she tell him about kissing Jack? Did he tell her about some slut of a nurse he's passing his time with? Did he propose? Did they—?

I could worm it out of her, but I want to wait and see how long it takes her to tell me. It'll be a measure of our friendship. Rio's more closed-in than she used to be, once upon a time Rio would tell me everything. Now she's as tight as a tick. Her old impulsiveness has become recklessness. Her old impish sense of humor has coarsened. Well, so has mine, I admit, but she started off sweet, and I never was sweet, not since I was thirteen anyway.

I admit it: it hurts my feelings to have Rio cold toward me. No, that's wrong, I don't mean cold, that's too much. She's just not quite as there as she used to be. I suppose I'm afraid that she is becoming someone who will no longer care for me as a friend. That would be hard. Much of the time I feel as if I'm only holding on because I'm here in this miserable ~~shit hole~~ dump with her.

So often the people talk about home, about wherever they're from and how they long to get back there. I wonder if anyone's noticed that I never join in. I'm in no hurry to get home, though I'd sure like to be somewhere other than here. It's confusing. What do I do, where do I go when this war is over?

I suppose it's a little pathetic, but once I talked

Rio into volunteering that was sort of the end of my plans. What's next for Jenou when the war is over? I suppose I'll have to get married. Pity I have no eligible males in my sights. And honestly, I don't really care about men, for once in my life. Maybe I've seen too much of them.

They're calling our group to board. Swell.

Dear Mother and Father,

I am unable to tell you anything about where I am or what I'm doing. But of course I am safe and sound, well-fed, and surrounded by great guys and girls.

I'm not sure whether this will get to you anytime soon, but I wanted to tell you first of all that it may be a while before I can write again.

And mostly I wanted to tell you that I love and miss you both. Even though it's perfectly pleasant here, I would far rather be home with you.

Love,

Rainy

Dear Mom, Dad, and Obal:

Well, we are finally ▮▮▮▮▮▮▮▮▮▮▮▮▮▮▮▮▮▮▮. Destination? I don't know. Right now we're all standing in line, and I'm writing this on the side of a truck. I've been assigned to a platoon as medic, which is what I signed up for. And everyone says it's beautiful where we're going.

You should not worry about me at all, really. I suppose you're seeing newsreels and listening to the radio and hearing all sorts of things about how it's going for us, but pay no attention to all that, it's mostly wrong, I think. I have plenty to eat, and I am getting along well. I'll be working ~~under~~ with a sergeant named Walter Green who I know, and who has been kind and very proper toward me. He's from Iowa. I didn't even know there were colored folks in Iowa. Walter says now he's here there aren't many left, that's for sure.

Okay, they're saying time's up if we're going to get our letters out. So I love you all very much and miss you all terribly.

Your soldier girl,

Frangie

PS: Obal, I forgot to tell you I had to crawl under a tank!

Dear Mother and Father,

I don't have much time, so this will just be a quick note. All is well, nothing very much going on, though we ██████████████████████████ , so it may be a while before I can write again.

I'm in good health and good spirits. I guess there was a news item that mentioned me, but you know that's all exaggerated. The biggest danger I ever face is sunburn. Well, that and the chow.

I saw Strand, which was nice. He seems fine, though a little worn down, maybe. He lost a man, and I suppose that's twice as tough when you're the one in charge. Well, that's war, I guess. But if you run into his folks don't tell them that, just tell them he was healthy and fine when I saw him.

I miss you. I miss home. I even miss the cows. But hopefully we'll get this war over quick and I'll be back there with you.

Your loving daughter,
Rio

10

First wave.

First wave.

The words won't stop torturing her. She will be landing with the first wave.

She is shaking, shaking down to bone and sinew, shaking down to the molecular level, one big tremble. Her teeth chatter in a dust-dry mouth. Her heart fades in and out, almost seeming to stop at times before pounding back like a panicked horse. Her breathing is a series of gulps and snorts, forcing air in and out of lungs that feel paralyzed.

"Lord Jesus, keep me safe," she prays.

According to her watch, a secondhand Timex, it is early morning, but it looks a lot like night. There are stars winking through gaps in high clouds. No moon, not that she can see anyway. From the railing of the transport ship she can make out nothing of the island itself, just a

144

sort of looming darkness within darkness that suggests mountains. But off to the left, the west, beyond the town of Licata, yellow and orange explosions mark the places where paratroopers are already engaged in battle. And something like a distant storm in the east marks the naval artillery covering the landing of the British and Canadian forces.

There are ships spread far behind hers, hundreds of them, a huge gray armada, only visible because of the phosphorescence of the water. The vast fleet should be reassuring, but ships stop at the water's edge while soldiers must go on.

Why am I so afraid?

It's the landing, she realizes, the absurdity of it. Madness! Little men and women on little boats trying to attack the massive, mountainous island. It seems ridiculous. It seems impossible. Surely the Italians and Germans are ready and waiting. They must have known this day was coming, and if they didn't guess it earlier, they must know it by now.

"Searchlights!" someone hisses.

Spears of white light stab at the ships from the beach, the circles of illumination crawling across wave tops before picking out a transport here, a destroyer there. In the light Frangie sees the nearest destroyer's guns swivel toward the beam. Everyone expects the shells to start flying from the shore. But nothing. The searchlights sweep and illuminate, like stage lights looking for the star of the show. But then, one by one, the searchlights go dark. And there is no distant sound of the big shore batteries firing.

From overhead Frangie hears the wind in the wires that hold a barrage balloon floating high to complicate life for German planes. No planes, not yet.

There is a small New Testament in her inner pocket where she also keeps her photos of her parents and her brothers. She touches it with cold fingers. She searches for a verse.

The Lord is my shepherd . . .

No, she's never liked that psalm. She's never liked picturing herself as a sheep.

Watch ye, stand fast in the faith, quit you like men, be strong.

She glances at the men nearest. Some smoke at a frantic pace. One chews gum loudly, snapping it. Others move their mouths silently in prayer. Most stare stonily into the dark.

The men are afraid too. And these are green troops who have not yet seen what a high-powered rifle round does to a human body. Their fear is of something they cannot fully imagine. They don't yet know how easily bones break and flesh melts and organs spill from . . .

She squeezes her eyes shut, tighter, tighter till stars and

pinwheels are all she sees. She opens them to see Walter Green looking at her through wire-frame spectacles.

Is he afraid? Or are sergeants not allowed to fear?

Walter Green tosses his cigarette aside and comes over.

"Hey," he says. "You okay?"

She nods too fast, not trusting her voice.

He says, "'Fear thou not, for I am with thee. Be not dismayed, for I am thy God. I will strengthen thee.'" Seeing her surprise, he adds, "Isaiah. If I'm not mistaken, he lived through a war with the Assyrians. Very bad fellows, those Assyrians. What are you scared of most?"

"Most?" She runs through a gallery of gruesome injuries. But in her imagination she is both the wounded and the medic. The medic whose fingers fumble and who can't remember what she's supposed to do. "I could make you a list," she says with an effort at lightness.

He lays a hand on her arm, looks her in the eye, and says, "You'll do fine." Then he leaves to deal with a shoving match between two of his higher-strung charges.

That's it, isn't it, Frangie thinks. *That's what I'm most afraid of. It's not just being hurt, though that's real enough. I'm afraid I'll fail these GIs. I'm afraid I won't be smart enough, brave enough . . .*

The announcement comes, and Frangie jerks out of her reverie and moves along with the men and the few women of her new platoon. She shuffles along till she comes to where Walter is checking men's gear.

"You okay now, Doc?"

She nods. "I want it to be over."

"Come on now, it hasn't even started." He winks, and she can't help but smile a little.

"Can't fight no war without Albert Huntington gets into it," a private says—presumably Albert Huntington, though Frangie doesn't know him or many of the men yet. She's new to this unit, having spent the last few months attached to a clinic where the work was largely the treatment of venereal diseases and injuries from bar fights and training accidents.

"I suppose it would be wrong to pray that all the Krauts just die," Frangie says, sort of joking, but also not.

"It's not wrong to pray for it to be over sooner rather than later," Green says, seeing that she is serious.

She nods and swallows hard and prays for just that. *Lord Jesus, bring this battle to a swift conclusion. And if it's Your will, take care of Your Frangie.*

The loudspeaker crackles to life. The final order is given. The mass of men and women murmurs and moves. Sailors and sergeants stand at the top of the boarding nets, which are slung over the side, hurrying and cajoling the clumsy soldiers.

"Come on, boys, it's just a net, you've practiced it before."

But Frangie has not practiced it before, and neither have the rest of them. Green troops, the greenest. Sergeant Green's green platoon. She climbs awkwardly over the railing, feeling helping hands steady the weight of the pack on her back and guide her feet.

Hands on the slick, wet rail.

"Don't look down, miss," a sailor says. "Climb down, but don't look."

She looks.

The landing craft below her is rolling in the agitated sea, banging against the side of the ship, rolling away to expose dark water, rising, falling. She is climbing down onto a moving target. The seasickness that has dogged her during the storm-tossed trip from Tunisia comes swarming back in the guise of vertigo.

Her boots catch on every rope. Her hands are sticky with tar from the nets but so cold she doesn't at first notice the wire-brush harshness that tears tiny slices from her palms and the meaty pads of her fingers.

Down and down, how can it be this far? She looks down as the boat rushes up, up, up as though to meet her before falling away again.

"Come on, Doc, you don't want to swim." It's a private named Jasper Jones who has occasionally helped Frangie out by letting her use him as a medical practice dummy. He's a gangly six-footer with big ears that won't look right until his face takes on some weight with age. Frangie likes him, but she's avoided him since it became apparent that he was thinking of her in romantic terms.

The last thing she's interested in right now is men. At least not men as boyfriends. Men and women as *patients* are her focus. Anyway, what kind of kids would they have? A beanpole and a midget? They would make a ridiculous-looking couple.

This is what I'm thinking of?

Better than so many other things . . .

She gratefully accepts Jasper's help as he reaches to guide her feet into the last couple of holes and then holds her steady as she jumps down into the rising boat.

"All set, Doc?"

"All set, Jasper. Thanks."

"Anything for you, Doc."

Of course he's doing the same service for all the GIs. Climbing down a net is hard; climbing down a net in full gear from a heaving ship onto a boat that is doing an impersonation of a crazy elevator is a whole lot harder.

Once the boat is loaded it veers away from the side of the ship and begins turning a big circle, waiting until more boats are loaded. The sea is rough, and once again seasickness threatens. Cold, salty spray lashes them.

"You scared, Doc?" Jasper asks.

"I am. Aren't you?"

Jasper laughs. "Me? Nah. The bullet with my name on it hasn't been made yet."

Another private shakes his head sadly. This is Paul Dixon, called Daddy D on account of his age, which may be as old as thirty. "You're a young fool, Jasper Jones, that's why you're not afraid," Daddy D says. "You are a young, know-nothing, been-nothing, done-nothing infant dressed up in a uniform that looks like it was a hand-me-down from some shorter cousin."

Jasper could take offense, but he recognizes the bantering tone. "Me young? Maybe to an old, old granddad like you. Weren't you in the Spanish-American War, pops? See the thing is, you being all old and dried up and wrinkled—"

"I do not have one single damn wrinkle—"

"You get closer to death, you get so you can see it through the mist, and that mist? That mist is starting to clear now . . ." There is some hand-waving here to simulate pushing through a fog. Jasper switches to an old man's reedy quaver. "And you're thinking time is short, time is short, it's all gonna end!"

Daddy D makes a wry smile at Frangie. "I am twenty-nine years old. Only in the damn army does that make me old." Turning back to Jasper, Daddy D says, "Difference between us isn't age, it's experience. I am a man. You are a boy. I have known the love of a good woman who knows how to be a bad woman; and I've known the love of bad women who know how to be worse women; and I have known the love of the worst women in Tuskegee, Alabama, and, son, those are some very bad, very, *very* bad women, women who used me up till I was a shambling wreck, a husk of a man . . ."

Laughter is spreading, even to Walter, a welcome, calming sound, though it sometimes comes through chattering teeth.

". . . staggering around the streets in my underwear calling on Jesus to take me home. You, on the other hand—" He's about to say something even more explicitly ribald, but he glances at Frangie and stops himself, finishing lamely with, "You, young Jasper, have experienced nothing."

Frangie wants to ask Daddy D what he knows about the Tuskegee base where she's heard they may be training colored pilots. But the back-and-forth is drawing the attention of other scared soldiers, giving them a few minutes of amusement in the midst of this mad circling and circling, so she makes a mental note to ask later.

"As much as I love to hear your Granddaddy Remus tales of the old days, the long, long ago when you could still interest a woman in your now withered-up—"

And on it goes until there's a whistle blast and the boat finishes its rotation and heads toward shore. The conversation dies.

The sea is still up, not the gale they sailed through to get here but still agitated enough that boats ahead and behind can completely disappear from view in the troughs between waves. The landing craft skids down the back of one wave, settles a beat, then powers up the slope of the next one. There's nothing but walls of black water to be seen at the bottom of the trough, and not much more at the top. Dawn has still not come, but the black of night is losing its absoluteness and there is the promise of dawn in the east.

Suddenly a nearby cruiser opens fire with its big guns, ejecting six-inch shells in volcanic eruptions of fire and smoke. They fly for long seconds . . . one . . . two . . . three . . . four . . . before blossoming as they strike a distant hill. In the dark where the hills are only shadows, the shells seem to be exploding in midair. Other shells from other ships blow up behind the small town of Gela, and sometimes land in the town itself.

"Eye-ties are catching hell," a soldier remarks.

"More hell they catch, the less we do," another soldier says.

Should I pray for the shells to strike true? Shall I pray for my enemy's death? Blasphemy, surely. But I do want them to die if it means I won't.

Now the guns of the fleet are firing with some steadiness, ship after ship enveloped in flame and smoke of its own making. Explosions that seem small compared to

153

the moment of their eruption on the invisible hills, on the barely visible towns to the north and dead ahead. The noise rumbles across the water joining the roar of boat engines and slapping waves. The flashes illuminate faces for snapshots of expression, here an open mouth, there wide eyes, a head lowered to kiss a rosary.

With all the noise, at first no one hears the Heinkels coming in out of the northwest until the antiaircraft batteries on the ships open up too late, chattering madly and sending thousands of red tracer rounds of small-bore cannon and large-bore machine gun fire to lacerate the sky.

"Planes!" Jasper yells.

"They aren't after us, we're small fry," Daddy D says. "We got other problems." He jerks his thumb toward the beach, a line of shimmering surf now, like someone had trailed a dripping can of silver paint through the night.

As if to make his point, a battery on shore seems at last to notice the tiny landing craft and begins lobbing big shells that come screeching overhead with a wind like a passing freight train before ripping up acres of seawater.

"There!" a soldier yells, pointing. "Dammit! They got one of our boats!"

Frangie sees the explosion that bursts from beneath the landing craft. The boat lifts clear out of the water before its back breaks and the boat falls in two pieces, *splash*, all revealed in the dramatic staccato lighting of outgoing artillery.

The Heinkels roar overhead, and a ship half a mile away blows up.

Jesus, make me strong. Father, Son, and Holy Ghost, make me strong.

Frangie is far from being the only one praying. She hears two voices reciting the Lord's Prayer.

Our Father which art in heaven,
Hallowed be thy name.
Thy kingdom come, thy will be done . . .

That's fine, Frangie thinks, *so long as the Lord's will is to keep me alive and let me do what I am here to do.* The navy's chaplain, back aboard the transport, gave confession to the Roman Catholics and a few Protestants who felt it best to cover every base. And Frangie has taken communion, so she does not fear dying outside of God's grace. But she does fear.

It is coming. It is coming. Death, riding a pale horse, death, death . . .

You'll do fine.

She begins running through her medical supplies, performing a mental inventory, a reassuring ritual, focusing on anything but her own fear. So many of this bandage, so many of that. So many pouches of sulfa, so many ampoules of morphine, so many splints. She has the full recommended ration of everything, plus all the extras she has stuffed into ammo pouches and pockets. Extra scissors? First pouch, left side. Extra sulfa? Both pockets of her jacket.

"Get ready!" the coxswain yells in a voice that sounds like it's coming from a twelve-year-old, but just then the boat comes to a sudden, shuddering halt, making a sound like a chalkboard being dragged over a hundred fingernails. Men fall forward and then back, staggering, grabbing for handholds. The engine dies, the coxswain curses and comes running down to look over the side.

"Goddamn sandbar!"

They are still a quarter of a mile from the beach. There are no life rafts, and there is no chance of swimming in the dark waves with their gear.

The engine is restarted and with lots of frightened cursing from the coxswain, the boat attempts to pull itself off the sandbar.

No dice. The water churns, the boards screech, but the boat does not move. Half a dozen soldiers strip off their gear and jump into the seething, waist-deep water and try to push the boat off, but the sand beneath their boots gives them no purchase and they are hauled back aboard, soaking and shivering.

They are a small boat, utterly helpless, a perfect target with the dawn now just beginning to paint the sky a soft and hazy navy blue.

The first shell lands fifty feet astern.

RAINY SCHULTERMAN—ABOARD HMS *TOPAZ*, NORTH ATLANTIC

"Wha . . . wha . . . where am I?" Cisco is suddenly awake.

He thrashes in his hammock and realizes he has been lashed into it with ropes, trussed up with all the knot-bending skill of a military service that has been tying nautical knots since the days of Sir Francis Drake and the Spanish Armada. Cisco is held in place by a virtual illustrated encyclopedia of knots.

Cisco's hammock is in the torpedo room, all the way at the front of the boat. It's a cramped, greasy space smelling of industrial solvents, unwashed bodies, stale tobacco, fresh tobacco smoke, farts, cheese, and oil. There appears to be a thin sheen of oil on virtually every surface, including on the tan canvas of the hammock.

The crew are dressed in a sort of liberal approach to uniforms, some of the men wearing neatly belted dungarees with shirttails tucked in, while others wear bulky fisherman's sweaters or stained shirts open at the neck with sleeves rolled up. The officers are only marginally more formal.

The submarine has refueled and provisioned in the Azores, and throughout the entire boat every nook and cranny is stuffed with powdery loaves of fresh Portuguese bread, pineapples, cabbages, bananas, onions, butter, and wheels of pale-yellow Azorean cow's milk cheese. They have also replenished their store of torpedoes, which lie sinister in steel racks just astern of the tubes, ready to be fed in. The torpedoes surprised Rainy on first sight, being much bigger than she expected, each just over 21 feet long, weighing 3,452 pounds, 750 pounds of which is the TNT warhead.

A passing sailor summons Rainy, who is just finishing dinner in the petty officers' (NCOs') mess. It is an amazingly cramped little room of upholstered benches completely dominated by a table, so seating oneself at the table requires a fair bit of twisting and squirming.

Rainy finds Cisco cursing a blue streak and threatening sailors who are entirely unimpressed but willing to kill some of the boredom by listening to him rant.

"Get me the fug out of these ropes!" Cisco demands in a roar.

"If you calm down, we can let you go," Rainy says.

"I'll cut your fugging balls off!"

"Shall I quiet him down for you, miss?" an eager blond-bearded seaman asks, brandishing a large wrench.

"Cisco, you need to get control of yourself," Rainy says. "They really don't like panic around here."

"Panic? Who's panicking?" He makes an effort to quiet down. The effort does not alter the murderous look on his face, but he stops kicking and squirming. At a nod from Rainy, the sailor with the wrench reluctantly unties him.

"Limey sons of bitches," Cisco snarls as he rolls out and stands up. But he does not threaten anyone further, and the gaggle of onlookers, disappointed not to have a fight, return to their duties.

Lieutenant Commander Alger appears, weaving his way with casual grace through the veritable thicket of forehead-smashing pipes, brackets, gauges, and water-proof doors. Rainy has already smacked her head twice, and she's a foot shorter than the commander.

Rainy has noted that no one salutes aboard the *Topaz*, but training compels her and she snaps a salute.

"Now, now, none of that," Lieutenant Commander Alger says mildly, returning her salute. He's in young middle age, with a jagged scar that crosses his lips and gives him a piratical air. His beard, neatly trimmed, is brown, like his hair. He has an impressive bent pipe of wonderfully rich polished wood. From time to time he emits a small cloud of sweet bluish smoke that Rainy would normally find nauseating but which at the moment is masking the strong body odor smell of the red-haired rating behind her. Lieutenant Commander Alger's expression and speech are alert, active, curious, and focused.

An intelligent man.

"We find the confined space really doesn't allow for a lot of saluting and snapping to attention," Alger says in a drawl that manages to be both upper class and casual. Then, with a sudden flash of wit, he adds, "You are also free to grow a beard and mustache."

Rainy smiles. "Thank you, Commander. I have a great-aunt who would take you up on that."

He's surprised by her quickness and nods in acknowledgment of her riposte. "How are you making do? Did you dine?"

"I did, sir, and very well. The pineapple for dessert was wonderful."

"I'm afraid the Azorean wine is not the very best, and the shops were plumb out of Madeira. How then is our civilian passenger?"

Rainy looks at Cisco, who is either intimidated by the captain's rank or by his posh English accent and remains momentarily passive. He takes the captain's outstretched hand, but scowls as he does it.

"He's less than thrilled, sir," Rainy says.

"Oh? Not yet enamored of the submariner's life?"

"Are we underwater? Right now are we underwater?"

Cisco demands, an edge of panic speeding his syllables and raising his voice to a near squeak.

"May I take it that you suffer from a touch of claustrophobia?"

"I just want to know, are we underwater?" The urgency is unmistakable and almost excuses the rudeness. Cisco is a frightened man, and Alger has dealt with frightened men before this.

"Not a bit," Alger says airily. "We are making eleven knots on the surface, with light cloud cover, intermittent rain, and moderate swell. If we were submerged, you would not be feeling that rising and falling of the deck."

"I want to get out. I need some air," Cisco says, eyes bulging and darting in every direction, a cornered animal looking for an escape.

"You may certainly climb up to the superstructure, the conning tower or con, I believe it's called in the American service, for a moment or two, once you have been briefed on our procedures."

"I don't give a damn about your procedures!"

The commander's pleasant informality evaporates in a heartbeat. The man with the mild expression, the diffident air, and the relaxed stance disappears, replaced by a taller, sterner, unsmiling officer with distinctly chilly blue eyes.

"Let me explain it this way, Mr. *Smith*." He uses the transparently false name Cisco's traveling under. "Should we spot a German plane or ship I will order the boat to dive. The men under my command know their places and how to reach them by the most expeditious means possible. A straggler, a civilian, blundering about on deck once we have begun our dive is quite likely to find the hatches battened and his shoes getting very wet indeed."

"You wouldn't—"

"Shut your bleeding mouth when the commander addresses you," a petty officer who is more grizzled beard and hair than face snaps in unfeigned outrage. "Pardon, sir," he adds, nodding slightly at the commander.

Alger takes no notice of his petty officer's outburst. "Rather than risk my men, I will, with the greatest regret, watch through the periscope as you attempt to swim to land," Alger says. Then, he is all casual friendliness again. "Sergeant Schulterman, may I have a moment? Jones, you will keep an eye on our passenger, won't you?"

Jones, the hairy petty officer—a sergeant by any other name—flashes teeth through his beard. "Oh yes, Commander, that I will."

"If he becomes unruly you may wish to place him into one of the tubes until he calms down."

Petty Officer Jones manages with some difficulty to avoid laughing in gleeful anticipation. Rainy follows the captain back toward the control room amidships.

The control room is hardly the roomy expanse Rainy has seen in war movies where officers have plenty of space to rush about yelling. The control room of a T-class submarine is the size of a long, narrow bedroom or parlor, a room where every square inch of wall (bulkhead) or overhead is festooned with an astounding array of equipment. It's as if some ambitious shopper has ordered every sort of pipe, dial, wheel, gauge, handle, cathode tube, switch, meter, or valve ever created by the human species and welded them onto every square inch of possible space. It's like being inside an explosion at a junkyard. There are spots where it seems to Rainy's bewildered eye that gauges have been attached to other gauges, which are themselves attached to still more gauges, with the entire assembly positioned carefully to make human movement dangerous to the point of impossibility.

Half a dozen sailors sit stiffly, facing outward or forward, eyes glassily focused on the slow sweep of a radar beam, or listening intently within headphones the size of coffee mugs. Others stand poring over a bright-lit chart on a sort of table not large enough to comfortably hold a tea service. As discreetly as possible the sailors look up from their stations to take in the fact that there is a female—an actual living, breathing *female*—aboard. Looks are exchanged, heads are tilted, eyebrows rise. But there are no whistles or catcalls—she's with the commander, after all. Alger checks in with one of his officers, perhaps his number two, Rainy is far from sure, then turns to Rainy and says, "Do you believe your passenger can be managed?"

"Sir, I barely know him."

"And yet you were chosen to accompany him."

"I follow orders, Commander, I don't write them."

He likes that answer well enough and forms a crookedly wry smile made more engaging by the scar that causes one side of his mouth to rise more easily than the other. "As do we all. As do we all. Well, Sergeant, you'll be bunking in the chief's room, hot-bunking as they say, meaning that the cot is yours when he pulls a watch. Then you should take what leisure you can in the petty officers' mess."

"I'll be fine, sir, thank you."

"It's important that you find a . . . a comfortable place."

Rainy grins. "You mean stay out of the way."

"I should never wish to be so blunt, but yes, in effect. There are sixty-one officers and men aboard the *Topaz*, and we are far from being a roomy craft." He starts to say something more, then stops himself and looks at her with frank curiosity, head back a little so he seems to be looking down his nose. "We do not have women in our service."

"It's pretty new for us as well."

"And how are you finding it?"

"At the moment very comfortable, sir."

"Is this your first operational assignment?"

"No, sir. I was in North Africa prior to this."

"Not in the action, surely."

Rainy smiles, recalling vivid memories. "Actually, I was in a battle, but purely as . . . well, as baggage, I suppose, kind of like I am now. But I was with a unit that comprised a number of women soldiers who performed very well."

"Indeed? Well. I hope *we* are not driven to such desperate measures." There's a bit of an upper-class sniff as punctuation, but Rainy takes no offense. She's seen news reports that more than 80 percent of Americans— including more than 75 percent of women—oppose sending women to war. She doubts that number is any lower in Britain.

After her brief chat with the commander, she and Cisco are instructed by Jones on how to behave in the event of an emergency, the essence being that they are to race without the slightest delay to the POs' mess and sit there without moving until instructed otherwise. There is a great deal of emphasis on showing them how to move like apes swinging from branches through the forest of obstructions.

"If you smack your head, you keep moving or you'll be trampled underfoot, d'ye hear me now, lassie?"

Rainy mentally maps the route from the conning tower,

down through the control room, and forward to the mess. Cisco scowls and looks furtively around. He keeps touching things, not moving them, just touching them, needing the reassurance of solid steel. There is plenty to touch, but at one point Jones grabs Cisco's hand in midair. "Not that pipe, my lad, you'd leave a layer of skin behind."

Cisco pushes to the front, desperate now for air, having used every ounce of his self-control to listen fitfully to Jones. He shoves past men hunched over their screens, spots a narrow steel ladder, and clambers up it. Rainy sees him outlined against gray-black, star-strewn sky above. They emerge into a semicircular space formed by chest-high cowling. Two sailors with massive binoculars scan the sky and the sea in every direction. Three more sailors stand by the four-inch gun just ahead and below them, scanning the horizon as well. They are peering intently at the water for the telltale phosphorescent trail of a periscope, since among the things submarines have to fear is other submarines. The dragon's snout bow pierces waves and sends foam boiling over the gracefully sloping deck to churn around the base of the superstructure.

"Cold out," Rainy says, hugging herself and hunching down inside her regulation army wool sweater.

Cisco clutches the steel cowling and breathes hard, like he's just run a record-fast mile.

"This is bullshit," Cisco says. "I'd rather take my

chances on the streets." He turns, looking for land, but the night is dark in every direction, with the Azores already far astern.

"Your father disagrees," Rainy says. "Anyway, you'll get used to it." But she herself is far from used to it. It takes the sudden access to cold night air to make her realize just how enclosed and cramped—trapped—she has felt down inside that steel tube.

A tube is what it is: a cylinder. The curves of the ballast tanks, the external tubes, the superstructure, the rudder and the screws and the hydroplanes are all added onto that essential steel tube, which is just a sort of long tin can, really, though built to take far more pressure without collapsing. A long tin can crammed with diesel engines and electric motors, batteries, stores of water and food, sixty-one men—and one woman now—and some rather large and extremely explosive torpedoes.

The trip from the Azores to Sicily is better than 2,200 miles. At a steady eleven knots (just under thirteen miles an hour) they can make it in about a week. Seven days in a steel tube full of men and head-bashing obstacles. Seven days with a panicky gangster. She shudders and tells herself it's only the cold air.

"I ain't going back down there," Cisco says defiantly.

"You're going to have to," Rainy says.

"The hell I do. I'm okay up here. Maybe a blanket or—"

A jet of icy spray slaps them both in the face.

"A raincoat. A poncho," Rainy says, completing his thought. "Look, Cisco, I know you're scared—"

He snarls. It's an animal sound accompanying an animal expression of bared teeth. "I'm scared of nothing!" Then he softens it just a bit. "At least no man. And sure as hell no skirt. It's just . . . I don't like tight spaces, never have, not since I was a kid." He finishes in a lower tone, a haunted tone that hints at some past nightmare.

"If you don't go down peaceably when the commander orders, they will not let you come back up. Consider that."

"I need a drink. I've got a bottle in my things, but that won't last long. They must have some aboard, right?"

But rum, while served on board Royal Navy ships, is doled out in precise amounts at prescribed times, and does not amount to much more than a single cocktail. The boat's medical officer has a better solution. After a long while, when it becomes clear that brute force will be required to get Cisco down, the medic climbs to the con and hands Cisco a small glass of amber liquid.

"What's this supposed to be?"

"Laudanum. Tincture of opium. Drink it down, now. It will settle your nerves."

Cisco swallows it and grimaces. "Damn, that is bitter."

Suddenly a klaxon sounds. *A-roooo-gah! A-roooo-gah!*

The loudspeaker comes on with a tense but controlled voice. "Battle stations, battle stations, dive, dive!"

The men on the gun disappear down their hatch in seconds, but it takes the medic and both lookouts—plus a moderate punch in Cisco's kidneys from Rainy—to shove Cisco, inconveniently bent in half at one point, down to safety. They close the hatch and spin the lock seconds ahead of a rush of water that gurgles over the hastily closed hatch.

The crew has already reached battle stations so the corridor is relatively clear as Cisco is dragged, literally kicking and screaming (and cursing), to his hammock.

Finally the laudanum kicks in and Cisco's movements become less powerful, less focused, his flow of curses and threats slows, and he offers only ineffectual resistance to being tied down again.

"This is going to be a very long trip," Rainy mutters under her breath. "And all of it probably a fool's errand."

Amateur.

RIO RICHLIN—OFF GELA BEACH, SICILY

It is not Rio's first rodeo.

It's an expression she has appropriated from Cat Preeling. *Ain't my first rodeo*, Cat likes to say when someone, generally a man, explains something in a patronizing tone.

Ain't my first rodeo. Ain't my first amphibious landing on a beach.

Rio's landing craft has been loaded and circling for the better part of a half hour. Dawn is breaking ever so slowly it seems, allowing just enough light to see that the boats of the first wave are reaching the beach and disgorging their troops.

"All right, we're going in," the coxswain yells.

The circling landing craft all line up abreast and race at full speed toward shore, smacking waves and banging their passengers around. The pink of dawn begins to give shape to the island ahead. Its most prominent feature is a steep, singular mountain that dominates the eastern end of the island. There is a small but clear plume of smoke twisting leisurely up from the top, smoke turned orange as the sun peeking over the horizon touches first the highest thing in view. It reminds Rio of Jillion's sketch, the curl of smoke at the end of Rio's rifle.

"Etna," Stick says. "It's a volcano."

"Like with lava?" someone asks.

"The whole island is just cooled-down lava. Etna created Sicily. But I don't think it's—"

The sea explodes around them, a vast gout of water. The defending Italians seem to be taking matters more seriously, and daybreak has improved their aim. Seawater rains down on them, running off Rio's helmet. Geer curses and urges Miss Lion deeper into his jacket. Everyone flinches as a shell passes overhead, howling like a racing locomotive.

Just ahead is another landing craft, much like theirs, but seemingly stuck and unable to move though its engines are churning the water into a small bubble bath.

"We're going to take some of them aboard," the coxswain yells down from his squat bridge, chopping his hand in the direction of the stranded boat. He gentles the engine and one of his small crew perches atop the ramp, peering down into the turbulent sea, trying to locate the limits of the sandbar with a length of rope and a lead weight.

"Looks like thirty feet, Skipper!"

"Got it."

"I make it twenty."

"Twenty it is."

"Getting hairy here, Skipper!"

The coxswain has his work cut out for him. He has to bring his boat in close enough to pass a line to the stranded boat, but not let the swell push him up onto the sand or send it crashing into the back of the other boat.

Geer yells, "It's a boatful of Nigras!"

"Throw 'em a line," the skipper shouts, and his crewman twirls a rope like a lasso before he sends it flying.

This activity, ever more visible as the sun threatens to leap into view from behind the horizon, attracts small-caliber fire from shore. At least one machine gun chatters away from a pillbox just beyond the sand of the beach, but the rounds splash harmlessly into the sea. They are beyond machine gun range, but not beyond mortar range, and someone with blessedly inadequate skill is firing, dropping rounds to their left, their farther left, behind, ahead, not yet zeroing in.

Rio is unnerved by the helplessness of being trapped in the boat, nowhere to run to, nowhere to dig a fighting hole, no cover, no control. No one to shoot. Any random shell . . . Tilo Suarez is working his rosary; Pang is mouthing silent words that must surely be a prayer. Rio thinks a quick *Take care of me, Lord*, but is too restless and worried to focus on divine intervention.

"Figures, fugging Nigras," Geer mutters. "Going to get us killed."

Pang says, "Looks to me like the guy driving the boat is white." This earns him a shrug from Geer.

The rope is secured and drawn tight across a mere twenty feet of water. Looking over the side, Rio can see the sandbar just below the surface, revealed and then concealed by each passing wave, like a fan dancer teasing. They try pulling the stuck boat free, but a cleat breaks loose and the rope has to be reattached, and now the effort focuses on getting the trapped GIs to crawl along the rope.

The rest of the platoon is just reaching the beach. Rio follows them, eyes squinting beneath an anxious brow. She can just make out a man she thinks may be Lieutenant Vanderpool, and is that Sergeant Alvarez beside him?

The rope is stretched, drawn taut by the engines now in low-gear reverse. A tall young private is bold enough to give it a try. For the first few feet he does fine, hands clasping, legs wrapped around the rope, face upside down and looking toward Rio. Then the swell pushes the boats closer, the rope slackens, and the soldier is dunked in the foam.

He pulls his way up, hand over hand, legs wrapped tight around the rope, and in a few seconds he is hauled aboard, spitting seawater and coughing. The second person across is a stocky sergeant, followed by a short young woman who moves with surprising agility.

"Hey," Rio says. "Don't I know you?"

Frangie Marr squeegees water from her face and blinks, clearing her vision. "Why, if it isn't Rio Richlin."

"Fancy meeting in a place like this," Rio says, and laughs, oddly delighted. "Jenou! It's Private Marr."

"What on earth?" Jenou says, and grins at Frangie. There is something reassuring about the chance meeting, a feeling that providence must be looking down kindly on them.

That warm feeling does not last. A fourth black soldier is coming across when the distant mortarman gets lucky.

BAM!

Ka-whoosh!

The round lands with eerie precision, right in the middle of the stranded boat. It goes through the deck, hits the sandbar beneath, and blows up. The stranded craft goes up in a jet of water, reduced to sticks and slabs of twirling plywood. Bodies fly up and outward. The man on the rope is whipped upward, loses his grip, and flies up only to fall in the deluge of water and shattered hull.

Sergeant Walter Green stares in horror. He grips the railing with both hands like a man ready to jump into the water. The surviving craft guns its engines and backs away, churning sand and water into tan foam, scraping loudly over the remains of the destroyed boat.

A body pops up from below, faceup, dead but with no evidence of trauma. Frangie reaches toward him, but of course there is no possibility of touching, let alone helping, him.

They take three tight turns around the scene and are able to pull one more injured man into the boat before finally racing away as more shells zero in on them. Blood turns their wake pink.

Frangie is on her knees in six inches of water on the bottom of the boat, kneeling over the injured man they pulled aboard. He's having some kind of spasm, his whole body twitching and jerking.

Frangie pulls a wrapped roll of gauze from her pouch and tries to pry the man's teeth apart. "I need help here!"

Rio is nearest so she drops down beside Frangie, sees what she needs, and manages with some effort to open the man's mouth. It is clenched so hard his teeth are likely to crack. Rio gets his jaw open just enough to let Frangie shove the gauze in and give the man something to bite down on.

"I'm going to check you over, Daddy D," Frangie says. "Richlin, can you hold his ankles down?"

Rio does, and the man's spasm lessens by degrees.

"I don't see any blood," Frangie reports. "No blood,

no broken bones. Most likely a concussion, unless . . ." She frowns. "Daddy D, you hear me? If you hear me, nod or blink or something."

There's a tight nod.

"Are you epileptic?"

There's a long pause, then finally, reluctantly, a nod.

"You can't be fighting a war with epilepsy, Dad, what are you thinking?" Frangie scolds. "Sergeant Green, Dad's got to go back to the transport."

Rio glances at Walter, who nods, but he's distracted, scanning ahead for other elements of his platoon as they close the distance to shore, a grim hopelessness in his eyes. She sees that his hands are trembling, watches as he closes them into tight fists, opens them again with the tremor gone.

They prop a calmed Daddy D against the side of the boat. There's nothing to be done about his sitting in water. And then the front of Daddy D's face explodes. Tilo yelps in fear and falls back. Rio and Frangie both recoil in shock. A random machine gun round has passed through the thin side of the boat and through the colored soldier's face. Rio does not immediately notice that the largely spent round has gone into her own left thigh. In fact, Frangie sees it before she does.

"You're hit!"

"No, I'm . . . Hey! What the . . ." Rio pulls at the hole

and the reddening cloth of her uniform trousers. Frangie pushes Rio's hands out of the way, snaps, "Let me do my job," has scissors out and quickly cuts an X in Rio's pants leg, exposing the wound. It looks nothing like what a machine gun wound should be. There is a simple hole but so shallow that the dull gray tail end of the slug is still visible.

Sergeant Cole and Jenou both come closer.

"Jesus, Rio, you're hit!" Jenou cries.

"I don't even feel it!"

"You will," Frangie says grimly. "But you were lucky. Luckier than Daddy D, foolish man covering up epilepsy, rest in peace. And him with children too, poor babies." Without a pause Frangie returns to Rio's wound, saying, "I'm not seeing much blood, so I think I can pull it out without risking a major bleed." Then, with a significant look, adds, "Or . . ."

"Or what?" Rio is fascinated by the wound. It doesn't hurt, but she is quite sure Frangie is right and that it will hurt later. There'll be a big bruise and the shallow hole will take some time to heal.

She glances up and sees the colored soldier, still sitting, portions of his face hanging down in tatters. There's a meaty hole where his nose should be, a red and pink and white hole, with an eye to either side and a blood-filled mouth below. But Hansu Pang has pulled a poncho from Daddy D's pack and is now spreading it over him.

"Or," Frangie is saying, "you could go back with the other wounded and be properly treated."

Rio stares blankly, not quite sure what's being suggested until Jenou says, "She's giving you a way out, honey. Take it!"

Then Rio understands. She can avoid the landing, perhaps avoid several days or even weeks of battle. She can lie on a nice clean hospital ship bed with sheets and hot coffee and . . .

Geer is looking askance at her, waiting, judging. Suarez looks worried. Even Sergeant Cole looks troubled.

"No," Rio says, shaking her head and frowning dismissively. "Do it now. Do it here."

"You'll most likely feel this," Frangie warns. She has her forceps in hand. With all the care she can manage in the vibrating, bucking, salt-spray-washed boat, she clamps the serrated teeth of the forceps onto a jagged protrusion on the metal slug. Rio winces. They are very definitely in range of small arms fire now, as if any further proof were needed, and bullets sing and buzz overhead.

"Okay, on the count of three. One . . ." She pulls the bullet out like a cork from a bottle of wine. There's some blood, but it's oozing, not pumping.

"Five minutes!" the coxswain yells down.

"What happened to counting to three?" Rio asks archly.

"Misdirection," Frangie says, but she's not chatty. She's

quickly breaking out a suturing kit, not so very different from the standard sewing kit.

"These won't be pretty stitches," Frangie says through gritted teeth. "No time for pretty."

"That's a shame, her legs are her best feature," Jenou says, and pats Rio's helmet comfortingly.

A part of Rio notes the fact that they've just seen a man's face blown off and while they are shaken, they are not panicked. Maybe it's the fatalism of veterans. Maybe it's the fact that it was just a colored man who died.

"Ow!" Rio yells as the needle goes in. This she feels, and she is incongruously transported back to the hotel room in Tunis, back to the moment when she crossed the line between girl and woman. There had been a similar sharp pain, a surprising pain, but one that did not cause her to pull back. She had been almost helpless beneath Strand, feeling the full weight of a man on her for the first time, feeling the discomfort as he accidentally pulled her hair with his arms straining beside her head, feeling involved yet distant in a way.

He had wanted it. He had wanted sex, but yes, so had she, there was no point deceiving herself. She could have stopped it at any point. She had wanted to know it and understand it, but looking back now she did not feel that she had been somehow transformed. She was no longer a virgin, and my God, her entire life she'd been told how terribly important it was for her to remain a virgin, that magic word. But what did it matter, really?

Strand, too, had suggested an escape, just as Frangie was doing now: Escape through wound? Escape through pregnancy? Was it some kind of omen that two people had now offered her a way out? Was God trying to tell her something?

Probably not, God, Rio thinks, abashed at the tension between thoughts of an all-seeing divinity and the forbidden thing she had done with Strand.

Anyway, God wouldn't kill her for fornicating. Would He?

I have a bullet hole in my leg, I'm three minutes from the beach, and I'm worried God will strike me down for fornication.

Steady, girl. Steady.

"Okay, I'm doing three more stitches," Frangie Marr says. "Go ahead and yell if you want."

"Richlin yell and admit she's human?" Cat teases.

Three more sutures follow and Rio almost does yelp in pain, but now she can't, can she? She can't without seeming to playact, to be someone the others didn't think she is.

I'm playing a role now. I'm an actor playing the role of warrior.

She looks around at the boat, at the scared, wet, shocked

faces and realizes, *Oh, they're playing too: pretending nonchalance and doing an unconvincing job of it.*

We're all scared to death and pretending to be brave.

The first time—her first landing on a hostile beach—she had wondered whether she was brave. She had imagined losing control of herself, throwing down her rifle and fleeing. She had imagined the shame of it.

Were they all thinking the same thing? Were they all terrified of a bullet like the one that had blown open the Negro's face, but more terrified still of the shame of running away?

"It's too wet for tape," Frangie says. "I'm going to wrap gauze around your leg and tie it off. It'll probably slip if you run around much. Try to keep dirt out of it. Check in with one of your own medics as soon as possible."

"All right, people," Sergeant Cole says. "Saddle up, you know the drill. Keep your weapons high and dry, keep your heads down. We rally on Lieutenant Vanderpool, he's a hundred yards down on our left."

The experienced soldiers have used condoms to cover the business end of their rifles, more to keep sand out than water.

Walter says, "We'll hang back until your people are clear, Cole. Best I can tell what's left of my boys are way off to the south. Good luck."

Cole glances at the poncho covering Daddy D. "Sorry about your men."

"It's war," Walter says, but there's a quiver in his voice.

"Ain't it just," Cole agrees sourly.

"Jasper, you ride back out with Daddy D," Green orders. "I want him cared for, best they can."

Jasper is too shaken up to argue. Almost his entire squad is dead. Rio thinks, *He's got no one to shame him into bravery now.*

Rio tests her leg. It works. She ritually checks her M1, checks the straps on her pack, checks her belt, and slaps her palm on the front of her helmet to get it seated just right. Then, an afterthought: she looks ahead at the beach, still two minutes away. She estimates. She has time.

"Jen! Get my knife out of my pack for me."

"What?"

"Just get it!"

The knife, the *koummya*, and its scabbard emerge. Rio has attached rawhide strips to act as a belt and quickly straps it to her uninjured right thigh, as high up as it will ride without bumping into her dangling canteen. She twists her belt slightly and tests her reach, dropping her hand several times to find the hilt.

When she looks up she intercepts a strange, cold look from Jenou. But there's no time to ask for an explanation, and anyway Jenou shakes her head in feigned amusement, killing the moment.

Jenou wants me to take the easy way out, Rio thinks. She doesn't understand. First Strand and now Jenou willing her to grab any excuse to go.

Neither of them understands.

The boat is in close, but the hull has not yet scraped sand. The coxswain drops the ramp, which splashes into the water, and the men and women of Second Squad go pelting out. Tilo, Pang, and Cat are in the lead, and the three of them fall from view, dropping straight down into eight feet of water.

"Goddammit!" Cole roars. "We're too far out!"

The coxswain throws the boat into reverse and starts to raise the ramp again. Cole strips off his pack, tosses his Thompson to Jack, and readies to jump in after his men. Rio is right behind him, tearing off her pack and tossing her rifle to Jillion, and, somewhat to her surprise, Geer is diving in as well. Geer has had the presence of mind to grab a rope.

Rio jumps feetfirst and plows down until the soles of her boots land on shifting sand. She opens her eyes underwater and spots Tilo, suddenly brilliantly lit by a star shell exploding high above them. He's desperately trying to get his pack off his back. His eyes are wide with terror. Bubbles escape from his mouth.

Rio kicks and glides toward him, drawing her *koummya* as she goes. Tilo nearly brains her with a panicky fist, but she slips past him, glides around behind, grabs his pack with one hand, and inserts the *koummya* between

Tilo's shoulder blade and the strap. One quick slice cuts through, and Tilo is able to shrug off the rest as Rio gets beneath him and pushes his head up into the air.

It's not so hard, Rio thinks. *Long as you don't panic.* Salt water stings the wound on her thigh.

Tilo manages to remove his own belt. He can swim well enough at least to keep afloat once unburdened. Rio surfaces, gasping for air, and gets a bellyful of salt water instead. She gags and coughs and looks wildly around to see that the boat is now forty feet away. The remaining soldiers are yelling a blue streak at the coxswain. Cole is bobbing a few feet away with Cat in the crook of his arm. Cat is sputtering and trying to yell, but white foam rolls over them both.

"Geer!" Rio shouts. "Geer!"

There's a porpoise-like eruption and Geer appears. He has an unconscious Hansu Pang in his arms and is fighting to keep him afloat. Tilo, now mostly recovered, swims to his aid, and between them they pass the rope around Pang, who is larger and heavier than he looks, and haul him like a fish toward the beach. The sand rises beneath them, allowing their boots to first touch and push off, and then to walk, fighting the retreating waves and allowing incoming waves to help to push them toward the shore.

It's like moving through molasses, as if the Mediterranean, having once tasted them, is reluctant to spit them out. Finally, Rio collapses face-first on the beach. She hugs the sand, gasping for air and retching up seawater.

Geer is astride Pang, pushing down on his chest, forcing water from his lungs. Suddenly Pang coughs back to life and Geer stands and steps back, as if now wishing to deny any connection to the weakly stirring GI.

Frangie Marr is running beside Walter Green, a hundred yards down the beach where the landing craft has finally beached. The boat is already turning back toward the transport.

And with that a badly shaken Second Squad, Fifth Platoon, is ashore on Sicily, minus a good portion of its ammo, some of its weapons, and way too much of its food.

But alive.

RAINY SCHULTERMAN—ABOARD HMS *TOPAZ*, TYRRHENIAN SEA

The first dive was just a test dive. As were the next three. Lieutenant Commander Alger and his officers are keeping the crew at the peak of training.

Cisco has spent most of a week drugged and lashed into his hammock. From time to time he's been allowed up on deck to blink blearily at the sun before being led on wobbly legs back to his opium dreams.

This is certainly a unique way to contribute to the war effort.

It is also troubling at a moral level. The medic has confirmed that laudanum can become addicting. He doesn't think it will happen in a week's time, but he admits he knows very little. He's not a doctor in any real sense of the word, just a medic, whose job is to deal with the various crushing and pinching and scalding and chemical inhalation injuries caused by the regular operation of the *Topaz*.

So between them, Rainy and the medical officer may be turning a gangster into a drug addict. For the war effort.

Lieutenant Commander Alger summons Rainy to the bridge.

"Sergeant, I thought you might like to know that we are just south of Capri, twenty-four miles from our target."

She's been expecting this. She nods.

"We are far closer to the Italian coast than we should like under normal circumstances. I'm rather hoping that Jerry's eye is focused on the fighting in Sicily and that he has few planes or boats to spare looking for subs. It's night and the moon has set, so I'll stay on the surface just a bit longer before submerging. We will pop up near the beach, get you and your . . . charge . . . ashore, submerge again, and creep away. I'd say that you should be ready to go in half an hour."

"Yes, sir. I'll be ready."

He looks at her with some affection. "You've done well this last week. It can't have been easy. Unfamiliar environment . . . your recalcitrant charge . . ."

Rainy smiles and gently touches the latest submarine-inflicted bruise on her forehead. "In another week I would have the hang of it."

"I'm certain you would. But there is a rather delicate matter to consider. I assume you will be going ashore in mufti. You understand that if Jerry or the Eye-ties capture you out of uniform they will likely treat you as a spy."

"Yes."

He seems taken aback by her one-word answer. "The mere fact that you are being put ashore in the vicinity of Salerno is a very dangerous thing. The Gestapo are brutes but not stupid. If they take you or *Mr. Smith* alive . . ."

Rainy is aware now of a hush on the bridge. It's never a chatty place, but there is now that hard-to-define feeling that all ears are eavesdropping.

"Commander, I've been issued a suicide pill."

The pill is a tiny glass capsule filled with cyanide in liquid form. It is sheathed in brown rubber to minimize the odds of it being accidentally broken. And it has been cleverly concealed by sewing it into the collar of the Italian dress she is to wear ashore.

"You seem quite sanguine about it," Alger says with a soft concern.

"I'm not thrilled about it," Rainy says with a sigh. "But I'm even less thrilled about being questioned by the Gestapo. I would be a female Jewish spy, and I don't think they would be gentle. I don't know that I would be able to resist. And I would rather die than cause deaths that might come of me spilling the beans."

Someone—she can't see who—mutters, "She's a prime one," in a tone she takes to be admiring.

"And what of *Mr. Smith*?" Alger asks. "Surely you don't

expect him to take an equally high-minded position?"

"No," she admits. "I considered that possibility and, well, I have a pistol."

Alger tilts his head, and his eyebrows crinkle in the middle. "Have you ever used a firearm in *that* way?"

Rainy shakes her head. Something about his concern combined with the doubts that have tortured her for this last week makes her throat clench.

"I see. It could be a very difficult thing to do."

"I would like to think it would never be easy," she says in a low voice. "But, Commander, with great respect, how is it different from what you do?"

Alger takes that on board, frowns, and nods slightly before saying, "You'll forgive me if I observe that there is regrettably a very long history of men fighting wars and doing the necessary. There is no such history with the gentler sex."

"You think that in a moment of crisis I'll hesitate because I'm a woman."

He inclines his head in agreement.

Rainy squares her shoulders, very aware of many eyes on her and of ears tuned carefully. "I am not a draftee, Lieutenant Commander Alger, I volunteered. I volunteered to kill Germans and to help rid the world of that monster in Berlin. I would be very sad to have to shoot Mr. Smith, though I've been tempted . . . But I believe if it comes to it, yes, I believe I can and will put the gun to the back of his head and pull the trigger."

Alger exhales long and slow. He makes a small, regretful smile and says, "Perhaps you will. I think it is a terribly sad thing to see that the madness of war has now carried women along too."

Rainy almost stops herself from saying more, but cannot. "There are women under German bombs in Poland and in Holland and in the Soviet Union. And more than a few in England. *They* never got to shoot back."

Alger takes Rainy's arm and propels her gently down what Rainy has come to think of as the obstacle course and guides her into his cabin. It's as close to private as any space on the sub.

Without preamble he says, "You know, of course, that this mission is absolutely mad."

Rainy frowns and says nothing.

"It's hardly unique. War is a series of foolish enterprises and a study of history is not reassuring on that score. I will tell you that this may be the most foolish. Sending a young woman with an unstable gangster—"

"I don't believe my sex has—"

He cuts her off with an abrupt chop of his hand. "I'm not talking about your sex, if you were an equally young man in the identical position I would still say that this is a reckless and foolish mission."

Rainy actually takes a step back, which brings her up against a cabinet. Even commanders have cramped quarters in a sub. She starts to defend her mission, but she can't do it honestly. Alger is right.

That's the damned thing: he's right.

"Of course it is understood that I am not referring to the admiralty when I say this," Alger says with a hint of irony. "But not everyone in this war has his eye equally fixed on the larger objective, or on the lives of the men—or women—under their command. Many officers are more interested in their careers."

She nods slowly and she agrees, but she is not ready to agree openly. She's a soldier on a mission. She has orders. She has no choice now, no easy way out.

He nods briskly. "Well, we shall submerge shortly and—"

Several things happen at once. The klaxon brays. A young officer sticks his head in the cabin, excited. "Contact, sir!" Alger spins away, and Rainy follows him back to the bridge, drawn by the excitement.

"Commander!" The sonar operator pulls one headphone back and half turns. "Screws closing fast!"

Rainy is instantly forgotten.

"Bearing?"

One lookout is already sliding down the ladder, the second just behind him as Alger raps out orders to dive. Within seconds the deck begins to tilt down by the bow.

The lookout says, "Looked like a spotter plane, Skipper, but it was just a glimpse."

The conclusion is obvious. A spotter plane has called their position in to either the Italian or German navy. Or both. The sonar operator confirms that he's hearing screws of a speed and type to indicate a destroyer coming on fast on an intercept course.

The periscope is sent up and Alger peers intently. "She's that Greek capture, the *Hermes*, if I am not mistaken. Take her down to ten fathoms and come around. Sergeant Schulterman, see to your charge."

Rainy spins away and runs up the corridor to find that the torpedo room crew has already taken Cisco's hammock down and the gangster has been made fast to a vertical bit of pipe.

It is a good thing he's tied because within minutes things go from merely claustrophobic to catastrophic.

The first salvo of depth charges explodes.

Rainy has seen a movie called *We Dive at Dawn*, which purported to show a depth charge attack. In the fictional submarine there had been a sound like distant thunder. Then lights had flickered, and the actors had swayed back and forth, and there had been a sound of galley pots rattling.

The reality bears almost no resemblance to that.

The exploding depth charges do not sound like distant

thunder; the pressure wave hits like a hammer, like some angry god is hurling great boulders at the *Topaz*. A gigantic aquatic beast is kicking the sub, and with each kick the bulkheads and deck and every gauge, wheel, bolt, and section of pipe strike at Rainy, as if the walls around her are trying to batter her to death.

The floor beneath her punches up at the soles of her feet, collapsing her knees. She falls sideways against the legs of one of the torpedo room crew. Somehow in the midst of what seems to Rainy like the end of the world, the crew is hauling on a length of cable, drawing a massive long torpedo toward its launch tube.

And suddenly the explosions stop.

Rainy climbs to her feet, muttering an apology to the man she'd fouled. There's blood coming from her nose, which feels numb.

The cessation of the catastrophic noise of the depth charges allows Rainy to hear Cisco. He is screaming, screaming, all self-control gone, screaming, head tossing from side to side, which gives his screams a rhythm, softer, louder, like a French ambulance siren.

One of the torpedo men snaps, "Gag 'im, miss, gag 'im. We'll be rigging for silent running soon!"

Rainy has no gag and her wits are scrambled. She grabs at the blanket peeking from the stowed hammock. But of course she can't tear it, the wool is too tough.

The word comes down, mouth to mouth, in loud stage whispers, "Rig for silent running!"

Cisco screams, incoherent gibberish sounds, lunatic sounds.

Rainy is wearing her borrowed Royal Navy peacoat. She shoves her right arm into Cisco's open mouth. He bites down hard, and she feels it, but right now the pain in her arm is the least of her problems. The second salvo of depth charges is sinking toward them even as the *Topaz* tilts precipitously downward. She can barely keep to her feet against the slope and leans into Cisco, arm still gagging him and . . .

Click-*BOOM!*

Click-*BOOM!*

The twin explosions hit harder, much harder. The torpedo being hauled forward is knocked from its cradle and smashes onto the deck. Twenty-one feet long, 3,452 pounds: it lands like a dropped bank safe.

For a terrifying moment Rainy freezes, expecting it to explode, but of course it has not yet been fused. The torpedo rolls slowly, inexorably left with men leaping over it to avoid being crushed. Then it rolls to the right, so Rainy has to grab the pipe Cisco is tied to and haul herself up and out of the way. The torpedo slams against that same pipe, and the whole thing pulls free and . . .

Click-*BOOM!*

Click-*BOOM!*

Steam everywhere, it scalds the back of Rainy's hand, she cries out, lands atop the torpedo with Cisco's weight atop her and Cisco screaming madly in her ear, thrashing and . . .

Click-*BOOM!*

Click-*BOOM!*

A different voice screams, a crewman, his hand crushed beneath the torpedo. Men race with rope and straps, leaping almost comically to avoid being crushed. An officer tears in yelling but in a ridiculous whisper, "What the hell?" which does nothing to help. Then, to Rainy, "Get that damned fool out of here and shut him up!"

Cisco is larger than Rainy, though not a large man. He has torn free of the broken pipe, bellowing all the while, rope hanging about him in loops. Rainy throws her arms around him, but he has the strength of panic, and it's like trying to tackle a charging rhinoceros. In this case, the rhinoceros is at least charging in the right direction.

Rainy uses Cisco's own momentum to bring him down. Just before the wardroom, still clinging to his neck, she times it carefully and twists with sudden violence so Cisco's momentum slams him headfirst into the heavy steel frame of a hatch.

He falls, not quite unconscious, but stunned, too stunned to resist as she guides him into the alcove of the

196

petty officers' mess. He is beneath the table. Rainy is on the bench. He starts to thrash again, and Rainy lifts her weight up on one leg, aims with the other foot, and kicks the side of his head with all the force she can muster.

At last, Cisco is silent.

And now it no longer matters because the destroyer is moving off, either convinced that it has killed *Topaz*, or convinced that *Topaz* is safely away.

They run beneath the surface. The mood is relieved but apprehensive. Crewmen laugh nervously and seem to be glancing over their shoulders, often at Rainy.

Her burned hand hurts terribly, and she can actually see the blisters swelling, thin flesh filling with liquid. Her nose is unfortunately no longer numb, but painful. A look in the back of a shiny spoon confirms what her fingers tell her: that she now has a broken nose to match her big brother Aryeh's. She touches it and is punished with a jolt of pain that takes her breath away.

There is some damage to the *Topaz*, and it is some time before Lieutenant Commander Alger comes to stand at the mess room opening to say, "You look somewhat the worse for wear."

Rainy doesn't have anything brave to say. She nods silently and presses gauze to her nose. The medic has given her a greasy cream to spread over her burned hand, but it does nothing for the pain.

"I wonder if, considering your condition, not to mention your panicky friend's condition, you would prefer to report yourself unfit to continue . . ."

Rainy shakes her head, but not without some inner turmoil. This is not how she meant to arrive in Italy. The whole mission is mad, she sees that now. Mad to send her with Cisco into enemy territory. Mad to risk exposing Allied interest in the area around Salerno. Mad to have no plan for what she is to do after she accomplishes her mission. Colonel Corelli is a fool. Agent Bayswater said so, Lieutenant Commander Alger certainly implies as much, and her own printed orders reveal his lack of planning.

It's a suicide mission.

My God, it really is a suicide mission!

Lieutenant Commander Alger is patient, but Rainy's silence has stretched on for quite a while. "You need to decide."

She decides. Stiff, pushing the words out, she says, "Sir, I have my orders."

Thirty minutes later she is on the slick deck. The night is not too cold, the water is calm, the *Topaz* lies half a mile off the coast of Italy. Hurried, spooked crewmen push a narrow rubber boat up through the torpedo-loading hatch, haul it to the side, and settle it in the water. Others are bent over the side peering intently at one of the hydroplanes. Cisco, battered, seemingly exhausted now, stands silent, staring as if dazed.

Rainy has taken off and carefully folded her uniform and left it in the care of the captain's steward. She now wears what can only be called a frumpy, faded dress of the quality one might expect an Italian woman to be wearing long into a war that has impoverished the Italian people. She wonders where Corelli's people found it. A rag bin? A secondhand shop? She has a too-thin and nearly useless knitted scarf around her neck and a thin wool coat. Her feet are in sturdy but graceless pumps, already soaked by the spray.

And thanks to the depth charge attack, they are late. The sun will be up in an hour, and the sailors have to row ashore and return, which will be no easy task with two oars in an awkward little boat. The boat slews alongside, two sailors already sitting in it, tethered only by a rope and anxious to get going: no one has forgotten either the spotter plane or the destroyer.

"Well," Rainy says, trying not to sound as worried as she is, "I guess this is it."

"I'm afraid so," Lieutenant Commander Alger says gently.

Rainy sticks out her hand, and Alger shakes it formally. "Good hunting, Sergeant."

"Thanks, Commander. It's been . . ."

She can't think of the right word, so Alger says, "Yes. Yes, it certainly has."

She is handed down into the boat where Cisco is

already seated. He's begun to revive, just a little, though he still seems abashed by the sailors and refuses to meet anyone's eye.

He's humiliated. That's going to be trouble.

Rainy is wet but not quite to the bone by the time the rubber boat grinds softly onto the beach. One sailor jumps out and draws the rope to steady the boat, while the other sailor hands Rainy out. Cisco jumps eagerly onto the sand.

"Careful with him, miss," one of the sailors says, nodding significantly at Cisco.

"Hey, screw you, pal," Cisco says.

In less than a minute the boat is lost to sight. Rainy takes a shaky breath. She has just landed in Mussolini's Italy on a harebrained mission with a seething, unstable gangster. Her face, hand, and shoulder all hurt.

Strapped to her inner thigh where a casual search won't find it is a Colt 1903, weighing 1.46 pounds and holding eight .32 caliber bullets.

Concealed behind a loosely sewn seam in her collar is her suicide pill.

It is still dark, but stars are already fading in the east. The only sound is the lullaby *shush-shush* of wavelets. The beach is empty. The closest lights might be miles away north, she can't tell.

"*Oy vey iz mir,*" she whispers, echoing her mother.

Oh, woe is me.

14

Harassed by intermittent shelling and occasional attacks from the air, the platoon assembles on the chaotic beach. Lieutenant Vanderpool, with orders to get them off the beach as quickly as possible, leads them inland. The 119th is spread out to their left, with Fifth Platoon holding the right of the line and Second Squad on the hanging end. There is no Allied force on their immediate right, not yet, as the division assigned that position has run into trouble getting their gear ashore.

SNAFU, Rio thinks. *Situation Normal: All Fugged Up.*

The division, accompanied by the single light tank they've managed to get ashore, bypasses the town of Gela and heads directly across the dry farm fields of southern Sicily.

Rio's first sighting of actual Sicilians occurs when three small children come running out of a farmhouse. The children are scrawny, haphazardly dressed in cheap, patched, ill-fitting clothing, and with not a shoe between them.

The nervous platoon trains weapons on them until high-pitched cries of delight, ear-to-ear grins, and manic laughter convince them that there is no danger from these three.

One urchin, a seven-year-old girl, tugs shyly at Jenou's leg while staring in a solemn way at the blood-soaked leg of Rio's pants.

"Give her something," Rio says to Jenou.

"What? Tips on how to dress? That outfit goes way beyond hand-me-down," Jenou says, but she fishes in her pockets and comes up with half a ration chocolate bar. The little girl falls to it immediately, gnawing at the rock-hard chocolate and grinning up in surprise and pure, undiluted joy.

"Careful it doesn't give you the runs," Jenou says point-lessly since there is no chance of the child understanding.

A woman comes rushing from the farmhouse, yelling in Italian, obviously scolding her children, waving at them to get back in the house. The house, in truth, is little more than a pile of mismatched stones, shabbier and less likely to be permanent than anything Rio has ever seen. There are no windows, just a low, crooked door and a roof of cracked tiles patched with tied bundles of straw.

The children ignore their mother, who slows as she

approaches. No grin from her. Her face is brown and deeply lined, her eyes dark with a thousand years of Sicilian suspicion.

"Keep moving," Cole urges his troops. "This war ain't over just yet."

They move along, and the children follow for a few dozen yards until drawn back to their mother.

They are in a sunbaked land of small farm fields, stone fences, donkey-drawn carts, scrawny cattle, and mostly dirt tracks rather than roads. Trees are few and far between, but prickly pear stands are everywhere, with large, flat ovals like beaver tails festooned with two kinds of needles.

Tilo cuts one with his knife and gingerly picks it up, careful to avoid the obvious pricks. But the large needles are not the problem.

"Ah! Damn! Ow!"

Hansu Pang says, "You got to watch the little hairlike prickles. They go right into skin and it's hell getting rid of them."

"Got a lot of them prickly pears in Japan, do you?" Geer asks.

"No, but they grow around the internment camp where my grandparents are." He says it without rancor, but it irritates Rio anyway, because she expects an argument to break out and she's instinctively unhappy about

203

any unnecessary noise. Sure enough . . .

"How the hell are your grandparents locked up and you're in the army?" Geer demands.

"I've been living in Hawaii, where people understand that we aren't Japanese but Americans." This time Pang's anger peeks out for just a flash before being smothered. "It's mostly in California that folks are being interned, not Hawaii."

"Japs are Japs," Geer says with a shrug.

"Thanks for saving my life, Geer, and also, fug you."

It is the first time Pang has defended himself in any way, and to Rio's relief, Geer lets it go.

They halt and crouch suddenly, hearing gunfire. But it's not close and not directed at them, so the march continues. Rio has no real idea where they're headed. Vanderpool told them the name of the village, but it's all Italian gobbledygook to Rio's ears.

Besides, Cat has noticed something far more interesting. "Hey, those are tomatoes!"

Every head swivels left.

"And they're ripe!"

Sergeant Cole yells something about mines, but no one pays any attention since it's unlikely the local farmers would be tending crops in minefields. An old farmer at the far side of the field looks as if he's considering protesting, but then gets back to his labor. They keep going in the same direction, parallel to the road, but now they are slowing to snatch fat red tomatoes from the vines, stuffing them into backpacks and shirt pockets and taking big bites from the most promising specimens. Soon the platoon is dripping tomato juice down mouths and necks, fingers and arms. First Platoon, farther on their left, is busily denuding their half of the same field and the farmer finally yells at them, but with no effect.

Rio does not join in; she's never been a great lover of raw tomatoes. Her leg wound is itching fiercely and at the same time aching and distracting her too much for cavorting through the fields. But a mile on, the tomato-stained, prickly-pear-maimed platoon spies a patch of watermelons, and this Rio cannot resist no matter the pain. She uses her *koummya* to slice open a melon heavy with sweetness and greedily gobbles it up, spitting seeds as she goes.

"It's like watching an especially disgusting machine gun," Jenou teases.

"What else am I supposed to do with watermelon seeds?" Rio demands.

Jack says, "You're supposed to spit them discreetly into your spoon and lay them on the side of your fruit plate." He winks and spits a seed about ten feet.

"Pitiful," Tilo says. "I can beat it."

The war is halted temporarily while Rio, Jack, Tilo,

and Cat compete to see who can spit a seed the farthest.

Sergeant Cole comes over, shakes his head in disgust, grabs a hunk of melon, chews, swallows, and spits a seed through the gap in his teeth that very nearly doubles Cat's record.

"I gotta teach you people everything? Now, get your butts moving, you've had your lunch."

Another hour on and the sun is taking a toll on the GIs. A water pump used to fill a cattle trough is worked eagerly to fill helmets with water, which they dump over their heads.

"That's better," Rio says.

"Your leg is bleeding again," Jenou points out. "Why are you being stubborn, Rio? Fall out and go back to the aid station."

"It's just a little blood," Rio says.

"She's right, you know," Jack says. "You should get that attended to properly."

"Richlin don't want to miss the war," Geer says. "Isn't that right, Killer Rick? You want more body count."

"Shut up, Geer," Rio snaps, not liking the nickname.

"That's why she won't swap out that big old M1 for a carbine," Geer says. "Can't shoot a man from half a mile away with a carbine."

This is too much like an insinuation of cowardice for Rio. She grabs his shoulder and spins him around to face her. "What is it, Geer? You think I'm afraid to do it up close? Because it was pretty up close and personal when we took out that Kraut mortar team."

Geer grins and holds up his hands in mock surrender. "Don't shoot me, Killer Rick. I surrender. You're right, you like killing at *any* distance."

"I'm doing my job. Doing what I'm told, same as you."

"And no reason why you shouldn't enjoy doing your job, right, Richlin?"

Rio is considering punching him in the nose, but she spots Jenou out of the corner of her eye. Jenou is standing with head down, unwilling to show her face.

My God, does Jenou believe that too?

"Knock it off," Stick says with the authority of his new corporal's rank. "We got actual enemies, we don't need to go looking for more here in the squad."

The column starts moving again, but not for long. There's what looks like an abandoned barn up ahead, a pile of stones with a collapsed roof. Platoon Sergeant O'Malley raises a clenched fist, calling a halt. The rest of the division is lost to sight behind a rise in the land off to their left. GIs drop to a knee or sit right down in the dirt. Rio squats and watches O'Malley, now conferring with Lieutenant Vanderpool.

Clearly the old sergeant doesn't like something about that barn. Rio tries to figure out just what exactly it is, because the same instinct is nagging at her. The land around the barn is not unusual: dry fields lying fallow, terraced vineyards bearing only stunted young grapes, prickly pear stands, two exhausted-looking donkeys standing mute beside a water trough. The sky overhead is clear blue with a blistering sun floating toward its zenith.

She glances back and only now realizes that the road has been climbing gently. That flat fields have given way to terraced fields as they've moved onto higher ground. It has the odd effect of making Rio a little homesick. Parched gentle hills, vineyards, dry yellow grasses and isolated patches of green, a blue sky and bright sun, these are Rio's natural habitat, at least whenever she gets out of Gedwell Falls into the surrounding countryside.

Then she spots something. There is a line of cypress trees, tall and narrow, like spear points lined up in a row. The line of trees would block their view of the barn if it had been extended just a half dozen trees farther. She squints and shields her eyes and sees several small disks the color of the red mud so familiar from basic training in Georgia—the raw, still-moist trunks of trees recently cut down.

Cut down to reveal the barn? No. Cut down to give the barn a clear view and field of fire over the road.

Cole looks worried. "Okay, people, listen up. The Loot and O'Malley are worried about that barn, and I agree.

It's a perfect site for an MG. Third and Fourth Squads are going to make it look like they've stopped for chow. First and Second Squads are going back down the road like we're heading for the beach. Then we're going to circle left and right respectively, and get close enough to put some fire onto that barn."

There are groans, but also murmurs of excitement.

"I hope it's Krauts and not just Italians," Cat says. "The Eye-ties might give up and then what? We're marching prisoners back to the beach."

First and Second Squads amble away, faux casual, rifles slung on shoulders, heading back the way they've come. A quarter mile down the road, around a bend, they halt. First Squad takes the left, Second Squad takes the right, which means walking off the road into a terraced hillside field. They walk upright at first, even taking time to pick the occasional very sour and unripe grape from the gnarled vines. But as they come around into sight of the barn they crouch low, walking bent over, which only exacerbates the pain in Rio's leg.

For about two hundred yards they are exposed, though far enough distant that they may avoid being spotted, and anxiously await the zipper sound of German machine guns. Then they are once more hidden from view by the bulk of the hill and can stand up and stretch strained muscles.

Soon they are back to where they can plainly see the barn, though now the surviving cypresses partly mask it. Here the vines are gone and the hill is covered in tall, desiccated grasses set off by the inevitable prickly pears. They are perhaps two hundred yards away from the target but not directly in line with the dark, gaping, threatening door.

Cole looks it over through his binoculars. "Can't see anything," he says. "Can't see any cover either. We can either go round this hill, which is going to take half an hour, or we just walk right in." He glances at his watch. He is supposed to have his squad in place in twenty minutes. "We'd have to do it at a run. What do you think, Stick?"

"Go around," Sticklin says without hesitation.

"What about you, Richlin?" Cole asks.

Rio actually jumps. "What? Don't . . . don't ask me!"

Cole sends her a sidelong look. "You know, Richlin, you won't be a private forever."

That thought bothers Rio more than the action ahead. It is one thing to follow orders; it is quite a different thing to take responsibility.

Cole quickly decides the matter: they'll go around the hill, even if it means running. This they do, running in ninety-degree heat without shade, running with gear rattling, with troops panting and tripping and cursing under their breath. It's worse for Stick, who still carries the big BAR.

Now the pain in Rio's leg is doubled. Every impact of boot on dirt sends a shock of pain shooting up her thigh into her belly. She grits her teeth, determined to go on, not to fall out. Part of her mind is still digesting the way Jenou looked at her, the way she *refused* to look at her, the way the usually protective Jenou failed to speak up in Rio's defense.

Jenou has known her longer than anyone but her parents. Does Jenou honestly believe Rio *enjoys* killing?

I could prove her wrong. I could fall out. I could go find a nice clean cot in an aid station back on the beach.

But she runs on, her M1 held chest high, canteen bouncing, boots pounding dust.

"So this is why we had all those five-mile runs," Jack says, panting.

Why didn't Cole ask Jack? Jack's a good soldier.

When they emerge, sweat staining their uniforms, they see the barn from the side. And they see the Italian light tank behind it.

Cole stares at his watch. "Three minutes," he says. "No time to send word back or bring up a mortar." On this side of the barn is a hole like a window except that it was clearly punched out from the inside, with stone bricks lying scattered beneath it.

"They'll have their MG on the road, most likely. We'll be getting small arms fire this direction. Unless they've got a second MG." Again he consults his watch. "If we jump off a minute early maybe the Eye-ties shift their fire toward us." He points. "We go straight across toward those prickly pears. We run like hell and hope they don't spot us. If we reach the prickly pears, we can put some fire on that light tank, make it hard for them to crank it up. Because if they get that thing started up . . ." He shrugs and shakes his head at that prospect.

Cole is putting them at risk in order to save other lives. *And that*, Rio thinks, *is why I'm happy being a private.*

"All right. Drop your packs. We'll go in two groups. Stick, you take Richlin, Castain, Pang, and Geer. Keep your heads low and run like hell," Cole says. "Keep some space between you. We'll follow on a ten count. On three. One. Two. *Three!*"

They break into a mad dash, moving more easily without their packs, Stick, Rio, Jenou, Pang, and Geer bringing up the rear.

Rio no longer notices the pain in her leg. She's pushing her senses forward and away from herself, willing her eyes to see inside the stony wreckage ahead, willing her ears to hear the first click of a cocking machine gun so she can drop.

They make it halfway before the rest of the squad

comes pelting after them. They run exposed now, with no cover between them and that shadowed, forbidding hole.

Rio spots an Italian officer, suspenders hanging, something in his hand, sauntering out the back of the barn toward the tank.

He is just a hundred yards away. If he but listened, he would hear the sound of their boots and their rattling gear.

He turns. He shades his hand and stares. His mouth opens in an astonished O.

"Richlin!" Stick says in a terse voice, and she drops to her belly and sights on the tan uniform. Much closer than her first kill, but farther away than others.

She is about to pull the trigger when the back half of the squad comes panting by, unaware that she is ready to shoot. They swarm into her field of view and for a moment the Italian disappears. When he reappears he is running and shouting.

Rio curses under her breath and jumps to her feet. She leaves a small patch of blood-red mud behind.

The Italian officer disappears from view, and now two Italian soldiers rush toward the tank. It is a pitiful thing by the standards of an American Sherman, let alone a massive German Tiger, but more than enough to tear up a column of infantry.

Stick slows to a deliberate walk and fires the BAR from

his hip, collapsing the two soldiers.

Now the machine gun they've been expecting to hear opens up on the two squads advancing down the main road.

B-r-r-r-r-r-t! B-r-r-r-r-r-t!

Geer throws a grenade in the direction of the tank. It explodes but only marks the side of the tank with a spray of smoke.

Rio runs, sees Jenou just ahead of her, Jenou firing her carbine at waist height. Jenou stops firing when Jack reaches the wall of the barn and flattens himself against it. He pulls a grenade from his webbing belt, yanks the pin, lets the clip fly, counts *one . . . two . . . three*, and tosses it through the hole. Two seconds later it explodes, sending a big cloud of hay fragments billowing out on a wave of smoke.

Rio runs and spots the Italian officer running at full speed away from the barn, away from the tank, seemingly heading for the hills and leaving his men to the mercy of the Americans.

Rio drops to one knee and sights carefully. The Italian bobs and weaves, dancing from one side of her rifle sight to the other. She pulls the trigger—*BANG!*—and a red stain appears in the Italian's lower back. She sees him grab futilely at it, like a man with an itch in a hard-to-reach spot. He runs another two steps and falls on his face in the dust.

"Cease fire, cease fire!" It's Lieutenant Vanderpool, audible in a gap between gunfire. "Cease fire!"

It takes Rio a moment to realize that the only ones still shooting are the Americans. There's a white handkerchief on a rake poking from the front door.

They take five prisoners. They'd taken prisoners before, but they had been Germans. These are Italians, and though they adopt appropriately sullen expressions at first they soften up pretty quickly once the GIs start offering them cigarettes. The Italians have a bottle of harsh red wine, which they offer around, and in no more than ten minutes the Italians are chatting among themselves and trying out a few words of English on the bemused Americans.

My brother he live Philadelphia.

New Jersey, me. One year, yes?

And, the always popular in any language, *Fug Mussolini, fug Hitler.*

Lieutenant Vanderpool claps Cole on the shoulder and says, "You violated my order on the time of attack. Was that deliberate or did you just misread your watch?"

"Well, sir, we saw they had that little tank . . ." Cole shrugs.

Vanderpool says, "Yep. Well done, Sergeant. You almost certainly saved some lives. Mind you, I'm not giving you carte blanche to disregard orders . . ."

"No, sir," Cole agrees, though Rio can see from his

glazed expression that he's a bit uncertain as to what *carte blanche* means. She's not quite sure herself. No doubt Jenou will know, and certainly Stick or Jack will. She makes a mental note to ask.

"Send a detail back with the prisoners." Vanderpool frowns, noticing the blood-soaked leg of Rio's trousers. "You wounded, Richlin?"

"I tried to get rid of her earlier," Cole says, "but . . ." Another shrug.

"Well, I like your spirit, Richlin, but you're taking these prisoners back to the beach and then you will take yourself to the nearest aid station."

Rio nods, then wonders if she should have saluted, so she does. The lieutenant salutes smartly in return, then with a smile he adds, "I appreciate the respect to my rank, but on balance I'd say we should dispense with saluting when we're on the line: kind of makes me conspicuous."

"Beebee, you go with her," Cole says.

"But, Sarge," Beebee protests weakly.

"Kid, as we were charging the barn you tripped, dropped your weapon, and if you was to look down the barrel of that weapon you'll see it's packed with dirt. So you stick to Richlin, she'll keep you alive. For today. Hopefully."

15

FRANGIE MARR—GELA BEACH, SICILY

Most of Walter Green's platoon is scattered, wounded, or dead, and since they will not immediately rush into battle, Frangie is loaned to the colored aid station, where she has worked feverishly since coming ashore.

The doctor, when he finally arrives, is harried, annoyed, and imperious. He's one of the few black doctors Frangie has ever seen, and she is drawn to the mystical power conferred by the letters "MD" that follow his name. He's also a captain, but that doesn't matter so much in a frontline aid station.

"Gunshot, through and through, perforated intestine. We cleaned and bandaged, morphine," Frangie says, nodding at an unconscious soldier lying on a stretcher on the ground. Moving on to a female corporal, Frangie says, "Broken tibia, simple fracture, we've splinted. This fellow here is, well, battle fatigue, I suppose. He almost drowned coming ashore, and his buddy took one in the chest. So . . .

And over here we have multiple shrapnel fragments in his calves, morphine. That fellow's lost two fingers loading a howitzer, he's bandaged."

She goes on through her two dozen patients, calmly updating the doctor.

Finally, the doctor says, "Good." Just that. Just "Good."

His name is John Frame, Captain John Frame, US Army Reserves, now returned to extremely active duty through no fault of his own. Frangie would give her next meal to be able to sit down and throw questions at him for an hour, but he does not seem to be that sort of captain or doctor or person.

"Okay," Dr. Frame says brusquely. "Transport him, him, him, her, and those two. The rest we'll keep for a while."

"Yes, sir."

There is paperwork to be done—this may be war, and this may be a combat zone, but the army is still the army and there are forms to be filled out. Outside the tent, out in the sunshine, Frangie finds a seat on an overturned food crate and props a clipboard on her knee.

She painstakingly fills in the forms and arranges with the beach master to get her sick and wounded out to the ship designated for colored wounded.

Then she gets back to work filling out papers on the

dead. There are three of those. They will be picked up by graves registration, who will keep the bodies until the powers that be figure out just what to do with them.

Not a job I would want to do, Frangie thinks. She'd rather be up on the line getting shot at than spend weeks, months, maybe even years trailing along behind the carnage identifying eviscerated, armless, or headless corpses.

I'd go stark raving mad.

Paperwork done, she returns to her ward to find the one nurse and Dr. Frame taking in a new patient. One glance tells her this will be another one for graves registration.

The nurse, a kindly older white woman from Arkansas, says, "We've got this, honey lamb, go find yourself a cup of coffee."

"And bring one back for me," the doctor mutters. "Two sugars."

Frangie does not hesitate. There is one lesson the army teaches that it wishes it wasn't teaching: never volunteer. If the doctor and the nurse want her to take a break, then she will sure take a break.

The beach is miles long, arcing toward the northeast and the town, and away to the south there is a long, low, stubby spit of land that Frangie vaguely believes marks a sort of rough boundary between the American sector and the Canadian and British areas.

The entire beach is like an upset ant mound, with soldiers, jeeps, half-tracks, trucks, cannon, tanks, impromptu fuel dumps where fifty-five-gallon drums are piled, and DUKWs (inevitably called Ducks) driving straight up out of the water onto the land.

"Wish I'd come ashore in one of those," Frangie mutters.

Daddy D, a nice man, a family man, his face split open like a melon struck with a hammer. That image joins others, many others. They're piling up in her brain, those images: a foot blown off by a mine; a gut wound oozing bile; a compression injury from a man crushed between two trucks; a man ripped in half a dozen places by wood splinters from a crate hit by a mortar round; a self-administered morphine overdose; broken eardrums; one self-inflicted gunshot wound where a soldier shot off his little toe for a ticket home. And even now, even with all that is here before her, the memory of that poor, doomed white officer all the way back at Kasserine.

All of that on top of the German typhus cases and gangrene and shrapnel injuries she had treated while being briefly held by the enemy. And all the mess that followed the battle in the Tunisian desert. And the usual maladies of garrison life: syphilis, gonorrhea, injuries related to drinking and fighting.

Her head is already stuffed to overflowing with blood,

brains, marrow, and human shit. Tears and screams.

And the dead, of course. The dead.

Frangie shields her eyes from the sun and sees for really the first time the vastness of the fleet. There are ships as far as the eye can see. Away north a destroyer is methodically firing. Away to the south there's an air raid, Heinkels and Junkers strafing and bombing. The explosions sound tiny and weak from here, but Frangie knows better, having been beneath similar air raids herself, and having had to cope with their effects. Above the fleet is a flight of two RAF Spitfires racing in from Malta eager to pick off the German bombers.

Frangie finds the mess tent and holds out her tin mess kit, which is then loaded with hot food—chicken-fried steak, green beans the color of her own uniform and even less fresh, mashed potatoes, a biscuit, and a lump of something gooey and red that is presumably cherry cobbler. She carries her food across the beach to a patch of sand partially shaded by a palm tree that leans precariously, having been knocked over by naval fire.

Until the moment the first bite reaches her lips she's had no idea she was so hungry. Now she shovels the food into her mouth, moaning with pleasure and washing it down with warm, brackish water from her canteen.

She pulls paper and pen from her pocket and sets her pictures upright in the sand, like a small art gallery.

Dear Mom and Dad and you too, Obal,

She feels bad, as she always does, not addressing her big brother, Harder, as well. Harder has been exiled from the family for his membership in a youth group aligned with godless Communists. She hasn't seen him in a long time since he's living now in Chicago.

Well, I guess it's all in the news now, so I suppose the censors will let me tell you that I am in Sicily. It's all pretty exciting, I can tell you. There are air raids and such, but of course I am not in any danger but quite safe.

That last is a lie repeated in probably 90 percent of GI letters home. No one wants their loved ones to worry. Or maybe no one wants to admit even to themselves that they're in real danger. But if it gives her mother a bit of relief, Frangie doesn't mind the little white lie.

I am helping boys who get hurt and learning a lot about doing that. I don't even have a gun—sorry, Obal. My most dangerous weapon is probably the morphine I give to the wounded. I see tanks and cannon and so on, but all of that is sort of apart. Like when little kids are playing in a sandbox and they don't really play together, just kind of play next to each other? Well, this is one big sandbox and the navy does what it has to do, and the army does what it has to do, and the medics and nurses and doctors, we do our duty too.

That sounds a bit high and mighty somehow, but it's too late to change it. And anyway, she is doing her duty, isn't she? She's saving boys' and girls' lives sometimes, though mostly she's patching folks up to send them back into the fighting where they might get hurt worse the next time.

They say the whole thing is going pretty well with—

The sound of planes is familiar, so she doesn't immediately dive for cover, not until she looks up and sees the familiar two-engine silhouette of a Heinkel, a dark cross against the sky.

She gathers her things and scoots to the base of the palm tree, where the shallow, torn-up roots have left a slight depression. She hopes the tree won't fall on her.

The Heinkel comes in low, met by a hail of small arms fire from the ground and chased by the antiaircraft guns of the navy. It drops two bombs, one of which falls near the aid station, sending up a cloud of yellow sand.

Frangie tosses the food tray aside, scoops up her pictures and unfinished letter, and races back toward the aid station tent. It's still standing, though it is coated with sand. A jeep being used to transport wounded men has been blown up pretty well.

There will be wounded.

"Sorry, Doctor," she says, rushing breathlessly into the tent where soldiers are now hauling their wounded buddies. "I didn't get coffee."

"Triage the incoming," Dr. Frame snaps.

Triage is the process of deciding who gets treated first. There are three categories. The "walking wounded" are low priority and will be patched up and sent back up to the line. The "hopeless" cases will be shot full of morphine and left to die.

The category of focus is on those hurt too bad for a patch-and-release but who may just live if given prompt treatment. Over the next hour Frangie makes swift, terrible decisions, choosing those who will be treated and those who . . . who will be given morphine to ease their passage to the afterlife.

Fortunately, only one soldier falls into this last category. His shirt has been torn open, revealing a mess of gray-blue intestines hanging from a jagged tear in his stomach. Red muscle, a layer of white fat, veins sticking out, arteries pumping weakly, skin ashen, draining the last of his blood away.

He's like one of the corpses she saw during training, one of the corpses after the medical students had been at it. The wounded soldier is a gruesome display of internal organs.

"What's your name, Sergeant?"

"It's me, Ma. It's me, help me, Ma, help me, I got hurt . . ." His voice belongs to a little boy.

She draws his dog tags out. *Gordon, William T. Blood Type A*.

"You're going to be okay, Gordon."

"Billy," he gasps. He blinks at her, seems to realize that she is not his mother, but then a wave of agony rolls through him, twisting his face into a fright mask, tensing his limbs. He cries out, a weak sound.

The smell of human feces billows up, and she sees the shit oozing from a tear in his pulsating colon.

"You're going to be okay, Billy," she lies, and lays a wet cloth on his forehead. "The pain will stop soon. Shh. Shh."

"Ma? Ma? Mommy?"

"It's okay, Billy, it's just a scratch, a million-dollar wound, you're going home."

"Mommy? Mommy?"

"Please, Jesus, help this boy!" Frangie cries out in frustration.

"Mommy?" Softer this time as the morphine penetrates

his consciousness, bringing a false peace.

The white nurse, Lieutenant Tremayne, is at Frangie's side. She takes Frangie's arm and leads her away just a few feet and forces Frangie to look at her. "Listen, you," Tremayne says, "you mustn't do that. You understand? We're here to help these boys, and if they hear you talking to Jesus they know they're done for."

The tension in Billy T. Gordon's body relaxes. Urine adds new stains to his trousers. There comes a long, slow, final, rattling exhalation.

"He was done for when he came in," Frangie says in monotone.

"Listen to me. Hey! You're a good medic, but you need to protect yourself, you hear me? I used to work the emergency room at Saint Vincent's, and I've had people die in my arms. You have to show them love and care, but you can't *feel* it. You'll go crazy otherwise."

"A handsome, healthy young boy . . . ," Frangie says. "Dies stinking like a sewer."

"And your tears don't change that," Tremayne says, and walks away.

Frangie stands by the dead man, refusing to be disgusted by the smell, refusing to move away. Her eyes fill with tears, and she knows she can't cry because she needs to be able to see clearly.

This is all we are. A bag of guts that can be ripped

open as easily as cutting into a sausage.

There will be more. More and more, stretching away into her future.

The tears spill down her cheeks, so it is through bleary eyes that Frangie sees Rio Richlin, her leg red from mid-thigh down to her boot, walking nonchalantly down the beach with another GI and half a dozen prisoners.

FRANGIE MARR AND RIO RICHLIN—GELA BEACH, SICILY

"That should hold," Frangie says, tying the last of her new stitches in Rio's thigh.

Rio sits with one pants leg rolled up above the wound. She and Frangie are on folding chairs, squashed down into the sand just outside the aid station. It's fine for the diminutive medic, but not so comfortable for Rio, who has to sit splayed out with one leg propped on Frangie's lap.

"Now sit still and I'll get a decent bandage on there."

"Thanks," Rio says. "So. How's the war treating you?"

"Fine."

Rio says, "Yeah. Me too."

Both start laughing.

Frangie worries that her laughter is somehow a betrayal of the wounded soldiers she's treated. "I suppose it's okay to laugh."

"I think it might be required," Rio says darkly.

"Just had a bad . . ." Frangie glances unconsciously at the cot, empty now. She's fallen silent too long and tries to pass it off with a wave. "Nice kid. Bad death."

"If I get it, I want it to be pow, right through the head," Rio says, and mimes the action of a bullet hitting her square in the forehead.

"Well, that makes a lot less work for us," Frangie says. She covers her mouth, shocked by her own callous-sounding reply.

Rio's face breaks open into a huge grin that starts off small and slow and turns into sunshine. Laughing, she says, "I wouldn't want to put you to any trouble."

Frangie picks up the bantering tone. "You shouldn't even be here, white girl, your aid station's up the beach."

"Well . . . I reckon I could walk on up the beach, but if I do I'm sure to run into some noncom or officer who wants to give me some work to do." Then, in a different tone she says, "I don't suppose you've heard of any mail coming ashore?"

"Nope. We only just got here." She winds gauze around Rio's leg. "You expecting something particular?"

"Maybe." Rio shrugs and her hand goes to the oilcloth packet in her pocket. She pulls it out, unfolds it, and takes out a photo, somewhat bent and ragged.

Frangie leans around to take a look. "My, my, isn't he handsome? You know . . . he looks a bit like Leslie

Howard, but with less forehead."

Rio frowns and looks closely at the picture. "I can see that."

"Are you two—"

"Just once," Rio blurts guiltily. This causes Frangie to clarify that she was asking whether they were engaged, to which Rio says yes, of course, she knew that and they aren't engaged, probably, she isn't quite sure because the last time they were together they were interrupted by the need to hop on ships and sail to Sicily.

Finally when the stammering dies down, Frangie says, "You know I'm a bit like a doctor—you can tell me anything and my mouth is a locked vault."

Rio nods distractedly, clearly flustered, embarrassed, and anxious to get away. But her leg is not quite done, and as she finishes the work, Frangie says, "He looks like a good sort of fellow."

"He is," Rio says automatically. "He's a pilot. He flies B-17s. He was able to get away and come for a quick visit and . . ."

Frangie suppresses a smile, but also stifles a murmur of disapproval. "Yes. I got that." The disapproval leaks out in her tone.

"I'm barely eighteen and I'm already a fallen woman."

"I took a drink a while back," Frangie confesses. Then adds, "We don't believe in alcohol."

"Coloreds don't drink?"

"Baptists. *Baptists* don't drink."

"Ah." Rio looks deflated. "You're the first person I've told."

"Not your friend with the unusual name?"

"Jenou? No, I . . ." Rio sighs and begins to roll her trouser leg down over the new bandage. "I feel like . . . Never mind. Thanks for the—"

"I've noticed the men never want to talk about it. About the war, you know, not fornication, they'll talk about fornication any day. But ask them about the war and they'll flirt or talk about baseball. Everyone complains, of course—"

"Of course," Rio interjects, nodding.

"But they never talk about what it was like before they managed to get hurt and end up here with me."

"My father is the same way. Even after he knew I was joining up he never talked about his war, not really. He just said to find a good sergeant and stick close, which was good advice, but I don't really know what it was like for him in the first war."

"Men," Frangie says.

"Soldiers," Rio counters.

"Just because men clam up that doesn't make it right or smart, does it?"

Rio frowns. "I don't know. I just know . . ." She's silent

231

for a long time, and Frangie waits, putting her gear away. "When someone asks me about it, I guess I just don't want to talk about it."

"You admit to being seduced, but you can't talk about the war?"

"I guess that doesn't make sense, does it? Maybe I'm not as ashamed as I should be of having . . . you know. I mean, I'm hardly the first girl to lose her virginity before marriage. But at the time . . ." She trails off.

"Does that mean you are ashamed of what you do as a soldier?"

"No! No, it's just that I've always known I would . . . you know . . . have s-e-x. I pictured it happening after I was married, and in some place more romantic than a cheap hotel room in Tunis . . . I pictured it being more . . . *important* . . . than it felt."

"The war makes other things seem small."

"Oh, fug the war!" Rio says with sudden anger. Then, abashed, "Look at my language! I never, ever even thought that word before."

"It's changing us, I guess," Frangie says. She shakes her head slowly, troubled deeply by the thought. "What will we be by the time we're done?"

"Alive, I hope." Rio rises to her feet and offers Frangie a hand, pulling her up.

"What do you do now, Richlin?"

"Find the guy who came down with me and see if we can't scrounge up some chow, check for mail, dig a nice hole for the night. Then in the morning, head back up."

"To the front line."

"It's why they gave me the rifle," Rio says. "You?"

Frangie holds up her bag. "Here, for now at least. It's why they gave me the bandages."

Rio does not find Beebee, which is no surprise in the chaos. It wouldn't matter except that Vanderpool and Cole have made her responsible for him.

Well, I didn't ask for that.

She cannot really dig a decent hole in the sand, so in the end she stumbles on an impromptu camp of lost or simply misplaced soldiers with a campfire in the lee of a barely head-high dune. It's dark by this time and rather than introduce herself, which will mean identifying herself as female, she stays to the gloom at the very edge of the fire's light, checking the faces for Beebee. When she fails again to find him, she spreads her shelter half out as a ground cover and curls up to sleep.

The night is warm, and it has been a very long day.

At first light Rio is up and once more looking for Beebee—who the day before had been trapped into doing some paperwork for their prisoners. She resents it in the extreme and walks the beach muttering about having to babysit the green kid instead of getting back to the squad and doing her job.

The beach is still a madhouse of noisy activity. A big LCU with its bow doors open disgorges a tank; planes roar overhead; a mired howitzer is being dragged and pushed out of the surf; crates and pallets lie open, disgorging their contents of ammo and food and blankets; a flexible fuel pipe is being squared away at a pumping station; a gaggle of reporters sit typing and smoking under a tent.

From farther inland come the occasional sounds of artillery or German bombs. Rio wonders idly where the American bombers are, shouldn't they be hammering the Krauts? But just then she spots a high formation, two big Vs of B-17s. She shades her eyes and imagines Strand up there in the cockpit of one. She imagines that he's looking down and wondering whether Rio is somewhere down on that confusing beach.

Then, finally, she spots Beebee. She has to blink twice to make out what he's doing, and even then she can't quite believe it. Beebee is leading a donkey cart. The donkey is small, mangy, and minus half of one ear, which looks to have been chewed off. The cart is small, a ramshackle wooden thing on what can only be bicycle tire rims. As she draws close she sees that the cart is nearly full. There is a forty-pound wooden crate of rations and a half dozen small metal ammo boxes, but it appears these are mostly there as camouflage, piled strategically to conceal the true treasure behind them: two big number-ten cans of peaches, four bottles of Sicilian wine, and dozens of tiny packs of Old Gold cigarettes.

"Hey, Rio," he says.

"You've been busy," Rio says.

Beebee shrugs, but he's obviously pleased with himself. "Also, I came across this." He takes something from his pocket and hands it to her. It's heavy for its size. "It's a whetstone for your *koummya*. Happy belated eighteenth."

"Well . . . that is very kind of you," Rio says, and means it. Her irritation at him is significantly reduced. "I guess we'd best head back to the platoon."

The donkey is reluctant to move and no threat or entreaty seems able to motivate him, but just then two ships open up, sending salvo after salvo over their heads, and the donkey seems to think that's a signal to advance.

It is soon clear that a serious battle is taking place a couple miles up the road. A passing jeep driver yells something about the Hermann Göring Division and Kraut tanks. The name Hermann Göring vaguely rings a bell for Rio—a chubby, smiling Nazi, as she recalls from newsreel footage—but the word *tanks* conjures up a much more compelling picture and adds hesitation to her next few steps. A Spitfire goes tearing away toward the action, flying just above treetop level. And thousands of feet above them fly three more B-17s.

Rio and Beebee (and the donkey, now named General Patton) reach the barn they'd shot up earlier. They are stopped by an MP, a thirtyish woman with the suspicious, slightly predatory look of a shopkeeper who thinks she's spotted a shoplifter. She warns them there is fighting up ahead.

"I think our unit's up there. We're part of the 119th."

"The one-one-nine?" The MP looks perfectly blank, aside from darting glances at the loot in the cart. Beebee gives her two of the small packs of Old Golds and the MP's memory suddenly improves. "The 119th have been pulled east, other side of Niscemi."

"Aren't the Canadians over that way?" Beebee asks. "I heard some officers talking."

The MP lights one of her new cigarettes, takes a deep drag, and says, "Kid, in case you haven't noticed, no one knows what the hell is going on."

"SNAFU," Rio mutters.

"Situation normal," the MP agrees. She gives them directions, which involve going back down the road to take a left turn on a road that's barely a line on the map.

"Great," Rio says with a sigh. They set off, keeping the pace set by General Patton, who, unlike his namesake, cannot be hurried. The war is happening, but not right here and not right now to Rio or Beebee. Rio worries about Jenou, all on her own, but the fighting seems to be north and northeast, so she's not worried enough to try and run. The sun is already hot, though it's not even midmorning. She's tempted to tell Beebee to leave the cart and release the donkey, but among the treasures on the cart is a five-gallon jerry can of water.

The road is more of a dirt track running between farm fields. They reach a watermelon patch that has clearly been trampled and despoiled, with rind and red fruit lying along the road for a quarter mile, evidence that at least someone has passed this way, even if it's not their platoon. This is heartening: Rio feels extraordinarily exposed out in the middle of open fields.

They pass an ancient, wizened peasant sitting on a stool watching a man and two women at work in a field.

"Niscemi?" Rio asks, making a chopping motion in their direction of travel.

The peasant says nothing, despite repeated queries, until Beebee hands him a pack of cigarettes, at which point the man grins so widely they can count all four of his teeth. It seems they *are* heading in the general direction of Niscemi. Of course they've been warned to pass well to the south of the town, and as they top a low rise they can see why. To their north tanks are moving along a road that according to the map will cut their own a mile back.

A German plane passes overhead, but has no interest in them. They hear distant explosions, but whether they are naval gunfire, bombs, or artillery Rio doesn't know. What she does know is that she's feeling strangely alone with Beebee and a donkey, on an island she'd never heard of six months ago, while men and women are fighting to her west, north, and east, as well as out at sea and in the air above.

At last though, as afternoon wears on and the sun beats down mercilessly, they come upon a new MP, a man who informs them that yes, at least some elements of the 119th are ahead in a stand of picturesque trees.

"What the hell?" Geer says. He's on guard.

"Aren't you supposed to ask us the password?" Rio says wearily.

"I sure would if I remembered it," Geer says.

"The password is *Old* and the response is *Gold*," Beebee says, and tosses Geer a pack of Old Gold cigarettes.

"So it is, so it is," Geer agrees.

The platoon is sprawled amid olive trees, staying to the shade. Jenou spots Rio, flashes an expression of profoundest relief, and says, "Back so soon?"

Sergeant Cole says, "Good. You're here. And you brought water. Well done, Richlin."

"It was Beebee. He's the forager."

Cole peers closely at Beebee. "A forager, are you? Well, well. You two find some shade." Then, in a louder voice, he yells, "Magraff! Grab this water and get everyone topped off."

Rio notes that Magraff has become the squad gofer, probably because she no longer has a carbine, having tossed it away or dropped it—again.

Rio drops into a patch of shade beside Jenou. She unlaces her boots and begins massaging her sore feet. "Guess who I ran into?"

"General Eisenhower, I hope. Did you mention to him that I'm really not meant for all this dusty marching around?"

"The colored medic, Marr. The one we picked up on the way in."

"It's a small war. How is she?"

Rio considers. "I don't know. Thinking too much, maybe."

"That thing that happened . . . the bullet that went on and nicked you . . . That was probably pretty hard for her."

Rio says, "I got the impression she was new to that bunch so they weren't that close, but yeah, she was a little down in the mouth."

She was also disapproving, and just a bit of a moral

scold, but Rio sees no point in mentioning that.

Jenou nods. "If there's one thing worse than infantry, it's all of that." She makes hand gestures that may be meant to convey medical care given to the wounded, but they end up looking like random, disturbed hand-waving.

Rio slaps Jenou's shoulder. "Did you miss me?"

"Not at all."

"Me neither."

Both laugh, and Jenou says, "My God, we're starting to sound like men."

"I used to worry I'd seem mannish," Rio says.

"Because of your . . ." And this time Jenou's hand-waving is more specific, as is the pitying look she aims at Rio's chest.

"No," Rio says, outraged. She gives Jenou a shove. "No. Because of my great, manly muscles, that's why, you catty witch."

For a wonderful moment, a golden suspended moment, they are Jenou and Rio once more. Rio feels it, feels herself back in Gedwell Falls, back at the diner stealing Jenou's fries, and vice versa.

I was a girl. I was just a girl. And after a moment's reflection, she silently adds, *Past tense?*

She is on the edge of saying to Jenou that Strand seemed quite taken with her inadequate figure and in fact spent quite some time exploring it in detail. However, that very thought, not even the memory, but the fact that she would think of saying something so vulgar, kills the fine nostalgic feeling.

Okay, Jenou: yes, I've changed. Happy?

This thought in turn sends Rio's mind off inventorying the ways in which she has changed. She's drunk alcohol with serious intent. She's cursed. She's killed. And she's had sex. She strives to connect those facts to memories of herself just, what, a year ago? Back then the only connection she had to the war was via her big sister, Rachel. Even after Rachel joined the navy it had all just seemed like some distant adventure to Rio. It had not been until that terrible morning when news of Rachel's death had reached the Richlin family that it hit home.

She remembers her mother's collapse on the living room rug. She remembers even more clearly the way her father stood in profile against the innocent sunlight beyond the door, slumped, wounded, silent. Being a *man*. Being a man? Or being an ex-soldier? Will it be different for us, as Marr suggested? Or will we have to turn into *them* just to get through this?

The two friends sit side by side, each lost in related but separate memories, when the conversation of Sergeants O'Malley and Cole penetrates Rio's reverie.

"We're infantry, not search and rescue," Cole says to O'Malley.

"That's what I told Vanderpool, and he said that's exactly what he radioed to the colonel, but the colonel explained that this was the goddamned army, not a goddamned knitting circle, whatever the hell that is, and he was to follow orders." He spat undiplomatically and added, "Officers. Jesus wept."

"Goddammit," Cole says, and his eyes veer toward Rio, who groans.

"Three, four men, tops," O'Malley says placatingly. "Send your corporal."

"Stick's foot is swollen to twice its size. Nettles," Cole says, disgusted. He looks again at Rio, and she actually turns around to see if he's perhaps looking at someone behind her. But no, there's only a tree behind her. And it's not a curious or idle stare: Cole is measuring her.

"Richlin," Cole says at last. "If that leg of yours is okay, you are about to volunteer."

17

RAINY SCHULTERMAN—SALERNO, ITALY

It is hot where Rainy walks as well, two hundred and fifty miles almost directly north from Gela Beach, Sicily, and perhaps a mile south of the outskirts of Salerno.

Rainy and Cisco huddle on the beach until the sun rises, not wanting to look suspicious walking in the dark. Then they climb onto the road, which runs very nearly as straight as a ruler toward the town.

At first the only traffic is a couple of Fiat trucks, both comically overburdened with open crates of vegetables and great bundles of what look like reeds. They walk far behind a donkey cart for a while, keeping pace with it until they see that it is stopped at a roadblock ahead.

"If I had a gat, I'd get up close and let 'em have it," Cisco says. He has returned to full, swaggering arrogance during the hours since they left the *Topaz*. But there's an edge to his swagger now, a defensive, angry edge.

Humiliation.

"We wouldn't win a gunfight," Rainy says with frayed patience. She had not liked Cisco on first meeting, she had frankly hated him aboard the sub, and so far he is doing nothing to earn a second chance. "They might have a radio or a phone. We don't want Italians running around the countryside looking for us."

The pistol strapped to her inner thigh chafes cruelly, and she bitterly resents having to wear the dress. Almost as bad are the shoes, which are not quite the right size and tend to crush her toes with each step.

"So what do we do?" Cisco demands. "You're the know-it-all."

"We have papers."

"Forgeries!"

"And I may be able to pass off my Italian," Rainy says.

"Yeah, well I don't speaka de Old Country," Cisco says.

She looks closely at him. His face is badly bruised and impressively swollen on his left side. Hers is bruised as well, and they look like they've either had a hell of an argument or been beaten up and . . .

"We were robbed," Rainy says, snapping her fingers. "We were in a cart, just like that one, bringing melons to market in the city and bandits . . . And you, you're so swollen you can't speak."

"But I can speak."

"For God's sake, Cisco, try to follow, would you?" she snaps.

"Hey, sister, we're in my country now—"

"A country where you don't speaka de language."

"I won't take that smart mouth of yours much longer," he warns. He waves his hand back and forth in a sideways chopping motion. A threat.

"Sure you will, because if you don't I'll give your uncle chapter and verse on how you handled the trip here."

They are face-to-face, eye to eye. Cisco breathes violence now; he is the real thing: a gangster. She has little doubt he could beat her in a fight despite her training in hand-to-hand combat.

Although, if I caught him by surprise . . .

In the end she gets her way, but she knows that her control over him is a slippery thing. He's not a Lucky Luciano type, which Rainy equates in her mind with a sort of general. He's at best a green lieutenant, a hothead with too much to prove. And he is not at all pleased to take orders from a female.

Rainy keeps her pace steady, eyes trained on three sleepy-looking Italian militia in ill-fitting green uniforms. They wear odd brown caps whose shape reminds Rainy of the fancy folded napkins at the Stork Club.

Only one of the carabinieri has a rifle, the main guard, while the other two lounge in chairs probably stolen from a local trattoria. The lounging men must be in their fifties. The one with the rifle might be fourteen at best. Italy is running out of men to put uniforms on.

"Papers," the child soldier demands brusquely, eyeing their bruises curiously.

"*Questo è il signor Rizzo. Io sono sua moglie.*" *This is Mr. Rizzo, and I am his wife.* It's a bit formal, but she figures anyone approaching an armed man would be likely to be formal. And she mangles the pronunciation in such a way as to suggest that her bruised face is the cause.

She explains to the guard that they have been robbed and her husband so badly beaten he can barely speak. The guard takes this in with the slowness of a dull and disinterested mind, then he summons the others, who saunter over trailing a cloud of tobacco smoke to be told the same story.

There follows ten minutes of sympathetic tut-tutting, followed by labored explanations that they can do nothing, nothing, *signora*, they have orders to stay here on guard. But when they are relieved they will naturally tell their superiors, who are certain to go rushing forth to find and arrest the malefactors.

Right.

Rainy has a pack of Italian cheroots supplied for verisimilitude and offers them around. And then they are on their way with barely a cursory glance at their forged papers.

The beach is still on their left, but it is increasingly obscured by one- and two-story houses and apartment buildings, with taller apartment blocks, some three and four floors tall on their right. They pass a hole-in-the-wall coffee shop, and the rich smell of coffee wafts toward them. Rainy sees a counter with a plate of pastries at the end and is suddenly famished, and although she's never been much of a coffee drinker, the smell is enticing.

"Let's stop in," Cisco says.

"Let's not," Rainy says regretfully. "I'm sure your uncle will feed us."

One of the advantages of having a battered face is that polite folk look away from you, and even the curious look first at the bruises, not at the eyes. Rainy keeps her head down and her eyes raised, glancing quickly into each face they pass, checking for signs of unusual interest. But the Italians in Salerno on that morning have better things to worry about.

Following the instructions Vito the Sack provided, they now turn inland, into the heart of the city. The sides of several buildings carry the painted slogan of the Italian Fascist party: "*Credere! Obbedire! Combattere!*"

"Believe, obey, fight," Rainy translates in a quiet voice.

"And there's the bastard right there," Cisco says. He nods toward a massive but time-faded stencil of Benito Mussolini, looking less stern than comical as someone has thrown a pot of paint at the portrait. The black paint struck Mussolini's eye and dribbled down so it looks now like absurdly long eyelashes drooping down to his chin.

"I never would have thought you cared about Mussolini one way or the other," Rainy says.

"The Fascists have been tough on our people. On legitimate traditional businesses."

"Organized crime."

Cisco shrugs. "You say *potato*, I say *potahto*."

They take a wrong turn and end up in a cul-de-sac of a cramped square facing the cathedral. Arched breezeways are to their right and left. The cathedral, the *duomo*, carries through the arches on its lower level before rising to form a plain peaked-roof middle. A square tower topped by a round bell tower looms up behind the church and to the right. It's grand by American standards, but a long way from being Saint Patrick's, the big cathedral on Fifth Avenue.

That thought carries Rainy away for a moment, far away, to New York. The New York of her father and mother, the New York of Halev. Homesickness swells within her, and she very nearly tears up.

A file of nuns walks past in ankle-length black with their faces framed by snow-white coifs and wimples. An old man with fantastically bowed legs hobbles by, leading a thin cow on a rope. There are more people in the street as the town comes to life.

Rainy is as curious as any tourist, and there is a part of her that keeps thinking, *Wow, I'm in Italy!* But she keeps her head down and eyes open. Two Italian soldiers, officers, both looking as if they've passed a night of debauchery, lurch past, blinking owlishly in the sunlight.

After another half hour they find the street and then the house. Cisco pushes in front of Rainy and bangs on the door. It is opened quickly by a squat man dressed in rusty black, who demands angrily to know who they are and why they are banging on doors.

"I'm Cisco Camporeale," Cisco says, and the guard's face goes blank in surprise.

"Camporeale?"

"Yeah. *Si.*" Cisco points at his chest. "*Me-o* am Francisco Camporeale, the don's nephew from America. You know? New York."

Something in that convinces the man, who lets them in and checks the street before shutting and locking the door behind them. They are in a cool, mildew-smelling entryway at the bottom of a flight of stairs. From up those stairs comes the sounds of clinking dishes and conversation, the sounds of a family at breakfast.

The guard apologizes with a shrug and pats Cisco down, looking for weapons. He looks disapproving when he finds none. He searches Rainy's bag but does not go further. He calls up the stairs, and a moment later a man in his late twenties, a sort of sturdier version of Cisco, comes galloping down, wiping his mouth with a napkin. He wears a white shirt with sleeves rolled up to the elbow, dark slacks, and what appear to be very expensive leather shoes. He is tall, olive complected, with brown eyes and an amazing shock of black hair. Each strand seems weighed down somehow and yet bounces with each step, letting a long strand fall down to bisect one dark, amused eye.

In Italian he asks who they are.

Rainy answers in that same tongue. The young man glances at her, looks away, frowns, and comes back for a closer look. Then, having apparently seen all he needs to see for now, he claps Cisco on the shoulder and in heavily accented but comprehensible English says, "Welcome, I am your cousin, Tomaso."

"Glad to meet you, Tom."

"How was your trip?"

"Fugging awful, and she's responsible." He jerks his thumb at Rainy. "So as family, *famiglia*, right? As your cousin, and as a made man, I got one simple request: give me a gun so I can shoot this Jew bitch in her smart mouth."

18

"There's a plane up-country, with survivors and wounded. With our usual good luck, we are closest. Pick three people to go with you," Cole says. "Vanderpool's giving you a radioman named Petersen."

It's a punch to the stomach for Rio. She does not want the responsibility. It is one thing to be chosen for a special patrol, that's bad enough, but it was a very different thing to be left to decide who should go. It is much too similar to picking teams in sports or deciding who you'll dance with: there is no way to avoid making someone feel left out, and no way to avoid being responsible for whatever follows.

It is a moment when Rio is suddenly called upon to offer an opinion on who is and who is not a reliable soldier. And whose life she will risk, and who she will leave in relative safety.

"Sarge, I . . . ," Rio begins.

"What?" he snaps.

"Maybe . . ."

"This is not a debating society, Richlin. Got it?"

Rio just nods, and Cole leaves her alone with the decision. On top of everything else, it's a test of her judgment with Cole watching and scoring. There are few things Rio wants less than to be found wanting by Sergeant Cole.

In any other circumstances it would be Stick leading the patrol. And if for some strange reason the choice had still somehow fallen to Rio, Stick would be her first choice to go along on that patrol. In her mind the hierarchy of who is and who is not a real soldier is clear: Stick, herself, Jack, Cat, and even the obnoxious Geer are soldiers now. Tilo means well despite his adolescent behavior, and he might make a soldier in time, but he's not there yet. Pang she doesn't trust, Magraff is worse than useless, Beebee is an unknown and green, and Jenou . . . She loves Jenou. Jenou is her lifelong friend. But in a fight?

It occurs to her to look at it from Stick's point of view. Who would Stick choose? It's a way out of feeling 100 percent directly, personally responsible.

What would Stick do?

Well, he'd pick Rio, of course. And obviously they were stuck with this Petersen fellow who she'd barely exchanged ten words with. And . . . and . . . Jack. Yes, Stick would pick Jack, because Jack is steady, reliable, not showy, and easy to get along with. But what would Jenou have to say about that choice? There would be many a wink and a knowing nod.

Another reason not to bring Jenou.

Jack, Jenou, Geer, Magraff, Pang, Cat, Tilo, and Beebee. Those were her possible choices. Magraff was a no. Tilo was annoying. Geer was a loudmouth jerk.

Pang? He'd done nothing wrong, said nothing wrong, and yet . . . And yet he looked like a Jap. That fact sort of squirmed around in Rio's head, making her feel wrong and yet helpless. Japs had killed Rachel.

And farmed peaceably all around Gedwell Falls.

And bought their fertilizer from her father's store.

And . . .

But not Pang. Not Pang. Despite . . . despite everything, not Pang.

Jack, yes, no matter what Jenou thought. And Cat. Cat was a rock.

Jenou, that was the essential problem. Jenou or someone else? Rio was not sure she could control Jenou, just as she worried about dealing with Geer. Geer was a jerk who wouldn't take orders from a woman, and Jenou might not take orders from her best friend.

Beebee? No. Too green. Still. Just like the first time she'd thought about it.

So it came down again to Jenou versus Tilo Suarez.

And yet . . . and yet . . . some nagging instinct told her no. She was thinking of feelings again, not military necessities.

Cole had said they were pulling a search-and-rescue mission, a plane down in the hills to the northeast. The crash zone was seven miles away. Who could march seven miles and carry extra water? Who would, if necessary, shoot with intent? Who would sneak up on a Kraut or Eye-tie guard and knife him in the dark?

Suddenly the choice was not between Jenou and Tilo. It was between Geer and Pang. Pang's presence might create conflict, especially with the radioman who had not dealt much with him. Geer, on the other hand, would be hard to manage but probably fit in better.

"Okay, people, listen up," Rio says in unconscious imitation of Sergeant Cole. "Jack, Cat, and Geer, we're going for a walk. Canteens topped off, rations for twenty-four hours, extra ammo, extra water, leave everything else, we have to move fast."

The radioman, Petersen, comes wandering over. He doesn't look like much, with a face so narrow he could be a flounder, but then his job is just to manage the radio. He has a pistol on his hip but no rifle and no pack. He has a single canteen and no ammo other than what's in his pistol. But of course the radio itself, the size of a backpack, weighs thirty-eight pounds, and with all that still only has a range of three miles. Three miles in open country, a few hundred yards in hill country.

Anyway, the radioman is not Rio's chief concern. Her chief concern is the carefully blank look on Jenou's face. It's the look Jenou gets when her feelings have been hurt but she doesn't want to show it.

Rio feels a flash of annoyance. She shouldn't have to be thinking about this nonsense. She shouldn't feel like she has to defend herself or soften the blow. My God, she's leading a patrol for the first time, which she sure as hell did not ask for, and her head is full of worry for Jenou!

Rio avoids looking at her friend and instead locks eyes with Cole, who is relighting his cigar and giving her a look of . . . what? Support? Sympathy?

They go over the map carefully, Cole, Rio, Jack, Cat, Geer, and Petersen in a circle.

"Whenever you're ready, Richlin," Cole says, and his tone is gentle. He knows what this means. He knows that for the first time responsibility is falling directly on Rio's shoulders—on the shoulders of an eighteen-year-old girl.

"Yep," Rio says. She takes a deep, steadying breath and says, "Let's move out. Geer? Take point. Cat, on our six."

In this, too, she is copying Cole, who always stays to the middle, the better to survive an ambush or minefield, the better to watch both ends of the line, the better to stay in touch with his squad. And she knows taking point will please Geer.

Does Cole have all these same sorts of worries about who and when and how? Does he take hurt feelings into consideration? For the first time Rio gets a glimpse of what it means to be the good sergeant her father talked about, the good sergeant whose job it is to keep you alive when an officer's orders are sending you in harm's way.

I am heartily sorry for any time I made your life harder, Jedron Cole.

The first mile or so is past twilit farm fields. The road is narrow but not overly rutted. Rio can see the hills rising ahead of them. Glancing back, she can see nothing of the platoon beyond Cat. Finding their first turnoff becomes a bit of a comedy as there are two very similar roads just fifty feet apart. But one turns out to lead nowhere except a tiny farm almost entirely surrounded by prickly pears, as if the farmer wants to strongly discourage visitors.

As it is the farmer comes out carrying a shotgun, but on being assured that they are *amici* and not Germans or Fascists, he insists on handing a wineskin around before giving them better directions.

They find the right track, but by now full dark has come. The road is barely a wagon track—at no time paved and with no convenient ditches to dive into should the need arise. They are exposed without cover, but fortunately hidden by darkness. Off to the southeast she sees distant flashes, and off to the southwest as well, but none are any more threatening than distant lightning.

After a while Geer raises a clenched fist, and they all take a knee.

"What is it?" Rio whispers.

"Hear that?"

Rio listens and breaks into a grin. "Cows, Geer."

"You sure?"

She holds up a hand he probably can't see and says, "Before I got calluses from humping jerry cans I got calluses milking cows."

They move on, and after a while, after she's sure Geer won't resent it as coming too early, she moves him back and puts Jack on point. Jack, Cat, Rio, Petersen, Geer.

If there are mines . . .

If there's an ambush . . .

No, she sternly warns herself. *You cannot protect your "backup boyfriend." You are in charge, Rio. You have a military objective, you have orders, you have the weight of it on your shoulders, and you cannot choose to expose only the people you don't like.*

This is not high school.

The track joins a better road for half a mile before veering away again onto what is likely a cattle path. This path meanders through prickly pears and olive trees, past ever-smaller fields of ever more random shapes. The angle of the slope increases until pretty soon Rio is feeling it in her calf muscles, and far more in her bandaged thigh. But of course she is the one to set the pace, so she cannot take it easy. She ignores the ache as best she can, and pushes out thoughts of Jenou's tellingly blank face and the image of Jack stepping on a mine, and focuses on the job at hand, which is to not get lost and to avoid wandering into either an ambush or a minefield.

The Milky Way shines cold and impossibly distant in a mostly clear sky, and eventually a sliver of moon rises as well. But still they fail to spot the four armed men who are walking the opposite direction and carrying shotguns, until Jack yells, "Drop it!"

Jack has his rifle leveled, and seeing this, every rifle in the squad snaps up. Even Petersen pulls his pistol. Had the Sicilian men been a bit more surprised the shooting might have started, but the men all keep their shotguns pointed cautiously down at the ground.

"Bandits," Jack says tersely.

"Yeah," Rio agrees, staring at four impassive Sicilian faces. "But they're not looking for trouble with people who can shoot back."

"*Bona sira*," one of the Sicilians says in the local dialect.

"Evening," Jack says.

"*Amici*," Rio says. "Americans. Yankees."

"*Si, lu capisciu, signore, signorina.*"

It sounds peaceable enough, and Rio orders her squad forward. The bandits are someone else's problem, not hers.

After a while they reach a crossroads. Question is, is this the right crossroads?

Petersen speaks up for the first time. "Miss . . . um, Private Richlin? We could try contacting them."

"What?"

"The plane. I thought you knew." There's a note of triumph in his tone. "That's why I was sent along. The downed plane still has a functioning radio, although their signal is weak. That's how we know where they are."

No, no one has mentioned this fact to Rio, although it's obvious once she thinks of it, which irritates her extremely. But there's no point in resentment, so she says, "Okay, try to raise them."

He swings the radio off his back onto the ground and squats before it. It's a rectangular object, painted the inevitable olive drab. There are a few knobs on the top and a hand piece snugged into the side. Petersen fiddles with it then lifts the hand piece.

"AAC 5348, AAC 5348, this is Ditch Digger, do you copy?"

He repeats it half a dozen times, each time waiting, hearing nothing but static or garbled transmissions from other outfits on the same frequency. He fiddles with his dials and tries again.

"No dice," Petersen says at last.

It was a waste of time, but it had been a good excuse to flop down and drink some water.

"Okay," Rio says. "We'll try again when we get to this lake."

The lake in question is about a mile and a quarter long, half a mile wide. The downed plane is supposed to be on the near side, halfway up the lake. And it has supposedly set some of the trees afire, so they should either have a flame or at least the smell of smoke to guide them.

But the ground is getting rougher. Sicily in general is rock with only a scrape of topsoil, and here the topsoil is even more sparse, so the ground is at least half-naked rock. The path weaves through narrower and narrower ravines, with rock and gravel and scrub grass walls rising ever higher around them.

Perfect for an ambush.

Rio scans the heights around them constantly, but unless a Kraut stands up to allow himself to be conveniently silhouetted against the stars, there is little chance of spotting anyone. In fact it is so dark they can barely keep to the path let alone spot enemies.

But then the air changes. She smells the difference immediately: water. Moisture in the dry air. It can only

260

be the lake, and indeed the path is now dropping away. On the downslope it is Rio's thigh and the muscle at the front of her calves that take the most punishment.

Plus, she has to pee, but somehow calling a pee break does not seem like the most Cole-like thing to do. She runs through her memories. Has Sergeant Cole ever halted a patrol to take a leak? Not that she recalls. But still, she can't be the only one who could use two minutes behind a boulder.

"We got some tree cover here," she says. "Let's take care of nature's call."

There follows an absurd rush as men and women disappear into the copse of trees.

One more thing to worry about: I am now the bathroom monitor.

In three minutes they are back on the move and soon see moonlight sparkling on water. Here the trees are thick enough to almost merit being called a wood.

There is indeed a smell of smoke—smoke and fuel. They fan out and wander south a bit, then turn back north and the smoke smell grows distinctly stronger. Then Cat points out that there is an unusual amount of fallen branches littering the ground. They gather around and stare down at the fallen foliage. Rio crushes pine needles, smells her fingers, and says, "It's fresh. Can't have been like this long."

They follow north and now it is unmistakable that the tops of trees have been sheared off.

"The plane coming in, crashing," Jack says. "It will have lopped off some treetops."

At last they emerge into an open, grassy field, and there in the moonlight lies the wreckage of a plane. The fuselage is in two pieces, the nose and most of the fuselage, and a tail section broken off at an angle and lying fifty feet away. One wing is torn off at the roots and nowhere to be seen. The other wing with its two engines is still attached to the main section of fuselage, but it has been twisted like a piece of licorice, so both engines are pointed down at the ground, with props bent all the way back.

It is a B-17.

This comes as a shock. Rio had formed the picture of a downed fighter, an RAF Spitfire or American P-38. She had not imagined a bomber.

A B-17. What Strand flies.

The odds . . .

There must be hundreds . . .

"Petersen, we don't want them getting jumpy and shooting us as Krauts. Try to raise them."

Petersen takes to his radio again, but again there is no answer.

"Sure that damned thing works?" Cat snarls at Petersen.

"Okay, we approach," Rio says. "They won't know the password so just try to sound, you know, American."

"Must I?" Jack says.

Rio pats him on the shoulder and says, "Think 'Yankee Doodle Dandy.'"

It's still a twenty-minute walk, or, more accurately, creep, along the shore, in and out of the trees, before they are close enough to be able to see the fuselage clearly. They are on the side without the wing, the landward side.

"Hey," Rio says in a loud whisper. "Hey, B-17! Hey!"

Nothing.

"Hey, Americans here," she says. Then she tries a low whistle, which she can't quite do, so Geer whistles.

This time Rio hears a rustling and bumping sound from the plane. But nothing more.

"Geer, back on point," she says, regretting that she can't walk ahead herself. Geer is American, unlike Jack, and male, unlike Cat, and a male American voice is what the crew will expect to hear, *want* to hear.

"Stay low," Rio says.

They advance in slow motion, soft steps, quiet steps, every weapon out and ready.

"Don't shoot unless you're sure," Rio reminds everyone. Just like Cole would. Like a cautious parent.

"Who's there?" a male voice calls out from the wreck.

"Americans," Geer says. "We're your rescue."

"Prove you're American."

Geer thinks it over for a moment then says, "Nineteen forty-one Series, Yankees over Brooklyn, four games to one."

Silence. Then, "Fug the Yankees!"

"You're preaching to the choir, brother," Geer says.

A second voice. "Who's married to Rita Hayworth?"

Geer turns and looks blank. "Anyone know that?"

Cat yells, "We don't know, except he's the luckiest man on earth."

Evidently that answer is close enough, earning a short bark of laughter. "Come on," the second voice says.

Rio signals weapons down and they advance, ducking beneath the up-tilted nose of the plane. Rio passes beneath then takes a step back to look up. As with most planes, the pilot has named his craft and painted a logo on the side.

The word *Rio* is in swirling red letters that ride just above the image of a pretty girl in a bathing suit holding an M1.

She freezes, staring up at it. The girl is dark haired, long legged, and rather more shapely than Rio herself, but all in all it's flattering. Flattering and . . . and terrifying.

"Strand?" she cries. "Strand?"

She pushes past Geer and Cat and stumbles into the little encampment the aviators have made—a tiny, well-banked campfire now out, two padded pilot's chairs propped against the lowered front landing gear, and an array of items salvaged from the wreck.

Two men are standing, one holding a pistol. One man lies on a blanket with a flyer's jacket thrown over him. But his face is visible in the moonlight.

Strand Braxton.

19

RIO RICHLIN—CATANIA, SICILY

Rio drops her rifle and rushes to Strand. "My God, my God, are you hurt?"

"Rio?" He seems strange and unfocused. But he smiles at her and touches her face as if reassuring himself that she's real.

"You know Fish?" one of the flyers asks.

"My girl," Strand says dreamily, smiling in that fuzzy way.

"He's got a broken ankle and a bad gash on his other leg. We gave him some morphine. Probably has some ribs broke too."

Rio takes a long look at Strand. How odd that she feels she can study him more closely now than before. There is something so unguarded about him now. He's vulnerable, Rio realizes, and there is a rush of sympathy, but along with the sympathy comes a less creditable emotion.

He looks weak.

Rio stands up. Everyone, the two other flyers and her own squad, even Geer, are looking at her. No . . . looking *to* her. She's in charge, even with Strand here, even with his crew, both of whom are senior NCOs.

The moment is heady and disturbing. It's exciting, thrilling even, and yet drops a ton of weight on her shoulders. She almost feels her boots sinking deeper into the dirt.

"We're here to get you out. Is Strand's—Fish's—ankle splinted?"

"Pablo Guttierez," one of the crewmen says. He's older, maybe thirty, wearing his flight suit and a bent, sweat-stained straw cowboy hat that looks as if he's worn it punching cattle. "We figure he's good to move. But . . ." He glances at the plane. "We had ten men. The waist gunners jumped even though we were too low. The belly man . . . I don't think we can get him out. But we have four . . . four bodies . . . that ain't been buried."

The four lie in a row. The belly gunner, who would have been in the bubble-topped ball turret beneath the fuselage, cannot be seen. That turret would have clipped treetops all the way down and then smashed like a dropped egg on hitting the ground.

Rio shakes her head. "We didn't bring entrenching tools. Make sure they've got their dog tags, and we'll leave them for graves registration."

Guttierez looks defiant, though the other fellow, Joe, seems ready to move out.

"Graves registration isn't going near them, miss. We never delivered our payload. You understand? We've got four tons' worth of five-hundred-pound bombs still in the bomb bay."

Rio, Geer, Jack, Cat, and Petersen all take a quick step back, as if an extra three feet of distance is all it would take to escape a blast. It produces a comic effect.

"And you figure with four tons of HE we want to stay around digging graves?" Geer demands. "You're fugging crazy." He shoots a look at Rio as if expecting her to argue.

"We need to make a stretcher for Strand," Rio says. "Then we need to get the hell out of here."

"I got rank here long as the skipper is, um, off his head," Guttierez says stubbornly.

"All due respect, Guttierez, but this is my patrol," Rio says. Her voice is soft but all the more definite for it. "I can't force you to leave, but I'm taking Stra—Fish, whatever the hell we want to call him, and we're getting out of here." Without a pause she turns to her detail. "Petersen, try to raise someone and report this in. Tell them about the bodies and the bombs. Cat and Geer? We're going to have to use your rifles to make a stretcher."

In ten minutes a scratchy, distant voice has acknowledged that they have the surviving crew, and Cat and

Geer have stretched canvas salvaged from the bomber to fashion a crude stretcher. They are just carefully rolling Strand onto the stretcher when Jack says, "*Shh!*"

Everyone freezes. Every ear strains. And most of those ears hear the noises that can only be men moving through the woods.

A terse whisper. "Jack! Cat! Check it out."

Rio feels she should go, feels it powerfully, but that's not what Cole has taught her. She's in charge, and that means sending others into harm's way.

Cat retrieves her rifle, and she and Jack plunge into the deeper darkness beneath the trees.

"No one makes a sound," Rio hisses. Spotting the pistol in Guttierez's hand, she adds, "And no one shoots until I say so."

She looks in every direction, taking in the terrain in quick glances. The lake defines their northern flank with a gravel beach mere inches wide. To their west is the trail of broken trees, and beyond that either safety or a German counterattack against the Gela beachhead. And east is where the sounds of moving men are.

South it is.

Trees, some tall by Sicilian standards, run in every direction. Hard soil. No ditches or depressions. Strand unable to walk. They can fight from the plane, but the plane is a massive explosion just waiting for an opportunity to flatten the woods and kill half the fish in the lake.

"Guttierez, Joe, any chance of getting one of your machine guns out?"

"Sure," Joe says, nodding, and moves briskly toward the plane. Guttierez has no choice but to follow.

"Geer?" She jerks her head toward the west. "Drop back, take a look in those fallen branches and trees, see if there's a place we can fight."

Geer takes off at a run.

"Should I call it in?" Petersen asks.

"No. The radio squawks." She sees Joe and Guttierez manhandling an awkward-looking machine gun—its mounting hardware half-removed—out of the plane's surviving hatch. She helps him hand it down and then takes a box of ammo from Joe. He climbs after it with a second box and a great belt of ammo over his shoulders like a shawl.

"It ain't great," Geer reports back, breathless from his run. "But there's a place where we could get behind a couple trees and dig in."

"Okay, get Joe and Guttierez set up there, and I'll drag Strand over while—"

Cat and Jack come crashing back at a full run, holding on to their helmets and yelling, "Krauts!"

Guns fire and bullets whiz by.

"How far back?" Rio demands.

"Three seconds!" Cat yells.

"Jack, help me get Strand. Preeling, Geer's that way, go, go! Geer! Preeling's coming to you!"

More firing, and this time the sound is much nearer. Rio grabs the shoulder of Strand's flight suit, Jack grabs the other, and they drag him back.

And Strand starts singing "White Christmas" in a low but audible voice.

As if spurred on by the singing, the firing becomes much more determined. A bullet plucks at Jack's sleeve. Another one cuts a furrow across Strand's chest.

"Shit!" Rio yells. "Strand . . ."

"*. . . and children listen, to hear sleigh bells in the snow . . .*"

"Leave him," Rio says, feeling like she's been stabbed in the heart, feeling a boiling panic within her, but relinquishing her grip, falling back onto her behind, spinning, crawling, rising, running, with Jack beside her and bullets so thick they could be a swarm of bees.

"Coming in!" Jack yells.

They reach two fallen logs, one angled over the other, forming a V with the point toward the attack. The logs aren't big, no more than six inches in diameter, but Cat and Joe have been busy dragging anything wood-like to this makeshift barricade. Geer is on his butt kicking dirt and rock into a barrier beneath the trees with the heels of his boots and cursing a blue streak.

Jack and Rio leap and tumble over the barrier, Rio plowing into Geer and twisting instantly to stand and fire back. *Bang-bang-bang!* Three quick shots to give the Germans pause.

The German fire stops, and Rio quickly checks her position. It's open on both flanks and behind. The beach is twenty yards to their left. The plane is mostly to their right now, a hundred yards away.

Enfilade, defilade.

Strand lies directly between the squad and the still-unseen Germans.

"They'll either come along the beach or circle the plane," Rio says. She's panting. They're all panting.

"Or both," Geer says.

"Petersen, make the call. Tell them we've made contact, force unknown. Joe, Guttierez?"

"Five minutes!" Joe answers. The two flyers are feverishly stripping the hanging bits of mounting from the machine gun. They'll have to rest it on the unsteady log.

German fire resumes, *bap-bap-bap-bap*, with bullets tearing through foliage and sending leaves and chips of wood flying.

"How many guys in the Kraut patrol?" Jack asks.

"Can't be more than a dozen," Rio says, hearing the fear and excitement in her voice.

"They're keeping us occupied while they flank us," Jack says.

"... *with every Christmas card I write* ..." Strand, of course, as the bullets fly inches above his nose.

"Beach or woods?" Rio asks Jack.

"Bloody hell," Jack says, and crawls toward the beach cradling his rifle.

"Petersen, anything?" Rio asks.

No answer.

She turns to find Petersen sitting up with his back against a tree, his radio propped in front of him. Petersen is staring. Unblinking.

Jack's M1 opens up, rapid firing, fast as he can squeeze them off. Rio still can't see the Krauts, but she can guess their approximate position. They're coming along the beach, looking for a quick conclusion.

"Right there!" she yells to the flyers, and chops the air to show direction. A bullet dings her helmet and ricochets away.

The flyers are ready, and their big .50 caliber blazes, stabbing tracer rounds into the trees.

"Watch your ammo!" Rio warns. "Short bursts, they aren't fugging Messerschmitts!"

For no more than a minute both sides blaze away, a mad cacophony of explosions, the *flit-flit* of passing slugs, the softer *thunk* of bullets hitting wood, and then a cry of pain from the Germans.

The Germans stop firing, and Rio yells, "Cease firing. Cease firing. Jack! Can you see them?" The air stinks of gunpowder, a cloud of it hovers around them.

"Just one," Jack yells back. "I think I got one of them!"

If there were a dozen Germans, then there are only eleven now. But on her side she has six people, one machine gun, and four rifles or carbines. If the Krauts have a mortar, this will be over as soon as they get it set up. But what are the odds of a Kraut patrol dragging a heavy mortar through the woods?

No, they have no mortar, and they have no machine gun either, though they have at least two Schmeisser submachine guns. But they may well have a radio and someone to operate it. Unlike Rio.

"Geer, check on Petersen."

Geer crawls back, and his report comes immediately. "Shot right through the radio," he yells and comes crawling back. "Deader than shit!"

Pull back and leave Strand to his fate, presumably at a German POW camp for the remainder of the war? Or fight it out, risking all their lives?

As if reading her thoughts, Guttierez yells, "I ain't leaving the skipper behind!"

The skipper meanwhile has lost the thread of the lyrics and is drifting into "Jingle Bells."

For just a split second Rio hates Strand Braxton.

Morphine. Not his fault.

Eleven Krauts to six, but those eleven are Wehrmacht.

They could be veteran troops, men who'd fought the Russians and British.

Professionals.

"Preeling. Get out on our right a hundred yards, and in three minutes you start blasting away. Throw a grenade but away from the plane," Rio says. "Jack, stay put."

"Certainly," he says. "It's damp, but the view is magical."

Despite herself, Rio grins.

Within the small shelter of the fallen trees it's the two flyers on the left, Geer and Rio in the center, with Jack on the left flank, Cat on the right. It's all Rio can do. If the Krauts flank far to her right, they can circle around and come up from behind, but there's nothing she can do about that. She doesn't have the people to cover every approach.

The math is terribly clear in Rio's mind. There is no way. The barricade is a joke, there's limited ammo for the machine gun, and she's likely facing veteran soldiers. No way. Sooner or later the Krauts bring up more men or call in artillery or simply flank them.

Her father's words come back to her.

There will come a time when you'll have a choice between staying in your trench and crawling out of it to save a buddy . . . When that moment comes, you stay down.

275

This is not a World War I trench, Father, and that's not a buddy, it's Strand.

Rio loosens the pins on two grenades. She pops a fresh clip into her rifle.

"Richlin?" Geer asks.

"Soon as Preeling opens up," Rio says, "you lay down fire. Keep it aimed high and to the right."

"What are you doing?" Geer demands.

She doesn't answer but crawls away toward Jack. "It's me," she hisses when she gets close. She finds him lying on a shore too narrow to quite hold him so his right shoulder is up against a low shelf and his left is in the water.

"You good?" she asks.

"Fugging lovely," he says.

"Stay here, Jack," she says.

"What are you—"

Whoompf!

Cat has loosed her grenade, and it is followed instantly by the sound of her carbine, joined quickly by Geer and the .50 caliber.

Rio pushes up, up to her feet, numb, a part of her mind dreamy and distant, while another part is focused with razor-sharp intensity. A deep breath and her feet are moving, moving, running, boots splashing the shallow water, digging sloppy divots in gravelly mud.

Branches whip at her face, thorns rip her uniform, she's

running, running, and now firing from the hip, *bang-bang-bang!*

The one thing the Germans won't expect: attack!

A dark shape ahead, a gleam of starlight on the iconic gray helmet and *bang-bang* and the German falls straight back. She leaps his dying body, with another Kraut ahead, firing at her. She sees his muzzle flash, hears the bullets, fires, fires, runs, and the Kraut is still firing when she plows into him, trampling him in her rush. Now she sees four, maybe five muzzle flashes ahead, coming from behind trees. She yanks a grenade free, pulls the pin, and throws it. She drops to the ground, hears shouts of alarm in German and then, *crumpf!*

Small branches pelt her helmet, and she's up instantly, rushing, no longer firing, waiting for targets.

There! Bang!

There! Bang! Bang!

Two rounds left in the clip. A German rushes in from her right firing a Schmeisser submachine gun from the hip, disciplined bursts that chop at the trees. Rio is moving faster than the Kraut can turn, and she tosses her second grenade at him, not fifteen feet away, too close—have to keep moving and *crumpf!*

Something big and thick and too soft to be wood hits her in passing, but she's beyond caring. There's a roaring in her head, a sound like a million waterfalls crashing, her

277

body is filled with lightning, she is unstoppable, invincible, unkillable, and she screams as she runs, screams, "Die, die, die, goddamn you!"

Two shots come in rapid succession, two shots that sober her up like a bucket of cold water thrown in her face. The shots are from behind!

She twists in mid-run to see the German she'd trampled earlier. He's up, and his rifle is leveled and smoking. And just a few feet behind him, Jack's rifle is also leveled, and also trails a faint wisp of smoke from the barrel. The German stands for what feels like an eternity, then crumples.

Rio stops running and realizes no one is firing at her.

"Cease firing!" she yells at the top of her lungs. With predatory alertness she strains to hear. The sound of men moving, but moving away. Are the Krauts pulling back? If so . . .

"Jack, with me!" she yells, and barrels back toward Strand, who has blessedly fallen silent. She drops beside him, lays her rifle on his chest, and grabs his uniform fabric. Jack, beside her, does the same, and side by side they haul Strand away. But it is inch by inch. Strand is a healthy-sized man and the soil is far from smooth.

Rio yells, "Geer, Cat, all of you fall back!"

"Artillery?" Jack gasps.

She nods. "Gotta be coming. They fell back to call it in."

They are no more than halfway back to the makeshift firing position before a whistling sound in the air proves her right. The round lands with shattering effect but off to their left, blowing the surface of the lake into a spout of water and mud.

How long for the Krauts to call in a correction? How long for their gunners to adjust?

They are at the fallen trees and must pull branches away before they can carry on dragging Strand. The second round of shells lands on the right line but sixty or so feet behind them.

"Cat! Turn south!" Rio shouts.

They are through the barrier but nowhere near escaping what Rio knows will be a murderously accurate artillery fire mission.

Jack squirms, hauls Strand onto his shoulders. Rio grabs Strand's legs and lifts and the three of them stumble away.

A whistle in the air.

"Down!"

They fall on their faces and Jack says something, which is lost in the noise of the explosion, but in the flash of light Rio sees what Jack has seen: a decently deep hole formed by a tree that's been ripped out by the roots. They crawl like worms and drag themselves and Strand into the hole.

Boom! Boom! Boom!

Shells are dropping like deadly rain, blasting trees and turf, and ripping the world apart like a giant throwing a toddler's tantrum. Hot, spent shrapnel clatters on Rio's helmet. Noise, noise everywhere; the ground itself is like the skin of a bass drum.

The firing stops suddenly. Rio speaks but can't hear herself. Jack's mouth is moving, but the sound might as well be coming through a heavy door it's so muffled.

She risks rising just enough to take a quick, shaky glance around. The plane lies there still, a new crater just off its surviving wing, its skin torn by shrapnel but not burning.

Of course: the Krauts want to take the plane intact, or at least the bombsight.

The Germans will move up now and finish us off.

Her thoughts are as clear as if they'd been carefully written out: with arty stopped, the Krauts will advance. They can't outrun the Krauts, not while hauling Strand.

One way, just one way to be sure.

Rio snatches a grenade from Jack's belt. She points at him and then at Strand, then chops her hand to indicate direction.

Jack is arguing, she can see it, though she still can't make out the words.

"Do it!" she snaps. "Far as you can!"

Then, uncertain whether her voice is pitched loudly

enough, yells, "Preeling and Geer! Get up here and help Stafford!"

Risking their lives to save Strand? Or just trying to complete the mission?

Jack is still arguing, but he's nevertheless begun dragging Strand again.

Rio's mind is a stopwatch. *Tick-tick-tick.* How long for the Krauts to advance from their fallback? How long for Strand and Jack to get clear?

How long for *her* to get clear?

Tick-tick-tick.

They'll come from both directions this time, circling the B-17.

Don't be a hero.

"I'm not, Dad, just trying to keep my people alive," she mutters as if he is standing beside her.

My people.

Tick-tick-tick.

Her hearing is coming back. She does not hear the advancing Germans, but she does hear Geer's warning, "Movement! More than before!"

Have the Krauts been reinforced already?

Geer and Cat have joined Jack, and the three of them have Strand by hand, hand, and ankle, leaving the injured ankle to drag and bang along the ground.

Strand is complaining in an aggrieved tone.

Tick-tick-tick.

Now.

Her grenades are fused for five seconds. Two grenades, her last one and the one she took from Jack.

Pull both pins. Hold down the lever. Run. Throw.

Five seconds to get away.

Impossible!

"Shit," Rio says under her breath, and races straight for the plane. In through the open hatch, the only way, otherwise the grenades might just scar the fuselage.

She runs and suddenly there are a half dozen Kraut soldiers ahead and they won't be bluffed a second time. She fires one-handed, from the hip, no chance of hitting anything, but maybe it will slow them down—and now the plane and the hatch and suddenly she's there.

She releases the first lever and tosses the grenade into the darkness inside the plane. The second follows half a second later.

Four seconds left.

One.

Run, Rio!

Two.

Too slow!

Three.

The stump hole! She dives, heedless, headfirst and the whole world blows up.

20

RAINY SCHULTERMAN—SALERNO AND POSITANO, ITALY

Rainy freezes.

"Let me have a gun so I can shoot this bitch in the mouth."

Tomaso tilts his head and looks at her quizzically.

Cisco says, "As long as she's alive, she's a risk!"

"If you kill me, the deal is off," Rainy says, though her voice is like the rustling of dry leaves. Her mouth is bone dry.

"The deal." Cisco snorts. "I'm here, I'm safe, that's all that matters."

But Tomaso flicks a sidelong look at him, a look full of distaste. "You don't think her people back in New York are going to take it out on Don Vito? On your own father, Cisco? They can tell the Nigras where you are, and for two hundred dollars US they can put a hit out on you. Not to mention busting every bar, flophouse, whore-house, and gambling joint Don Vito controls."

Tomaso's English is too good, despite the accent, too *slang* to have been learned from books. He's been to America.

Rainy breathes.

"This is business, not personal bullshit," Tomaso scolds Cisco. "You make a deal, you keep the deal. Otherwise there's no business, *capisce*?"

Cisco is furious, furious and afraid. Rainy turns a cold stare on him and says, "Best if we all keep our mouths shut. Right, Cisco?"

It is not a subtle threat, and Cisco hears it. So does Tomaso, who raises a curious eyebrow but does not ask any questions. He says, "We're having breakfast. Come upstairs, have some coffee and a *cornetto*. Don Pietro will decide what happens next."

He sweeps his arm toward the stairs, and Rainy, followed by Cisco with Tomaso bringing up the rear, climbs a long, steep staircase that opens onto a hallway. The kitchen door is open. An old woman is brewing coffee in a stovetop espresso maker. A younger woman is washing dishes.

Past the kitchen—Rainy nods to the old woman—is the dining room. It's a pleasant, homey room. There's a long, mahogany oval of a table decorated with a lace runner. The table is piled generously with croissants—*cornetti*—and assorted pastries. There are pots of jam, a lump of yellow butter, fine china cups and plates, and expensive silver.

Three men are seated, two obviously muscle, and one, at the head of the table with his back to a window and thus haloed with sunlight, who is much older and unmistakably in charge.

Don Pietro Camporeale has less sinister energy than Vito the Sack. He's more elderly, for one thing. But what he lacks in physical energy he makes up for in sheer, stolid, graven-image intimidation.

Rainy is tough-minded, skeptical, unimpressed, and confident in her own abilities. But Don Pietro is something she's never encountered before. He seems to warp the fabric of space, as though he radiates an intense gravity that causes every eye to turn to him, causes every thought to focus on him, has every other person in the room hanging expectantly on his word.

He is polite, even courtly. He speaks no English, so Tomaso translates even though Rainy understands the don's Italian perfectly well. Don Pietro has a voice that starts out hearty enough but soon grows hoarse, like many old men. He could be sixty, he could be ninety. His expression never changes. He is not startled, fascinated, puzzled, annoyed, happy, sad, or angry. He is a perfect unemotional void projected onto a hound dog's face.

And yet, his eyes . . . He seldom looks at her, but when

he does Rainy knows, by some sub-logical sixth sense, that he is not seeing an American soldier, or a spy, or an ally; he's seeing an object, a thing, a piece on the chessboard where he is the grand master.

Don Pietro nods at one of his bodyguards, and the man puts down his cup and pulls an envelope from the pocket of his jacket. He slides it across to Rainy.

Don Pietro (as translated by Tomaso) says, "You have delivered my brother's son. We have now given you the information you sought in return. Our transaction is complete."

"Yes, sir," Rainy says. "But I still have to get the information to my superiors. I have to get to Rome."

"We have made no bargain that includes aiding you. No bargain that includes sheltering you. Francisco"— he glances at his nephew with obvious distaste—"I am certain has also made no such promise. As I said, our business is satisfactorily concluded."

Panic gnaws at the edge of Rainy's mind. This is Italy, enemy territory, a country overrun by various Fascist police forces and intelligence people, not to mention the German Gestapo. She has a little money and a pistol, and other than that, nothing but her orders—orders that direct her to contact a certain person at the neutral Swedish Embassy in Rome, or, failing that, to find some other way of passing her information along.

I'm not the hero of this story, I'm the fool.

"Don Pietro," Rainy says in Italian now, hoping her use of his tongue will make him more favorably disposed to her. "It was no easy thing getting Cisco here to where he is safe with you. I had hoped—"

"Hope is for fools," Don Pietro says with a very slight wave of his hand.

"Is honor also for fools?" she demands, her heart in her throat. It's a challenge to Don Pietro, a challenge to a man who can snap his fingers and end her life.

But Don Pietro doesn't blink. "Honor requires keeping to the deals we *make*. This I have done."

She sees that he is ready to move on to a different topic. If that happens, she's very likely done for. He won't risk letting her fall into the hands of carabinieri or the Gestapo, she realizes in a moment of startling clarity: that could end up making trouble for him. So he'll have her killed. Maybe not right away, maybe not until he can pin it on someone else, but she will be killed—of that there is no doubt.

For a moment she is paralyzed by this realization. She is bargaining for her life, not just her mission. While she's frantically searching for something to say, Tomaso steps in.

"Perhaps there is some other service she could perform."

Her first reaction is gratitude. But then, despite the fear growing inside her, she realizes this is *planned*. Don Pietro has made clear her likely fate: death; and Tomaso now offers a way out.

"What other service?" she asks, dreading the reply.

"The don grows tired," Tomaso says, though Don Pietro has shown no evidence of weariness, merely boredom. "Let's discuss this between ourselves."

They make their polite good-byes to the evil old man and pass by a glaring Cisco. They walk down worn stone steps into a pleasant, walled garden. There is a hedge of well-tended roses and a fig tree whose fruit is just a week or two from ripeness. There isn't much to see in the garden, but there is a stone bench in the shade, and it is there that Tomaso explains.

"You are not Catholic, I take it," Tomaso says.

"No. I'm Jewish."

"Then you would have no particular objection to dealing with a difficult priest."

"You want me to talk to a priest?"

"No," Tomaso says, smiling at the thought. "We want you to eliminate him."

Rainy stares at him, dumbfounded. She has expected any number of possibilities, largely having to do with sexual services. And now, absurdly, she is almost abashed to find that this plays no part in the don's considerations, or apparently in Tomaso's.

"I'm not an assassin."

Tomaso shrugs. "No, but Francisco is. He very much wants you gone and silenced forever."

"He's claustrophobic."

"I'm sorry, I don't know that word."

"Cisco has a deep-seated terror of confined spaces. He panics. I mean, really panics. Raving, screaming, pants wetting." She owes Cisco nothing and getting the information out there alters his motivation.

"And you arrived by submarine." Tomaso smiles privately and nods. "Yes, he'd want you dead for having witnessed that. And by telling me you think you'll eliminate his need to eliminate you. Clever, but not *very* clever. Cisco is not a great believer in reason."

"No," she admits. "But I'm still not a killer."

"Not yet," Tomaso says, and pats her knee. "It's something that's only really difficult the first time. It becomes easier. And this priest really is a very bad fellow, he's getting his flock up in arms against certain businesses we wish to extend into his village."

"You're moving in on a new territory, and the priest is trying to stop you."

"Exactly. You're very quick, you know, very quick for a . . ."

"For a woman?"

Tomaso laughs his easy, genial laugh. "I was going to say for an American. No Italian man needs to be schooled on the subtlety of women." He laughs at some private memory. "But sometimes feminine delicacy may cause women to be slower to reach unpleasant conclusions."

"What unpleasant conclusion?"

"Come now, we don't need to be explicit."

"Kill or be killed," Rainy says. "That's the conclusion, isn't it?"

Tomaso sighs and shakes his head, but it's not a negative, it's amusement and disapproval. "I abhor threats."

"Me too, when they're directed at me," Rainy snaps.

Her heart is thudding in her chest. She has difficulty breathing without gasping or sobbing, but her mind is still alert. There is a door in the garden wall. And there is a man armed with a shotgun beside that door, and probably another just outside on the street. She has a pistol that will be very awkward to draw from beneath her dress with Tomaso beside her. Anyway, a pistol versus at least one and likely two shotguns is not a good bet. Then, too, even if she somehow escapes into the streets, how long before they find her? Minutes? A half hour at best?

Two things are obvious. She can refuse and die right now, if not by Tomaso's hand then by Cisco's. Or she can stall for time by agreeing.

Option two seems a much better choice.

First she has to struggle some more, pretend to be appalled, pretend to come slowly to the idea, pretend to talk herself into it. Too-quick agreement will just show she's planning a double cross.

Tomaso waits patiently—or is it cynically—as she makes a show of convincing herself, complete with expressions of outrage, which do not move Tomaso at all.

In the end she is driven in a beat-up tricycle truck from Salerno by Tomaso and one of his thugs. The passenger compartment is absurdly cramped, so she is squeezed miserably between the beefy driver and the compactly muscular Tomaso.

Despite the impossibility of her position, Rainy is aware that the drive is spectacularly beautiful. The road winds north out of Salerno before turning west along the coast. It is a narrow, even precarious road, which at places lances through small, steep, seaside towns, creeping down streets so tight that at one point Tomaso simply reaches out of the window to grab an orange out of a shop display. He peels it with a pocketknife, cuts a dripping section, and hands it to Rainy.

In other places the road seems to almost hang in midair. There's usually a low stone wall along the seaward side, but the ground drops away so steeply that she can't see anything below but the sparkling Mediterranean. A single careless turn and the little tricycle truck will likely plow straight through or over the wall and go tumbling down onto picturesque homes.

"Beautiful, isn't it?" Tomaso asks.

There's no point lying. "The most beautiful place I've ever seen."

This earns her a thoughtful look. "Have you traveled much?"

Rainy hesitates—it is in her nature to reveal as little as possible—but she can't see the harm and she needs Tomaso's friendship, if such a thing is even possible. "I'm from New York City. It's a different sort of beauty, more man-made, larger, grittier, but still beautiful at times."

"Yes," he says. "I've seen it. But New York is all about the works of man, and here we have the perfect melding of man and nature. The sea, the steep cliffs and hills, the brightly colored homes. And of course the food is better here."

"The coffee certainly is," Rainy allows, straining for affability.

They stop at last on the street outside a whitewashed, three-story building. Its door is wide, open, and inviting beneath blue, aquatic-themed tile work. A sign in matching cobalt-glazed letters spells out Hotel Alto Positano.

"A hotel?" Rainy asks. She's been expecting some dank hideaway in which to be instructed by this charming murderer on the business of assassination.

"Certainly a hotel, and a good one too, I believe. It is

run by a friend. I must be honest and tell you that he will not allow you to make telephone calls or mail letters." This last comes with a regretful shrug. "Here the authorities will not trouble you. You are not an American and certainly not a Jew—though I have no such prejudices, many of the great men of our business are Jews—Dutch Schultz, rest in peace, Bugsy Siegel, Meyer Lansky. But for our purposes you are Irish, a neutral, on a retreat following some unfortunate event."

"What unfortunate event?"

"You have been living in Rome and your engagement to an Italian man was broken off at the last minute, so you have come to romantic Positano to take your mind off your sadness. And perhaps find some other, more amenable, more marriageable fellow."

"Like you?"

He makes one of the faces only Italians can make, an expression that manages to combine romanticism, resignation, amusement, and a cool distance, all in less than a second. "It would explain why I may sometimes come to call on you during your stay."

"Right," she says tersely, and begins to climb out.

Tomaso puts a hand on her arm. "Miss Schulterman, you must have no fear that I would exploit . . ."

She nods tightly and the two of them go in, leaving the driver to light a cigar and unfold a newspaper.

Tomaso walks Rainy to a room that is nothing special:

white walls adorned only by a crucifix and a portrait of Mussolini, a tile floor, a sagging bed in an iron frame, the tiniest sink she's ever seen in one corner beneath a milky square of mirror.

But the view . . . the view is breathtaking.

Even after the stunning drive along the coast from Salerno, Rainy is not prepared for what now unfolds below her. The Mediterranean is genuinely blue, almost placid, and it sends up sudden reflections that dazzle and make her look away to avoid being temporarily blinded.

The town of Positano rests mostly on the side of a hill, which at the bottom is quite steep and by the top becomes sheer cliff. Stucco houses and hotels painted ochre, sunflower, pink, tan, and white cover the hill—all but that last hundred feet of cliff, and even there a terrace has been cut into the rock to allow one last house to be supported. Many of the buildings, almost all in fact, have arched galleries or graceful balconies facing the sea, and on virtually every one there are green plants of a type Rainy cannot name. Palm trees grow here and there on larger terraces.

Looking down there are the roofs, some flat, others gently pitched and covered in Spanish tile. Then, just before the beach, where at last the land levels briefly before touching the sea, there rises a dome, presumably a church. At a glance it is gold, but on closer examination it looks as if it is covered in fish scales, colored shingles that form abstract mosaic patterns of gold, faded green, and dark blue.

Tomaso steps beside her on the balcony and nods. "Yes, that is the *duomo*. There you will find Father Patrizio." He steps back inside, unfastens his coat, and draws out a long and clumsy-looking pistol. He lays it on the bed.

Rainy stares at it and up at him.

"It's a .22 with a silencer, a quiet but not silent gun, and deadly at close range. Tomorrow morning you will go to confession. You will shoot him through the grating in the confessional. *Pop, pop, pop.* Three times. Quick. You will leave the gun behind, and I will pick you up a block away. You will be taken directly to the Swedish Embassy in Rome. If something intervenes on the first try, you will make a second attempt the next day."

"Once the priest is dead, you'll kill me," Rainy says.

Tomaso steps close. There's a flinty look in his eye. "I have given my word. Don Pietro has given his word. We have kept our word to this point, and you have the information you sought. Now we embark on a new deal, a deal that we will also keep. So do not treat me with disrespect, or I may forget that I am a gentleman."

He runs his hand up her arm, raising goose bumps in their wake. He touches the side of her face, pushing the springy hair back to see her neck. "Unless, of course, that's what you would like?"

Rainy shakes her head no, not trusting her voice, because as much as she fears Tomaso, as much as she knows him for what he is, there is something undeniably . . . compelling . . . about him. The touch of his hand leaves fear but also excitement in its wake.

"Pity," Tomaso says. "And now I must go. You see therefore that I am a man of my word. I hope you are a woman of your word." With that he leaves, closing the door gently behind him.

It's a very convincing performance, and for several seconds Rainy is almost willing to buy it. The side of her face where he touched her burns, and she wants to touch it herself. But the effect lasts only those few seconds before cold logic sobers her up to reality.

She walks back out onto the balcony and ignores the beautiful view. Instead she focuses on the railing, and the similar balconies below and to each side of her.

Wherever she goes she knows she will be watched. If she is to warn the priest and escape with her life, she'll need to avoid the watchers. Will they expect her to try and climb down? If yes, she will *certainly* die. If no, she will only *probably* die.

Rainy sits on the edge of the bed, puts her face in her hands, and cries. Then, with tears of frustration and fear released, she begins to plan.

RIO RICHLIN—CATANIA, SICILY

Rio is up in the hayrack in a private space she has shaped for herself by moving a few bales. She has a forbidden copy of a scandal magazine with Judy Garland on the cover and a headline promising juicy tidbits.

Hay surrounds her. Hay aroma fills her nostrils—that and the rich smell of cows. She cannot hear them, the cows, which is strange because cows are always making some sort of noise, lowing, shifting position, farting. She's sure they're down below and not out in the field, but she can't hear them because there is a ringing, a very persistent ringing, and now the hay bales are falling and she along with them and . . .

What? Wh . . . What is . . .

Blink. Is that the ground? She's looking down, seeing the ground and a pair of boots. The boots are running noiselessly. They turn to bypass a large branch lying on its side. Her middle is compressed. Her legs are dangling.

She can see, she can feel, she cannot yet put it all together.

And then she does.

"Put me down!" Rio yells.

"Hey! She's awake!" She can feel the vibration so she knows the sound comes from the person carrying her, but the words sound far away.

Rio is lowered to the ground, an action made more difficult by her attempts to jump down on her own. She's been carried, over the shoulder, by someone, and then, lying on the ground and looking up, she sees a face in shadow but still recognizable.

Jack.

"What happened?" she asks, panicky, and begins checking her body.

"You blew the fug out of everything." This from Cat, who is panting, sweating, and looking shaken.

Rio nods, straining to hear and straining, too, to remember. She glances around. A huge fire burns no more than two hundred yards away. Smaller fires blaze away to the left and right and beyond the spot where the plane had been. Around her an eerie scene out of a natural disaster, like some newsreel clip of a tornado's aftermath. A wide circle of trees has either been knocked flat or stands burning.

The bombs.

"Strand?"

Jack jerks a thumb to indicate Strand lying on a make-shift stretcher. Cat and Geer have obviously been carrying it and have set it down to rest while Rio regains her wits. Strand is breathing, she can see his chest rising and falling. The two flyers are standing nervously, peering at her with something between disapproval and amazement.

"Where's my rifle?" Rio demands.

Geer lifts it off Strand and tosses it to her. She catches it just ahead of the trigger guard and automatically slides the bolt to check that she has a chambered round. The brass cartridge glows warm in the firelight.

"All right," Rio says, still woozy and not completely sure what has happened. "Let's get moving."

Jack is directly in front of her. His blue eyes are absent their usual mischief, and in the orange light they seem very serious. He says something, but it's in a low voice and she can't quite hear it.

She taps her ear and says, "Sorry," in a too-loud voice.

Jack shakes his head very slightly. His expression is unreadable. In a much louder voice he says, "Never mind," which she does hear.

"I'll take a turn carrying the stretcher once we get clear of this place," Rio says. "Let's move."

And with that she levels her rifle and leads the way into the trees beyond the blast area.

The trip back is much slower than the trip to the site.

Strand is not small nor particularly light, and rifles do not make the best stretcher poles. But finally they strike a road and hail a passing deuce-and-a-half whose driver takes pity on them.

An hour and a half after being picked up they are back with the Fifth Platoon, which has been pulled off the line and back to the beach for a rest. There are as yet very few tents set up, and soldiers are passed out in sleeping bags or simply lying atop shelter halves. The night is warm, and the dawn, just peeking from behind distant Mount Etna, promises to be downright hot.

Sergeant Cole and the rest welcome their buddies with the usual sincerity as expressed in wry looks, teasing insults, and indifferent nods or waves.

Beebee and a new guy from another squad are detailed to carry Strand to the nearest aid station. Cat leads Rio down to the chow tent.

"You got blood coming out of your ears," Cat points out with no sign of concern.

Alarmed, Rio touches her ears. "It's dried. Mostly."

"I didn't say it was pouring out." Cat walks beside her and then suddenly stops, reaches over, and hugs Rio in an awkward sideways way. "You did good back there." The clinch is over in a second, leaving Rio not knowing quite what to say.

"Thanks. I guess."

They reach the chow line, which seems to be a permanent fixture regardless of mealtimes.

"You blew the living shit out of the Krauts," Cat says.

"You know . . . dammit, SOS again? Isn't this breakfast?" SOS is the abbreviation for Shit on a Shingle, the gooey, creamy mess of meat, milk, and flour the chow line has been featuring almost without a break. "Just as I was tossing the grenades it occurred to me, what if the bombs don't all go off at once, what if the first explosion just throws them all around the place."

"I hate to tell you, but that's exactly what happened. Bombs flying through the air. *Whoosh. Boom.* Sheer dumb luck one didn't land on us. People wouldn't be using words like *splendid* then, would they? Tell you one thing, any fish in that lake is either dead or has the worst headache of its life."

"Splendid? What are you talking about?"

"Stafford."

"I couldn't hear a thing, not then. Much better now."

"He said you were absolutely splendid. Very English too. They can say words like *splendid* and it doesn't sound nearly as silly."

They carry their loaded mess kits to a spot where a tent side provides a scrap of shade. It's only midmorning, but already the sun is riding high and hot. Then, because she has to hear it again, Rio says, "What did he say? Exactly?"

"Well, once we saw you were alive he said it was the finest thing he's ever seen. That you were bloody marvelous. Then, later, the splendid thing."

"Oh."

"Oh?"

"What am I supposed to say, Cat? Hooray for me?"

Cat shakes her head. "You are a pain in the ass, Richlin, you know that? Half the time you're playing little miss milkmaid, and the next minute you're GI Jane, which is all fine, but now you're getting bitchy about it."

"I am not bitchy," Rio protests through a mouthful of food.

"You used to be fun, that's all."

"I have to be fun too? What, am I not smiling enough?" She gets up and knocks the remains of her food into a slop drum. Then without a word to Cat she heads back.

Cat trots after her. "Jesus, Richlin, since when can't you take a joke?"

"You know what, everyone can drop dead!" Rio rages.

"Yeah, well fug you too, Richlin."

Rio's still furious when she rejoins the platoon, now coming down to the beach, and Jenou, seeing a white-faced fury she's never seen before on her friend, pulls her aside. "Are you all right? How's Strand?"

"What's that supposed to mean?" Rio hisses.

Jenou blinks. Looks at her like she's seeing a stranger

and says, "It's supposed to mean, 'How is Strand?'"

Rio is breathing fast, panting almost, wishing she could have some privacy, somewhere away, somewhere she can think without being judged. Anywhere. Literally anywhere so long as it's not here.

"You're upset," Jenou says. She looks around, mirroring Rio's desire for privacy, but there is none to be found on the crowded beach. She does the best she can, puts an arm around her friend and draws her closer to the path the tanks are following up from the LSTs (Landing Ship Tank). The noise of engines and the clanking of tracks will shield them from too much snooping.

"Something's bothering you," Jenou says.

"Yes, you. You're bothering me. And Cat. And everyone."

A tanker riding atop his vehicle winks at them and says, "Hey, honey, want to see what I've got for you?" and grabs his crotch.

In a flash Rio draws her *koummya* and with amazing ferocity says, "How about I cut it off and look at it later?"

The shocked tanker just gapes at her, twisting to continue gaping as his tank rattles away.

"I'm sick of people looking at me," Rio says angrily, as if picking up an ongoing conversation. "I see how you look at me, Jen. I know what you think. You think I'm not acting like me, but I'm still me!" She almost impales herself jabbing with the *koummya* for emphasis.

Tears fill her eyes and make her even more angry. But tears have a power of their own to subvert rage and leave only sadness and hurt to rise to the surface.

"Come here, honey," Jenou says, and holds her arms open.

Rio shakes her head almost violently, spilling the tears down her cheeks and sending one to land on Jenou's chin. "I'm not crying."

Jenou accepts that gravely and lowers her arms. "I understand. You don't want to act like a girl. You have to be big, tough Rio Richlin."

"I did it with Strand."

"You were tough with . . ." The silence stretches and stretches as slowly Jenou realizes what she means.

The confession seems to hang in the air between them. It takes Jenou a solid minute before she can ask, "You mean, just now, after he crashed?" When Rio doesn't answer she says, "Tunis? *Tunis?* And you didn't tell me?"

"I knew how you'd react. Like it was this terribly important thing."

"It's not?" Jenou is flabbergasted.

Rio shakes her head and wipes furtively at a tear. "Look around us here, Jen." Rio waves a hand to encompass the beach and the whole island and indeed the whole war. "Look at all of *this*. What's important compared to *this*? What does anything matter when we're doing *this*?" Each "this" sounds like a curse word.

"But, honey, Rio, we're going home someday. We're going home to Gedwell Falls, and so is Strand, and it's not like either of you can just forget what happened. My God, this means you have to get married."

"Really?" Rio's laugh is a sneer. "Suddenly you, Jenou Castain, are the voice of morality?"

"Well, no, but I've never—"

"You lie!"

"Don't you call me a liar!"

"You've told me you . . . you . . . ." But Rio's memory is not giving her what she wants. She's searching and not finding any moment when Jenou ever actually said she'd lost her virginity.

Jenou shakes her head and looks at Rio sideways, as if tilting her head will show her a new picture of her friend. "Everything *but* that," Jenou says. She makes a cross over her heart. "Hope to die."

Rio closes her eyes and stands swaying, tired, so tired. And more than tired, disturbed, twisted around inside. There's a rage boiling inside her again, a rage with no target, a rage she can't put into words.

Do not start crying again!

"Well, it happened," Rio says at last. "And I killed more Krauts. A lot more Krauts." Suddenly Rio drops to her knees. "I'm tired. I'm really tired, Jen."

She slumps sideways and falls instantly asleep, curled up in the sand twenty feet from passing tanks.

Jenou summons Cat and together they carry a completely unconscious Rio out of the line of traffic. They erect a shelter over her and Cat finds Jillion to borrow a piece of paper.

Rio sleeps for fourteen hours and wakes to find herself sore, stiff, and in desperate need of a latrine. And she finds Geer's Miss Lion curled up beside her.

She crawls out of the shelter and sees the note Cat has pinned to it.

Danger: Explosives! Disturb at Your Own Peril!!!

Rio tears the sign down and goes in search of chow, which is, once again, SOS.

FRANGIE MARR—GELA BEACH, SICILY

"I've got a request for a field medic," Dr. Frame says. "Some of our boys are heading up to the front. There are three qualified medics who could be seconded to a company and go up."

"I'll do it," Frangie says quickly.

Dr. Frame steps close and in a low whisper says, "You aren't my first choice, Marr. You're good, you give a damn, and you work your ass off. I'd rather keep you here."

For what feels like an embarrassingly long time, Frangie just stares at the caduceus on his collar. It is without a doubt the best compliment anyone has ever paid her. Ever. And for a terrible few seconds she feels she might start crying. And when she remains silent—not trusting herself not to start blubbering—Frame shrugs and says, "But I guess the boys at the front deserve the best care. Some of the field medics . . ." He lets that hang and shakes his head in a woeful way.

Frangie nods, the maximum she can do right then. She turns away quickly, just as a tear goes rolling down over her cheek. And an hour later—there is paperwork to be done—she presents herself to Fourth Platoon of the all-black 407th Battalion, and its new platoon sergeant, Walter Green.

"You my medic?" Green asks, and his face is all welcome and smiles. "Thank the good Lord. At least there'll be someone I know by name." He grabs her arm in a friendly sort of way and guides her to meet a white officer, a lieutenant who can hardly be twenty-two. The lieutenant is sitting on the hood of a broken-down jeep.

"Lieutenant Waterstone? This is Corporal Marr, the medic they sent us."

"A girl?" the lieutenant says with no attempt to hide a condescending smirk. He looks her up and down and adds, "A girl and a midget besides."

But from Green's posture Frangie gets the impression that this may be a bit of an act on the lieutenant's part.

"Yes, sir, she's a small one," Green says complacently.

Waterstone hops down from the jeep, and Frangie sees that he is at best three inches taller than her. In fact, the three of them standing together are practically an advertisement for *Short Folks Monthly*.

"You know what I think?" Waterstone says, chin thrust

308

out in a belligerent echo of the Mussolini posters all over Gela town. "I think short people got something to prove, so they tend to be a bit tougher than your tall, lanky folk like Private Jellicoe, here."

Private Rufus "Jelly" Jellicoe is the lieutenant's runner, no more than nineteen, six foot three inches tall and most of that in his legs. He grins at Frangie and gives her the inevitable up-and-down, followed by an even wider smile.

"All right, Jelly, show her what we have by way of medical supplies. Marr, we're moving out in three hours. We're supposed to start some trouble on the flank of a Kraut tank column, so you make sure you got what you need. Jelly will give you a hand."

The march to the front is hot and dusty and, worst of all, passes by a melon field where previous units have left nothing but rinds now black with flies. The grumbling has that combination of profane bitterness and wry resignation common to all GIs, with some extra remarks about "crackers" and "rednecks" who don't even leave a single damn melon behind, the greedy sons of bitches.

They are to help capture a stretch of road, but by the time they are in position word comes that the Germans have withdrawn. And now, from his lofty perch, General Patton has given orders for a quick march over the hills to Palermo, the largest city in Sicily, and from there to Messina along the northern coast. There are rumors of tension between the American commander and the British commander, Montgomery, rumors that delight the gossip-starved GIs. The word quickly comes down that this race to Palermo is very much about sticking one to the Brits for taking over some road the Americans were to use. And while there is some grumbling about that, there's also a keen competitiveness with the condescending British. They've all been expecting to fight Germans, and now it seems they are to be part of a footrace.

This sounds just fine to Frangie, who has very little to do unless there's a fight, and the soldiers seem to embrace the idea as a sort of lark. The main hope in the short run is that they can capture an intact melon field, or better yet some hidden store of Sicilian wine. At the very least they hope to spend the night in some comfortable villa like the ones the senior officers seize for their headquarters. And then, if they reach Palermo, the reasoning goes, surely there will be wine and women, and Messina can take care of itself.

A column of trucks picks them up—a wonderfully welcome luxury—and drives them back the way they've come, then west toward a spot north of Agrigento, where they join a column that stretches all the way back to the beach. Tens of thousands of GIs, hundreds of tanks, hundreds of trucks, all watched over by newly arrived American P-38 fighter planes zooming overhead.

The plan of advance is to move at top speed—never better than fifteen miles an hour and usually much slower—up the road until they run into opposition. The column is shelled from time to time, and when this happens they all dive off the trucks and into a ditch—if one is available—or simply into what is mostly empty, hilly grassland. When the shelling is done, the column starts off again, no recovery time, no licking of wounds, just push the burning vehicles aside and *go, go, go!*

By the time evening rolls around they are well into the hills, far from the beach, and moderately far from Agrigento. Sergeant Green's platoon—Frangie's platoon too, she corrects herself—is sent down a side road to a tiny village that will command a view of the main column when the sun comes up the next morning. Nothing has been heard from the village, but the officers do not like its position athwart their line of march.

But the journey is all by truck, so to Frangie it's all pretty much the same. On the ride she tries to get to know the men in her truck, and they are all men with just one woman GI aside from Frangie. The squad sergeant is Peter A. Lipton, known by everyone as Pal. He's a fidgety man in his late twenties, old to be wearing buck sergeant's stripes, and his face forms a permanent scowl. The lone woman, Annette Johnson, is the corporal, a seemingly emotionless woman and almost as burly as Cat Preeling.

Neither Lipton nor Johnson has any interest in Frangie—she's "the new guy," frequently abbreviated to FNG, as in Fugging New Guy, or less frequently, Bambi, after the Disney cartoon movie (which Frangie has not seen).

But she strikes up an easy conversation with a fellow Oklahoman named Andy Hinkley. Private Hinkley is from Broken Bow, Oklahoma, a small town near the Arkansas border, which he cheerfully describes as "six Nigra families being eyeballed by a thousand crackers, half of which own sheets with eye holes."

Frangie has never been to Broken Bow, and Hinkley has never been to Tulsa, but they are two Sooners in a truckload weighted heavily toward Tennessee boys.

"Is it true ya'll ride buffaloes and shoot Injuns?" one of the Memphis boys asks, looking to start any kind of trouble, anything to beat the boredom.

"Injuns were mostly run off back when," Hinkley says, not interested in arguing but certainly ready to go jab for jab. "My grandpap was shot by an Injun arrow. Right in the neck. Would have killed a Memphis boy, sure, soft living and all, but being a tough old Okie, my grandpap just pulled it out and threw it right back so hard it pierced the Injun chief right through the eye. Went straight on through and killed the medicine man too."

Frangie laughs, a sound that brings smiles to more than one face. She has a great laugh; a whole body laugh that doubles her over.

"Which eye was that?" Memphis demands.

"Why, it was his left eye. Grandpap had already cut out his other one with a bowie knife, which—"

"Here we go." Memphis rolls his eyes.

"A bowie knife, I say, which Grandpap took off Jim Bowie himself in a card game in Baton Rouge."

The tale of Hinkley's grandfather, elaborated on in a free-form saga that makes little allowance for time and space, what with Grandpap also having been taught to handle a sword by the Marquis de Lafayette, learning to speak Comanche from Pocahontas (by whom he had three natural children), and surviving the Battle of Little Big Horn by passing himself off as a lunatic.

It all reminds Frangie of riding on a hay wagon at a church social when she was just seven. Then she had teased her big brother, Harder, who even as a young teen was a skeptical soul and willing to voice doubts about God and even President Roosevelt, so long as someone could be found to argue with him.

"Your grandpap gets around," Frangie says to Hinkley when he finally runs out of steam, somewhere in the Chinese opium wars.

"Well, we're a rambling bunch, us Hinkleys. Look at me. Here I am in Sicily."

"Well, I guess that proves it," Frangie says.

"Can't argue with facts," Hinkley says solemnly.

Ahead is the first village they've come across, maybe

six or seven miles off the main road. It's like many Sicilian villages, built on a hill, approached by a steep, serpentine road that leaves them exposed to possible fire from above.

A squad is dismounted and sent ahead on foot in a cautious reconnaissance. Frangie watches their progress until they round a corner and disappear from view.

A rush of rag-clad children appears and surrounds the trucks, begging and staring. One little boy wants to touch one of them and Frangie obliges by shaking his hand. The boy grips her hand and with his other hand touches the black skin of her arm, rubs it like he's trying to get the color to come off.

An ancient man, gnarled, his spine twisted, armed with a well-used walking stick, hobbles to Lieutenant Waterstone, standing beside his jeep. There follows a conversation of sorts, in hand gestures and frustrated looks. Some of the urchins go over to offer more hand gestures, but at least one of the girls can read a map and points with great certainty to the map, then up at the road, then back at the map.

Sergeants Green and Lipton are summoned forward, and they confer with the lieutenant and with various gesturing, nodding Sicilians who have grown into a small crowd. Moments later Frangie's squad and another are summarily tossed off their comfortable trucks and made to march steeply uphill into the town.

"Locals say there's a couple 88s right in the town square up ahead," Sergeant Green explains as three dozen GIs surround him. "We're going ahead. Now listen. The locals are behaving themselves, so you all watch who you're shooting and don't shoot unless you see a Kraut or Eye-tie uniform."

They form a column in two sections, one walking ahead, one hanging back a few hundred yards. Frangie is with this second group. They enter the town proper, walking along streets so narrow and overhung with balconies that the trucks would never have made it. Here, too, children walk along, importuning in singsong voices, at first charming and then irritating the GIs. After a quarter mile, though, the urchins fall away and a tingle climbs Frangie's spine. The streets are empty but for a single old woman in black carrying a net bag containing wine, a ripe pepper, and two onions.

From within the homes close on either side, Frangie hears the sounds of laughter and argument, the clatter of pots and pans, and she smells wonderful, exotic smells, garlic and basil and frying fish. But the shutters have been closed up, and aside from an occasional eye peeking through a slat, there is not a Sicilian to be seen.

No one has to tell the GIs to be alert, the air practically vibrates with menace. They near what has been described to them as the town center. Lieutenant Waterstone consults his map again, and sends half his force, including Pal Lipton's squad, down an alley, intending to flank what they believe is the German position.

Silence but for the sound of boots on cobblestones. Every rifle at the ready. Eyes searching, searching every doorway, balcony, window, and roofline.

A sudden loud, braying laugh and out of a doorway steps a German soldier. He has a slice of pizza in one hand, a bottle of white wine in the other, his Schmeisser slung over his shoulder.

The German freezes. Gapes. Reaches for his weapon. Thinks better of it, turns to run, and Walter Green, late of Iowa, takes quick steps, runs, grabs, and hauls him backward, off-balance, by his uniform collar. Green has his knife. There's a blur, a pitiful yelp that becomes a gurgling sound, and a fountain of blood. The blood sprays across the cobbles and up the wall beneath a defaced picture of Mussolini.

Green bears the man's weight for a moment and lowers him almost kindly to the ground, where the rest of the German's blood fills the gaps between cobblestones, first spraying, then pulsating, then trickling.

But a second German has escaped, disappearing at a run up steep, narrow steps.

Frangie steps around the dying German, forcing herself to look down at him, trying not to step in his blood, and that's when the firing starts. There's a loud bang, and Frangie Marr suddenly sits down.

Noise everywhere, guns firing, yelling, the rush of men toward cover. Frangie feels stupid sitting, ridiculous, gotta get up, and Lipton twists and collapses. The wall behind Frangie is chewed by machine gun fire while other bullets spark as they strike the hard cobbles to go singing away.

Frangie tries to stand, but her legs aren't working quite right, and neither is her mind, which is not making sense of things, not quite figuring anything out. She knows she should try to help Lipton, who is bellowing in pain and being dragged off the middle of the street by Jelly, who trips, slips, turns to get back to his sergeant but is scared off by bullets everywhere, everywhere. It's like someone kicked over a bee's hive, zipping and buzzing. And now Frangie's crawling toward Lipton, hands slipping in the dead German's blood. *No, no, can't be, he's way back there*, but her hands are definitely red with blood.

Can't even crawl, stupid leg.

Lipton is yelling, "Get back, goddammit!"

Well, he doesn't mean her, he wouldn't blaspheme that way at her, so she crawls on, fuzzy in her mind, until she reaches him. On automatic, without a conscious plan, she yanks up his shirt and sees the brutal belly wound, blood seeping, not spurting. Nothing to do but bandage him up, and she sets about this task with rote movements,

movements that are muscle memory now, the pinching out of bits of uniform cloth, the sulfa, the careful folding of . . .

Very tired, that's what she is, very tired.

And now a bullet wound that's taken off a chunk of a man's shoulder, and then . . . and a bleeder . . . pressure . . .

A little rest.

Just a little rest.

Frangie means to lie back, but she falls and her helmet smacks the cobbles, jarring her so she tries to . . .

Can't . . . arms . . . Can't . . . um . . . Should . . .

The sky is a narrow band of royal blue, late afternoon shifting toward evening's navy blue.

Frangie closes her eyes.

23

RAINY SCHULTERMAN—POSITANO, ITALY

The Italians dine late, eight o'clock, as Rainy knows from her own study. So at eight o'clock she goes out looking for a meal and the instant she steps out on the street, she notices a man with a round, pockmarked face following her.

She is stared at a bit in the trattoria she chooses—unaccompanied women are even rarer in Italy than in the States—but as a tourist this eccentricity is passed off with a shrug by the locals who, after all, can't expect foreigners to understand anything, really. Harder to explain are the obvious bruises on her head and face, but perhaps her rumored ex-beau is the sort to slap a woman around a bit, hardly unusual.

She eats a small green salad, a dish of ravioli, an excellent piece of fish—she is unable to translate the species name—and a small dish of intensely flavored berry gelato.

This takes two hours, during which she pretends to

read a book she found in the hotel lobby, Agatha Christie's *Appointment with Death*. It is not a reassuring title.

After dinner she walks down through the town, paying particular attention to the church. Her watcher will expect that. Then she makes the steep climb back to the hotel, retrieves her key at the front desk, and returns to her room. She leaves the light on for twenty minutes, then turns it off.

Darkness.

She stands listening at the window. Water drips in the little sink. Someone in the room to her right is humming. Hooves clatter on cobblestones. The wind rises, singing through the ironwork of her balcony railing. A truck. The buzz of flies or mosquitoes, hopefully not the latter. A quick, flitting sound as a bat zooms past, banking sharply.

And far deeper, way down at the threshold of hearing, so it's more a feeling than a sound, the slow, inexorable rhythm of the sea trying with infinite patience to swallow the land.

Midnight.

Rainy sits in the dark, waiting. Waiting for every light to go out in the town below. Waiting and thinking. About her father, who, without meaning to, has basically gotten her into this fix; her mother, who Rainy imagines haranguing her postmortem after she's killed by the Gestapo, telling her in Yiddish-English-Polish that she brought this on herself; Aryeh, a million miles away on the other side of the world on God knows what hellish island.

I wish I believed in praying. I'd pray for Aryeh.

And myself.

And she thinks, too, about Halev. And, strangely, about Captain Herkemeier, an early supporter of her . . . what to call it? Job? Career? Both Halev and the captain are very smart, very perceptive men and for some reason this strikes her as funny, and in a bad impression of John Wayne's cadence she says, "That's how I like 'em, pilgrim: smart and perceptive."

The sound of her own voice is reassuring.

Two a.m. She stands at the balcony door, hidden from view but able to see out. Barely a light anywhere. No sound of traffic. The humming from next door has become snoring.

Rainy gets her bag and stuffs the silenced .22 into it, barely, with about two inches of silencer sticking out and looking like a piece of plumber's pipe. She steps all the way out on the balcony and looks down: three balconies, all dark. She goes to the bed, strips off the sheets, and carefully knots them end to end. Not long, but maybe long enough. She tugs at the knot a few times—it would be a long fall if the knot came undone.

She loops the sheets over the bottom post of the railing

and climbs over, squats down in an awkward pose. She loops the handle of her purse over her head, grabs tight to the two sheets together, and with her heart in her throat she hangs in midair, willing herself not to gasp or cry out.

Or fall.

She slides down to the balcony below, hands burning on the sheet. Silence. Either no one is home or they're sound sleepers. The drag of the purse on her neck cuts off her blood and makes her woozy.

She hauls the sheets down after her and repeats her maneuver. This time her foot kicks a chair and she half falls in panic, landing hard, freezing, listening, waiting. This balcony's door is open. She hears breathing from within.

Next balcony and there's no problem but for her hands cramping and already starting to blister. The steam burn on the back of her hand feels as if the flesh must split open at any moment. The final drop takes her down to a balcony from which she can step off onto a concrete retaining wall.

And then she is on the street below the hotel. She looks up: getting back up there will not be easy. There may be no way back.

It's not hard to find her way to the church, it's all down-hill and that intriguing dome is the tallest thing around. There's a small plaza between the church and the beach. Empty. No, wait!

She strains to hear, flattened against a wall. No, it's just wind.

Dammit, Rainy, don't panic!

Finding the entrance to the church is harder than she'd expected, but find it she does, only to discover it is locked. This is strange, shouldn't churches be open all the time for . . . well, whatever Christians did in their churches? She's momentarily disheartened.

Do priests live at their churches? Of all the things she's studied to prepare her, this question has never come up. Keeping to the shadows within shadows she follows the walls of the church until she finds a door in the building adjoining and connected to the church. It's also locked, but this lock is smaller, small enough to . . . *click!* Yes! Who knew you really could pick a lock with a bent hairpin? For a moment she savors the small victory. She is surprised—pleasantly—to discover that the lock-picking course back at the Army Intelligence school was actually useful.

Noise! Boots on cobblestones, a patrol?

She ducks inside and closes the door behind her, stands there and listens as the boots—two men, she guesses—pass by. Now she looks around. It's an entryway, an old black bike leaning against the wall, a narrow stairway leading up. Step by creaking step, she climbs, her silenced .22 in her hand and leveled.

At the top landing there are two rooms, one is a parlor

practically stuffed with books, the other is a bedroom. Both doors are open, and there's a small candle burning in a glass lantern in the parlor. She takes the lantern in one hand, her gun clamped under her chin, opens the bedroom door. Breathing. A snort and a mumbled snatch of indecipherable sleep-talk. A man asleep, a mop of iron gray hair on a small decorative pillow. A bottle of grappa beside the bed. A small glass.

She creeps up to the bed, points her gun at the man's head, and says, "Father Patrizio?"

The breathing stops, a different snort, a sudden upward lurch that smacks his forehead against the silencer and a cry of surprise and pain.

She lets him focus, collect his wits, and push his hair aside before repeating, in Italian, "Father Patrizio?"

"Yes, yes, what is it . . ." He stops, staring at the gun.

"Please don't cry out. I'll put the gun away if you promise not to cry out."

He nods. She shoves the heavy, long thing back into her bag.

"Who are you? What do you want?"

"I've been sent here to kill you."

It's an unusual introduction, but after some more confusion, they move to his parlor and he pours them each a small glass of some sweet wine. Rainy, with her usual efficiency, fills him in on the details.

"I don't really understand your religion, but if a good Catholic can't kill a priest, then surely sending someone else to do it is the same thing morally."

"I doubt you wish to discuss theology, *signorina*. Or my parishioners' sometimes strange notions of it."

He's old, maybe in his fifties, with an old, faded scar down one side of his face, deep-set eyes beneath a cliff of forehead. He's tall for an Italian, maybe six feet. He's wearing a white nightgown and should look ridiculous but does not.

"No," Rainy agrees. "What I want to do is get to Rome without having to assassinate anyone."

"It's five hours by automobile. Depending of course on how many roadblocks the Fascists have up."

"I don't seem to have a car. Just a gun," Rainy says.

"I . . . that is to say, the parish, owns a small truck. I use it to visit outlying parishioners. The sun will be up in . . ." He checks a wall clock. "Three hours. Confession starts an hour later."

"If they don't see me by eight, they'll check my room."

"That may be enough. I'll miss confession, but I'll leave a note that I was called away to see a sick parishioner."

"Just like that you're going to help me? And believe me?"

The old priest laughs for the first time, a booming sound quickly stifled. "Young lady, I'm a priest, I have been lied to more times and by more people than I could possibly count. I know, um . . . there's an American word . . . something to do with bulls."

"Bullshit?" she says in English. "Um, sorry, I shouldn't—"

"Exactly! I know bullshit when I hear it. If your story is this bullshit, then it is very good bullshit. And I don't like to comment on a woman's appearance, but you seem to be somewhat the worse for wear."

Twenty minutes later they are in a minuscule vehicle that might be called a truck, but which manages to be even smaller than Tomaso's truck. Thirty-five minutes later they are waved through their first roadblock by a sleepy guard who nods at Father Patrizio's collar, crosses himself, and accepts a quick blessing. A second roadblock is tougher. But a third, just as they enter Rome, is not even manned. The guards can be seen drinking coffee in the cold, acid light of a bar.

"I leave you here," Father Patrizio says as he pulls over on a side street. "Just ahead is Saint Peter's. If you have the opportunity, you should see it." Seeing her arch look, he laughs and adds, "Even Jews are allowed inside. I promise the floor will not open and plunge you into hell. And it is really quite spectacular."

She shakes his hand. "Thanks for the ride, Father."

"Thank you for not killing me," he says. "I will pray for you."

For some reason that starts the tears filling her eyes as she tumbles out onto the morning streets of Rome.

Rome! One of the three great Axis capitals. The second heart of darkness in Europe. She has a map, a tourist map, but Roman streets bear only a vague relationship to maps, and it takes her until 11:30 before she reaches the Swedish Embassy and gives the guard there the name of the man she is to meet.

The Salerno artillery emplacements are in her pocket. She has only to hand the paper over and then . . .

And then?

And then, she has no idea.

FRANGIE MARR—SICILY AND PORTSMOUTH, UK

Am I hurt?

She sees through one eye, but as if through a sheer lace curtain, everything fuzzy, details all blurred.

She can hear, but only the low tones, the vibrations of loud voices, the deepest notes of explosions.

Sky overhead. Blue.

Shapes moving around her. Green.

Pain comes from everywhere at once; it has no specific location, it's everywhere and everything.

Am I dying?

She knows she's moving but realizes she's not the one doing the moving. She's being carried. She's on a stretcher, a stretcher that crushes her between two rifles.

She raises her head to try and see what has happened but her head won't move and the very thought of trying it again is exhausting. Everything is exhausting.

Lord, don't let me . . .

* * *

She feels pressure on her eye, her one working eye, her left. The pressure is firm but restrained. Something wet. Something that stings.

She pries open that left eye and sees the face of the nurse, Lieutenant Tremayne. Tremayne is cleaning the blood from her eye.

Tremayne's gaze meets hers. Tremayne is saying something, and Frangie can hear it if she strains her attention, tries to focus, watches her lips move . . . move . . .

Sleep.

Awake again.

Sleep.

Awake and now she sees Dr. Frame.

"Listen, Marr, I've eased off the morphine so I can explain things to you. The pain will come back, so try and understand me." He's speaking patiently, slowly, like to a child. "You took a grenade. Friendly fire, from the look of the shrapnel. Someone must have dropped it. You have a compound fracture of the right femur. That's what will cause the most pain. You also have a perforated lung, perforated right kidney, burst right eardrum, contused right eye, and you can only count to nine on your fingers—you lost a ring finger, but on the right hand, so you can still wear a wedding ring someday."

Frangie says, "Mmm?"

"You will probably live, Marr, and if you live you may be all right."

"She'll be fine," Tremayne murmurs, not approving of the doctor's bluntness.

"She's a medic, she deserves to understand," Dr. Frame says. "You're being evacuated either back to North Africa or to England."

"Mmm. Eh?"

And suddenly, as if waking from a dream to find your body has been set afire, Frangie feels a wave of pain—a sickening, mind-spinning wave of pain—and she knows it's only the beginning.

The doctor sees her face twisting with pain. "Okay, that's enough for now, Marr. Nurse?"

Frangie does not feel the jab of the needle. She does feel the way the wave of pain slows and crashes and dribbles down to become nothing but bubbles and bubbles and . . .

She's in a bed, not a cot. There are sheets beneath her fingertips. Something strange about her hand. Something strange.

It's dark, but the dark of lights turned down low, not the dark of night. Above her a bulb burns dimly behind a glass shade protected by a wire cage.

She turns her head. Exquisite pain stabs her temples, rockets around her head, and spreads in echoes through her body. A deeper, more compelling pain rises from her leg to dwarf the headache.

She sees beds in a row with hers, how many she can't

tell. A hospital? A horn reverberates, a far-off, melancholy sound. A nautical sound. Is the slight rolling motion just her imagination? Is it a symptom?

No, she's on a ship. She's being evacuated. That simple logical deduction is immensely reassuring: her brain still works. It's confused, it's drugged, but it still *works*.

"Where?" Her first complete word. She can hear that it's an actual word, not a moan.

A man's face swims into view. Not a black face, but dark, maybe an Indian, like from India, she isn't quite . . . She refocuses. It's not a quick or automatic process, she has to think about it, to *focus*.

Yes, a dark but not African face.

"Well, hello, young miss."

"Hello." A second word.

"How are you feeling?"

"Hurts."

"Yes, I suppose it does." There is a fruitiness to his English, a musicality. "Now, listen to me. Can you hear me, love?" He covers one ear and then the next as he speaks. "Do you hear equally well through both ears?"

She shakes her head, a mistake that brings back the stabbing pain. "Right not as good."

An entire sentence!

"But you do hear through the right ear?"

"Yes but ringing."

"That should go away in time."

331

Frangie notices a bag of whole blood hanging. The nurse follows her gaze. "You have just come from surgery. You lost some blood; we are replacing it."

"Hot. I'm hot."

"You have a fever, love. There was some sepsis, which would have been arrested earlier, perhaps, had your people not wasted twenty-four hours before evacuating you."

"What?"

"There was only the field station for blacks. It took some time to find a ship willing to admit you to their sick bay. But you are now aboard a Royal Navy ship, bound for Blighty, so all's well, eh?"

"Can I have some water?"

"Not just yet, I'm afraid, your fluids will be through IV for now. But here, you can take this chip of ice."

The ice chip is a tiny bit of heaven. She savors it as it melts on her tongue.

"The surgeons were able to get most of the shrapnel out of you. Not all, but most. Your leg has been set."

He goes on for a while, but with the ice chip gone Frangie has time to focus on one very important thing that drives away all other thoughts.

I'm alive!

The voyage takes seven days. Frangie has very little awareness of passing time because now the great danger to her is the fever spreading from a tiny piece of shrapnel that ripped through her intestines. What she knows of the voyage is a drugged dream, a fantasy whirl of white-clad doctors and nurses, light and dark. Sometimes she sees only ghosts. Sometimes she is not on the ship at all, but back home with her mother and father and Obal, and Harder's there too. Sometimes all she sees is red.

There are the sounds of bells, the constant thrum of engines, rubber-soled shoes squeaking on painted steel, murmured conversation.

And the pain. And the burning.

Eyes open.

Frangie sits up. The pain in her head is still there, but it no longer stabs at her. The pain in her leg is deep and gnawing, but it no longer threatens to overwhelm her.

She looks at herself, at her torso and legs. Two legs! One on each side. That's good.

Hands? Yes. But one is bandaged and there's a gap in that bandage where her right-hand ring finger should be.

With stiff and awkward fingers she pulls aside the blanket covering her. She's dressed in loose pajamas that bulge here and there from the bandages beneath.

"Good morning, pet." It's a different nurse, a woman this time, also a brown face, but perhaps from some other part of the far-flung British Empire. The nurse whips out a thermometer, sticks it under Frangie's tongue, takes her wrist, and counts pulse beats against her watch. The nurse pulls out the thermometer and holds it for Frangie to see. "Ninety-nine point four, and that is a very good thing. The fever has broken, and we may hope it does not return."

"Can I have water?"

"Orderly? Water, please. We'll be sending you ashore soon."

Frangie gulps the water, the sweet, clean, beautiful, luscious water.

If I live a thousand years, no water will ever be sweeter.

"Where ashore? Where are we?"

"We are lying at anchor off Portsmouth. England. As soon as there's a place at the mole, we'll go in and offload you all."

"Thank you." The nurse nods and starts to move away, but Frangie grabs her hand, wincing at the pain of stiff, unused muscles. "Really. Thank you. Thank everyone."

Tears fill Frangie's eyes and now it's emotion not pain that swells through her, sadness and relief and gratitude. Emotions she can't even name. Just . . . just . . .

I'm alive.

I'm alive!

They tell me yesterday was Hitler's birthday. And here I forgot to even send him a card.

You know, it's funny, I think the folks at home have almost forgotten about old Adolf already. They showed us a newsreel and a movie earlier tonight. The movie was Meet Me in St. Louis, *which of course led various wits in the audience to yell out to Judy Garland that they'd meet her anywhere so long as it wasn't Germany.*

The newsreel was a lot of triumphant talk, pictures of long lines of German prisoners, burned-out German cities, the Stars and Stripes waving over German rubble, stirring images of Shermans and Mustangs and B-17s all heading toward Berlin.

But everyone knows it's the Russians who will take Berlin. And everyone dreads being shipped off as soon as they're well to invade Japan. Can't the Japs just quit? Don't they see we're tired of killing?

But I'm getting ahead of myself. Sicily was a bump in the road, a nasty little bump, but one that came with wine, cheese, and juice-dripping melons, so there was that at least. And although it was hot and dusty, the Eye-ties had about given up. The Krauts fought hard and well—they always do—and in the end the bickering American and British generals let the bastards escape to Italy before we could crush them like insects. The Krauts escaped North Africa, and then they escaped Sicily. They're clever at escaping, but they won't escape the Russkies.

The 119th didn't do much fighting in the latter part of Sicily, and of course the whole shooting match was over within six weeks, start to finish. Rio was made corporal and was not happy about it. Stick got three beautiful stripes and was now Sergeant Sticklin and took over the squad. Sergeant Cole got an extra stripe and took over as platoon sergeant when O'Malley broke his spine falling drunk off a bluff. The handsome Lieutenant Vanderpool became Captain Vanderpool and, much to the regret of every female (with the possible exception of Cat Preeling), was shipped off to take some advanced training.

Meanwhile there was the dull routine of garrison duty for the platoon, first in a proper town and then in a remote mountain village. With the fighting over, uniforms had to be proper, boots spit-shined, ties knotted *just so. But everyone got three hots and a cot, and it beat getting shot at.*

Mussolini, that strutting fool, was overthrown by his own people. There was a celebration—we all managed to find something alcoholic to mark the occasion. And for about a day we had the illusion that the whole thing might be over pretty quick. But the Krauts swept down through the boot, pushed aside the few Italian Resistance fighters, and effectively made Italy far more dangerous than it had been when it was only ill-equipped, half-starved, and completely despondent Italians.

Rio got her first Purple Heart.

Frangie Marr spent those weeks enduring two more operations to pull out the last bits of shrapnel. She got a Purple Heart too.

And Rainy Schulterman? After narrowly avoiding arrest by an eager patrol, she made her way to a picturesque little town outside Rome to await the invasion.

We were all awaiting the invasion, and somehow we had convinced ourselves Italy would be easy.

Easy.

I want to put my fist through a wall just thinking of it. And it is with a sense of mounting dread that I tell myself to stop stalling and get on with telling that story. We are perhaps halfway through my long tale of war and woe, but there were laughs and fun too.

Yes, there was fun sometimes. Even in Italy.

Two more lines before I reach the bottom of this sheet of paper. The letters are getting sketchy, and I'll need to change the ribbon in the typewriter.

And then, Gentle Reader, I will tell you about Italy.

Bloody, goddamned Italy.

PART III

OPERATION AVALANCHE
THE INVASION OF ITALY

RAINY SCHULTERMAN—GENAZZANO, ITALY

Rainy is dressed all in black, just another young Italian war widow walking the two miles to the nearest market, string bag at the ready to carry bread and wine and olives and maybe a small piece of fish. There is a food shortage in Italy and it is growing worse; there is no shortage of women in mourning in Italy. The older ones were still in mourning from the last war; the younger ones mourn soldiers lost in this war. Italy has much experience with mourning.

Rainy had stolen the clothing months earlier from a drying line on the outskirts of Rome, just outside the Porta Maggiore, a double arch of stone that long ago—very long ago—had formed a gate in the Aurelian walls on the eastern edge of the ancient city. It had been worth the risk taking the clothing—people didn't look at women in mourning, they were all but invisible.

She had walked out of Rome in her purloined outfit and, after two days spent walking and hiding at night in barns or sheds, she had at last collapsed, exhausted, in a weed-grown cavern cut long ago into the hillside just beneath a vertical rise precariously topped with three- and four-story apartment houses. And there she lay for three days as a fever made her teeth chatter and her body ache. Lay there without food, the only water coming from a trickle down mossy stone walls that she had to crawl to and lick. On the fourth day, as the fever began to break, while Rainy was too weak to even crawl to water, a boy and girl, brother and sister, found her.

They had summoned help, and in the end she'd been half carried, half dragged to a church and given over to the care of hard-faced but kind nuns. A day earlier and they would have found her raving in English as the fever twisted her mind into pretzels of illogic. But with clean water and bites of bread and cheese, she had managed to stick to Italian.

It wasn't Italian that would fool a local but for the fact that Italian has so many dialects and regional accents. She told the nuns she was from the Venezia area. That she had come south to visit her dead husband's commanding officer in Rome, but that he had turned her out without so much as a glass of wine or a hundred lire.

The nuns believed her, or pretended to. The nuns had fed her and bathed her and washed her filthy mourning weeds.

She had concealed her guns—the silenced .22 and the gun that had chafed her thighs so cruelly—in the cave. She had transferred her suicide pill to her stolen dress and it had, to her amazement, survived a thorough washing. And she still had money, concealed in the false bottom of the purse she had kept.

With her strength recovered, Rainy had stayed with the good sisters until the reverend mother had suggested that she should register with local authorities to avoid any problems arising.

Rainy had taken this as a sign that it was time to move on. In the night she took bread and cheese, several tins of sardines, and two bottles of wine, then she left two thousand lire—which she believed to be about twenty dollars—pinned with a note that said simply, *grazie,* and snuck away.

She retrieved her weapons and walked up into the hills outside Genazzano, looking for and eventually finding an abandoned stone house that leaned back against a thirty-foot escarpment. The back wall of the house was the cliff face, rock and dirt. She could easily see why the house had been abandoned—there was a two-foot hole in the roof where a slab of stone had fallen from the escarpment. The rock still sat there like an odd artwork in the single room. The hole in the roof at least let in sunlight, which was pleasant until the autumn rains started, and

343

then the entire room could be flooded an inch or more deep.

Not pleasant, not in the least, but better than the alternative. And surely the Allied landing would come soon.

As she walks into town, Rainy keeps her head down and avoids eye contact with other people on the street. Genazzano is a small, hilltop village of no great distinction, cobbled streets, faded apartments and homes, with few shops beyond the necessary. The limestone walls still bear the iconography of the now-deposed Mussolini—portraits, slogans, exhortations—but these had all now been defaced. Mussolini no longer ruled Italy, the German army did.

Though Rainy avoids contact or conversation her presence is of course known to the locals. Strange women with "Venetian" accents simply don't appear and take over abandoned properties in small towns and go unnoticed. But small towns have a habit of secrecy, especially when it comes to the police, and with the police now lacking all authority she feels she might be safe, at least from that direction.

Rainy enters the bakery, the *panificio*. She waits her turn behind two other women, nods to the baker's clerk, who says, "*Signora?*"

"*Pane, per favore.*"

There is only one type of bread currently available—a

foot-long, flattened dome made of equal parts wheat and sawdust—and no one is allowed to buy more than one. But the formalities must be observed, and she must state her preference as though she has a choice. Rainy takes her loaf of still-warm bread and crosses the narrow street to the *drogheria*, the grocer. It is a small, dark shop with few shelves and even fewer things to be found on those shelves. She gathers a can of sardines, a packet of dried beans, pasta, a can of tomatoes, and a single garlic bulb. She is running low on cash and is very careful to husband it, but the grocer has been keeping his customers alive on credit so he is always happy to see her and her lira notes.

Since arriving in Italy, the land of fabled foods, Rainy has lost twelve pounds between the fever, her constant hunger, and the exercise of walking to and from town, as well as her optimistic and probably doomed effort to revive a long-neglected garden. She is thin but not weak. If anything, Rainy has hardened—there are few better exercises than climbing hills.

And she has perhaps hardened in mind as well, or at least deepened. Long, long days and nights with no one to talk to, no books, newspapers, or radio have forced her to think more deeply about many things: the war, God, her family, Halev, her future.

She is contemplating college as she climbs the long slope

back to her borrowed home, shifting the net bag from hand to hand every now and again. The pistol, retrieved from the cave, is still strapped to her leg and she's quite used to it now, would feel naked without it.

Back at her temporary abode, Rainy uses the rusted knife with a broken-off tip she'd found in a drawer to cut off a hunk of bread. She slices a wedge of cheese, considers the sardines, and decides to save them for later. Instead she piles the cheese and a half dozen olives on her slab of bread, sticks an opened bottle of red wine under her arm, and goes outside to eat atop a stone wall beside the well. The weather is fine, just a bit chilly but sunny and very clear.

A bite of cheese. A bite of bread. An olive. A swig of wine.

"Life could be worse," Rainy says. She has long since stopped worrying about talking to herself, though for safety's sake she talks to herself in Italian.

"It will be worse soon," she answers herself, taking on a glum tone. "You're down to three thousand, four hundred and seventy lire." Perhaps thirty-five dollars in round numbers, and the prices are rising as the shortages worsen and as the authorities have ceased to show much actual authority against price gouging and profiteering.

Thirty-five dollars in cash is more than most people in Genazzano have, but most of them have jobs or farms, and all of them have local family and connections to help out.

If only she had some idea what was going on in the war. The local newspapers are censored and useless, good only for reading between the lines. It's clear that the Allies have taken Sicily, but beyond that, no news at all. No news and of course no letters. Her parents must think she's been captured or killed; she's never gone this long without writing to them.

Halev . . . well, he's surely found someone else by now. Not that they really even had more than a friendship. Halev owes her nothing, and she owes him nothing. But she cannot quite bring herself to dismiss Halev—friends, family, the memories of home have become vital to her survival.

She worries at times about her father and Vito the Sack. No doubt Tomaso and his father are furious that she's escaped without killing the priest, but her deal was with Vito Camporeale to deliver Cisco, and she delivered Cisco. So no one should have any beef with her father.

From the stone wall, Rainy can look out over most of a mile of road. The road twists and turns along escarpments, through woods, behind occasional homes, but for the most part she can see anything or anyone coming this direction. Twice she has seen German vehicles passing on their way west to Rome.

There's very little else to do aside from picking insects off the scraggly, never-to-ripen carrots and peppers in the garden. Her days are full of silence. Her nights are full of the small sounds that cause her to wake suddenly and check the door. She lives in fear of the sound of tires on the gravel outside, of slammed car doors and German voices.

But mostly she is bored. Somewhere the war goes on, but she is no longer in it.

Missing, presumed dead. So sorry, that girl had promise, what was her name? The little Jew with the hair like a bird's nest and the odd name. You remember. Snowy. Or was it Breezy?

A car passes by on the road below, driving fast. Ten minutes later, an oxcart moving slow. The oxcart driver stops his beast, goes to the side of the road, and unbuttons his fly, needing a pee.

Rainy looks away, and it is this bit of delicacy that almost causes her to miss the open car. But she hears the engine and looks back, then peers intently as the car slows to maneuver past the stopped cart.

Four men in the car, none in uniform. She should breathe a sigh of relief, but something is wrong, very, very wrong about that car and those four men. She can't see the spot where the car would have to turn off onto the driveway and reach the house, but instinct is screaming at her to run, so she races for the house. She grabs the rest of her bread and the bottle of wine, piles out of the side window, and runs to the shelter of the nearest trees.

The car pulls up when she is still exposed and in the open.

"Halt!" a voice shouts.

She runs, low bushes whipping her bare legs.

Voices yell in German. A shot! More yelling, angry, berating. *Alive!* she translates. *Take her alive!*

The suicide pill is in the pocket of her dress, but surely it's not . . . no, it can't be . . . She fumbles for her pistol.

She glances back. Two young men, both fit, neither hampered by women's shoes. They'll be on her in ten seconds.

The pill is in her fingers. The gun in her hand. *My God, no, it can't have come to that. It can't be . . . not now . . . not yet!*

She fires fast, without aiming, hoping to make them cautious.

And then, turning to run again, Rainy trips, throws out her hands instinctively. The suicide pill flies free, but she tracks it, sees it peeking from beneath a fallen pine twig. Rainy grabs for it, footsteps so close now, her fingers find the pill, raise it to her mouth, and she is hit from behind, a knee in the spine. Electric pain shoots through her body.

She has a split second to see the shoe that smashes into the side of her head, sending her consciousness spinning through the void, twirling, dragging her down and down. The second punch finishes the job.

Rainy lies crumpled, unconscious on the ground, her wine gurgling out onto the pine needles. Her gun beside her.

26

It is Rio Richlin's first battle briefing as a corporal, an NCO, a noncommissioned officer. Corporals aren't always included, but Stick has brought her along and Rio is very sensible of the compliment.

Sensible of the compliment . . . and resenting it. She had not asked to be made a corporal, had not wanted to be made a corporal, had argued with Cole and their new lieutenant, and had been told to shut up and do what she was told.

That part at least she understood.

In addition to the NCOs, their new lieutenant, Frank Stone, is there. No one knows much about Stone yet aside from the fact that he looks almost absurdly young, smokes like a fiend, blinks a lot, and seems to have a chip on his shoulder.

The main hold on the tank deck of the LST has the feeling of a warehouse made of steel. It is a vast oblong box stuffed full of Shermans, twenty tanks in all, plus two half-tracks and a couple of jeeps.

GIs are berthed in rectangular cells all around the outer edge of the boat. This ship has a nominal capacity of 217 men, which is nonsense—there are soldiers crammed everywhere. The upper deck is crawling with soldiers. The busy sailors have trouble at times pushing through the crowds of soldiers to reach their stations and genially curse the men and women in green as "sand fleas," "lub-bers," "clumsy bastards," and more, but never with real animus. The sailors know that soon these soldiers will be ashore . . . and they will not be.

Twenty tanks, something like 305 men, barrels of oil, ammo—the contents of this one ship could start a war all by itself, Rio thinks.

The colonel, a West Pointer, has given a little rah-rah speech and turned the briefing over to Captain Jesus "Paco" Morales, also a West Pointer, a shinily bald, broad-shouldered officer in a spotless uniform. Morales urges the two dozen noncoms to line up around a low sand table. The sand table is a lovingly sculpted diorama of the Salerno beach.

"Okay, men. And lady," Morales begins. "We have a tough one here, a real ball-buster, begging your pardon, Corporal."

Two specific references to Rio—she is the only female

present—and both times every head but Stick's swivels toward her.

Rio is aware, very aware, of being an object of great interest. The army as a whole has not changed its opinion of women soldiers. The army, to put it simply, *hates* the idea of women soldiers. This hatred is expressed in a variety of ways: from verbal harassment to crude attempts at seduction down to the more subtle means of slur and exclusion. But Rio Richlin is not just the only female NCO—a very unwilling NCO—at the briefing, she comes with a *reputation*.

So curious eyes, many but not all hostile, take in her stance, her expression, her uniform, and her *koummya*, then add in the stories that have circulated about her, including the fact that she refused to ship out after being injured. They reach various conclusions, mostly that she is some sort of freak of nature, a standout, a very odd duck, probably a man hater, likely to end up an old maid, and more on that same line.

"As you can see, we have a very long stretch of beach, almost twenty-five miles end to end. We've had a bit of luck with some intelligence giving us a notion of Herman's positions."

Herman, like *Jerry, Kraut, Heinie, the Hun, the Natsee*, and more, is a common term for the Wehrmacht, its officers, the German people, and Adolf Hitler himself.

Morales likes to mix and match his slang terms.

"We are facing a full panzer division," Captain Morales says. "Fortunately twenty-five miles of beach is a lot for a single division to defend. Unfortunately the Hun is clever and experienced. They have broken the Sixteenth Panzer Division into four mobile battle groups, roughly here, here, here, and here. And eight reinforced strong points: here, here, here, these three here, here, here." With each "here" he stabs his pointer at a place on the sand table. "They've got massed artillery on almost every high spot: here, here, here, and possibly here."

There is a discontented murmur from the NCOs, many of them experienced combat soldiers, though there are some green hands too. The experienced sergeants see nothing but problems ahead: a long beach swept by artillery, a beach that opens onto a triangular plain bordered to the north by mountains, to the south by mountains, and to the east by more mountains. The goal is the city and port of Naples, *Napoli* to the Italians, and Naples is thirty-five miles north from Salerno along a road that is in plain view of mountainside artillery almost every inch of the way.

Rio focuses all her attention on the sand table, trying to commit every detail to memory, willing it to sink deep into her brain. But she spares a glance at Stick, solemn and engaged, and hopes that any life-or-death decisions will fall on his shoulders, not hers. And just beyond him, head tilted, cold cigar in his mouth, is Sergeant Cole. There is reassurance in those two. Cole is a soldier's soldier, and Stick is close to achieving that same status.

"Damn river," Cole mutters.

"Speak up, Sergeant," Morales says, looking sharply at Cole, who is not in the least intimidated.

"Well, sir, it's that river."

The sand table shows a winding stream, the Sele River.

Morales nods. "You are correct, Sergeant, the river is a problem. It splits our battlefield and at least at the start there will be Brits on one side, us on the other. We need to close that gap pronto or the Hun will drive his tanks right down through us."

Lieutenant Stone says, "Nothing we can't handle, sir."

This bravado is to be expected—you don't get far in the army by displaying doubt, not if you're an officer—but there is an inaudible, invisible, and yet unmistakable coolness coming from the combat veterans. They are men and woman who have actually fought tanks, and they don't talk lightly about "handling" them.

Stick speaks up. "Sir, even if we take and hold the beach and the valley, isn't it mountains and rivers all the way from there to Rome?"

Lieutenant Stone aims a furious look at his most junior sergeant, but Morales nods. "Yes, it is, Sergeant. There's something Napoleon said to the effect that Italy is a boot, you have to enter it from the top. Unfortunately, that option is not open to us."

"We'll get it done," Stone says.

There is more of the same back-and-forth, practical concerns having to do with logistics, and optimistic talk of Day One objectives, Day Two, and so on. None of the combat veterans, from Cole down to Rio, believes any of it. The sand table, unlike reality, does not come complete with German 88s raining down.

Almost two weeks later, weary, footsore, and jaded, Rio is convinced of the physical accuracy of the sand table and painfully aware of the irrelevance of the timetable. She and the 119th were spared the worst of the landing, not being first wave, or even second wave, for once. The earlier arrivals ran into a wall of German artillery, machine gun fire, and air attack, but by the time the 119th joined the battle, the Germans were counterattacking.

That had been rough, but it was fighting from foxholes and prepared positions. In the end it was the massive firepower of American and British naval gunfire and planes from Sicily that hammered the German tanks and broke up their thrust.

But now the job is to expand the beachhead and begin the push north toward Naples and Rome beyond, which, for the 119th, means pacifying dozens of small villages and strongpoints held by a determined enemy rear guard.

Rio lies wedged between sharp stones that had once been someone's home or shop, with an intermittent hail of machine gun bullets chipping away at the stone like some mad sculptor. She is reminded of a saying she'd first heard from Stick: *No battle plan survives first contact with the enemy.*

Naples was the Day Three objective. They are beginning Week Three, and they are still some distance from Naples. How far, Rio does not know. What she does know is that she is facedown on the ground wishing she could dig a hole through the cobblestones beneath her.

Rio's squad landed on the beach below Salerno at full strength, twelve men and women: Stick, Rio, Jack, Jenou, Tilo, Geer, Cat, Pang, Jillion, Beebee, Sergeant Cole, and a replacement. Rio had exchanged no more than a few words with the replacement, a woman named Karen Scalzi. Scalzi had stepped on a mine on her first day ashore. She hadn't died, but she would no longer be able to count to ten on her toes.

Now they are eleven, and Cat has come down with dysentery, so half the time she is squatting behind whatever cover she can find. She should have been sent back, but she kept saying, "I'm okay, dammit, I'm fine, just don't fugging look at me!"

"No one's looking at you," Tilo had wised off. "We're just trying not to smell you."

The heat does not approach the Sicilian heat, September having brought some moderation in temperature, but for hours they've advanced at a crawl through the heap of rubble that was once a town. The town has been worked over by naval gunfire, tank fire, and P-38 and P-47 ground attack planes. It was home to not quite a thousand people, but now every roof is blown away or collapsed. Scarcely a wall stands without ending in ragged crenellations at the top, here and there splintered wooden beams stick out or up, doorways have all been kicked in, windows have all been blown out, and if any civilian is left alive it is a miracle.

The full platoon is spread down both sides of what had almost certainly been the main street of town, now a tumbled, almost impassable jumble of fallen stone, all of it painful to lie on.

A Sherman tank burns behind them, burns too fiercely for anyone even to think about extricating the dead tanker whose charcoal body lies draped across its forward deck.

Rio is on point. She hears Stick clattering through the rocks, followed by sniper fire, to drop beside her.

"What do you see, Richlin?"

Rio and Stick are side by side, faces inches apart, both sheltering behind the same chunk of lathe and plaster. Rio risks a quick pop-up glance, drops hastily, and says,

"That wall there, the building where the street turns? That high window, top floor? Machine gun. There's maybe a second one farther on, I think. And you know about the—"

Boom!

A small explosion rearranges the rubble twenty feet ahead, temporarily obscuring their view with dust. Rio and Stick crouch low and let the shards of rock pelt their backs and helmets for several seconds.

"Mortar," Rio says.

"Yeah, kinda noticed that. If the Krauts get a spotter and a radio up in that window they'll murder us," Stick says. He surveys the terrain ahead. "Can't get another tank in here."

Rio shakes her head. "Not if they've still got that 88 up around the corner."

"Okay," Stick says. "Take Stafford and Suarez and scout to the right, see if there's a way to flank 'em."

"Yep." Not the answer she wants to give, but what can she do? There are two stripes on her shoulder now.

For a moment, just a brief, very strange moment, Rio realizes that despite her self-doubt she does actually know what Stick means. She knows how to do the job, knows what risks she should take and what she should avoid. It's a strange moment, a moment out of time, a quiet, self-aware moment.

She crawls backward, not easy to do in these rocks. She makes a turn at what looks like a safe place and is nearly hit by that high-up machine gun. She decides to jump up and run, hunched over with bullets pinging and ricocheting off the rock around her.

The squad is a series of helmets barely poking up, like so many gophers who've dug their hole in the middle of a rock quarry.

"Stafford, Suarez. We're taking a walk," Rio says.

Two of the helmets begin to move and soon they are three, all prone, face-to-face, legs splayed out in different directions, hugging the ground as machine gun fire chips stone above them.

"We're going to scout down that alley to our right," Rio says.

"Won't that just be fun," Jack mutters under his breath.

They set off at a crawl until they are out of the direct line of fire, and then it's the familiar stooped run, take cover, stooped run, take cover, till they are well within the alley. The alley is so narrow Rio can touch both walls without stretching. At least here they are safe for a moment. Tilo lights a cigarette.

"Give me a puff," Rio says, and takes the cigarette from Tilo. She draws the smoke in. She doesn't smoke, not really, she tells herself, just the occasional puff. But she no longer chokes and coughs from the smoke. She started up after the mission to rescue Strand, and while she does not carry her own pack of smokes, she is beginning to irritate people with her cadging of a puff here, a complete cigarette there.

They creep down the alley, which opens onto a narrow street. This street seems less damaged—it's still possible to see patches of cobblestone not covered by rubble. But they proceed cautiously since they cannot see beyond a curve ahead. But then they happen on an extraordinary sight, a surreal sight: there are dozens of big, white and tan loaves of Italian bread, and many more fragments of bread outside a burned-out bakery. It's like a snowstorm of bread crumbs. A solitary crow has found this bounty and casts a jaundiced eye at the advancing GIs, following it up with a harsh warning croak.

"Someone blew up the bakery," Tilo says. "If we find a cheese shop and a wine store, we're set for the duration." He stuffs a fat, crusty loaf in his shirt. The heel sticks up under his chin.

The alleyway being only moderately filled with rubble, they advance, Rio hugging the left side, Jack and Tilo on the right. They measure each step, one foot in front of the other, heel to toe, heel to toe, rifles at waist height, training side to side, eyes scanning ahead, up, right, left.

"I'll be damned," Tilo says. "There's my bottle."

Rio hears him.

Rio says nothing. She is focused on a sound from ahead, maybe a rat, maybe a civilian, maybe . . .

Suarez grabs the bottle, which is sitting quite undisturbed on a dusty table outside what must be a bar.

Bang!

To ears accustomed to everything from tank fire to 88s to the massive explosions of naval gunfire, it sounds slight. Slight but terribly close and intimate.

Rio slams her body against the wall and yells, "Stafford, Suarez, down!"

"Shit!" Jack yells.

Rio spins to look and sees Jack rushing to Tilo, who sits on the ground. His face is black with soot. His uniform is smoking. His right arm hangs twisted all the way around, like he's trying to reach the far side of his lower back. Blood gushes from the chewed meat of his shoulder.

Rio rushes to him, but *bam-bam-bam!* a German rifle drives her back.

Tilo says, "I think I'm all right."

Rio on her belly now, Jack on his, both pressed against their respective walls, bullets everywhere, and Tilo stares blankly ahead. He looks baffled and amused, as though something unexpected but entertaining has occurred.

The firing stops.

Rio glances frantically around, looking for a way to get to Tilo, maybe to grab and drag him to cover. But there is no cover, not close enough.

A single bullet hits Tilo's half-severed arm, knocking it free of the arteries and tendons holding it. The arm lies on the cobbles, seeming to point at Rio.

Seconds tick.

"What do we do?" Jack calls to her in an anguished voice.

A second, carefully aimed bullet hits Tilo in the chest. There is the cleaver sound of steel on flesh and paradoxically it knocks Tilo forward so he sits bent over as if examining his shoes or doing a sit-up back at Camp Maron.

A pause. The sniper is waiting for the pressure to mount, hoping a new target will present itself.

"Stay put," Rio tells Jack. If she can just time it perfectly, grab Tilo's shoulders, haul him back over the cobbles to the door opening . . . She calculates the time. No way it's less than seven or eight seconds, more likely ten or fifteen.

Suicide.

Jack drops back down the street, back to where he can cross without being shot, and sidles up to Rio's side.

"No way," he says, panting.

The sniper fires a third time. And a fourth. Tilo falls backward now. The loaf of bread in his shirt is soggy with blood.

"You fugging Kraut asshole, he's already dead!" Rio cries.

The unseen German sniper shoots Tilo a few more times, maybe hoping to goad them. And Rio is ready to be goaded, panting and sobbing in frustration and rage, but feeling Jack's arm on her shoulder, hearing his voice, "He's dead, Rio, he's dead. We can't help him."

"I'll kill that Kraut bastard," Rio says. The threat is hollow, and she knows it. They may well get the sniper, but Tilo will still be dead.

"We have to go back and warn Stick that Jerry's booby-trapped the place."

"Goddammit, Suarez," Rio says, half like she's yelling at him, half like she's mourning. But she turns away into the shelter of the alley and in a few minutes finds Stick and the squad, much where she left them.

"Where's Suarez?"

"Stayed behind," Rio says with a quick, furious wipe of her eyes. "Booby trap and then a sniper."

"Suarez bought the farm?" Geer asks, an almost tender note in his usually abrasive voice. He reaches to the cat—no longer a kitten—that rides inside his shirt.

"We have to get out of here," Jillion says in a trembly voice. Like all of them, her face is covered in dirt, grease, sweat, and plaster dust. It makes the terror in her wide eyes even more insistent. "We gotta go back and tell Sergeant Cole we can't get through."

She's not wrong.

Jesus Christ, I lost Suarez!

Stick says, "We pull back, that Kraut up there'll see it and have an MG sitting down on this very rock, and we'll have to pay twice for the same rubble. No, we are not pulling back, to hell with pulling back, we're finding a way through!"

If only I'd seen Suarez reach for that bottle.

Should have. Could have.

Didn't.

It's a sickening, grinding thing inside her, a weight, like she's swallowed a cannonball. She feels a poison spread through her body, a sapping weariness. It will swallow her up if she lets it. It will grow and consume her, she knows that, and she fights it down, fights it down like a seasick person straining not to puke.

He's dead, he's dead, he's dead, and he's lying there chewed up like a . . .

Tilo Suarez has joined Kerwin Cassel in whatever place dead soldiers go to. Maybe heaven. Maybe hell. Maybe oblivion. Tilo would have wanted none of those choices. Tilo would only have wanted to go home.

He's dead, just like Cassel, but with one terrible difference: she was leading the patrol.

Tilo's death is on her.

27

Jenou says, "What about we make our own path?"

"What?" Rio snaps at her. It's getting harder to ignore a growing distance between them, a cordial, polite, but definite distance.

No time to worry about that, there is a war on.

I lost Suarez.

Jenou's eyes flare and she almost turns sullen, but she shakes her head and says, "Listen, maybe this is stupid, but instead of crawling down the street in the open, why don't we go through the walls between all these buildings?"

"Because they're walls?" Cat says.

"We blow a hole in 'em with grenades," Jenou says. "Look at the angle: Krauts can't see through walls, right? All these buildings have connecting walls, so we can push *through* them while still being covered by the exterior walls facing the street."

"Huh," Stick says thoughtfully.

Rio, already regretting snapping at Jenou, says, "Could work."

It's not Jen's fault Suarez is dead.

"Probably six, seven walls," Beebee estimates. He's holding up well aside from having dropped his rifle and almost shooting a major when the gun went off. That incident of course led to a lot of teasing but also a more general acceptance of him as part of the platoon. Any enlisted man who can make an officer leap into a chow line steam table full of bacon is an instant hero.

"Okay," Stick says. "Here's how we do it. Richlin, Castain, and Preeling—maybe you'll find a toilet, Preeling—blow out the walls. But we synchronize our watches, then every time you toss a grenade, we throw one here too, maybe the Krauts only count that as one and they don't figure out what we're doing. Get set up, send Preeling back, and let us know. Then Preeling fires two quick rounds as a signal, count twenty seconds exactly, then *bang-bang*. Got it?"

They had it.

Rio, Jenou, and Cat crawl to the nearest doorway on their right. Easier said than done, given that rubble practically chokes the doorway in question. A mortar round lands on the burning tank, turning the charcoal body to fine ash. Once inside they find a barbershop with a single swivel chair, shattered jars of pomade and perfume and hair dyes that fill the narrow room with a sweet chemical stink. The wall they need to blow up is fronted by built-in cabinetry and a long mirror.

"That's a complication," Jenou says.

They are able to stand, the three of them, now that they are no longer in the line of fire. Rio has the feeling this may be the first time in three days she's stood all the way up. Cat rushes to the back of the shop and yells back, "My God, there's toilet paper!"

"Take whatever you don't use!" Jenou says. There is a chronic shortage of toilet paper.

Rio and Jenou, side by side, stare at their reflections in the barber's mirror: two young women, uniformed, covered in dust, faces white with sweat-streaked plaster dust, helmets low on their foreheads, rifle and carbine respectively propped on hips, and in Rio's case a big knife strapped to her thigh.

Jenou sighs. "I remember when I used to be sexy."

Rio nods and sighs. "Dear Strand: this is a picture of me at work."

Cat's back in three minutes, by which time Rio and Jenou have broken the mirror with blows from their rifle butts—great fun—and have begun to yank the cabinet free of the wall.

"Okay," Rio says. "Ready, Cat?"

Cat runs back to the doorway, aims her rifle up in the air, squeezes off two shots.

Rio stares fixedly at her watch. "Cat, Jen, back to the bathroom."

"Oh, I don't think you want to go in there," Cat warns.

"Fourteen seconds," Rio says.

"Come on," Jenou says, grabs Cat by the arm and pulls her along, saying, "It's okay, Cat, we know your shit stinks."

"Not yours, though," Cat says.

"Of course not," Jenou says. "Mine couldn't."

Suarez has not yet been dead an hour and already the teasing, the mordant GI sense of humor, is back. Days of mourning for Kerwin Cassel; an hour for Suarez. In another month or two will anyone even pause to take note of a new death?

Rio has a grenade in hand. She pulls the pin. The fuse doesn't light until she releases the clip and she counts the seconds down. Nine. Eight. Seven. Six.

On five she releases the clip, hears the fuse pop, rolls the grenade against the base of the wall, and leaps to join her friends in an admittedly fragrant bathroom.

CRUMP!

Crump!

Two grenades, one right here, loud enough to make their ears ring and raise a fine dust cloud, the second one outside, separated by perhaps half a second. Will the Krauts fall for it?

The hole in the wall isn't all they'd have liked. It is not a doorway, just a hole barely big enough to crawl through. Rio points her rifle into the dark hole and fires off a whole clip, eight rounds. No response.

Rio sticks her head through the hole, calls for Jenou to hand her a flashlight, and points the beam around.

"Looks like the entrance to an apartment building," Rio reports. "Stairs and mailboxes." She squeezes through.

A tiny, wiry-haired dog stands its ground and barks furiously at her. "Hey, boy, relax. They should name you Lucky, pooch. I could have shot you."

Jenou fishes a bit of cracker from her pocket, kneels, and hands it to the dog. The dog eats it greedily and immediately starts barking again.

"Ingrate."

They repeat the process six more times. Sometimes the explosions are so closely timed they are indistinguishable. Other times there's a full second between. Rio wonders what the Kraut sniper can possibly be making of all this.

But at last they reach a looted grocer's, every shelf empty. Through the jagged glass-ringed hole where the store's front window had once been she can cautiously look out and see a doorway into the sniper's lair.

"Cat," Rio calls.

"She found another toilet," Jenou says.

"Okay, then you go back and tell Stick we've got a ten-foot gap between this spot and that door." She points.

Jenou runs off, and Cat returns looking both embarrassed and belligerent. "Hey, if I find a toilet I'm using it."

"I didn't say anything."

They wait in the dusty silence of the eerily vacant shop.

"Suarez, man," Cat says. "That's FUBAR."

"Yeah."

"He was okay. Pain in the ass and all, but . . ."

"Yeah."

Jenou comes climbing laboriously back through the various grenade holes. Stick and Jack are with her. As the five of them contemplate their objective, Rio says, "I got the door."

"No," Stick says.

"What do you mean, no?" Rio demands.

"You're not fighting the war by yourself, Richlin," Sergeant Sticklin says, and a part of Rio's mind marvels at the authority in his voice. He's always been a serious, mature sort of person, but he's becoming something more. It seems unimaginable that Rio would ever be able to master that sort of voice herself.

Jack says, "Yeah, Rio, let other people play. I'll go."

"Whoa," Rio says, ready to object.

Stick holds up a hand, silencing her. "When you're sergeant, you'll make the call," he says.

Rio says, "But . . ." and looks anxiously at Jack. The extremely vivid image of Tilo Suarez fills her vision. But another part of her mind takes in *When you're sergeant* and files it away for later contemplation.

Jack is already in position. "You suppose that door over there is locked?" He sounds calm, even casual.

"Nah, sniper's gotta think some of his own boys might try to get in," Cat suggests.

"Fingers crossed," Jack says. He winks at Rio. He takes a deep breath and leaps through the shattered window, four fast steps and he's at the door. He turns the lever handle and is inside in less than three seconds. Rio is right behind him, not waiting for Stick's permission.

There is no fire from above. The sniper has not seen them. Yet.

A stairwell rises to the second floor, one long flight without a landing. They creep up, Jack at the front, his M1 at his shoulder, finger on the trigger. From directly overhead they hear the German firing.

The steps end on the second floor, some kind of warehouse or storeroom. Papers and account books from the look of it—and from the fact that it hasn't been looted. It takes a few moments for them to locate an exterior iron ladder that seems to be the only way up. Up they climb, one at a time, rifles slung, in full view of their comrades below, who have their rifles ready for covering fire.

Jack reaches the top. There's a very narrow platform and a door. Jack waits until Rio is perched beside him on the precarious ledge, facing the low, wooden-slat door.

Jack makes hand motions: *you go right, I go left.* Rio nods. The door has a latch, not a handle, and Jack presses down on the piece of metal.

Locked!

A yelp from beyond the door, the sound of rapid movement. Jack says, "Grab me!" Rio grabs his shoulder, supporting his weight as he leans back far enough to fire two rounds into the door handle. The door flies inward, and Jack tumbles after it.

Bang! Bang!

Rio pushes past a crouching Jack and sees a German soldier dead, facedown across his machine gun, killed in the act of swiveling it toward them.

"See?" Jack says to Rio. "Easy."

The intensity of Rio's relief surprises her. "Nothing to it."

But then a bullet comes zinging in through the shot-up door. "It's the other one, the one who got Suarez," Rio yells. She takes a quick peek and sees that from this angle the second sniper is in line of sight behind a roof parapet a hundred yards away.

Rio fires at him but then reconsiders. The sniper almost certainly has a scoped rifle, and she is not going to win a bullet-for-bullet exchange.

"Hey, Stick!" she yells down.

His voice comes floating up. "You okay?"

"We're just swell," Rio says. "Can you send up some rifle grenades?" She looks at Jack. "You have any blanks?"

He fishes in his ammo pouch and produces three. They look like regular bullets but with the end crimped down and with no slug.

"All out of antitank grenades," Stick yells. "You want the bazooka?"

Rio looks around, considering. The space is too cramped for a bazooka—there's nowhere to vent the back end of the bazooka, and they're likely to cook themselves or at the very least start a fire. "We'll try with frags," Rio calls back.

Three grenades and an adapter come up with Jenou. The space is cramped with three of them. Rio attaches the grenade launcher. It is a steel tube about six inches long that slides over the muzzle and snaps in place like a bayonet. There are half a dozen raised rings around the launcher.

The adapter is a short, squat tube with a simple gripping spring that cradles a grenade. Rio slides a grenade into position in the adapter, sighing as she pushes it onto the fourth ring—the deeper the seating, the more power, but also the more recoil.

She crouches beside the low door, peeks at the distant sniper, and gets a stone splinter in her cheek for her pains.

"He's good," Stafford says. "You'll need covering fire."

Rio looks around, muttering, "I wish I could prop it against something. Damn recoil."

"How about him?" Jenou suggests, indicating the dead German.

They drag the dead man into place. Rio sets the butt of her rifle against his bent back.

"Okay. On three."

Jenou and Jack stand ready with their weapons. It's going to be cramped and dangerous firing through the doorway while Rio is aiming the rifle grenade.

"One. Two. Three!"

Jack and Jenou blaze away, Rio sights the rifle grenade and fires. The recoil punches the dead German hard, and the three of them twist out of the line of fire.

Two seconds of flight and *bam!*

Rio glances out, sees plaster dust and a little smoke beside the sniper's window. Close. Not close enough.

"Another," Rio says, and reloads.

The same routine, but this time the sniper is expecting it and his fire drives the three of them back behind cover before Rio can aim.

And then, a distant *pop-pop-pop*.

And a voice yelling, "He's down."

Rio looks out and sees Hansu Pang waving from the sniper's perch. Stick has taken advantage of the distraction to run up the back street and send Pang up to the roof of an apartment building and shoot the unaware sniper.

Tilo is avenged.

Maybe now we can retrieve his body.

Another day of the war. Another small, nasty firefight that would never make it to the history books. Another few hundred yards of rubble gained.

The full platoon, forty-six men and women now, after losing Suarez and the replacement, and the several wounded, spends the night in a church that must have been quite beautiful once. The roof is partly collapsed, but there are still hints of gilt and paint suggesting the ceiling was once a work of art. The cross is gone from the altar, as are the usual vestments, candlesticks, censers, and chalices. A painted plaster Madonna has lost her Baby Jesus and part of her face. Another saint stands looking up toward heaven though some joker has hung a grenade from her hand.

The pews are cots now, GIs sprawled along them. There's a campfire going on the slate floor just before the altar steps. The smell of instant coffee tugs at Rio's awareness.

"Hey, I found the wine!" a guy Rio knows only vaguely

as Skip announces, proudly waving four bottles, two in each hand.

Rio flinches, recalling Tilo's glee at seeing the bottle of wine.

"That's sacred wine, you damn heathen," says Cat.

"Not if it ain't been blessed and had words said over it," Skip retorts.

"Well, let me try a little," Cat says with a broad wink. "I can tell you whether it's holy or not. Won't take me more than half a bottle. If I don't burst into flames by then, you can safely drink a little yourself."

Rio sits with her back against a cold stone pillar, feet toward the fire, boots off, socks laid as close to the fire as they can be without catching fire. With her are Jenou, Jack, Cole, Jillion, Hansu Pang, Beebee, Geer, and two guys from other squads, one of whom is using his bayonet to open a can of hash.

Jenou raises her canteen cup. "To Suarez."

Those who have beverages raise them. The others just nod.

"I don't like him still lying over there in the street," Rio says.

Sergeant Cole gives her a sidelong look. "Graves registration will be here tomorrow. Engineers are there sweeping for booby traps now, that comes first."

"I knew it was nuts there being loaves of bread out,"

Rio says. "Wine just sitting there. I just didn't . . ."

No one says a word of comfort, no one says a word of reproach. It was not really her responsibility; they all knew about the possibility of booby traps. But it was her detail and she has left a man dead, and that fact cannot be dismissed.

"Where's Miss Lion, Geer?" Cole asks to get them all past the moment.

"Sent her back with the water truck to the quartermaster back down the hill." He sighs. "This is no place for a lady."

"No ladies here," Jenou says glumly.

Geer starts to argue, then raises his canteen cup in Jenou's direction and falls silent.

Jenou pulls her book from her backpack and turns so she can read by firelight.

"Jenou Castain, bookworm," Rio marvels.

"Well, fashion magazines are kind of sparse," Jenou says absently.

Jack says, "It's September. Back to school."

That earns a meager laugh followed by a gloomy silence, which is broken by Jillion Magraff, who offers up a bit of impromptu poetry.

> *The one-one-nine*
> *always on the line,*
> *Shootin' up the Kraut,*

Runnin' in and out,
Pissin' in our pants,
Eatin' out o' cans,
Wishin' we were home,
Feelin' all alone.
The one-one-nine,
Where life is j-u-u-u-s-t fine.

That earns some laughs and even some applause. Magraff is a useless soldier, worse than useless really, downright dangerous. But she can be amusing at times when she isn't fleeing in terror or sunk in a distracted funk drawing in her little sketch pad.

But Cat, too, has some skill with verse, and she offers hers up as a song set to the tune of "Yankee Doodle."

Yankees came to Africa,
To run away from Heinies,
Floated off to Sicily,
To run a race with Limeys.
Yankee doodles keep it up,
Yankee doodle dandies,
Mind the mortars and the mines,
And keep your shovels handy.

"Hold up there, Preeling. Who the hell are you calling a Yankee?" Geer, of course, dropping into the group, but welcome since he's brought a new bottle of the possibly sacred wine. Rio takes a long pull.

"You, you hillbilly," Cat says. "We're all Yanks as far as the Krauts are concerned."

Geer considers this for a moment. "Yeah, okay. But it doesn't set well with me. Not at all."

At which point Cat produces her second, and last, verse (so far):

> *Yankees went to Italy,*
> *To visit Mussolini,*
> *Found the bastard's run away,*
> *And left the German meanies.*

This time most people—including Geer—join in the chorus.

> *Yankee doodles keep it up,*
> *Yankee doodle dandies,*
> *Mind the mortars and the mines,*
> *And keep your shovels handy.*

Then, someone across the church, a man with a very fine voice, perhaps even a professional voice but certainly worthy of any church choir, begins a mournful Bing Crosby song.

Be careful, it's my heart.

It's not my watch you're holding, it's my heart.

That earns less appreciative whistling and more respectful applause. He didn't quite pull off Bing's lazy drawling croon, but it is well done nevertheless. The mood turns wistful and even, in some cases, thoughtful.

Rio retrieves her dry and toasty socks, puts them on and her boots as well. She never wants to be caught fumbling with laces if trouble starts, but the front line has moved past them for now and short of an air raid—or a sudden counterattack—there is no real danger on this night. Probably.

She bunches her coat up into a pillow and closes her eyes. She has acquired the combat soldier's ability to fall asleep any place, any time, within seconds. Usually. But now she lies back listening to voices, some familiar, some not.

They'll have us up again tomorrow, just you wait and see if they don't . . .

I'm going to open my own garage. I'm good with engines, don't know why I'm not in some motor pool instead of here . . .

Yeah, that's one pretty girl, Henricksen, you're a lucky guy . . .

FUBAR as usual, it's all FUBAR . . .

Tell you exactly what I'm gonna do. I got me a bass boat, fourteen-footer, gonna fill it up with tackle and beer and some boiled shrimp, see, and just drift down the bayou. And I won't even mind if I don't get a nibble . . .

If you shoot me in the foot, I'll shoot you. We'll say it was just some beef over cigarettes or something . . .

Fugging Suarez, man . . .

She ain't waiting for you . . .

If the bullet's got your name on it . . .

I miss . . .

I wish . . .

Home . . .

28

FRANGIE MARR—US ARMY HOSPITAL, PORTSMOUTH, UK

"This one's a Nigra. What am I supposed to do with her?"

"Chief says coloreds go to the Sixth."

"How in hell am I getting her there, we only have . . . Never mind. Three more, that's four. That's a load."

"Yep. Get 'em an ambulance. You'll need a colored driver. Make sure you put 'colored' on all the paperwork."

Frangie hears it all as if it is a distant radio play. She is on a wheeled gurney, parked for the moment in a bustling corridor of a stuffy building with walls painted green halfway up and tan the rest of the way. She has noted the paint. She has noted the ceiling. She has noted the dim lights and the smell of alcohol swabs and ammonia.

She is a package for the moment, a bit of parcel post awaiting an address. She tells herself it's good for a medic like herself to know what it's like for the soldiers who survive and can reach a hospital. But mostly she is bored. Bored and worried and depressed.

She had lain offshore on the British ship for three days before being off-loaded and sent on her various bewildering journeys through converted warehouses, on and off trucks, in and out of ambulances, fed haphazardly, treated with minimal kindness and no personal attention, seldom addressed and never by name.

She was an object to be handled, shunted here and there, always accumulating more carbon copies on her chart.

Depression has taken hold. It feels now as if her brain is a dull, heavy thing made of iron. She seems to have to consciously think about breathing, not because of her injuries—though deep breaths do hurt—but simply because breathing seems a pointless chore. She starts letters she does not finish. She has just enough—barely enough—energy and focus to thumb through a handful of magazines she's lifted and concealed beneath her sheet, some English, some American, all months out of date.

One picture in a three-month-old *Life* magazine holds her for several minutes. It's an advertisement of sorts for International Harvester. It's one of many war-themed ads, this one showing a color sketch of an army field unit, men in the foreground working to repair a tank. It catches her eye because the tank is strangely tilted on the edge of a crater in a way that reminds her of the tank she crawled under. There are a dozen or more men, many shirtless, all wearing obsolete World War I helmets.

All white, all men, she notices. International Harvester does not seem to think their tractors are ever used by coloreds or women, though Frangie has seen both.

Frangie idly thumbs all the way through the magazine. There is a shockingly revealing photo of actress Burnu Acquanetta, nude behind carefully positioned venetian blinds. She is called the "Venezuelan Volcano," though every black person who follows Hollywood knows she is just a colored girl with some Indian mixed in. *Life* magazine would never have allowed a similarly risqué picture of a white woman. Frangie feels a little . . . immoral . . . just looking at the picture.

The magazine also has photos of a union hall, workers awaiting defense jobs. Here there are women, but no black faces. Then, there's an article and photos of farmworkers. All white. Defense workers. All white. Soldiers and sailors and airmen, and all are white. Here and there stands a woman soldier, never photographed, usually drawn as voluptuous and made up in a way that in Frangie's experience the real female soldiers are very definitely not, lipstick being of little use on a face that hasn't been washed in a week.

There's a feature article on eight couples where the husband is off at war. In all eight pictures both man and woman grin like idiots, like they're looking forward to it all. *My, won't war be fun!* And all are white.

In the entire magazine, of hundreds of drawings and photos, thousands of faces, three are black: the seminude actress, a reporter for a black newspaper shown taking notes, and an illustration with a slave in the background.

Not until she turns to a women's magazine—*Woman's Weekly*—does she see anything about women at war. But the article is mostly nonsense while the drawn illustrations are absurd: women in tight-fitting uniforms, top buttons open, hair out of a shampoo ad, lips luscious and red, carbines cocked at improbable angles.

"Not sure which is worse," Frangie mutters.

After a full day of being shuttled this way and that while reading the magazines cover to cover and then back again, Frangie lands at last in a makeshift hospital in the countryside north of Portsmouth. It is a former Home Guard camp, two dozen long, narrow, hastily constructed huts, three of which have been designated with stenciled signs as a "Colored Ward."

She is still weak and weighed down by feelings of sadness, which she knows from her training are common in injured soldiers. But knowing her depression is common does nothing to lessen it.

"Marr, Francine, Corporal," a chubby black nurse reads from Frangie's chart.

Frangie nods, not bothering to explain that she's usually called Frangie.

"Well, Francine, it seems you're going to live and walk and eat solid food. You're slated for a nice long rest and rehabilitation."

"They're not sending me home?"

The nurse shrugs and smiles. "Believe it or not, the generals and such never do ask me my opinion on who should go home."

Frangie nods.

"Got the blues?"

Frangie shrugs. But now the nurse is frowning. "Marr. Marr. That's an unusual last name. I have the feeling in the back of my head that I heard it somewhere before."

"Maybe so," Frangie says flatly. Then, with an effort, "What's your name, Nurse?"

"Carmela DeVille." The nurse waits, expecting a smile, then, slightly crestfallen, says, "That's not really my name. I do like the sound of it, though. I'm Joan Lewis, pleased to meet you. I'll have dinner brought round, you missed the usual dinner hour, but I will plead medical necessity! You need a good, healthy hot meal."

Frangie falls asleep minutes later—or at least into a hazy, unsettled, restless dream state—and wakes after an indeterminate amount of time to a voice that pierces right down to her sleeping subconscious.

"Jesus H. Christ. I don't believe it."

A male voice, a confident but concerned voice. A voice that sounds . . .

She opens her eyes and looks up at the face of her brother, Harder Marr. He is holding a metal tray piled high with creamed chipped beef, mashed potatoes, corn, and a biscuit.

She stares at him with the suspicion of a person just awakened from a dream and still not sure whether they are seeing reality.

"Harder?"

"You are no more surprised than I," he says. Then he grins tentatively. "Say, are you allowed to talk to me?"

"I don't see Daddy here, do you?" She holds out her arms. He sets the tray down on her legs and hugs her.

Then he lifts her medical chart, lets out a low whistle, and says, "You must be tougher than you look, Knee-high."

"Knee-high? No one's called me that since . . . you know, since you left."

"Left? Who left? I was kicked out." He says it without obvious rancor, more in amusement.

"What are you doing here, Harder?"

He shrugs. "The draft board caught up to me. So here I am, like most Negroes, working as an orderly. Private Harder Marr: cleaner of bedpans and deliverer of trays.

I put it in one end, take it from the other. Though I do wash my hands in between."

Frangie grins. "My goodness it's swell to see you, Brother."

"It's good to see you too, Sis."

It is said by both with emotion verging on tears. Years have passed since Harder's politics caused him to be disowned by their father. Harder is older, more serious-looking now, worn perhaps, tired but not defeated. He is the tallest person in the family, nearly six feet, and the lightest-skinned with features that seemed to be an uneasy cross between white and black, but Frangie knows there's hardly a colored family that doesn't have some white blood somewhere in their past.

"Well, the head nurse will skin me if I dawdle," Harder says with a roll of his eyes. "But I'm off shift in a couple of hours. I've found a place out of doors that's not too unpleasant, if you're up for a ride in a wheelchair."

"You have no idea what I'd give to see the sky," Frangie says.

She sleeps after that, is awakened to be jabbed with a needle, sleeps, wakes again to be poked at by a doctor who communicates solely, it seems, in grunts. But the tenor of the grunts is satisfied. It seems her fever has left her weak and exhausted, but her wounds are all healing satisfactorily. The cast on her leg makes the flesh beneath it itch like mad at times, but that will come off in a few weeks, most likely. In the meantime she is to relax.

As evening comes on, Harder comes to fetch her. He has a thermos of coffee, a pair of sandwiches wrapped in a British newspaper, and a piece of venetian blind slat wrapped in gauze and tape.

"What's that for?" she asks.

"There are one or two things we lowly orderlies know that you medics don't," he says. Then he demonstrates the ease with which his segment of wrapped blind can be slid down inside her plaster cast, providing a gentle but outstandingly effective scratching tool.

"My goodness, Harder, they should give you a medal for inventing that!" She unconsciously adjusts her vocabulary, which has begun to slip perilously close to the common soldier's dialect. A certain four-letter word for sexual procreation is often used as verb, noun, adjective, and adverb (often modifying itself). So she consciously reaches for safe expressions, expressions an untainted Frangie would use. *Goodness. My, my. You don't say. Well, I never.*

Harder pushes her wheelchair along the ward, past cot after cot filled with colored soldiers. It's a cheerful enough ward since most of the soldiers are past the point of danger and only waiting for bones to knit together, skin to close, dysentery and malaria to calm and recede.

Virtually everyone here will be back with their units within a few weeks.

The air outside comes as a welcome surprise, a face slap of damp chill. Harder has brought a blanket, which he tucks efficiently around his sister. Evening is coming on, with mist blurring but also magnifying the stars, so they seem to twinkle with unusual brilliance. They push down the central line of mud road along a sort of board-walk that runs past identical long huts.

It is all much more peaceful than Frangie is used to. An ambulance rumbles by, but there are no tanks or half-tracks, no antiaircraft batteries being hastily shifted, no jeeps loaded with self-important officers.

It is far from a garden spot, being a vast field of mud barely punctuated by the few surviving patches of green turf. But beyond the camp there is the forest, and beneath the line of trees are three fires burning, campfires, each sil-houetting men and women standing, hobbling, or rolling. As they get closer, with Harder struggling to push the nar-row wheelchair wheels through mud and over ruts, Frangie sees that one of the fires has a distinctly darker-skinned complement and, to her delight, she hears a guitar.

"That's Willie playing," Harder says. "He's an orderly too. If Bertha May is off duty, you'll likely hear her sing-ing. Beautiful voice. Like an angel."

There is something in his tone that makes her turn to

look back at him. She sees a wistful half smile, eyes gazing into some imaginary vision.

"Bertha May, huh?" she prompts. "I suppose she's some ancient nurse . . ."

"Bertha May? Ancient? Not at all," he protests. "Quite the contrary, she's the most lovely . . ." He stops. "Oh, I see your game. Oh, you have grown tricky in my absence, Knee-high. But you're wrong, there is no romance going on here." This is said with a degree of conviction tinged with bitterness, a bitterness confirmed when he adds in a low mutter he must think she can't hear, "More's the pity."

Around the campfire are a dozen men and women, more or less equally split. Harder is greeted with waves or shouted greetings. It's clear he is liked, and Frangie finds this immensely gratifying. She's had no choice but to guess what Harder's life has been like these past years of separation, and her imagination had led her to dark assumptions. That he is respected and liked, here at least, relieves her mind.

Willie is a picker, not a strummer, with each note crystal clear, mournful, but with an edge of wry humor, and he accompanies himself in a tenor that seems at odds with his rotund and ancient (by army standards) form.

A good mornin' little schoolgirl
Can I go home with you?

Harder checks that the blanket is keeping Frangie warm, and despite her protests that she is fine, perfectly fine, he pushes her so close to the fire she expects within a very short time to actually burst into flame.

They share a cup of coffee and politely refuse the bottle of brandy being passed around.

"How is the family?" Harder asks with stiff nonchalance.

"Well, Obal is practically grown up. If by grown up you mean that he has a paper route and is crazy determined to get every one of his customers a nice, dry paper perfectly deposited on their stoop."

Harder grins. "Obal *working*?"

"You would not credit the seriousness in his letters."

"And Mother?"

"She's fine. Worried like any mother, I suppose. She's still sewing a little, but she has a second job packing parachutes. And you know Father was hurt, I suppose?"

Harder shrugs. "I'm not much concerned with him."

"Well, be that as it may, he has a new job dispatching taxis, and now he's doing something at the defense plant as well, I don't quite understand what it is. But it seems everyone is quite prosperous."

She makes no effort to conceal her own wry bitterness. She volunteered for service to help her family with expenses; now her sacrifice is unnecessary, while she is stuck in the war, like it or not.

"I was amazed they let any Negro carry a gun," Harder says. "There was a lot of pressure from the NAACP and Eleanor Roosevelt and various other do-gooders."

"You don't approve?"

He shrugs again. "As a way to demonstrate that Negroes are not cowards or fools, it's a good thing. But I'm not sure the fellows who get a leg blown off are grateful."

"I suppose not."

"And for what?" Harder asks rhetorically. "Everyone knows the Italian campaign is a sideshow. The real fighting is on the Eastern Front. Soviet comrades are dying by the tens of thousands fighting the Fascists in the most inhuman conditions."

At the word *comrades* Frangie glances around nervously.

"No need to worry," Harder says, dripping sarcasm. "The capitalists have decided they quite like Communists . . . so long as they're dying. But never fear, as soon as the war is won our capitalist overlords will turn against them again. Probably start a whole new war."

Frangie winces, wishing she had managed to avoid anything political, but Harder barrels ahead.

"This war is not at all what most folks think. The real war is between the Fascists and the Communists, with the capitalists doing the absolute minimum. The capitalists want to see the Fascists destroyed because they threaten British colonies. The Nazis want to replace the colonial order with an even greater evil, so we fight them. But make no mistake, America is being used to defend the evils of colonialism and imperialism. And the only ones truly standing for the rights of working men and women are the Communists and Comrade Stalin."

Frangie doubts this is quite true, but there has never been much point in arguing politics with her brilliant, verbose, and rather strident brother.

"Our people, Negroes, colored folk, we're being tricked into believing that we can change things by serving in the capitalist army. But back home, white defense workers are striking to stop colored folk getting paid equal. They're using the tools of unionism to deny us our rights, which is an unholy perversion of . . ."

It goes on like this for a while, and Frangie tunes out the words, maintaining an attentive expression even as her memory drifts back to the day when a thirteen-year-old Harder had ambushed her with water balloons.

". . . and has Jim Crow changed? Not a bit. Just last week a fellow in Louisiana was lynched, strung up by night riders in front of his children by the light of a burning cross."

Frangie wonders if she should break into his peroration on the topics of race and class and the exploitation of workers, but she knows she can't hold her own in any sort of political discussion. What she feels is that his fervor burns too hot to last. And she worries that his outspokenness will land him in trouble sooner or later.

". . . since the days of the Greenwood riot. It's the same as ever—"

"Have you learned anything about those days?" she breaks in, seeing an opportunity to get away from radical politics.

"About Greenwood?" He frowns and seems to be looking in her eyes for the answer to a question. "What do you know of it?"

"Only what everyone knows, I suppose," Frangie says.

"Mother hasn't ever . . ." He lets it hang.

Frangie has a squirming feeling of discomfort. "She doesn't talk to me about it. I know she was there at the time, and Daddy was up in Chicago visiting his sister."

Harder has stood all through his long, fervent political survey, but now he sits on a moss-coated log so he's at eye level with her. "Haven't you ever wondered about it?"

"I've wondered, but . . . she's always seemed like she didn't want to talk about it."

"I'm not surprised. She had a very bad time of it. She won't talk, but others have, down through the years. I fought many a schoolyard skirmish because of it."

"But . . . but because of what?"

"My God, you really don't know."

"I don't . . . I don't even know what you're talking about."

His face is serious now, grim even. His gaze meets hers

and won't release her, and the back of her neck tingles.

"Have you never wondered why I look like this?" he asks, almost pleading.

"Look like what?"

"My skin. My nose. My hair. My eyes."

She stares at him, and the tingling spreads from the nape of her neck down over her shoulders and up her cheeks.

"Good lord, little Frangie, my sweet sister. Do I look like Father? Do I look even a little bit like Father?"

Frangie's head is moving slowly, side to side in negation, in denial, in a preemptive, protective reaction to what she senses coming. She doesn't want what's coming. She begins moving to the music, trying to focus on the Robert Johnson song Willie is now playing.

Woke this mornin' feelin' round for my shoes,
But you know by that, I got these old walkin' blues.

But Harder has never been one to read subtle cues. His voice is relentless, cold, determined to tell it all. "They caught hold of Mother. She was newly married, just seventeen at the time, and they caught hold of her as she was fetching groceries."

"What do you . . ." But she can't say more, her throat is swelling shut, her heart pounding like a great bass drum keeping a funereal time. Because all at once, she knows.

"She was raped, Frangie. Many times, by many white men."

"Jesus, no."

"She was close to death for weeks."

"No, no, Jesus no, Jesus no," Frangie pleads, imploring Harder through a screen of tears.

Harder takes her hand but his expression is remote. "Did you think Father kicked me out for my politics alone? No, although he has a fool's unthinking rejection of the party. No, Knee-high, every time he looks at me he *knows*. My face is a constant reminder that I am not *his* son."

29

The slap is backhanded. The ring cuts her cheek, a new cut to join the dozens already there, some partly scabbed over, others fresh and oozing blood.

Her ankles are tied to the feet of the chair. Her hands are tied behind the chair back. Her left eye is swollen closed. Blood clogs both nostrils so she can only breathe through her mouth.

Her stolen black dress is in tatters. The collar is so saturated by both fresh and dried blood that it looks as if the fabric is rusting.

"Again, Hans." The Gestapo officer has a soft voice, an insinuating, regretful, but slightly bored voice.

Hans is a big brute in a sweat-stained uniform, which he has covered with a long, white butcher's apron. It protects his uniform from the flying sprays of blood that are an occupational hazard for Hans. He wears leather gloves to spare his knuckles, and he wears a fat gold and

399

emerald ring, a ring that looks as if it was looted from a rich dandy's home. Hans has shoved the ring down over his gloved pinkie. He's an expert at the backhanded blow that will bring the emerald into contact with flesh. But this is a less artful, more brutal blow, a punch, a clenched fist not to her face but to the side of her neck. It snaps her head sideways and sends waves of pain into her shoulder and rocketing up through her brain.

For a while she is lost, wandering on the dreamlike border between nightmare reality and eerie, unsettling visions. She has tried to focus her thoughts on a single happy moment, her date at the Stork Club with Halev. But that memory has become fragmented, so she can no longer summon long passages of happy conversation and now can only hold on to snatches, moments, and then only for a few seconds at a time.

"Let's begin again."

"My name is Rainy Schiller," she says, her voice whistling slightly through broken teeth. "Serial number—"

The slap is almost perfunctory this time. The Gestapo man has accepted that her name is Rainy Schiller. That she is from New York. That she is an American soldier. And he has memorized her serial number.

He has not accepted her lie that she is in Italy solely to meet an Italian Resistance member named Xavier Cugat. In fact, Xavier Cugat is a bandleader known for his Cuban rhythms. It's not even an Italian name, but it was the first Latinate name Rainy had come up with. She'd thought of giving them Tomaso's or Cisco's name, but that sort of cleverness could turn around and bite her.

The Gestapo agent, Heinrich Berman, remains convinced she knows more, and after weeks of interrogation, freezing cells, little food, and no sanitation, Rainy would happily tell him everything, anything . . . if she can be sure the Allies have landed in Salerno. Once the landing is secure, her secret is of no value.

If she can confess, she will be taken to the grim courtyard she can see from her cell, and like so many she has seen over the course of these terrible weeks, she will be placed against a wall, have a lit cigarette placed in her mouth, and be shot.

She is afraid to die, but death is preferable to this. Her body is one massive bruise. Her face is bruised, cut, and swollen so she is barely recognizable. She is filthy and stinks so vilely that Berman keeps the window open at all times to allow fresh air. Her dress and underthings are matted with dried vomit, piss, feces, and menstrual blood as well as the blood of beatings. She had just started her period when she was captured. It is this fact alone that saved her from being raped as a sort of Gestapo "welcome." And now she is far too vile an object for that particular indignity.

On a few occasions she has heard distant explosions and has begun to hope that it might be approaching Allied artillery, but it could just as easily be bombs. In the early days of captivity, she had applied her intelligent mind to the task of seeking escape, but her cell door is thick wood, and the bars on the tiny, dirty window are strong and firmly fixed in stone. That window is at her head level when she stands on tiptoes, and it is placed directly beneath and behind the stake where the condemned are tied. Her view is of the feet of the doomed, and the three or four black-uniformed SS riflemen beyond. Again and again she has seen the condemned dragged in, often barely able to stand. Time and again she has seen the execution squad line up, cigarette smoke rising from faces sullen with drink. Time and again she has heard the orders snapped out, seen the rifles rise, heard the crash, seen the feet splay sideways, seen a body slump. Watched blood run down like rain across the glass.

After the first beatings she knows escape is a pipe dream. She can only walk in a shuffle, and even the simplest thoughts require all her energy. Her focus drifts. Her thoughts splinter and go off in tangents before petering out in futility.

Her best future now is death: bullets are quick. She has come to envy the dying.

At first she had tried to keep their spirits up, crying out, "Be strong!" in Italian, as most of those executed now are Italian partisans. But that bravado is miles beyond her now. That Rainy is gone. That Rainy has been beaten, leaving only this filthy, despicable, weak creature.

"How did you come to be in Italy?" Berman asks in his bored voice.

"Parachute," she says, and flinches, awaiting the blow that arrives instantly.

"Who was your contact?"

Some time later she is aware of being dragged, limp as a doll, and pushed to fall against the stone wall of her cell and slide, delirious, to the floor.

Some unmeasurable time later, when she reluctantly leaves the realm of swirling nightmare and returns to her worse-than-nightmare reality, she senses a change in the air. At first she has no idea how she knows something is different. The effort to focus takes all her energy, and she drifts in and out of full consciousness. She hears a gunshot. It makes her frown. It's not right. Wrong sound. Wrong direction.

She hears a yell in Italian, *No, no, no, no. Mercy! I have a family!* The cry is cut short by a gunshot, then in quick succession, a second shot.

Cell doors are opening and not slamming shut. Too many feet in the corridor.

Slowly the truth comes to her: they're shooting prisoners in their cells.

A cell door opens, quite close by. The man in the cell

next to hers yells and curses in a language Rainy does not recognize.

Bang. And a second gunshot immediately after. *Bang.*

One in the heart, one in the head.

The key rattles in her own door.

I'm going to die.

I'm going to die right now.

Right now.

Fighting terror and pain and weakness, she rises as stiff as a very old woman.

The cell door opens.

Hans is there with a smoking Luger pistol in his hand. A second guard stands behind him, swaying drunkenly.

Rainy searches her mind for some brave final phrase and can only summon up Nathan Hale's words. Through broken teeth and swollen lips Rainy tries to say that she only regrets having but one life to give for her country, but her tongue is thick and her throat is constricted and whatever comes out it is no great, inspirational speech.

Hans steps in quickly. He places the Luger's barrel against her forehead. His blue eyes stare hard into her one open, brown eye.

He tightens his finger on the trigger, right there, inches from her face. Then he twists the gun sideways and fires.

BANG!

It's a hammer blow against her head, and she falls

straight back, hitting the stony floor like a sack of meal. Hans steps over her, straddles her, so she is looking up at his towering figure as he takes careful aim for the second shot.

BANG!

The bullet hits the stone beside her ear, sending stone chips into the side of her face.

Hans looks down at her.

She stares up at him.

"This bitch is dead," Hans says in German. Then, his lumpish face twisted into a nasty grin, he whispers, "Xavier Cugat. Funny." And he turns and walks away.

Hours pass. Rainy lies absolutely still on the floor. The cold threatens to make her shiver, but she can't show any sign of life lest some passing German see that she still lives.

She listens intently. More gunshots. Then trucks. She hears them through the window, which means they are pulling into the courtyard. There comes the tramping of feet. Snatches of conversation in German that is all urgency and bravado.

After an eternity, the trucks drive away.

She continues to lie still, slipping in and out of reality, losing all track of time. When she is lucid she listens, but all of the familiar sounds are gone now. She hears a bird. She hears distant explosions. A rat scrabbles curiously in through the open door, and in earlier times she would have leapt at it, wrung its neck, and eaten it raw. She's eaten rat before this, and beetles and moths too. But she's too weak to try to catch this rat.

Hours pass. And her voluntary stillness becomes involuntary: she doubts she can possibly stand. She knows she cannot escape even if she can stand. She is too weak, and the weakness this time feels fatal. Rainy is sure she will never move again.

Is that why Hans did not kill her? Was he leaving her to a longer, more painful death by starvation? Or is it that he appreciates the way she'd managed to make a fool of Hans's superior? Had her life been spared because a Gestapo thug liked to rhumba?

Time loses all meaning. There is no longer any line between nightmare and reality, between disconnected subconscious fantasy and awareness. So when Rainy hears strange voices, she is not excited. They cannot be real. The phrase "fugging slaughterhouse," in an indignant Bronx accent, can only be a dream.

"This one's a woman," a different voice says. "Fugging Nazi animals. It stinks like a goddamn latrine in here."

"I guess these Eye-ties are sorry now that they joined up with Hitler."

From deep within the lurching madness of her shattered mind, Rainy says, "Fug Hitler."

It's a mumble, barely a sound, but a voice says, "Hey! This one's alive!"

There is a rush of activity. She sees boots—GI boots—coming and going, and then a face comes swimming into view. A young woman with her helmet tipped back.

"Hey there, honey, I don't speak Eye-tie, but you just lie still there till we get a *medico*."

Rainy's eyes focus and from far away comes a tingle of recognition. But it fades as she spies the canteen on the young soldier's hip.

"Water," Rainy begs.

"Hey, that's English. You mean this, right?" the GI asks, pointing to her canteen. She unbuckles it, screws off the top, and dribbles a thin stream into Rainy's mouth.

Rainy swallows desperately, swallows and swallows until she coughs.

More soldiers, more voices, more blurry, shifting faces.

"Are you real?" Rainy asks in a hoarse whisper.

The soldier flashes a smile. "You do speak English."

"Are you *real*?" Rainy insists.

"As real as I can be," the soldier says. She sits on the floor cross-legged and cradles Rainy's head with her hand, lifting her just a little to take more water. "Who are you?"

Rainy has been asked the question hundreds of times, each time telling the same not-quite-true answer, the answer that would not identify her as a Jew. Now she has a hard time making herself say her name. She has endured hell for her secrets.

But the soldier, the impossible *American* soldier, leans down over her and says, "Listen to me, honey. You're safe. You're safe."

Rainy cries without tears and sobs, her body shaking with the emotion of it. The GI is patient, waving off an officer who seems to want her to move on.

At last, after so long that Rainy is certain that the soldier will leave if she doesn't speak, she quells her sobs long enough to say, "Sergeant Rainy Schulterman. US Army."

Dear Mother and Father,

A friend is writing this for me since I banged my hand a bit and the fingers are stiff.

I know you must have been very worried since it's been quite a while since I was able to write. But please don't worry, I am perfectly fine. In fact, I've run into some old friends from Africa, one of whom, Jenou Castain, is writing this down for me.

Someday I will tell you all about my adventures over these last couple of months.

No time for more right now, they have me hopping! Just know that I am all right. And that I miss you terribly and remain your loving daughter,

Rainy

Dear Mom,

I am sending this letter by way of Pastor M'Dale

because I don't want Daddy to read it. You'll know from the letter I sent addressed to you both that I am in England now, having been slightly wounded. What I did not mention in that letter is that Harder is here working as an orderly.

I don't quite know how to say what I need to say next. So I guess I'd better just blurt it out: Harder told me what happened during the riots. I understand a lot more now than I did. I understand why Daddy can't deal with Harder, even though I wish he could. And of course I understand Harder better too.

But most of all I feel I understand for the first time how hard your life has been. Mother, I am so sorry for any time I vexed you. I am so sorry for so many things. I know you forgive me, you always do, and if you would rather we never speak of this again I will honor your wishes.

But since you aren't here to shush me, I want to say something. You kept us safe from all the pain you've felt. You kept all that bottled up, and because of it I got to grow up happy. If I am a mother someday I hope to do half as well.

Please don't worry about me, I am well away from the fighting, completely healthy aside from a very itchy cast on my leg, and I doubt I will be near the fighting again. You must never worry on my account.

Harder is fine, full of all his usual passion and wild ideas. But he is liked and respected here, though he's only an orderly. He still has a way about him that draws people.

Well, that's it for now. I won't mention Harder in the letters I write to the whole family. But if you wanted to write to him you could send it to me, and I will pass it along to him.

Pray for me.

Your loving and grateful daughter,

Frangie

PS: Pray for the boys and girls I care for too; they need it more than me.

Dear Mother and Father,

Well, I'm a corporal now, and they're threatening to make me a buck sergeant eventually. It means some responsibility, which I'm not keen on. I think I like following orders rather than giving them, although you know, strictly speaking, NCOs don't give "orders," they just carry them out. So I suppose whatever happens it won't be entirely my fault.

We lost a fellow named Tilo Suarez a few weeks ago. It was very sad, and I've been going over and over in my head what could have been done, by anyone, to save him. Sergeant Cole says I have to accept it and move on. He says we have to put all our feelings in a box and only open that box at some later time. But these people are my friends now, not just fellow soldiers.

I am sorry, I am rambling on, aren't I? And I don't have time to start over or I'll miss getting this posted, and who knows when the next mail call will come.

Daddy, I remember you saying that I should find a good sergeant and stick by him. Well, I have two now, Cole and Stick. I am in good hands, and I am not worried so I hope you won't be either. I'm writing this from the shadow of a sheer and amazing mountain topped by an incredible monastery. It's all very beautiful.

Love always,
Rio

Dearest Rio,
Finally I am in a place where I can write: England! Of course I can't tell you where exactly without risking the censors marking the page up with their black marks, but I am fully recovered and reassigned to ███████.

My darling, I loved our time together in Tunis. It was magical. I won't say more here where prying eyes see everything, but I want you to know that it was no meaningless pastime for me.

I wanted to say that when we last met, but Guttierez tells me I was singing Christmas carols. I was a little out of my head, as I guess you noticed. Ha-ha.

Anyway, darling, I hope the future will see us together, you and I. I hope also that you know I will always try to do the right thing by you. I would say something more definite, but my love, I am leery of making promises when our futures are so fraught with possible difficulties.

But my love for you is undiminished. Always and forever yours,

Strand

30

"Okay, huddle up," Sergeant Cole says. He's just come from a briefing with the captain, and the expression on his face is grim in the gray, cloud-filtered light. A chilly drizzle falls, dripping down helmets to slide down ponchos, and from there to soak trouser legs and the tops of socks and inevitably boots.

Cole's cigar is lit and clouds of blue smoke billow forth from time to time, sometimes lingering beneath the brim of his helmet. They are six men and one woman: Sergeants Cole, Sticklin, Alvarez, and Coelho, and Corporals Petrash, Marder, and Richlin. Everyone but Alvarez is smoking, including Rio. All are caked in mud, the men all whiskered, and Rio is nearly as dark from smoke and dirt. Eyes peer from beneath helmet brims, white-rimmed eyes in darkened faces.

Winter has come with rain and hail and still more rain. Italy from Rio's perspective is made of jagged rock, rubble, and mud, and life is a story of cold and wet and hunger and exhaustion. Each day the proportions change but the essentials do not.

"Here's the deal. We are starting the big push on Monte Cassino."

No one is surprised, but neither is anyone happy at the prospect. For weeks after taking Naples they have fought their way closer to the massive, forbidding rock topped by the awe-inspiring monastery. Monte Cassino lies directly alongside the only usable road to Rome. From that high perch the Germans see everything, and their gunners can pick off tanks or trucks with effortless accuracy.

Monte Cassino *must* be taken.

Monte Cassino *cannot* be taken.

"There's this river up ahead that some are saying is the Volturno, and others are saying is just more of the Rapido." Cole waits, letting this sink in. Earlier a Texas outfit had tried to cross the Rapido and had come very close to being wiped out before withdrawing, having achieved none of its objectives.

"I don't much care what they call it. They say it's not very wide or deep, but it's too deep to wade across and the water is running pretty fast. And, well, you know about the Texans."

Stick spits rainwater that's run into his mouth and says, "Sarge, we've all been patrolling that stretch of river, and we can't even get a recon patrol across. The Krauts have wire everywhere and mines, they've got MGs dug in and mortars and 88s sighted in."

Cole sighs. He relights his cigar with his Zippo, and in the light of the flame he looks older, Rio thinks. Not a little older, a lot, as if he's aged twenty years. "Yeah, the brass knows all about it. But this is a broader movement—Free French are attacking as well. And we'll get arty."

"Great," someone mutters. "At least we'll have crater holes to jump into."

"Look, I'm not here to bullshit you," Cole says. "This isn't a garden party. Engineers have marked lanes through the minefields, *mostly*, so as long as no one panics maybe we can avoid those at least. But don't assume. Engineers make mistakes, and it's not unknown for Kraut patrols to move the markers."

Rio listens closely to every detail, but her heart is sinking. She knows what matters and what does not. Will the target be softened up by artillery? Yes. Will there be cover? No. How strong is the enemy? The Wehrmacht is never so weak you can relax, but intel says they're not expecting the Allies to attack.

"Unfortunately they can't get the boats anywhere near the river by truck, so we have to carry them from a drop-off."

"How far?" Coelho asks.

"About a half mile, I reckon."

"What the hell?"

"That's right," Cole says, raising his voice just a little to quiet the din of outrage. "We're carrying the boats across open country in full view of Kraut artillery, although it's dark enough and we'll have smoke. Then we put 'em in the water and cross the river." He spreads his hands. "That's my orders. No one's happy about it."

"It's fugging suicide," Sergeant Alvarez says. "You know goddamn well this is FUBAR."

"This entire goddamn campaign is FUBAR," Sergeant Coelho says. "General Mark goddamn Clark does not know what the fug he's doing. He's as big a glory hog as Patton, but only half as smart."

No one jumps in to defend the general, who is seen as more interested in reaching Rome and riding through the streets like some Roman emperor of old than in the lives of his soldiers. Cole lets the anger burn down to glowing coals before adding, "Yeah, and just so you know exactly how FUBAR this is, our flanks will be hanging in midair. Once we get across—"

There's a bitter snort.

"Once we get across, we've got a series of objectives. A series of hills—"

Rio almost smiles. Cole always pronounces it "OB-jec-tives."

417

"Better and better," Alvarez says. "Cross this flooded field in the freezing rain, through minefields, paddle across to reach barbed wire and more minefields, and then la-di-da into the hills and every goddamned inch of it under Kraut shells."

"Well, Alvy, you've explained it perfectly," Cole says dryly.

This earns bitter, cynical laughter.

Rio says, "What's the terrain like?"

"Open from here to there, farm fields, cross-country. There are some tree trunks still standing along the riverbank, but the fact is there's not six inches of real cover between here and the far bank of the river. And none on the other side either."

Rio falls in beside Stick as they slog back to their squad.

"Listen, Richlin, this is a bad deal. You know it, I know it. But we can't let on to our people."

"You don't think they'll figure it out pretty quick?"

"Sure they will. But we can't have anyone hanging back. So you and me, we put on our war faces and keep discipline."

"Whatever you say, Stick."

Rio is weary, they all are. Too many fights in too many villages; too many holes dug only to fill with rainwater; too much time spent cringing in muddy fields as artillery dropped around them; too many snipers firing from too many well-concealed positions; too many night patrols sneaking along that river in the dark with Kraut machine gunners firing at any sound; too many hikes past the bodies laid by the side of the road for graves registration.

Weary. Down to her bones.

The lunacy of the plan is instantly clear to every member of the squad, but Rio keeps a stern look on her face and refuses to join in with the loud grousing. She hasn't asked to be made corporal, she doesn't want the job, but she'll do anything for Stick, and he's asked her to back him up.

They are trucked to yet another muddy field—having to get out twice to push trucks whose wheels have sunk to the rims in the soup—where they find the boats. Boats . . . and craters.

Rio has her hands full trying to locate two boats in the roadside dump that have not already been holed by shrapnel. Jenou is with her, shining a flashlight to inspect the boats. At least a third will never float. "This isn't good, is it?"

"No," Rio says softly.

"Jesus."

"Scared?" Rio says it in what she intends to be a joking tone, as if expecting Jenou to deny it. But it comes out sounding like a challenge.

"Sure I'm scared," Jenou says. "I'm not you, Rio, all right? Is that what you want me to say? You want me to kiss your butt and tell you how brave you are? Fine. You're braver than I am, Rio. You're a better soldier. Goodie for you."

Rio stares at her. It is not the response she expected. She'd just made a little joke. They all joked about their fears, didn't they? Did Jenou actually believe Rio wasn't worried?

"We have a job to do, Private Castain."

"Well, aren't you a good little corporal?" Jenou sneers. "What the hell do you think you're proving? Is this about being as good as the men? Or is this about being better than me?"

"I'm just doing my job," Rio insists.

"Your job? I'm your friend, Rio. Remember? You and me? Jen and Rio?"

Rio kicks the side of the boat in frustration. "What do you want from me, Jenou?"

Jenou stares for a moment, meeting Rio's angry gaze before dropping her own, so she ends up looking at Rio's *koummya*. "I don't think I'm going to make it, Rio. I feel it. You know? I feel it here." She taps her chest. "If I'm going to buy it, I want to know I've got a friend who will mourn for me."

"Christ, Jen, you're not going to die," Rio says dismissively.

Jenou's belligerence is all gone, the flash of anger burned out. In a soft voice she says, "What if I do, Rio? What if you do?"

"What the hell is the point of worrying about it? I don't see Geer or Pang or Stick moping."

"No," Jenou admits. "They're all busy being men." She says that last word with a strange mix of condescension and affection. "We're not men, Rio. We don't have to be men."

Rio shakes out a cigarette and arches her body over it, shielding it so her Zippo will light. The flame lights her face, an eerie light, like something out of a Dracula movie. "Don't we?" Rio asks, exhaling smoke. "You ever think maybe it's the other way around? Maybe men are that way because they grow up expecting they might someday find themselves in some shithole getting shot at?"

Jenou draws back, confused, and Rio plows ahead, angry in her own turn now. "You think if we grew up imagining the day we'd be ass-deep in mud with our buddies getting picked off, we'd be sharing our deepest emotions? You and me, we grew up imagining our first kiss and planning our weddings. They grew up playing cowboys and Indians, playing war. So yeah, they keep their distance from each other, they don't expose themselves to . . ."

"To what?"

"Pain." The word comes through gritted teeth. She

grabs Jenou's collar and yanks her close, close enough that no one else can hear. "It tears my guts out, Jen. Cassel. Suarez. It's like a . . . it's pain, that's all. And you want me to be little Rio from Gedwell Falls and share my every thought with you? You think I don't know you could get hit? You think every goddamn patrol we go out on, every fugging little village, you think I forget it could be you next?"

Rio releases Jenou and steps back. She takes a deep drag on her cigarette, but a drop of rain has extinguished it. "We're in this now, Jen. We can't go home. We're here, and we're in this, and any moment some Kraut could . . . Grab a fugging bottle of wine . . . make the wrong step . . . and what do you want to do, have a nice chat about it? You want me to spill my guts to you and tell you I'm scared too? Want to ask me again what it was like, shooting those Eye-ties?"

Jenou says nothing, and Rio yells, "Stick! These two look okay!" Then, her energy gone for now, she says, "Jen, you don't get it. It could be you. Or it could be me. You really think the smart move is for us to get closer?"

Jenou shakes her head slowly. "Okay, Rio, have it your way. I just have one question, and I want the truth."

"Yeah?"

"What *was* it like. For you. The first time you killed a man?"

Rio is quiet for a moment, ignoring Stick who is coming over with the rest of the squad. In a barely audible voice she says, "It was . . ." She shakes her head, smiles ruefully, and says, "I liked it. That's the truth of it. I felt powerful. And I *liked* it." She forms a bitter half smile. "That's what you wanted me to say, isn't it?"

The two friends look into each other's eyes. Jenou nods very slightly and says, "See, that's the thing, Rio. You were made for this. You talk about the men growing up expecting something like this, well, you didn't expect it, but you took to it fast enough."

"I'm just trying to get by."

"We're all just trying to get by, but we aren't all Killer Rick."

"You want to feel bad every time you kill one of those bastards who are trying to kill us?"

Jenou shakes her head. "No, Rio. We'd all go nuts. I'd go nuts. I'm just . . . I'm scared, and I want to make sense of it all. It's got to mean something, doesn't it? If I get it, I want to die thinking it made some kind of *sense*."

"Yeah, well, after it's all over you can write a book about it. Call it *Jenou Castain: My Wartime Adventures in Africa, Sicily, and Italy*."

They are silent for a while as Stick breaks the squad in two to carry the boats, and they wait for the signal. Then, with forced humor, Jenou says, "Of course they might make a movie of the book. I'd have to be played by Veronica Lake."

"Yeah? And who plays me?"

"John Wayne in a dress," Jenou says instantly.

This is somehow both preposterous and funny, and despite the rain and the cold and the exhaustion and the fear of what is coming, Rio's slow smile appears.

"Fug you, Jenou."

"Yeah, fug you too, Rio."

"Just keep your head down," Rio says, and reaches for Jenou's cold hand. "You'll be okay."

"Whatever you say, *Corporal*." The hand squeeze is quick and furtive.

With rain falling and night dropping the temperature to near freezing, they carry the boats: five or six soldiers to each boat, soldiers already weighed down by their gear, soldiers with fingers numb with cold holding the slick wet gunwales, feet slipping in mud. They set out like some bizarre parody of an amphibious landing, a long line of men and women staggering abreast as they haul their awkward loads forward.

It's almost funny at the start. And then the first artillery rounds start to drop from the sky, flying in from the town of Monte Cassino at the base of the massif and from hillside positions behind the far bank of the river.

Rio's squad has one of the boats, all hands gripping,

slipping, reattaching, slipping again. Shells scream in, and they drop the boat and lie facedown, hugging the mud.

Then it's up and grab and stagger until mortars start to fall, and then it's facedown again.

Up and down.

Up and down.

Then Lieutenant Stone calls a halt, and they sit in the mud as the American artillery opens up. For thirty minutes the distant 105s and 155s plaster the riverbanks and the positions beyond as they sit watching, hoping against hope that the artillery will do their work for them. A green kid yells, "That'll teach 'em! Leave some for us!" But the veterans know better. The Germans are dug in, and while the rain of shells will kill some, it won't kill enough.

And the American artillery does nothing to discourage the German gunners. A boat from Fourth Platoon is hit, making splinters of it and hurling men and women aside.

"All right, move out!" comes the order.

Rio sees Jillion crying freely, eyes red in the light of an explosion. She sees Jack, grimly determined, one foot in front of the other. Geer, strong as usual, cursing constantly. Jenou, having a hard time of it, hands coming out in blisters. Beebee has turned into a decent soldier with a talent for locating things, but he's small and the weight is hard for him. Pang is at the back, holding on with both hands, probably bearing more than his share of the weight. Cat has the bow, probably also carrying more than her fair share.

Rio sees more hands slipping and calls, "Down boat."

They drop the boat and fall to their knees or bend over, gasping. Canteens are drained, crumbs of biscuit retrieved from pockets and shoved into greedy mouths. A flask makes the rounds, a swallow of raw brandy that provides the only hint of warmth.

"Up boat!"

Another group is hit, their boat sent tumbling to crash into Sergeant Alvarez, wounding him. The calls for *Medic, medic!* sound across the field.

Trudge, trudge, trudge.

"Down boat!" The boats and their human transportation look like some strange sort of spiders: too many legs hauling a swollen, ungainly body.

A shell lands fifty feet away, and no one bothers to cower as clods of wet earth patter on their helmets and shoulders. A second round is closer, and they hug the ground again.

"Up boat!"

They are helpless. They are ants waiting for the shoe that will crush them. Rio spares a glance at Jenou. Her mouth is set, her eyes narrowed, determination on her face.

The next round and Jenou could be . . . Rio shakes off the image, but it is too vivid, too awful to dismiss entirely.

Ahead, a few stumps of trees mark the bank of the river, and now they are coming within range of small arms fire, so sniper rounds, outrunning the noise of their firing, come *flit . . . flit . . .* striking dirt, rocks, and at least one round punches a hole in the boat itself.

They are in the crosshairs of long-distance as well as close-range fire now. The position is impossible.

Impossible.

But then there is a screaming artillery round with a different pitch, as shells arc overhead from the Allied artillery behind them. The banks of the river erupt in smoke, almost useless smoke with the German gunners all zeroed in, but it will baffle the snipers, for a while at least.

Rio sees Jenou trying to light a cigarette, but her hands are shaking so badly that Jack does it for her. A distant part of Rio's mind notices that her friend has acquired the habit too. How long has Jenou been smoking? Why hasn't Rio noticed? Is there anyone left who hasn't acquired the habit?

She looks at her brothers and sisters, peering at them each in turn, anything to distract from the fear rising inside her. This is not like staying strong in the heat of battle, this is helplessness. It is not the first time she's been under artillery fire, but never has she had to simply walk through it, unable to shoot back, unable to take cover, unable even to run away.

"Up boat!" Rio says, trying to make the words sound like the previous twenty iterations, but to her own ear her voice sounds strained.

They run forward now, short, fast steps, feet slipping, boots so caked up with mud that each foot weighs ten pounds. No stopping this time, all the way, all the way!

BOOM! BOOM, BOOM, BOOM, BOOM!

The 88s screech in, falling like meteors, sending up yards of dirt and leaving craters and mangled bodies behind. There is an eerie scream of pain off to the left, but the source is invisible because now they have at last reached the smoke. Rio glances up just as a falling shell punches a hole through the smoke and shatters a denuded tree that sends splinters flying, one striking Jillion in the stomach. It sticks out, an elongated triangle of wood. It's as if someone has thrown a dart at her. Jillion releases her hold on the boat, and Rio does as well, rushing to her.

Jillion stands plucking at the splinter and says, "It doesn't hurt."

Rio tugs experimentally at the big chunk of wood, then unzips Jillion's coat and the two of them see that the splinter has pierced her coat and blouse but somehow caused nothing more than a slight scratch.

For the first time that Rio can remember, Jillion smiles.

"Missed me!" she says.

They grab back onto their boat and shuffle forward into gloom, following Stick's boat, which has pulled ahead, hearing the river before they see it, and stepping into it when their momentum carries them too fast down the near bank.

It's no Mississippi, the Rapido or Volturno or whatever the hell it is, in fact it's less than thirty feet across. But the banks are steep and the water is swift, swollen with rain. It nearly yanks the boat away from them, and indeed Rio sees some other squad's boat go bouncing past, empty of men.

Orders are being shouted down the line: they are to board and push off immediately. Small arms fire—rifles and machine guns—now blaze away through the smoke from the far bank. They are too near the Germans on the other side for the 88s to be used, but now the mortars get serious about their work, dropping behind the platoon and walking slowly, cautiously forward to pound troops trapped between artillery-scoured fields and the river.

Stick yells, "All set, Richlin?"

Rio says she is, and they begin to pile into the boat. A bullet hits Jillion in the eye and blows out a chunk of her skull. She falls backward in something like slow motion, landing on her back in the boat.

"Medic!" Jenou yells, but there can be no possibility of

429

helping Jillion. She is dead, unquestionably dead, with the pink matter of her brain floating in the swamped bottom of the boat like chum.

The boat moves into the water, driven by the few oars they've managed to get into the water, and is instantly seized by the current, which drags its head around so all their paddling together barely straightens it out. They can do nothing to stop the boat's momentum in the direction of the distant Mediterranean.

They row like mad but the far bank, glimpsed only in brief tears in the smoke and fog, is running swiftly past.

A machine gun finds them and half a dozen large-caliber holes are poked just below the waterline, so water begins to pour in.

"Row, row!" Rio yells. "Left side row! Right side—"

A mortar shell douses them in buckets of freezing water. More shells land behind, beside, blasting the river, knocking the oar out of Geer's hand, twirling the boat again so now it faces upstream and the machine gun bullets pluck at the water.

Cat pushes the stunned Geer aside and paddles madly with the splintered remains of Geer's oar, but now Rio can sense that whatever hopes they might have had are diminishing quickly. No sooner do they have the boat turned in the right direction than Rio realizes there is eight inches of water in the bottom. The boat lies lower in the water and is infinitely heavier.

"Jen! Help me bail!" Rio cries. Jenou is pulling something from inside Jillion's coat and stuffing it in her own.

Jack yelps, "Shit!" and a red stain appears below the unit patch on his shoulder.

Jenou and Rio use their helmets as buckets, throwing water as fast as they can, and with Jack now cutting away his sleeve to get at the wound, they are down to just two oars actively slapping at the water. The boat, caught in an eddy, twirls a complete 360-degree turn before machine gun bullets turn the bow to kindling. The boat slides almost gratefully below the water.

"Get your gear off!" Rio yells, and every hand is busy shedding packs and ammo belts and coats as the water comes swiftly up over their laps.

Rio plows through to Jack and says, "Is it bad?"

His face is pale and his eyes wide, but he says, "Just a flesh wound," like some British cowboy in the wrong movie.

Then the boat disappears beneath them, and they are swimming, though most of their motion is a result of the current, which carries them along like flotsam.

They are past the town when at last Rio feels ground under her feet and drags herself up the far bank.

She looks around. She is alone.

A voice barks an order in German, and she sees two

gray uniforms and two leveled rifles.

Rio raises her hands. One of the Germans rushes off upstream, presumably to seize another prisoner of war, leaving Rio under the puzzled eyes of just one soldier. She is exhausted beyond all caring and sits straight down in the mud, showing every sign of being defeated, but also sitting sideways so her right leg is hidden from his view. She twines her fingers and holds them on her helmet, the universal sign of submission.

The German seems quite unconcerned, not at all the attitude of a soldier who believes he is in danger. He's a medium-sized fellow in his twenties, his uniform clean, though wet, and his boots only slightly marred by mud.

The river rushes by, and Rio sees the debris of failure: boats, half-constructed segments of a pontoon bridge, and American bodies float past. No wonder the German is relaxed; it must have all seemed a pitiful effort to them.

The full weight of it descends on Rio. The assault has failed. GIs are dead and all for nothing. And she is a prisoner.

"*Zigarette*?" the German asks, advancing toward her, lulled by her passivity and no doubt by her gender.

Rio nods wearily. The German taps one out of his pack, hands it to her, and leans close with a lighter.

The *koummya* slides easily out of its scabbard. Rio stabs upward, right into his belly.

"Ah! Ah!" the German cries, and staggers back, blood staining his uniform. But he is far from dead and brings his rifle up to aim as Rio, summoning a last, desperate measure of strength, pushes herself up, throws a stiff left arm to push the muzzle away, and stabs him again.

This time the blade stops short on ribs, so she twists it and leans into it, using her weight to force the point through cartilage and into the vulnerable organs beyond. Too close, too close to avoid seeing his face, the surprise, the hurt as if she's betrayed him, the incomprehension, that moment of *no, not me, not me!* And then the dawning fear as he begins to understand that he is dying, dying right here, right now.

Rio cannot twist the *koummya*, trapped as it is between ribs, but she saws it back and forth as his blood pours over her hand. She sees the light in his eyes go out.

He falls, and she has to put a boot on his chest and pull hard and work the handle back and forth to get the knife out of him.

When she looks up she sees Jack watching her. She meets his gaze, unflinching, and wipes the blood on the German's uniform. She rifles through the dead man's pockets. A letter received. A letter in progress, unfinished. A photo of a wife and child, a girl Rio thinks, a daughter, though it's a very formal pose and the baby is all in white lace without obvious signs of gender.

She takes the German's canteen and drains half of it before offering it to Jack. She takes the German's Schmeisser submachine gun, checks the safety, works the bolt, and slings it over her shoulder.

"What now?" Jack asks.

"I guess we swim back across or spend the war in a POW camp."

"Swim it is," he says.

RAINY SCHULTERMAN—FIFTH ARMY HEADQUARTERS, NAPLES, ITALY

Rainy sits in a uniform that is her proper size but which now hangs loose on her. Her head is shaved bald. In fact, all the hair on her body has been shaved to get at the lice and bedbugs and scabies that are part of the legacy of her imprisonment.

She is in a waiting room, ready to be called in for her first real debriefing.

They have given her forty-eight hours before being asked to recount her . . . what to call it? Adventure? Ordeal? In that time she has showered and showered again, eaten, drunk, slept . . . and awakened screaming in a voice filled with rage.

She's seen doctors and psychiatrists and ignored their questions, questions that, it seems to her, are impossible to answer.

How do you feel? they want to know.

Is she supposed to give a one-word answer? How does she *feel*? She feels as if she's a lump of slow-burning coal. As if she might start crying and never be able to stop. As if she would gladly dig her fingernails into the throat of the first German she came across and choke the life from him. As if she's not real, that she's a Rainy puppet, a hollow, lifeless thing being dragged along by strings.

She feels brittle, as if her skin is a hard candy shell and the slightest tapping might break her open.

She feels inexpressibly sad, though sad for what, exactly, she could not possibly say.

But it has begun to dawn on Rainy that the questions have a single purpose: to discover whether she is fit for duty, will soon be fit for duty, or will simply never be fit. The wrong answers will send her home, back to some safe, stateside billet. Unless . . . unless those are actually the *right* answers, the answers she *should* be giving.

You've done your part, she tells herself.

More than your part.

Home to her mother and father. Home to New York. Home to life and ease and safety and maybe romance and . . . But it's all sour, all of it impossible, there is no going home, there is no going home until . . .

Until what, Rainy?

Until what?

Until she no longer feels empty? Until she is herself

436

again? Because she can't go home yet, not like this, not as this person.

She can't go home, because there are no Krauts in New York. The Krauts are *here*. The Gestapo is *here*.

A staff sergeant calls her name and holds a door open for her before hurrying past her to turn a plush wingback chair that slides easily on the polished parquet floor.

The ceiling, far above her, is an arch painted with cherubs and men and women in Renaissance clothing. No doubt it is a scene from the Christian Bible, but she cannot decipher the symbology and doesn't care to try. The headquarters is in a seized villa of some magnificence, and this is but one of the many floridly decorated rooms.

A captain sits to her left, a colonel sits behind the desk, and it takes her a few beats before she realizes he is her former captain and now Lieutenant Colonel Herkemeier. He still checks his creases compulsively, but his eyes are full of compassion and . . . and respect? Regret? Pity?

What is clever, kind, decent Jon Herkemeier seeing when he looks at her?

There is also a female corporal taking notes, seated tactfully off to Rainy's right and slightly behind. All three are Army Intelligence, but Rainy quickly intuits from the start that her mission is seen differently from here than it was from Colonel Corelli's office in New York.

She gives a stripped-down account of her mission, her

escape from Positano, her flight from Rome, her time in Genazzano. She takes a pause before going on. She wants to give a controlled, professional account, knowing that if she lets herself become emotional she may be unable to go on.

Even the barest retelling takes her thirty minutes, all accompanied by the scratch of pencil on paper from the corporal stenographer. The questions begin.

"And there was no plan of action, no plan of withdrawal after you completed your mission?" the captain, an older man named Fraser, asks.

"No, sir," Rainy says tightly.

"I find that hard to believe," Fraser says, and Rainy's eyes flare, a warning.

"How then did you decide how to proceed once you had delivered the document? The very useful document," Herkemeier asks gently, sending a significant look to Fraser, who takes the hint and sits back, looking abashed.

"I started walking. I knew the gangsters might come after me for alerting Father Patrizio. And of course the Krauts. The Germans, sir." She turns away slightly, and it is only the stenographer who sees her grimace of hatred and for a moment the stenographer is so startled she loses her place. "I walked out of Rome, not knowing where to go, but I figured the countryside would be safer than the city."

"You simply walked? But surely it was many miles?"

"There are plenty of refugees on the roads, sir, some fleeing Rome in expectation of our arrival. I kept to myself, spoke as little as possible, slept at night in barns or under bridges. Three days and I reached a little village called Genazzano."

Herkemeier snaps his fingers, and Fraser unfolds a map. "Here it is, sir, almost due east of Rome." The captain points.

"My God, that must be forty miles!" Herkemeier says.

"Yes, sir. I hadn't eaten much, and the countryside was picked bare. I had to steal a chicken from a farmer. Then I found a cave. And I got sick, and some children found me . . ." Her voice trails away as she remembers the chicken. She'd wrung its neck, a far more difficult task than she'd imagined. Then she'd made a mess of butchering it, using a sharp-edged piece of tin roofing as a knife.

"Anyway, some sisters, some nuns, took me in for a while until I was better. But I couldn't stay there without endangering them, so I walked until I found an abandoned farm. I meant to wait there until our forces arrived."

"Yes, well, our forces are all hurry-up and very little planning, I'm afraid," Herkemeier says with savage disapproval. "Rather like your mission."

"Yes, sir."

"Please go on, Sergeant," Herkemeier says with a frown of worry.

"I guess someone gave me up," Rainy says. "One night

a staff car pulled up. I ran, but . . . but not fast enough."
Then, feeling obscurely as if this was disappointing,
added, "I shot at one of them. But I missed, at least I think
I did."

Should she tell them that her last conscious act had
been to reach for her suicide pill? Would that help or hurt?
Would she seem mad? Unstable? Unreliable?

Was that what she wanted?

*Home to New York. Home to my father and mother.
Home to see Aryeh and Jane's baby, my niece. Home to
Halev. Food. Warmth. Safety.*

"What happened next?"

"Well, sir, I wasn't raped at least, but they beat me.
Fists and rifle butts that first time. I think it went on for a
while. They were angry. Very angry." She shook her head,
trying to refocus. "I woke up in the cell where the soldiers
found me."

"You were weeks in Gestapo headquarters," Herkemeier says softly.

It's his kindness that sets Rainy's chin to quivering.
Tears flood her eyes and spill down her cheeks. At the
same time her hands are clenched painfully and her teeth
grind together and her breathing becomes ragged as she
fights down the urge to sob openly.

"Yes, sir," she manages to say.

"They questioned you—"

"I gave them nothing!" It's a scream, a scream of rage, mountainous, vast, impossible rage. Fraser jumps in his chair, but Herkemeier never takes his soft, concerned eyes from her.

"Name, rank, and serial number?" the captain suggests.

"No." Rainy stretches the word into an animal growl. "They'd have known Schulterman is a Jewish name and then . . . I guess I thought things would be even worse then, but also they didn't expect it. See, they thought I told them the truth, and I didn't, you see, I held it back, and I held it all back, I lied and lied, and it is so hard to keep the lies straight, see, Colonel, keep the fugging lies straight—that was the hard part, because you can't sleep and you just hear the screams and you see the men shot down, bleeding, and . . ." She brings herself up short, painfully aware that she sounds crazy, that she sounds . . . emotional.

With great effort Rainy finds a version of herself, an earlier copy of Rainy Schulterman, a calmer, dispassionate, self-controlled version. As if she is an actress playing a role, she steadies herself and says, "I had no useful information I could give them. I fabricated things to let them think they were getting somewhere."

"I believe that's enough for now, Sergeant," Herkemeier says gently.

Rainy shoots to her feet, wincing at the innumerable bruises that stiffen her body. She salutes and prepares to about-face, but Herkemeier says, "Just one moment, Sergeant Schulterman." He stands. "I will tell you that I have had and still have many doubts about the part I played in getting you into this. But by God, Rainy, I have no such doubts about you. Well done. Damned well done." He returns her salute sharply, and she flees the room as sobs take hold.

RIO RICHLIN—RAPIDO RIVER, ITALY

"I want you to know, I'm relieved you're not suggesting we stay on this side of the river."

"The Krauts are on this side," Rio points out.

"Precisely," Jack says.

It's easy enough to say swim, but it turns out to be rather more difficult. The current is powerful, and the river bends in places so it threatens to bear them right back to the same shore farther downstream. They walk in silence, searching for a place to cross, creeping through the night, guided by the sound of water on their left and the frenzied sounds of battle and machine gun fire behind them.

The squad may be back there fighting, if any of them made it ashore, but Rio and Jack tacitly acknowledge that they will search for a ford farther from the battle, not closer to it.

He thinks I'm crazy.

No, Rio, he thinks you're "splendid."

At times the stumps of burned trees and the tangle of blasted shrubbery obscure their view of the river, which in any case can be better heard than seen in the deep darkness. This is a blessing because from time to time a boat or a body comes floating by. None of the bodies are German.

Rio fears looking over and seeing Jillion's body . . . or Cat's . . . or Stick's.

Or Jenou's.

She pushes that thought away as far as she can, but it doesn't work. Jenou was in the water, the water that boiled with machine gun bullets.

Not Jenou, please, God, not Jenou. I told her she would be okay.

Rio and Jack walk for perhaps a half mile, creeping silently, alert to possible German patrols, before coming to a place where they can get at the river and where the bend ahead is toward the right, which should help them to land on the opposite shore. They fashion a sort of tiny raft out of small branches woven together and buoy it by draining their canteens and sealing them tight to act as floats. Weapons and gear, excess clothing and boots are all piled onto the raft, which rides way too low in the water to keep anything dry, but is better than nothing.

Jack strips down to just his boxer shorts, and Rio down to her identical pair plus her army bra. The night is cold, and they are shivering violently before they even touch the icy water.

"Nothing for it but to j-j-jump in," Jack says, his teeth chattering.

"Yep," Rio acknowledges with equal dread.

They hesitate at the water's edge, but a machine gun opens up just fifty yards upstream and that motivates them. The water is brutally cold, just short of turning solid. They each keep a hand on the soggy raft and paddle with the other hand, but it is soon clear that paddling is irrelevant—the river will decide where they go. So they roll onto their backs, extend their legs downstream, and are carried along, pushing water rather than paddling, pushing themselves, willing themselves out of the faster current toward the onrushing far bank.

They land, teeth chattering so badly neither can speak. They empty the raft, put soaking-wet uniforms on over soaking-wet bodies, fill their canteens from the river, drop in water purification tablets, send up silent prayers that their ammo is not all waterlogged. Then they head back east, back toward the sound of guns.

Rio's watch has stopped, and she sees condensation under the crystal. "W-w-what time you th-think?"

Jack shakes his head violently. "No idea." His face is

as white as a cotton sheet, his lips blue. Rio imagines she looks much the same—like a walking corpse.

Ahead they see distant orange and yellow flashes and hear the short, sharp explosions, the sound flattened by distance.

"That way," Jack says, and chops the air. "If we d-d-don't f-f-f-f, shit. Can't t-t-alk."

They set off across a plowed field, furrows all but invisible underfoot so they must step high and heel first or else trip.

"Fug!" Jack yells. "Freeze!"

"Already freezing," Rio snaps in a cold-rattled voice.

"Mines."

"What?"

"My foot hit something metal."

The cold is forgotten. Rio looks around, considers where they are, considers that the engineers have cleared only those minefields along the main line of attack—which will not include this field—and says, "Bad."

Jack, about ten paces ahead, kneels slowly and feels in the dark. "Yeah. Bloody hell, we're in a minefield."

They can try to perfectly retrace their steps—not likely to work in the dark—or sit still and hope for help when the sun comes up.

"Stay there," Rio says. "I'll feel my way to you." She, too, squats down and begins to feel through the mud for the telltale touch of steel. Once her immediate circle is cleared, she sets off crawling toward Jack, who has likewise cleared his immediate area—except for the mine he's already found.

Rio's little finger brushes something hard and too smooth to be rock. She says, "Got one." She carefully feels her way past it and places her helmet gently over the mine to mark it. At last she reaches Jack, and now the cold has overcome the warming effect of adrenaline, and both are shaking so badly they can barely speak.

"I think it doesn't go off until I lift my foot," Jack says.

"I heard that was bullshit," Rio says as calmly as she can. She lowers herself to the ground and begins to probe with numb fingers. Jack's mine is not hard to locate. It is a cylinder about six inches tall, topped by a stem that adds a couple more inches and holds the trigger.

"You didn't step on the trigger," Rio says, exhaling relief. "Your toes are just up against it. Don't move, and I'll disarm it."

For this she needs a pin of some sort, and the only pin she can find is one from her own grenades. "I gotta toss it," she says to Jack. "So squat down but don't move your foot yet."

"You think you know how to—" Jack begins, but Rio has pulled the pin and whips her grenade away, as far as she can throw it. It lands, they wait, counting, then . . .

"Dud," Jack says. "Possibly a result of us drowning the lousy thing."

Rio awkwardly slips the pin into the hole on the mine's stem, just as she'd been taught to do a million years ago in basic training.

"Thank you, Sergeant Mackie," she chatters under her breath. "It's safe, Stafford. You can move."

But of course they can't move far, not in a minefield. And anyway their small reserve of ambition to move on is now all used up. Rio lies down in the mud and Jack lies beside her, and without needing to discuss it they press their bodies together to hold on to what body heat there is.

"I s-s-spose a fire w-would be bad," Jack says.

"Not for the s-s-snipers."

"Nothing to burn anyway."

For a time they work at scraping out a shallow depression, but the mud just slides back in. And then the rain starts up again, rain that forms a crust of ice on their clothing but melts on contact with the soil to add to the soupiness of the mud.

"Pigs in mud," Rio says, disgusted by the state of her own body and uniform. The only thing not black with dirt on Jack is his red hair. "We sh-sh-should sleep."

"G-g-o ahead, I'll keep watch."

"Kinda doubt anyone is going to sneak up on us,

Stafford; we're in a minefield."

"Excellent point," Jack concedes. "You know," he says in a lighter tone, "this could be quite romantic if you weren't covered in filth and didn't stink like one of my socks."

"You're not exactly Prince Charming yourself," Rio says, and both stifle laughter.

For a while they lie side by side on the ground, gazing up at falling rain or away toward bright yellow explosions and the deadly streaks of tracer rounds. Both are freezing except for the places where their bodies meet.

"Do you miss England?" Rio asks after a while.

She feels his shrug. "I've barely been there in years, aside from our training stop. But yes, I suppose I do."

"You could probably transfer to the British Army now."

"Trying to get rid of me?"

She doesn't answer directly but says, "I miss home."

"Not enjoying scenic Italy? You live in some sort of rustic splendor, I recall."

"Gedwell Falls. Northern California, the part where Hollywood isn't. Small town. Me and Jenou and Strand."

"Yes, the pilot last seen singing 'White Christmas' while everything around us was blowing up. I remember him vaguely. Is he all right?"

Now he feels her shrug. "I got a letter from him. He's in England, recovered, waiting to be sent out again."

"Bomber pilots." He sighs. "If only I'd thought to join the Air Corps."

"What? And miss this?"

They lie silent for a long while until Rio begins to suspect that he has fallen asleep, which outrages her: what kind of person can sleep in this? They are spooned now, Rio behind him, her body pressed to his back, one arm draped over him, and Rio thinks it's quite nice in an awful sort of way. Then he begins to twist around, bringing them face-to-face, so apparently he can't sleep either.

"Tell me one thing, Corporal Richlin. Are you engaged to him?"

Part of her wants to laugh. The question comes out of the blue, and she doesn't have a ready answer.

"I don't know," she admits.

"Do you . . . do you intend to be?"

"That's up to him, isn't it?" she evades.

"I see. If he asks. If he proposes. I don't wish to . . ." He seems unable to find words for what he doesn't wish to do.

"I don't know," she says again. "I don't know anything, Stafford. Jack. I don't know why I'm here or what's happening or if I'll be around tomorrow or dead like Suarez. Or Cassel. Or Magraff. Jesus. I can't even . . . I mean, what's the point, Jack? What's the point of thinking about later?"

"It's what keeps me going, I suppose. Later has got to be better than now."

His face is inches from hers; she can see the glitter of his eyes. They speak in whispers.

"We should catch some Zs," Rio says, mostly as a way of shutting him up.

"Just tell me, Rio."

"Tell you what?"

"Do you love him?"

She takes a long time to answer as she spools through memories of Strand. Their first awkward date. The plane ride they took. The picnic. Their first kiss. And the hotel room in Tunis.

What can she say? What can she say when she has slept with Strand? Can she answer anything other than, *of course I love him*?

In the end she says, "I'm not sure love is a thing I can do anymore." She means it to be airy and flippant, but it sounds sad.

"Love isn't a *thing* you do or don't do, Rio. Love is everything, and it swallows you whole or it's not love."

Is he seriously flirting with her? Here? Now? With both of them side by side in a freezing hog wallow?

She forces a small laugh and twists away from him, pressing her back against him, feeling his warmth on her numb backside. "And how do you know so much about love, Jack Stafford?"

He lays his free arm over her and wraps it chastely around her belly. "I just do," he whispers to the curve of her neck. "I just do."

33

The first crossing is accomplished only by a small American force, which is then stranded when the main force falls back in disorder, and is then killed or captured by the Germans.

Rio has missed this particular tragedy by the time she and Jack make it back to the platoon.

"What. The. Hell," Geer says on seeing them stumbling through the rain. Geer is in a deep hole with Pang. The two of them are standing in eighteen inches of water. Pang is patiently bailing with his helmet while Geer is shoving mud into a sort of dike meant to keep water from simply flowing unimpeded into their foxhole.

"We thought you two were dead or captured," Pang says, and grins.

Jenou and Cat are in a second hole—there are foxholes of various depth and complexity dug all along the sector, many of them having started as shell craters. Cat has managed to find a few sticks and has used them to give some angle to her shelter half, creating a sort of sagging, pitched roof so rain runs off onto the ground . . . before draining right back into the hole.

Jenou climbs sloppily out of their hole and runs to Rio. She runs with arms outstretched and Rio goes to receive her hug, but at the last minute Jenou passes Rio and embraces Jack.

"We missed you!"

"Oh, very funny," Rio mutters.

Jenou relents and throws an arm around her friend and says in a low voice, "Goddamn, Rio, you scared the hell out of me." Then in a yell, "Stick! We picked up a couple of replacements!"

Stick appears, a sodden, mud-covered, and exhausted man. But he has energy enough to smile and clap both Jack and Rio on the back. "Where have you clowns been?"

"We spent the night in a minefield," Rio explains.

"Might have been better off staying there. We're getting ready to make another push."

"Everything okay?" Rio says it with an emphasis Stick understands to mean, *Has anyone else been wounded or bought the farm?*

"You saw Magraff?" Stick asks in a low voice.

Rio and Jack nod.

"We thought it was her *and* the two of you. Although

Castain kept saying you'd just lit out for Berlin to shoot old Adolf all by yourselves. Damn, you have no idea how good the two of you look! Now, dig a hole."

"It's just like the parable of the Prodigal Son," Jack says. "Except for the part about digging a hole."

"The Krauts haven't forgotten we're here," Stick says gloomily. "They hit us every few—"

He stops because the whine of falling shells is suddenly audible and with a soggy *BOOM!* a section of mud erupts.

Stick runs for his hole, Jack dives in with Geer and Pang, and Rio slides down into the soupy filth with Jenou and Cat.

"They better not blow off my roof!" Cat warns loudly, as if the Germans can hear, and as if they'd take heed.

The barrage lasts only a few terrifying minutes. A man from another squad is hit while trying to use the latrine. They hear his screams mixed with cursing. "I was just trying to take a shit, you Kraut bastards!"

When the shelling stops, Rio asks, "I don't suppose there's any chow?"

"They set up a field mess back past where we picked up the boats, but it got blown to hell," Jenou says. "Beebee's got a little fire going, don't even ask me how." She rises cautiously, lifts a corner of Cat's rain cover, and nods in the direction of a scrap of canvas showing above the lip of a crater.

"Guess I'll see if he's got any coffee on," Rio says. "Then I guess I'll dig a hole."

"You're welcome to join us in our warm, comfortable, dry establishment," Cat says. "So long as you dig out that end and help us bail."

Rio slithers up out of the hole, not an easy maneuver, and runs to the crater where Beebee has managed to set up a tidy lean-to atop a flat rock that's been exposed at the bottom of the crater. It's not dry, nothing is dry, but he has managed to get a small hidden fire going and has a pot of coffee brewing over an empty can filled with sand and gasoline.

Beebee looks up and says, "Hah! That's five bucks Geer owes me. He bet you were captured. Coffee?"

He pours a few inches into her canteen cup, and she drinks it with reverence—the first warm thing she's felt in twenty-four hours, aside from Jack.

"First one's free," Beebee says. "A refill costs three smokes."

Rio carries her steaming cup back to Jenou's hole and proffers a sip to her and Cat. For the next hour she digs out the right side of the hole, then bails for a while.

"Now it's just like the Plaza Hotel," Cat says contentedly.

"The very finest of mud-filled holes anywhere," Jenou agrees.

They are still joking around, Cat and Jenou, partly no doubt energized by Rio's reappearance. But Rio sees something dark and dangerous in their eyes. She wonders if they see the same on her face.

"We're going up again?" Rio asks.

Jenou nods. "Stick says the captain asked about pulling us off the line for a while, but no dice. We're fighting this war alone."

"The engineers have a Bailey bridge slung, so no boats this time, but we'll be crossing in single fugging file," Cat says. And then she mimes a machine gunner. "*Bap-bap-bap-bap*. Like ducks in a shooting gallery."

Both Jenou and Cat are doing their best to put on a brave face, but Rio sees the signs of deep strain. No one has slept in at least thirty-six hours. Nor has there been a hot meal. Or a single instant of escape from the rain and the filth. And with all of that, the artillery, and Magraff's death, and the assumed deaths of Rio and Jack, strain is understandable.

The squad is down to nine: Geer, Pang, Cat, Jenou, Beebee, Stick, Rio, Sergeant Cole, and Jack.

There comes the supersonic screech of artillery falling, and for ten minutes the three young women crouch in freezing water, keeping their heads down below the horizontal flight of jagged shrapnel. As long as a shell doesn't land right beside them or drop right down into the hole they survive, but it's like playing dice with life itself. The odds are against coming up snake eyes, but it is possible, all too possible.

When the shelling stops, Stick calls out from his hole to take roll.

"Just like school," Jenou says, and yells, "Present!"

Then they are called to help unload an ammo truck, hauling wooden crates off the tailgate, humping them awkwardly to deposit them up and down the thin line formed by the platoon. They unload quickly, despite their weariness—no one wants to be standing next to an ammo truck when the German gunners spot it through the rain.

But with the job done, Rio is sick with exhaustion, both sleepy and bone-weary.

"Ammo," Cat says.

"Yep," Jenou says.

This big of a distribution of ammunition—loose .30 caliber for the M1 Garands and the BAR, shorter .30 caliber carbine rounds, grenades in fragmentation, smoke and incendiary models—signals an action is coming.

The three of them mechanically top off their rifle and carbine clips and stuff loose bullets and grenades in wherever possible. For once Rio is not worried about topping off her canteen. There is no shortage of water.

Now they have a nice, fresh ammo crate the size of a footstool, which they set atop the mud at the bottom of their hole. It clears the water by three inches and they decide to rotate, each getting an hour in turn to sit on it.

Rio goes second, and the instant her butt hits wood she's asleep, her body jerking automatically when she starts to fall forward.

When Cat rouses her Rio sees Jenou leaning, one foot in the slurry, one foot bare. When Jenou pulls off her sock, Rio sees puffy white flesh coming off with it. Jenou's big toe is swollen and she wonders aloud whether piercing it would release pus and lessen her pain. Or whether any puncture wound in these conditions is likely to lead to far worse infection.

An hour's disturbed sleep has done little to clear Rio's mind, rather it deepens her descent into a sort of dream state. Her thoughts are fragments of memory, images without narrative: her family, Strand, the induction center, Jack, a much younger Jenou, dry hills. It's that last image that captures her attention, and for a while in imagination she is hiking up a hill covered in desiccated, yellowed grass, set off by a small stand of trees. The sky is blue. A red-tailed hawk rides the wind, looking for an unwary mouse. A biplane floats overhead, and there's Strand waving down at Rio as she rides a black-and-white cow to the top of the hill.

Rio jerks awake. "What?"

She has slumped right down into the slurry, and Jenou is shaking her shoulder.

"Time," Jenou says.

Darkness has fallen. The rain is a slow drizzle, almost a mist now, as if the sky is down to the last of its moisture. Rio crawls up out of the hole and to her left and right more soldiers rise from the mud, like a parody of creation: *And the Lord God formed man of the dust of the ground . . .*

But not dust, mud.

The squad forms up on Stick, and the platoon as a whole forms up to either side of Cole, who is beside Lieutenant Stone. Rio hasn't seen the lieutenant in a while, and he does not look good. His earlier restless energy seems to have been sucked right out of him. Beyond them in the dark the rest of the division is on the move. They slog forward, a long line of men and women, silent but for the squelch of their boots, back to the river.

The engineers have managed to set up two narrow pontoon bridges. The Germans haven't blown them up, which is ominous, for it can only mean the Germans are waiting until they have living targets.

"Okay," Cole says. "We're second across, behind First Platoon."

"Can't believe Stone didn't volunteer us," Cat says.

"He's growing up fast," Stick says, and it's almost enough to make Rio smile. Dain Sticklin, who started in basic with her and Jenou, is now the wise sergeant.

First Platoon steps onto the swaying, unsteady bridge,

holding the guide rope, which is very little help. The German gunners wait patiently until the lead element is almost across, and then the fire comes pouring down, knocking GIs left and right into the water, where they flounder and cling and try to swim, or float away, dead.

"Now!"

And Cole's platoon rushes down the bank, and they start yelling, yelling to keep their courage up, piling pell-mell toward the bridge to get it over with, a headlong rush to destruction. But now they have a bit of luck, as an American mortar lands a lucky shot and knocks out the nearest machine gun nest.

Rio runs, staggers as the bridge moves beneath her, rights herself, and runs, with Jenou just ahead and Pang behind. A second machine gun sends a line of tracers arcing toward them, but it's farther away and by some miracle the squad reaches the opposite shore, where they flop down, panting.

The next squad isn't so lucky. Rio sees two of their people knocked like bowling pins into the churning water.

Allied artillery has opened up well beyond the river, hitting the Germans in the rear, doing nothing to stop the small arms fire but playing hell with the Kraut mortars, which, nevertheless, keep firing. Beebee cries out in pain as a piece of hot shrapnel scrapes a quarter inch of flesh from his thigh.

"We gotta push in!" Cole yells.

Stick says, "Come on," and they are up and clambering hand over hand up a slippery slope, smoke suddenly everywhere, smoke torn by renewed rain. Ahead there must be a German position, a dark lump revealed only by the light of tracer rounds.

Rio is on her belly now, almost swimming through the mud, legs pistoning, elbows digging, her rifle in the crooks of those elbows.

"Smoke!" Stick shouts, and Jack and Jenou both throw smoke grenades toward the presumed but invisible machine gun. The smoke billows, blinding Rio at least as much as it must be blinding the Germans, but she crawls on until stopped by a soft but heavy obstacle.

Her face is inches from a corpse, bloated and reeking of feces and decay. A corpse in American uniform.

She crawls around it and already the smoke is dissipating, but there's Jenou on her right, on hands and knees, her carbine slung over her back. The Germans have spotted her, and Rio sees the little splashes of bullets landing all around her friend.

Rio fumbles for a smoke grenade of her own and throws it as Stick yells, "More smoke!"

And this time, as soon as the smoke pours forth, Rio jumps to her feet and runs, hunched over, trips—another body—rolls away, gets up again, and runs. Jack is ahead of her with Pang and now, in a tear in the smoke, she sees plain as day the muzzle protruding from beneath a log roof piled high with dirt.

The opening is narrow, tough to get a grenade in, so she drops to one knee, aims, and fires off a whole clip at that muzzle.

Pang slams into the bunker, just to the right of the hole. In a desperate voice he cries, "Fire in the hole!" and twists to almost gently roll a grenade inside.

It's an incendiary and explodes in a shower of white phosphorous, so the firing hole is suddenly a brilliant greenish-white gash of mouth. Rio tries to push a fresh clip in her M1, but it jams from grit amid the mud.

A German soldier, screaming, pushes out through the firing hole. He's been hit by the white phosphorous, which burns without regard to water, burns like acid through the German's uniform.

Rio sees his face. A fright mask of agony as the chemical eats into his body in a dozen places. He sees her. He looks at her, pleading and crying something in a begging voice.

He wants me to shoot him.

Geer shoots the burning man in the neck, turns a savage grin to Rio, and shouts, "My turn!"

Rio climbs to her feet and follows Geer forward, a dark shape wreathed in smoke and rain and darkness.

Suddenly Geer falls into the earth, and Rio realizes there's a trench ahead. Geer is bellowing and guns are blazing and Rio raises her rifle, remembers it's jammed, and stares helplessly as Geer faces three German soldiers, the four of them blazing away at close quarters. Jenou is standing at the lip of the trench behind the three Krauts, and she fires carbine rounds *pop-pop-pop-pop!* into their backs and necks and heads. Geer, miraculously unhurt, clambers up out of the trench raging at the top of his lungs. Jenou jumps the trench, Rio just behind her, Pang and Stick off to the right.

They've broken through the first line of defenses, but there's no one coming up from behind to strengthen them. Now the Krauts are to their left and right as well as ahead, and the air is practically a solid object, a ceiling of lead as the squad hugs the ground, shaking, and Geer continues to rave, "I'm comin' to kill you! I'm comin' to kill you!"

For long minutes they are paralyzed there, unable to so much as lift their heads. Then Sergeant Cole is trudging up from the river, leading two squads, all firing into the darkness over Rio's head.

But it's no good, it's no good, the Germans are too strong, too dug in, too determined. Cole yells, "Fall back!" and then twists wildly and drops to his knees.

Rio yells, "Cole!" while crawling to him, and then

pushes him down as tracers arc toward him. "Where are you hit?" she demands.

"Leg. My goddamned leg."

Blood pours from his calf, the red stain joining rainwater as Rio tears the fabric away from the bullet hole. She practically faints from relief.

"Through the meat!" she tells Cole. "You'll live."

"Tell Stick to fall back," Cole says through gritted teeth.

"We are," Rio assures him. "Come on, you can crawl."

And they do crawl. Back to the riverbank, not onto the bridge that is clogged with dead and wounded, but pulling themselves along through the water by gripping the sagging hand rope.

Back across the river. Again.

There is no respite from the far shore, with continual German fire, so they crawl and then stand and run hunched over, Pang and Rio each with an arm around the hobbling Cole.

Behind them, the Americans draw back from the river and call in artillery, which now blasts the water and the mud and makes the ground tremble, but it does not force the stubborn Germans to fall back.

An ambulance sits with engine idling behind the scant cover of a stone wall. Medics are working feverishly to bandage and splint and pile their charges into the steaming, overstuffed ambulance.

Rio sends Pang to fetch ammo and haul it back forward. "We got plenty of .30 cal, get all the smoke grenades you can carry! And see if they have any more of those limey phosphorous grenades."

The medics offer Cole a syrette of morphine as they quickly bandage his leg, but he waves it off. "Later. Listen to me, Richlin, Stick's got his hands full, so get your ass back up there."

Rio nods, overwhelmed by the stark fact that they are piling Cole into a newly arrived jeep. "You'll be okay, Sarge," Rio tells him. "You'll be okay."

"It's not me I'm worried about," he says. He feels in his pocket for a fresh cigar, but what appears is a swollen, soggy mass of brown leaves. "Well, hell."

He's leaving us.

He's leaving me!

"Sarge," Rio says, and emotion chokes her. "I . . ." What can she say when she has so much to express? There is not the slightest doubt in her mind that she's gotten this far, stayed alive this long, because of the gap-toothed man before her.

Her father had told her to find a good sergeant and stick to him. She had found that sergeant. She had stuck to him.

And now . . .

Cole sticks out his hand. She shakes it.

"You'll do fine, Richlin. You're a natural."

Suddenly there's the captain cursing a blue streak. "Back up to the line, damn you all, get back forward!"

Rio ignores him until the jeep guns its engines and goes tearing off into the night bearing Sergeant Cole.

"Bye, Sarge," Rio says.

Pang comes struggling by, loaded down with four steel ammo boxes, two in each hand, and a heavy satchel slung over his shoulder. Rio lifts the satchel, peeks inside, can't see, so thrusts a hand in to find the familiar and somehow comforting shape of the British-made white phosphorous grenades called SIPs and nicknamed thermoses for their cylindrical shape. They go trudging forward, their hearts in their boots.

"How is he?" Stick asks anxiously when they rejoin the others.

"Million-dollar wound," Pang says.

A lieutenant neither of them knows runs out of the gloom and says, "What platoon?"

Stick tells him, and the lieutenant says, "We're making another push. Right now."

"The hell we are," Stick says. "Where's Lieutenant Stone?"

"He caught a frag. He'll live, but he's gone and I'm it and my goddamned orders say to move up!"

"Shove your orders up your ass. Sir," Stick shouts.

"Listen, Sergeant, we've got a whole platoon across upstream, and they're catching it on both flanks."

"Fug!" Stick yells.

"Now!" the officer bellows with the eerie energy of terror.

And without a word to his squad, Stick starts forward on his own, unwilling to ask anyone to follow him. Rio hesitates and sees Cat looking to her as if for guidance.

"Shit!" Rio snarls and goes after Stick.

Back to the river.

Back stumbling across GIs dead and dying.

Back to the bridge now mostly gone, but with the hand rope still in place so they pull themselves across, fighting the current, pushing floating dead men and women aside, some cursing and blaspheming, others praying, most just putting one foot in front of the other.

Again, they climb the far bank, and the Germans only then spot them. The fire is less this time. The phosphorous in the German bunker has flamed out at last, and they spill into the reeking bunker.

For the first time in an eternity, they are out of the rain. Two German soldiers lie dead. One still burns, his uniform wicking melted human fat into a flame.

With shaking fingers Rio taps out a Lucky Strike and settles it in the corner of her mouth. She pulls out her

Zippo and lights it, letting the smoke fill her nostrils and disguise the stench of burning flesh.

"What now, Stick?" Geer asks.

"The Krauts will counterattack, try to push us out," he says. "So we don't let 'em. Castain, check that Kraut MG."

"Barrel's bent," Jenou reports. "And the ammo's mostly cooked off from the phosphorous."

"Okay, Cat, get the BAR set up here." Cat has inherited the BAR. He points to the crawl hole that forms the entry to the bunker. "Get as far up as you can without exposing yourself." Then, to Rio, "Richlin, up on the roof, take Geer with you. The rest of you, dig in on both flanks."

Rio climbs atop the bunker, up onto logs covered with mud held together by straw that had been crushed down into the seams between logs. It's not a comfortable firing position, prone on those logs, but it gives her a good field of fire. Without needing to discuss it, Rio takes the left, Geer the right. Twenty yards away, Jenou digs a hole with Pang, and on the other side, Geer's side, Beebee digs in with Jack. Stick stays in the bunker to help feed Cat and watch the firing hole, which now points back toward their own forces, but which might be turned by determined Germans.

It is not much of a position, Rio reflects, but farther away on both flanks the Americans are making similar preparations for the counterattack, which is not long in coming.

This time it's the Germans who favor smoke to cover their assault. They appear like creatures from a nightmare, emerging from smoke and fog, their Schmeissers chattering, their Mausers *pop-pop-pop*ping, tossing their twirling, baton-like grenades.

Cat's BAR erupts first, followed instantly by the rifles and carbines of the rest of the squad.

Mortar teams start dropping their bombs on the advancing Germans with decent marksmanship that blows holes in the smoke and produces screams of pain.

Rio aims and fires, aims and fires, aims and fires, and for every two rounds she fires, a German soldier falls dead or wounded. Geer beside her is, as usual, cursing as he shoots, but shoot he does and with some accuracy.

Days of mud. Days of rain and cold. Days of cold canned food. And above all, days of helplessly marching into prepared positions to be gunned down. It all forms a burning core in Rio's heart, and at last, at long last, the boot is on the other foot. Now she is the one with some cover. She is the one with altitude. She is the one who can lie there taking aim and taking a life with a twitch of her right index finger.

They keep coming, even as a welcome breeze wafts the smoke away and multiplies Rio's targets.

She kills and laughs, kills and yells, "Hah!" She kills and yes, yes it is pleasurable, yes, she is enjoying it. Yes, each time one of the gray-uniformed Kraut bastards drops she exults, she gloats, and aims and fires, curses when she misses and bares her teeth each time her bullet finds German flesh.

A chant has started off to the right somewhere, voices yelling, *Die! Die! Die!* and for a while the squad takes it up, yelling, "Die!"

Rio hears Jenou's voice, her husky alto yelling "Die! Die!" as Jenou stands in her thigh-high hole, stands foolishly exposed but heedless, her carbine level, muzzle blazing, brass flying away, magazines dropped, and new ones popped in.

It is pure and clean: infantry against infantry, rifle against rifle, and Rio pops in a new clip and fires again and again, a chest here, a head there, a scream, a gurgle, a wounded man flinging down his rifle to run away and taking Rio's round in his spine, a coward's wound.

Now the German advance wavers. They are tripping over the bodies of their own dead. Someone, somewhere, maybe the captain, maybe just some keyed-up GI, yells, "Advance!"

Up come the Americans, up out of foxholes, out of their appropriated German bunkers, up from the slick banks of the river behind, men and women in dirty green, walking forward firing from hip and shoulder, and the Germans break.

A fell roar goes up, an animal sound, a brutal, murderous noise that tears from hundreds of throats, from hundreds of GIs tired of taking it and lusting to dish it out.

Cat Preeling, looking like some comic book illustration, her helmet gone somewhere, her BAR at her hip, walks forward like the messenger of doom, firing and yelling something wordless.

It can't last long, they all know it in their hearts, all except the green kids. This is the Wehrmacht on the run, but the Wehrmacht never runs except to reach yet another prepared defensive position.

They push the Germans back a quarter mile before reaching the next line of bunkers and firing positions, and there the disciplined German fire forces them back down into the mud.

34

RIO RICHLIN—MONTE CASSINO, ITALY

They take the next German position, and the one after that. Day after day the rain falls and the mud slides and the artillery drops out of the sky and maims and kills.

Day after day, night after night, one firefight after another, they move along the ridges that lead to Monte Cassino, to the taking of that great and terrible massif with its gloomy, ethereal monastery.

Three times Stick has asked Lieutenant Stone, who has reappeared after treating a minor wound, to demand they be taken off the line. Three times Stone has told him that the captain isn't having it, because the colonel isn't having it and the general isn't having it.

The squad moves like zombies, no longer capable of conversation, no longer really capable of thought. They fire and throw grenades and they fall in the mud and lie there, so gone, so destroyed they might as well be dead. And yet, they rise when Stick calls them or shoves them or kicks them, and they advance.

Everyone is sick. Some have picked up malaria, others have dysentery, there are cases of pneumonia and frostbite. Men and women alike find their feet have gone numb, the flesh a puffy, disintegrating white. They urinate and defecate in their fighting holes rather than risk a sniper's bullet and sleep in their own filth. They are no longer men and women, they are beasts, unshaven, dirty, stinking, grunting beasts.

Sometimes a soldier has had enough and simply throws down his or her weapon and walks toward the rear. Some keep walking until they get back to Naples, where many hide or join in black market activities. But most who walk away come back after a day or two. It upsets the officers, but the GIs understand—they all know it could be them in a week, or a day, or an hour.

Rio no longer has any sense of how many days have passed, no clear notion of how far they've advanced, and very little hope of something that could be called victory. Sometimes, from some positions, she can look up and see the monastery through the rain, and it never seems any less far away. The more they push toward it, the farther away it seems, for after each hill, there is another hill; after each German position, there's another. On and on, and endless repetition, always moving forward and somehow never getting anywhere.

At last comes the word.

Stick pulls back a corner of the tattered shelter half over the hole Rio is sharing with Jenou and Jack and says, "They're taking us off the line. Move out in five."

It should be time for relief, even exultation. But emotion is an impossible luxury now. So they pack up their gear and clamber up out of their hole and trudge downhill, downhill for the first time in . . . in forever.

Rio walks asleep, or very near to it. One foot moves in front of the other with the regularity and mindlessness of a machine. She walks past rows of bodies laid by the side of the road, bloated, decayed, gruesomely torn bodies that have lost their power to move her.

Off the road, in ditches, on the stony sides of ridges, lie the German dead. All have been stripped of souvenirs, so their uniforms lie unbuttoned and askew. Here and there a dead Kraut has been propped against a tree or a rock so some grim joker can stick a cigarette in his mouth, or scrawl a clever sign and hang it around his neck.

One German, his head gone, has been leaned against a blasted German 88 and a cardboard drawing of Adolf Hitler has been propped on the stump of his neck to suggest a dead Führer.

After an eternity they stumble onto waiting trucks and are hauled like cattle to the rear staging area a mile away at the edge of a town that is now little more than a rock quarry.

And suddenly, there is hot food. There are proper tents

with channels dug around them like moats to keep out the water.

Rio makes it no farther. She falls face-first onto a cot and is asleep before her body hits the canvas. No dreams. Nothing. She is destroyed, finished, drained of every last ounce of energy, a body without a mind.

When she wakes it is to the sound of hail pelting the roof of the tent. She is still in her vile uniform, her boots still on her feet, weighed down now with dried mud rather than wet.

Her body is a single, unified mass of aches and bruises as she sits up, blinks owlishly in the gray half-light, and sees Jenou in the next bunk, writing in the back of Magraff's sketch pad. That fact should surprise Rio, but what draws her attention with far greater force is that Jenou is wearing a clean uniform. A damp uniform, but a clean one.

"D'jget that?" Rio mutters, tongue woolly.

"Well, hello, sleeping beauty," Jenou says.

"Fresh gear?"

Jenou nods. "Uniforms, hot chow, and a shower, which is available for women from ten a.m. to . . . Well, you could just make it." Jenou sets down the pad, stands up, gives Rio her hand, and hauls her to her feet. "Follow me."

The shower is a fifty-five-gallon drum raised on a plat-form, with four pieces of pipe welded in place, each ending not in a showerhead, but in a simple valve that releases a moderate stream of icy cold but mud-free water. The four shower pipes are set up in a canvas-walled enclosure. An official stenciled sign reads: *GI Janes Only, 10 to 2.* An unofficial, handmade sign below reads: *Any male organ found on the premises between 10 and 2 will be removed and sent to the mess tent.*

Rio finds a scrap of soap resting in a mess kit on the ground. But before she can employ soap she first lets the water sluice away unbelievable layers of filth, filth in every crack and every orifice.

And then: soap.

Rio is crying by the time she lathers the soap and covers her hair, her face, her body—every inch of her body. Soap! *Soap!* The smell of it. The feel of it. It's a small, slippery piece of humanity and civilization. She lathers and rinses, and then does it all again.

When at last she can no longer take the cold, she finds Jenou standing by with a neatly folded and astoundingly clean uniform.

From there it's to the mess hall tent, where Rio would have happily devoured her weight in SOS without a complaint. But the cooks have done better, layering on scrambled eggs (powdered) and sausages and wonderful, fluffy, freshly made biscuits with butter(!) and jam(!). And of course, there is coffee. Coffee! The magical beverage. There's a great, steaming tureen of coffee, all the coffee in the world, and it's hot, and it's not made from instant, and it contains no tiny pieces of gravel or leftover corned beef.

Rio eats and drinks like an animal, shoveling, swallowing without chewing, until she is full. And then she keeps eating and drinking but uses her fork and spoon.

Jenou doesn't say much, just sits patiently, watching her friend eat and drink. When Rio is at last sated, Jenou says, "You're going to want to sleep some more."

"I slept plenty," Rio says.

"Uh-huh," Jenou says, and leads her back to the tent. Rio says she just wants to close her eyes for a minute and wakes up ten hours later.

It is night when she opens her eyes. For a while she can't tell where she is. It takes a while before vague memories of soap and food come floating up to her conscious mind.

She sits up and looks around her. Jenou, asleep, snoring lightly. Cat, asleep, snoring not so lightly. Jack sitting in his cot, writing a letter by the light of a small candle. Beebee counting something on his cot and arranging things in short stacks: packs of smokes. Stick, passed out, facedown in his cot.

"Where's Geer? And Pang?" Rio asks, dreading the answer.

Jack sets his letter aside and smiles crookedly at her. "She lives! As for Geer and Pang, I believe they are playing poker in another tent. Quite healthy, I assure you, though I imagine they'll both be broke when they get back."

"How long?" she asks in a hoarse voice.

"They pulled us off the line three days ago," Jack says. "Since then we've all been sleeping, eating, and sleeping some more, though not all at the same time. I'm told I was medically dead for twenty-four hours."

He still has the red hair and the freckles, but the boyish mischief is gone now, or at least weighed down. His eyes are deep, sunken into his skull. There's a twitch at the corner of his mouth, a tic in his cheek that nervously simulates a mirthless smile. He's still Jack, but a different Jack, older, sadder perhaps, but enough of Jack that he still bothers with a wisecrack.

Rio wonders what she herself looks like. How much does her face show what she has been through? There's a blank deadness to her emotions, a distance from the world around her as if she's standing on the other side of a sheet of frosted glass and can see people only dimly, hear them as if from a distance, touch them not at all.

"When are we going back up?" she asks.

Jack shakes his head. "The 119th took forty percent casualties, half of those KIA. Rumor is they're going to ship us out."

"Out? Where?"

Jack shrugs. "Home. At least, my home, England. But it's just scuttlebutt."

"What happened?" She jerks her chin toward the tent opening, but Jack understands her meaning. She means the massif. She means the monastery.

She means Monte Cassino.

"Attack failed. We hold some positions, but Jerry chewed up the Frogs on our flank, and well, you know what happened to us."

"Then they'll send us back."

He shakes his head. "I don't think so. Anyway, not you." There's a ghost of his old smile. "The general wants to see you."

Rio's feeling numb, but this cuts through and makes her sit up sharply. "What?" Her first thought is that she is in trouble—very serious trouble, unprecedented trouble, if a one-star general is asking for her.

Jack shrugs. He clearly knows something he's not saying. "Standing request for you to go see the general as soon as you wake up."

This is even stranger: generals do not summon corporals. That's odd enough, but if a general *does* summon a corporal it comes with a "right now," not a "wait till she's awake." She can't quite process the thought: *A general? Wants me?*

Whenever I happen to wake up?

"What the hell?" she mutters, and climbs stiffly to her feet. "What time is it?"

"About 1900 hours. It looks later than it is."

Rio wishes for three things: coffee, a smoke, and for Jenou to somehow accompany her. It's like being called to the principal's office, and she wants a friend along. But of course it will never do: the summoned one goes, not the summoned one plus her friend. Anyway, Jenou is currently dead to the world.

But Rio does manage a smoke, and she swings by the mess tent and captures the last half cup of coffee, en route to the general's tent, which is . . . no idea. She has never really seen this camp, which is a confusion of tents and vehicles and men, some rushing about, others drifting half dead.

She asks an MP and gets directions. The HQ is two tents strung together, with an MP guard at the pinned-back flap. Rio is sure she smells cooked beef inside. The general is having his dinner, a great, juicy steak no doubt, him being a general. But on being informed that a Corporal Richlin is there, the great man calls her in.

Brigadier General Rufus Valdosta is a bespectacled man with sparse hair combed over a skull that shines in the grim light of a kerosene lantern. His uniform is clean but basic GI with none of Patton's swaggering embellishment or Mark Clark's elite tailoring. Valdosta is a fighting general, an Army Reserve major given temporary rank and thrust into a position for which he, like most of the army, is barely prepared.

He is at a foldable table, sitting on a camp chair. Rio is obscurely pleased to see that what's on the plate before him is not a steak as she'd imagined, but SOS: creamed beef on toast. He's drinking coffee, and there she spots the only sign of privilege: his coffee has been lightened with milk or cream.

Valdosta stands to accept her salute, puts her at ease, and offers her coffee. "Or maybe something stronger? I don't indulge in spirits myself, but I don't begrudge others."

Rio refuses both, feeling way too far from comfortable to be able to calmly sip coffee and nibble cookies. An aide brings a second camp chair, and Rio sits, moving like an old woman as joints and muscles complain bitterly.

"You've had a time of it," Valdosta says.

"Yes, sir." Rio flashes on Mackie, way back in another life, telling her new recruits that 90 percent of what they needed to say was "Yes, Sergeant." Now it was "Yes, sir," but the principle was the same: you never went far wrong answering in the affirmative.

"Well, Corporal, I don't mind telling you that when the Supreme Court in its wisdom decided to send young ladies to war, I thought it was the damned foolest thing ever. I still regret it extremely. I suppose I've always thought of war as a male vice and was grateful that at least half the human race could be spared it."

He takes a swig of his coffee, and though she hasn't asked for it, a cup arrives for Rio. She is grateful for its warmth and the comfort of familiarity in this extremely unusual environment. No cookies arrive, and she is vaguely disappointed.

"That said, I am a man of reason. I follow the facts. Women soldiers are on average almost but not quite as effective as the male—they fall out for exhaustion at a higher rate. And we've got the new problem of soldiers getting in the family way, or at least claiming they have so they can catch the bus home. And needless to say, army doctors are not gynecologists. On the other hand," he says, pursing his lips and frowning, "the females get in fewer bar fights, catch a lot less clap, and never desert, at least not for long."

Rio adopts a deliberately blank expression, concealing her guilt at the mention of bar fights.

"As for you, young lady, Corporal Richlin, I have the great honor to inform you that you have been recognized for valor."

Rio doesn't know what he means by this, but she feels certain it demands a "Thank you, sir."

"Don't thank me." He pushes his plate away, hauls a leather briefcase up onto his table, fiddles with the buckles, and then searches through papers within. And finally says, "And here it is." He lays the paper down and taps it with his forefinger. "Don't thank me, thank the captain, the two lieutenants, and the two sergeants who have all attested to your actions in Africa, in Sicily, and now here in Italy."

Mystified but staying cautious, she says, "Yes, sir."

Then he smiles. "You don't understand what I'm saying, do you? Your kind never does. Richlin, by order of the President of the United States, you have been awarded the Silver Star for gallantry in action. And by God, having read the record on you, I don't doubt you deserve it." He stands, and so does she. He sticks out his hand, and she stares at it for a few seconds before reaching, almost frightened, to shake it.

"Sir, I . . . The platoon, the whole outfit . . . Stick, I mean, Sergeant Sticklin . . ."

He waves her to silence. "Like I said, your kind never does understand why they're getting a medal. I've had the pleasure of handing out a few such, and I've never yet had one where the soldier didn't try to throw all the honor onto his brothers." He dipped his head. "Sisters too, now."

She nods and means to say *Yes, sir*, but a lump has

formed in her throat, and, to her horror, there are tears in her eyes.

"This is the first time for one of your, um, sex. You and a couple others. They want to make a bit of a show out of it, I'm afraid, so you'll find orders waiting for you to take transport to England, and there you can have the whole kit and caboodle."

The dreaded tears spill and run down her cheeks, and Valdosta, noticing, says, "Well, so you are still a female, I see. I suppose I'm old-fashioned. I'm used to female tears, but I freely confess I had not known females had it in them to be so fierce: I'd have been much more cautious around Mrs. Valdosta and not slept nearly so soundly back in Missouri."

Rio can't help but smile at that.

"You'll be made sergeant, of course, probably should have been by now, but better late than—"

"Sir! General, I . . . I'm sorry, sir. Permission to say something?"

"What is it?"

"Don't make me a sergeant. Please. I'm happy . . ." That word stops her because of course she is not *happy*, but now she's stuck with it. "I never even wanted to make corporal."

He stares at her for a long while, and Rio can see that his mind is elsewhere, remembering, reliving. He shakes his head at last. "Don't like the weight, eh?"

She shakes her head. "I just want to do my job."

"Well, young lady, this is my division, the one-one-nine. And it's been hit pretty hard." He's heaving the words up, sighing, pushing past his own emotion. "Pretty hard. It has taken terrible casualties, casualties taken because I sent it into battle and kept it there. The 'job' you speak of isn't just going in harm's way yourself, it's sending others there too. People you know, maybe even friends. You're brave, you're tough, you can fight. I guess now we'll see if you can lead."

Rio heads out into the dark, out under an eerie and surprising sight: the clouds have cleared, a little at least, and she sees stars overhead, actual stars!

And in the distance the impossibly steep massif of Monte Cassino, and the tall, forbidding walls of its monastery.

Jack is waiting for her, and Jenou and Cat are awake.

"So?" Jack says.

Rio shrugs.

"You're an official hero, and all you can manage is a shrug and a look like you swallowed Geer's cat?"

Miss Lion has been retrieved from the quartermaster, who fed her while Geer was on the line. She lies atop a snoring Geer, glaring at everyone around her as though she's a watchdog and she doesn't like the look of any of them, no, she definitely does not.

Hansu Pang comes up and extends a hand. "Congratulations, Richlin."

"Thanks, Pang, but—"

"Come on, Richlin," Cat says with a groan. "Cut the humble act, we have important business to deal with." At that she produces an almost-full bottle of brandy. "It's a damn celebration, whether you like it or not."

"They're talking about making me a sergeant," Rio says wonderingly.

"About time," Jack says.

Cat uncorks the bottle, which wakes Geer, who in turn smacks Stick on his back. "Come on, Stick, we're drinking."

They pass the bottle solemnly, like a ritual, like some parody of holy communion. Cat, Pang, Geer, Jack, Jenou, Beebee, and a sleepy but smiling Stick.

"They're sending me out early. I guess you all follow later," Rio says.

"We hate to lose you," Stick says sincerely. "Even just for a while."

"They can't force me to take a promotion, can they?"

"Well," Geer drawls. "They can force you to leave your home and come wallow like a hog in the mud of Italy, so I'm guessing they can force you to do whatever the hell they like."

There's a bit of teasing after that, various members of the squad competing to come up with examples of how much better it'll be once Rio is gone.

Won't have to listen to her bitching about SOS.

You know those sneaky farts no one admits to? That's Richlin.

Who's going to steal all my smokes once Richlin's gone?

Eventually it's just Rio and Jenou, and they leave the smoke-filled tent for fresh air.

"Whoa," Jenou says. "Are those stars?"

"Yeah, shocked me too."

"You know, Rio, chances are you won't end up back with us."

Rio shakes her head. "I won't let that happen."

Jenou laughs. "I'm not sure a little tin star on your chest will give you godlike powers, Rio."

"I'll do my damnedest," Rio protests. "I'll refuse to fight."

"Honey, don't be a fool. You're going to be the first woman ever—*ever*—to earn the Silver Star; they're not going to send you back to the line. They'll trot you around like a show horse for the newspapers and the cameras and probably have you giving speeches and sleeping in fancy hotels, ordering up steak and lobster."

Rio takes a step back. "That's bull."

Jenou sighs and shakes her head. "Well, maybe not, I don't know. But we better face up to the fact that this may be good-bye, at least until the war is over."

"No!" Rio cries. "No, that's not right, that's nuts. We're in this together. You and me, Jen."

"Sweetie, all we've done is get on each other's nerves."

"Fug that, we can get on each other's nerves and still be friends, can't we?"

"I don't know."

That answer cuts Rio like a knife.

Jenou sees her reaction and squeezes her hand. "You're a genuine, certified, grade-A hero now, Rio. Me? I'm just a plain old dog-faced soldier." She takes a beat before adding, "Well, a very pretty dog-faced soldier."

"You're my friend, Jen," Rio says, urgently returning Jenou's pressure on her hand. "You have to always be my friend."

"I'm not the right friend for someone like you."

"You fought as hard as I did," Rio insists. "You put as many Krauts in the ground as Geer or Cat or me."

Jenou nods, accepting this, and even smiles in gratitude. "Let me make it clear for you, Rio. Like I said, I don't expect I'll make it through this war. I used to. I used to think . . . hell, we all did, didn't we? Used to think it couldn't happen to us? I don't believe that anymore. When I catch it, I don't want you to be the one who sent me."

"You think I'll get you killed?" Rio feels hurt by the suggestion, but it's instantly clear that she hasn't understood.

"No, I don't think that. I mean, sure, it could be you, but it could be anyone or anything. But if it is you, it'll eat you up inside. That's part of it. The other part is that I've been leaning on you." She straightens her spine and holds her head high. "I'm ready now."

"Ready for what?"

"Ready to stop leaning on you, my best friend. My brave, fearless best friend. The sister I never had. Funny thing is, once you accept the fact of death, you stop being afraid." She sighs and tilts her head back to look at the stars and says, "I don't like any part of this whole goddamned war, but I'm ready now to pull my own weight. You've become a hero, Rio, and to my amazement, I, Jenou Castain, have become a soldier."

Rio parts the next morning, with tears from Jenou, and the inevitable jokes and gibes and nonsense from the others.

Rio, seated in the back of a truck, waves to Jenou and Cat and, coming to stand beside them, Jack.

Jack makes a fist, places it over his heart, and bows to her. Then he disappears as the truck column obscures Rio's view.

FRANGIE MARR—US ARMY HOSPITAL, PORTSMOUTH, UK

"Just hold it still, Frank. How many times do I have to tell you to hold it still?"

"Well, it hurts, Miss Frangie!"

"Nonsense. Goodness, you'd think you were the only person here with a bullet wound. Look at me!" She holds up her right hand, now with just four fingers and a tiny stump. "When I got hurt, I was a perfectly obedient patient."

A nurse walking by says, "Uh-huh," in a sarcastic voice.

Frangie cuts the old, yellowed bandage with a pair of blunt-tipped scissors. The wound was a through-and-through on Frank's right arm, with the bullet managing to pass between the ulna and the radius, chipping the ulna but not breaking either bone.

Frangie uses gauze, alcohol, and distilled water to carefully clean the wound, teasing away dried blood and shreds of cotton.

"How's it look?" Frank asks.

"How's it look to you?" Frangie teases. Frank is a staff sergeant, a tough soldier by all accounts, but he does not like the sight of his own blood, not even a little. He keeps his head averted, arm propped on the little tray that Frangie carries from bed to bed. "Looks good to me," Frangie says after he refuses to respond. She leans close and sniffs the wound. "Smells good too."

This is a trick she's picked up from one of the doctors, a pacifist from Cincinnati with too much experience with gangrene. *You'll smell it before you see it*, he'd told her.

Having long since become stiffly ambulatory, Frangie has begun to help out on the ward, replacing bandages, taking temperatures, doling out medication, and holding hands and offering reassurance.

Her broken leg still aches when she stands or walks for too long, but she is long past the need for morphine. There's a new, smaller cast on her leg, but aside from that, and the missing finger, and some shrapnel scars scattered around her body—little arcs or twists or dimples of pinkish flesh against the black—she shows no obvious signs of her near-death experience. She has lost fifteen pounds—quite a lot on her small frame—but paradoxically this makes her seem larger, somehow, harder and stronger.

In fact she has taken advantage of the sketchy rehabilitation equipment to begin a regime of strengthening her arms, legs, and back. Her wounds, and the subsequent illness, have left her feeling vulnerable. Her experience has also had two seemingly contradictory effects on her thinking: on the one hand she feels the pain of her patients with exquisite sympathy, sympathy so deep it almost seems to make their wounds hers.

But on the other hand, she now knows the difference between serious pain and the mere discomfort Frank is feeling. And while she is patient, she is not above teasing the less stoic patients.

"Yep, looks fine. Should be no problem now having Dr. Stuart saw that thing right off."

"What? What are you . . . Oh, dang it, Miss Frangie! You're trying to get under my skin."

She grins as she finishes winding a new bandage around his arm. "There you go, you big baby."

They call her Miss Frangie. She's not a nurse, she's not a doctor, nor is she an orderly like Harder. She has no official position in the hospital and is essentially a volunteer, but far more capable than the barely trained British women who so generously volunteer. Somehow "Miss Frangie" has become her title, position, and name, all in one.

Every day she checks in with the officer on duty to see whether her orders have come through. But day after day the answer is the same, "Nope. Nothing for you, Miss

Frangie. Guess you'll just have to stay here."

Here is not a bad place to be. She follows the war news on the BBC and in the papers, and between the official reports and the rather less optimistic tales she hears from wounded soldiers, she knows what's happening in Italy. It does not sound like anything she wants to be a part of, though she worries about Sergeant Green. And the rest too, but mostly Walter Green.

Here she has a nice clean bunk in an overheated room she shares with three American nurses and a Polish anesthetist, all female. Every morning there is a hot breakfast followed by a hotter shower. Her uniforms are professionally laundered and pressed and contain no lice. She has no gear to haul, no trucks to unload, no paperwork to fill out, and aside from the occasional air raid warning, no reason to be afraid.

Best of all, she is getting to know Harder better. He is fire to her soothing balm, but once she lets him have his rant about the oppressed workers and the valiant comrades in the USSR, he can be great fun. They talk, they play board games or cards with patients, they work, each in their own function, and they take walks into the village.

And they talk about Tulsa, Oklahoma, in June of 1921. They talk as well of the lynchings that used to happen several times a week, but have died down a bit since the twenties, though Harder of course had a long list of more recent atrocities. He's doing that as they walk—slowly, given Frangie's leg—through the little village. It's cold, but not miserably so, except when the breeze freshens and cuts through their field jackets, and even through the very welcome scarves knitted and donated by British women and folks back home.

"They lynched a soldier out of Fort Benning. Lynched him in full uniform!" And his stories are not limited to lynchings and burnings. "They promoted three colored men at a Packard plant up in Detroit? Just three. Twenty-five thousand white workers went out on strike. Know what they said, those patriotic white boys? Said, 'We'd rather see Hitler and Hirohito win than work alongside a Nigra.'"

"Maybe all this"—she waves in a way meant to encompass the village, the hospital, the air base beyond, and the entirety of the war—"will change things."

Harder laughs cynically. "Nothing is going to change, Frangie. Nothing changes without revolution, a socialist people's revolution."

Frangie steers the conversation onto safer ground by pointing to a flight of bombers passing by overhead, on their way to Germany.

Harder is still a fire-breather, still naive in Frangie's eyes, despite his grand allusions to Marx and Lenin and the Soviet this and the Soviet that. Most difficult of all for

Frangie is the fact that he sneers at the faith she relies on. The *opiate of the masses*.

And yet, much of what he says gets through. The tales of lynchings, of beatings, of castrations, of the fear that pervades the South and has now moved north as black people follow the defense industry jobs into Chicago and Los Angeles and Detroit.

She has not forgotten the white sergeant who tried to rape her. She has not forgotten the slurs and the open hatred she's gotten from white troops. She does not ignore the fact that even now white officers command black troops, and white generals try their best to assign black units to the most demeaning tasks.

And now that she knows the truth of Tulsa in June of 1921, she cannot look at her own brother's face, at the color of his skin, without being forced to imagine their mother's suffering.

There are good white people, she tells herself. She's met good white people. And all people, all people of all colors, are the children of God, all sinners, all in need of redemption through the blood of Christ. But her imagination tortures her, playing again and again what must have happened to her mother, over and over like an eternal newsreel, each image more lurid and horrifying than the one before.

They cut deep, those images.

"Miss Frangie?" It's a corporal striding purposefully toward them from behind.

"What is it?" she asks.

"Colonel wants to see you."

This is tantamount to being summoned to meet Moses or Franklin D. Roosevelt. Frangie has had no dealings at all with the base commander. No reason on earth why she should, she's a lowly detached medic awaiting orders. The distance between Frangie Marr and a colonel is vast and unbridgeable in her mind.

"But . . . why?" she asks.

The corporal shrugs. "Colonel tells captain, captain tells lieutenant, loot tells me, and here I am telling you."

Frangie glances at Harder for support, but Harder just frowns, no doubt annoyed at having his latest sermon interrupted.

Frangie follows the corporal to a jeep and is then driven to the air base and the HQ building, a grand estate that has been ceded to the military by its owner, an earl or a count or whatever—Frangie has never been clear on what those titles mean.

Her fear grows with each minute of the trip. Has the colonel somehow gotten word that she's talking revolution with her Communist brother? One thing is certain: it's trouble. She is in some sort of trouble.

But apparently the trouble can wait as she is told to

take a place in the small waiting room outside the colonel's office. She takes a seat. A white lieutenant, also waiting, sniffs noisily and moves ostentatiously to the seat farthest from her. But the colonel's secretary brings her a cup of tea with milk and sugar in the British style, which she's come to like.

She waits and sips and wishes she had something to read. The lieutenant is called in. She waits some more. The lieutenant leaves. She waits as a pair of privates arrive and are shown immediately into the office. She waits as they emerge with relieved smiles on their faces.

Frangie waits as six different individuals are shown in, one after another, and the hours slowly tick away on the wall clock. Finally, at what must be the last hour of the colonel's day before heading off to dinner, she is summoned. The kind secretary shows her in.

The colonel is Air Corps, tall, distinguished looking with gray temples and extravagant, sandy eyebrows.

She advances to an imaginary line on the floor before the colonel's desk and salutes.

The colonel looks at her with what feels to Frangie like naked hostility.

"So you're the little Nigra who crawled under a tank?"

He has not returned her salute, which leaves her standing at attention, right index finger on her right eyebrow, waiting.

"Sir?"

"I don't suppose we need to ask how it happens that some coon gets himself trapped under a tank."

"I . . . Sir, they told me he—"

"Goldbricking, if I know my Nigras. Avoiding work. Is that it, Marr? Was he shirking?"

"I don't believe so, sir. I think he was green and didn't—"

"Are you contradicting me?" He finally tosses her an indifferent salute.

"I only know what they told me, sir," she says, lowering her hand at last.

"Well, *I'm* telling you: he was shirking, like you people do. Isn't that right, Marr?"

He is directly challenging her to contradict him. Frangie feels herself melting into her boots, withering beneath his hard glare. "If you say so, sir."

"You're goddamned right about that: if I say so. And I do say so, and do you know how I know? Because I know the Nigra, that's how. I grew up on a large farm in Mississippi, and we . . . employed . . . your kind to pick cotton and never once did I see a Nigra really work hard."

It was not a question. No answer is possible. So she stands at attention feeling small and helpless and bewildered.

"Now this," the colonel says. He holds up a piece

of paper. "Goddamn insult to the white boys out there giving their lives for freedom. They won't be getting a medal, you can be damn sure of that, because they don't have the president's wife nagging and bullying for them."

Now Frangie is left to pick out words and phrases and try to piece them together, make some kind of sense of them. But her mind is at sea, lost and confused.

"You have anything to say other than yassuh, nosuh?"

"No, sir," she says.

"At ease." He twirls the paper toward her. She makes a grab at it but misses and has to stoop to pick it up off the floor.

"Take that and get your black ass off my base. Dismissed."

Frangie flees the room, and the building, and finding no transportation waiting, begins the long, chilly walk back to the hospital on her aching leg. She waits until she is well clear of the HQ estate, clear off the manicured grounds, out onto the hedge-lined road with the sun dropping fast and the shadows lengthening before she tries, at last, to read the paper.

It is a set of orders for her.

It takes her several tries, starting, stopping, and restarting, to make sense of the official language.

She is to take the earliest available transportation to

HQ First US Army Group (FUSAG) at Dover, United Kingdom. There is some detail—a unit, an officer she's to report to—but still Frangie can make no sense of it until she sees two words:

Silver Star.

She stops walking. Stops breathing, as she reads:

The President of the United States, authorized by act of Congress, has awarded the Silver Star to:

And then, centered on the page, her name and her rank. And below that, what is labeled as the citation, which begins:

Corporal Francine Marr distinguished herself for gallantry . . .

It goes on to describe how she had crawled beneath the tank. And then it talks about the day she was wounded in action and *"Despite her own severe wounds, and with indifference to the enemy fire directed at her, Corporal Marr continued to treat injured soldiers . . ."*

This last part baffles Frangie. She has a vague memory of trying to close a man's stomach wound after she'd been injured, but the citation makes it seem she'd done more than that. Apparently she had treated three soldiers, saving one from almost certain death, before succumbing to her injuries and being evacuated.

"Well," Frangie says to no one but a horse standing in the field. "I wonder what Harder will make of this?"

36

RAINY SCHULTERMAN—NAPLES, ITALY

Colonel Jon Herkemeier comes to see her every day. Sometimes he takes his lunch with her in the room they've given her all to herself. She has a balcony wide enough to accommodate a table and two chairs and, weather permitting, Rainy likes to be out of doors. Today, however, will not be an *al fresco* day. It is raining steadily and, like everyone else who thought Italy was always warm and sunny, Rainy has long since been disabused of that notion.

Rainy's quarters are as luxurious as a five-star hotel. The room has high ceilings framed in massive wooden moldings. There are oil portraits on the wall, mostly gloomy, dark things showing various Italian notables in Renaissance tights and early-nineteenth-century uniforms. But one has caught her eye, a portrait of a thirtyish man with a bulbous nose and protruding eyes and an expression that suggests he is inclined to be amused. In fact he looks as if he is preparing a witty remark and will deliver it just as soon as the artist leaves him alone. It's said to be a genuine Antonello da Messina, not an artist Rainy has heard of, but evidently somewhat famous.

She has taken to talking to the portrait at times when she needs distraction. She calls the man Pip, for no real reason except that he looks like a Pip, and she enjoys saying the word with its two percussive Ps.

"Well, Pip, I don't think I like the weather in your country. Say what? With a name like Rainy I should love this weather? Say what, old Pip?"

She has been given no duties, she is on R and R, rest and recuperation. Military Intelligence has better facilities for such things than regular GIs would get—no villas for regular GIs, and there was a time that might have bothered her, but she doesn't have the energy for fairness. Her days are spent reading books from the villa's library. She's already worked her way through Machiavelli's *The Prince*, an Italian translation of *The Great Gatsby*, and most of Dante's *Divine Comedy* in the original Italian.

When not reading books she reads and rereads letters from home with all their worry about her and all their relief that she is well. Aryeh has even managed to write, though reading between the lines, Rainy fears he is having a hard slog in the Pacific. Curse words have started to slip into his speech, and snide remarks about "our lords and masters with the stars on their shoulders."

She has the freedom of the villa but rarely ventures out. Her face is no longer swollen, but her bruises are still in evidence, and while she is recovering her strength, she tires easily and walks hunched like an old woman, holding on to the marble rails as she goes up- or downstairs. Her hair is just starting to grow back in. Her appearance causes people to stop working and stare after her with sober, concerned expressions.

So she mostly stays in her room and is able to have her meals brought to her there. Breakfast with Pip. Lunch with Herkemeier. Suppers with Pip and a book. Day after day.

Now she goes to her balcony, staying under cover so the rain sheets just in front of her face. She closes her eyes and savors the chilly mist. And when she opens her eyes again she sees Colonel Herkemeier hurrying through the garden, his briefcase held above his head to shield himself from the downpour.

"It's not lunchtime yet, is it, Pip? Oh, you don't have a watch? Not invented in your day, eh? Well, sorry, old fellow, but I don't think they'd like me painting one on for you."

Two minutes later a very damp and somewhat out of breath Herkemeier knocks on her door.

"How are you today, Rainy?" he asks, a standard greeting—they have set titles aside for now—but that is not a standard expression on his face. Herkemeier has something he wants to tell her, and it shines from him.

"What's going on, Jon?" she asks.

He lays his briefcase on a side table, opens it, withdraws an envelope, and draws out several sheets of paper.

"You might want to sit down," he says.

She takes his advice and sits in a remarkably uncomfortable but no doubt valuable antique chair.

He remains standing, unfolds the pages, and begins to read. "The President of the United States, authorized by act of Congress, has awarded the Silver Star to Sergeant Elisheva Schulterman, US Army."

He lowers the paper to gauge her reaction. When she stares blankly he goes on.

"Sergeant Schulterman parachuted behind enemy lines in North Africa during . . ."

He reads and Rainy stares, first at him, then at the rug, then up at Pip, who is amused, as always. The citation begins with her parachuting behind enemy lines in North Africa. Then it talks of a secret mission that had her landing in Italy months before the Allied invasion at Salerno. This part is short on detail—secrecy, of course—so there is no explanation of the nature of her mission, only that it was of "the greatest importance to the war effort." And it mentions heroic resistance to capture, and resistance to torture at the hands of the Gestapo.

Torture. She hates hearing that word.

Her hands tremble on her lap. Tears blur her vision. Words are impossible.

"It's a *first*, Rainy. There's never been a female Silver Star recipient."

She nods.

"They're flying you to England to get the award. Probably from some general. They'll make a big deal about it in the press, it being the first time women soldiers have—"

"There are others?"

He nods. "Word is three women are getting it. You and two others."

She takes this in and nods again. "That's better. I don't want to . . ." But her thoughts trail off and leave her words hanging.

"This is a big deal, Rainy. This will mean something."

She nods, yes, yes it is a big deal, she understands that.

"They'll probably ship you home, have you do interviews and sell war bonds for the duration, and—"

"No." It comes out fast, automatic, uncensored.

"No? What do you mean no, you can't refuse a Silver Star!"

"I'm not shipping out," she says. "I'm not going home."

Now Herkemeier takes a seat, pulling a chair close to her so their knees almost touch. "Rainy, you've been through hell. You've done enough, more than enough.

My God, a Silver Star is barely adequate to—"

He stops when he sees that she is shaking her head, side to side.

"I'm not quitting," Rainy says. "I'm not quitting. I didn't enlist to sell war bonds and talk to reporters."

"Rainy, listen to me, this is the sort of thing that advances the cause of women in the military, not to mention . . ."

She holds up a quieting hand. She tries to master her emotions and fails, so her voice is heavy with feeling and all too near to tears. "I am not done, Jon. I am not done." The second repetition rises in tone and volume. "You think I'm going home? You think I'm just going to go back to my old life? You think I'm going to run? Like those bastards have licked me?" Tears stream down her face, unnoticed by her, but her voice is hard, even harsh. "I'm not done, Jon. I am not done!"

"Rainy, what do you mean?"

She leans forward until her tear-streaked face is within inches of his. Her eyes are bright and feverish. She knows what she must look like, what she must sound like, but she doesn't care.

"I came to kill Nazis," she grates. "I came because I thought killing Nazis was the right thing to do, the good thing to do, but that's all over now, because it's not really about right or good, is it? I've seen what they *are*. You

haven't. All due respect, I've seen them, I've *seen* them."
Her voice rises again, edging toward hysteria. "I've
smelled the evil stink that comes off them. I've—"

Herkemeier leans back, unable to face her intensity,
not knowing what to do or say in the face of this combination of rage and tears.

"Day after day, and week after week, I watched those
bastards murder people, people whose blood drained
down and I saw it, and I heard it, and I listened to the
screams and sometimes I screamed too. I screamed and
I cried, and I told myself if somehow, by some miracle,
if I ever . . ." Sobs break up the flow of words. "I swore.
There was a woman, Jon, they raped her, night after
night. And an Italian partisan, they tore his fingernails
out and . . . him screaming and crying and those bastards
laughed." She stops herself, mastering her emotions, trying to find the old Rainy, the controlled Rainy, the calmly
determined Rainy. But when her words come they still
tumble out, forming no sentence, and making only the
rawest emotional sense. "I swore. It was a holy oath. I
don't care if . . . It was a *holy oath*. If I ever . . . I would
not stop. Never, never, never, never! I would chase them.
To hell. I would . . . I would find them . . . I would kill
them. I would kill them until there were none left to kill!"

The silence that follows seems to vibrate from the
walls. Her hands are twisted together on her lap. Her lips

are drawn back, a dog with teeth bared.

Now too quiet, almost inaudible, so Herkemeier has to lean forward, she says, "Don't let them do it, Jon. Don't let them send me home. I'm not done. If they send me home, I'll use a fake name and sign up for infantry."

Herkemeier's expression is shocked, but beneath that he is sad. He shakes his head slowly and looks at her with infinite pity. "Rainy, you're not fighting this war alone."

"Not alone," she says. "Not alone, but I am still fighting this fugging war and no one is stopping me."

Herkemeier sighs and stands up, moving heavily as if he were an older man. "Sergeant Schulterman," he says, "you will go and receive this medal."

She waits, ready to rage.

Then, with a heavy sigh, he says, "Afterward . . . well, I'm being reassigned to England myself, that's where the action is moving. Afterward, if you still feel this way— and I hope for your sake you don't, Rainy—but if you do, come see me."

Rainy feels a fierce surge of some emotion that is like joy but much darker. A rational part of her knows she may be sealing her fate. A part of her even groans inwardly at what her parents or even her brother would say, if she told them. But they were not there with her in the cell, or in the interrogation room. They were not *there*. Herkemeier was not *there*. The voices screaming in the night were there, and now they were in her, in her memory, and she knows with terrible certainty that those voices will always be with her.

I will not forget you. I will kill Nazis for you. For each of your voices shrieking in the night, for each of you whose blood I watched spilling down that wall.

As if reading her mind, Herkemeier says, "Revenge is a dangerous quest, Rainy."

He leaves, downcast and worried. But his mood doesn't concern Rainy, because she knows she has convinced him.

He'll help me. He'll help me kill Nazis.

"Hah!" she cries, exultant now. A Silver Star? That will help her get the tough assignments. It will help her get close to *them*, within range of *them*. It will make it possible, with Herkemeier's help, to hurt *them*.

Rainy cocks an eye at Pip. "You think I've gone round the bend, don't you, Pip? Well . . . Well, maybe I have. But you know what, old Pip my friend? I feel a hell of a lot better."

37

FRANGIE MARR, RAINY SCHULTERMAN, RIO RICHLIN— RINGWOULD, KENT, UK

The ceremony is to take place in Dover proper, but given that Dover has been bombed repeatedly—though not recently—plus the fact that there is scarcely a spare bedroom to be found in a town overrun with GIs, Frangie, Rainy, and Rio are housed in a pub's rented rooms, in the tiny village of Ringwould, just northeast of Dover and south of Deal.

It is the land of the famous white cliffs. The army driver who picks them up at the airfield drives along the shore for a while so they can admire the cliffs—which are indeed snowy white except where creeping foliage has added splashes of green.

Their room—just one room—has two single beds and a chair. Staring at the room, it is Frangie who is most uncomfortable. Her first thought is that she should volunteer to sleep in the chair. She is, after all, a Negro, and neither of the white girls with her is likely to want to share a bed.

But she can practically hear Harder in her ear telling her that she's acting like a second-class citizen. British hotels are not segregated—which is not to say that the English aren't racists, but their treatment of blacks tends to be condescending and insulting without quite reaching the levels of open hatred Frangie would have expected in the South, and, if Harder's right, much of the north, back home.

Rio solves the problem. "I got the floor."

"The floor?" Frangie protests. "What do you mean?"

Rio shrugs. "I've been sleeping in mud. Cold mud. A nice, clean floor is pure luxury."

"Still cold, though," Frangie says. "I can see my breath in here."

"Yeah," Rio says. "But there's a fireplace." Wood and kindling have been piled in the fireplace, and Rio drops to her knees and sets about lighting it with her Zippo. "There you go."

"Did you open the flue?" Frangie asks, as smoke begins to fill the small room.

"The what?"

Frangie reaches past her to an iron knob set in the wall that opens the flue. Smoke swirls then is sucked up the chimney.

"We're here for tonight and tomorrow night," Frangie says. "I'll take the floor tomorrow night."

Frangie and Rio are easy together, having a long acquaintance. Rainy is also slightly known to both of them from Tunisia, but this Rainy is somehow different than the determined, confident young intelligence sergeant they'd known back then. This Rainy is polite but quiet. And more than quiet—distant, as if nothing is quite real to her, as if she's sleepwalking.

They toss their bags onto the floor, and Rio excuses herself to the bathroom down the hall.

Rainy sits on the edge of one bed and belatedly says, "I could take the floor."

"We could draw lots," Frangie suggests, wishing the whole matter settled. It is beyond strange to be spending a night in a white pub with two white women. It feels transgressive and maybe a little bold. It also feels very insecure—either of these two could tell her to get out, to find somewhere else to stay, to go sleep in the park, if they chose to.

Harder has lectured her on the internalization of anti-Negro feeling. She had daydreamed through most of that, like most of his lectures, but bits and pieces of what he's said have stuck. She can't deny that she's doing just what he said: *unconsciously collaborating in our own oppression.* But at the same time, there's a question of fairness—she knows little of what Rainy has endured, but suffering is all over the Jewish girl's face. Her eyes, which Frangie recalls being alert with a questing intelligence, are still intense, but now there's something hard in them as well. Something very hard that frightens Frangie a little. In any event, Rainy Schulterman looks like she needs a decent bed and a good sleep.

As for Rio Richlin? The freckle-faced farm girl Frangie first met back in basic training is still there, somewhere beneath the leathery hide of the tough soldier she's become. And she's seen Rio since then, so the change seems less sudden. Frangie's not even put off by the fact that even now, with the three of them in fresh-pressed class-A uniforms, Rio has her curved knife strapped to her thigh.

Rio has changed, but Rainy is almost a different person.

Something happened to that girl.

Rio returns from the bathroom and grins. "It flushes," she says with great satisfaction. "Civilization."

They repair to the pub proper, finding a table in a corner. It's early for drinking or eating, so the room is empty but for a foursome of British Marines chain-smoking and nursing pints of ale and two old men playing chess.

The room is warm, both in temperature and style, with dark wood beams contrasting with whitewashed plaster walls. The bar boasts three taps and a few sparse bottles of harder stuff. Rio appoints herself to provide the first round and comes to the table carrying three pints of golden-colored ale.

"I think I'll just have tea," Frangie says.

"Tea." Rio snorts. "Come on, Marr, don't be a party pooper."

"Is this a party?" Frangie wonders aloud.

Rio raises her glass to her lips, takes a drink, smacks her lips, and says, "It is now."

Frangie relents and tastes the ale, which is cool rather than cold, and very bitter, but somehow pleasant despite that.

Rainy drains half her glass and says nothing.

"So, here we are," Rio says. "Three heroes." The tone of irony is unmistakable. She clinks her glass against both of theirs and says, "To warm rooms and cold beer."

"Yes. I mean, cheers," Frangie says.

"We should eat," Rio says. She's trying to inject some life into the glum group—Frangie awkward and skittish, Rainy just . . . in another world. "Barkeep! What's for chow?"

The barman has dealt with enough GIs to know that "chow" is food. He comes from behind the bar, a middle-aged man with a wooden leg, and stands beside their table. "We've got shepherd's pie with very little mutton, steak and kidney pie with more crust than meat, and fish and chips."

"Is the fish real fish?" Rio asks.

"That it is, miss. Jerry isn't sinking fishing boats at least, and we still get the occasional potato from the north."

"That's it then, fish and chips." Then, frowning, she adds, "Please," a word she obviously knows but which now seems strange, a relic of ancient times.

The barman stumps away, and Rio follows him with her eyes. "Probably lost that leg in the last war," she says in a low voice.

"Below the knee," Frangie says, her experienced eye taking in the bend of his knee. "That's best. I mean, if you have to lose a leg."

They sit in awkward silence for a while until both Rio and Rainy are well into their second pint and Frangie is a quarter of the way through her first. Even Rainy makes an effort to be slightly more conversational.

"So," Rainy says. "Zero eight hundred tomorrow."

Rio nods. "Yep."

"Aren't you nervous?" Frangie asks.

Rio sighs, sits back in her chair, and says, "Nah. Not about the ceremony. Just about what comes after."

"And what's that?" Frangie asks.

"You must have gotten the same talk we did," Rio says.

"You know, tour the country playing hero and getting folks to buy war bonds."

"Not the whole country," Rainy says acidly. "College towns, parts of New England, San Francisco, and Los Angeles. New York, of course. The parts of the country where women soldiers are more . . . acceptable."

Frangie shakes her head, eyes down to conceal her amazement at their lack of understanding. "No, I didn't get that offer."

"Well, they probably just haven't gotten around . . ." Rio lets it trail off as the truth begins to dawn. "Because you're a Negro?"

Frangie shrugs, wondering if there's even any point. But she likes Rio. She admires Rio's courage, and her refusal to pretend to be something other than what she is. And, too, she likes the fact that she can be the tough warrior and yet completely naive at the same time. There is still something *girlish* about Rio, notwithstanding what Frangie knows about her.

A fallen woman.

Well . . . judge not that ye be not judged.

"Well, Rio," Frangie begins, "I guess if you take all those places where maybe folks can stand the idea of women soldiers, you'd have to subtract at least half because as much as folks don't like women soldiers, they like colored women soldiers even less."

Rio surprises them all (including herself) by banging a palm down on the table and making the glasses jump. "You're wearing the damned uniform! You're fighting the same damn war!"

"Yes, but I am the wrong color."

"Wrong color," Rio snorts. "And the Krauts are the right color?"

"Dog and pony show," Rainy says. She taps out a cigarette, offers one to each of the others, and lights it. "You think they'll send you around looking like you do, Richlin? They'll slather on the makeup, they'll stuff your bra, and they'll find a way to show off your legs. They won't want some woman who looks like you do."

"Like I do?"

Rainy leans across the table on her elbows, smoke rising from her lips. "You know what you look like, Richlin? You look like mama's sweet little baby girl who kills Krauts. It's in your eyes. You know it, you've seen it in other soldiers, you know the look. Well, they are not going to want *that look*. They are not going to want scary Corporal Richlin, they're going to want sweet Rio the milkmaid."

"Nah, people aren't that stupid," Rio says. "They know—"

"They know shit," Rainy snaps. "People back home don't know a damned thing about the actual war. Anyway, the way they look at it, the whole point of fighting the war is to keep all the things they like about America. And killer milkmaids and Negroes who walk around with a Silver Star on their chest, well, that's not what they think we're fighting for."

Rio blinks. Until this moment it has never occurred to her that she represents something . . . unacceptable. Unacceptable even to many of the most open-minded people. Rainy's cynicism has the ring of truth, and now she can imagine it. Back in Gedwell Falls, in the town square, local girl Rio Richlin on a bunting-bedecked bandstand talking about how many Krauts she's killed.

People would applaud, no doubt. But then, when she'd climbed down off that bandstand and walked around town, people would give her sidelong looks, and avoid her, and talk behind her back.

"Well . . . well, damn," Rio says, deflated.

"I'll get this round," Rainy says, and gets up to go to the bar.

"She's laying it on thick," Frangie says, "but she's not wrong." Then, in a whisper, "Is she all right? There's something . . ." She shrugs and looks uncomfortable.

"That's right, you don't know," Rio says with a significant look. "They rescued her—not meaning to, you understand, some platoon that just happened to be the ones to liberate Gestapo HQ."

Frangie is shocked. "What was she doing in Gestapo HQ?"

Rio shakes her head. "You don't want that answer. I know, and I wish I didn't. I'll just say, whatever stories you've heard about those Gestapo assholes, the truth is worse."

Frangie sneaks a look at Rainy, leaning against the bar and waiting as the barman pours three beers. "The poor girl."

Rio follows the direction of Frangie's gaze and says, "Yeah. Sergeant Schulterman is not having a good war."

Frangie has not kept pace with the other two as the beer flows. She's just starting her second by the time Rio and Rainy are well into their fifth, sweating, cursing freely, and slurring angry words.

At one point Rainy, voice sullen and brutal, says, "I'm not going home. I'm not. Fug that. I'll go home when they're all dead. Every fugging Nazi. I'll go home after I've stuck a pistol into Herr Hitler's fugging mouth and pulled the fugging trigger."

Rio laughs savagely at this and nods agreement. Frangie's attention is drawn to a group of four young GIs, all privates, all in crisp, clean army uniforms with nary a stripe on their sleeves. They are all young men and obviously in tearing high spirits.

Until they spot the three women.

One of them, a gangly youngster with a mean grin, comes over, leans on their table, and says, "Ladies. You look lovely this evening. But there seems to be a Nigra stinking up your table and—"

In less than three seconds Rio has knocked his hands away, which causes him to topple forward off-balance, grasped the back of his head, and accelerated his fall, slamming his face hard onto the table surface. Blood spurts from his nose. He yells, and Rio shifts her grip to one of his ears, which she twists viciously.

"See that ribbon on her uniform, you pimple?" Rio says, turning his head to look at Frangie. "That's a goddamned Purple Heart. You come back tomorrow and there'll be a goddamned Silver Star alongside it, you snot-nosed little shit."

The other three start forward, ready to come to the aid of their companion, but they stop upon seeing a look from Rio. Frangie thinks it's about the same look that a doomed gazelle sees on the face of a lioness.

"He's just a little frisky, Corporal," one of the cleverer among them says quickly. He retrieves his bleeding friend and guides him toward the men's restroom.

"Thanks," Frangie says. "But it doesn't bother me. It's water off a duck's back."

"Really?" Rainy asks her, peering with the special intensity of the inebriated. "That doesn't bother you?"

"Maybe a little," Frangie mutters. "You get used to it."

"You shouldn't," Rio says. "You shouldn't get used to it."

"You sound like my brother," Frangie says, feeling extremely uncomfortable.

And yet, isn't she right?

Isn't Harder right too?

Rio raises her glass. "Here's to not getting used to bull-shit."

For the first time Rainy smiles. It's a wry, mocking smile, but it's her happiest expression yet. "Well, Corporal Richlin, you may just be in the wrong organization if you don't like bullshit, because as far as I can tell the US Army runs on a full tank of bullshit."

Rio reveals her slow-building but still sweet and rather amazing smile, clinks her glass against Rainy's, and says, "I do believe you are correct."

"Although," Rainy says in a more somber tone, "that doesn't apply to the GIs." She takes several quick breaths, steadying herself. "Saved my life, GIs, and I will never—" She can't go on. Rainy shakes her head, dashes away tears, and says, "I best hit the sack. Alcohol makes me weepy."

They let her go, secretly relieved to let her carry her pain and rage off to bed.

"Just let me find one of those Gestapo bastards in my sights someday," Rio says with a controlled anger and a deadly eagerness that scare Frangie. Then, switching gears entirely, Rio says, "But she's not wrong, is she? About what they'll have me doing, I mean. Giving speeches in high heels. Pity. Jenou—you met her—Jenou would probably love it."

"Jenou. She's the blonde with the . . . the *figure*?"

That gets a laugh. "The figure. I'm going to tell her you said that, she'll love it. Yeah, that's Jenou. Although . . ." Rio frowns. "I guess the truth is, she's pretty much a GI now, herself. She's changed a lot."

"And you haven't?"

They stay in the pub until closing time, finally abandoning war talk and army talk in favor of talking about mothers and fathers and siblings; about school and teachers and principals; about church socials, Fourth of July fireworks, jazz, boyfriends, real or potential, about Rio's cows and Frangie's menagerie of injured creatures.

Home, always home.

A million miles away, Frangie thinks. *And can any of us ever really go back?*

A car collects them the next morning after a night in which Frangie and Rio ended up squeezed together in one bed, with Rainy in the other and no one on the floor.

They are driven—frowzy, tired, somewhat hungover, and a little embarrassed by their soul-baring—to an

RAF airfield that's been turned over to the American Air Corps. The base is chosen because it affords ample open space and can produce a band to play various martial and patriotic tunes, one of which strikes Rio as oddly familiar as they march out onto the field to take their places.

"Did some Scots come into the pub last night?" she whispers to Frangie.

"With a bagpipe," Frangie whispers back.

"Did we sing with them?"

"Yes," Rainy interjects from behind the other two. "I was woken up by the sound of a cat being strangled, a bunch of Gaelic, and two out-of-tune sopranos singing about Scotland the Brave."

It is chilly and damp. The grass is wet beneath their polished shoes. There is a reviewing stand with a few dozen civilians, no one that any of them knew. There is a color detail holding the flags of the United States and Great Britain, as well as the flag bearing the insignia of the First US Army Group.

The band is to the side of the reviewing stand, playing their trumpets and tubas and banging their drums, none of which helps Rio's head.

And penned in together by a rope, a dozen or more men and some women, with cameras flashing and news-reel cameras turning and stubs of pencil scratching away at notepads.

They follow an officious sergeant who marches them out into position, facing the reviewing stand. And they stand there for twenty minutes at ease, which is only slightly less relaxed than being at attention—waiting, waiting, ignoring shouted questions from the reporters while the band plays on.

Did you kill many Germans?

How's it feel being a woman soldier?

Have you got boyfriends?

Finally they spot a convoy of staff cars and jeeps and a single British lorry coming straight across the grass landing strip. One of the staff cars wears a red flag with the three gold stars of a lieutenant general.

"Jesus Christ," Rio whispers through seemingly tight lips. "Is that Old George himself?"

The general is a brisk, energetic man in his late fifties, wearing his army cap with its three shiny stars at a rakish but still proper angle. His uniform is a study in elegant tailoring. He wears high, polished brown leather cavalry boots, and—if any confirmation of his identity was required—two ivory-handled revolvers.

General George S. Patton is surrounded by a gaggle of colonels, majors, captains, and lieutenants, who follow him like so many sparrows flocking around an eagle. He glares at the three women, and none of the three is in any doubt about his mood: Patton does not want to be there.

But then the young female who'd driven the British lorry walks confidently over, and to the astonishment of every single person in attendance—particularly Rio, Frangie, and Rainy—Patton executes a sincere bow as the young woman offers him her hand. He kisses her hand before stepping back, a big, slightly terrifying grin on his hard face.

Staff rush to bring a microphone forward and a nervous captain begins the proceedings by announcing the names of those in attendance. The next to last name mentioned is that of General Patton.

The final name is "Second Subaltern Elizabeth Windsor."

"Oh my God," Rainy breathes. "The princess!"

"The *what*?" Rio and Frangie echo, too surprised to be discreet.

"Elizabeth Windsor. *Princess* Elizabeth, the king's daughter!" Rainy is not easily impressed. The general has not cowed her. She's dealt with colonels and generals, but this finally cuts through her cynicism and a smile slowly appears.

They are called to attention—they're already at attention, proximity to a lieutenant general will do that, but they take this order as a sign that it's time to stop whispering.

Their names are read out one by one, followed by the

official summaries of their actions. And then, all at once, Rio is face-to-face with Patton, who gives her a sideways, thoughtful look before taking the medal from one of his aides and pinning it onto the lapel of her uniform. The lapel being more discreet under the circumstances than pinning it on her chest.

"Congratulations, Sergeant Richlin," Patton says with bare civility.

"Corporal, sir," Rio blurts as the general is moving away.

He stops, comes back a step, leans toward her, and says, "Young lady, if I say you're a sergeant, then you're a god . . ." He glances guiltily toward the princess, clears his throat, and starts over. "If I say you're a sergeant, then that's what you are."

Princess Elizabeth steps to her and extends her hand, smiling radiantly, just a teenager herself, Rio realizes.

Completely confused, Rio attempts a curtsy but has no idea how to manage it, so ends up looking like she's got an itch.

"Now, now, none of that," the princess says with a high, musical laugh. "You're Americans, and we settled all that some time ago."

Rio swallows, says nothing, bobs her head, and the moment blessedly ends as Patton and Elizabeth move on to Rainy.

"Congratulations, Sergeant Schulterman. Fine work," Patton says, and pins her medal on.

On reaching Frangie, the general seems to take a breath and hold it, as if unwilling to breathe her air. His eyes are cold and dismissive, but he says the right words of congratulation.

"Congratulations, Sergeant Marr. Good work."

The princess is more gracious, and she holds Frangie's hand in hers for a long time as she speaks about helping to keep our brave boys—and girls too—alive and healthy so they can return to their loving families.

And then they are done, marched off the field as the band plays "Garryowen."

Squeezed into the backseat of the closed car that will carry them to a reception at the enlisted men's club, Rio says, "I do not want to be a sergeant. No, I sure as anything do not."

"Pay's better," Rainy observes.

But for Rio it feels like a punishment. She had not wanted to be a corporal, and this is infinitely worse. She wonders now if she shouldn't accept the offer of stateside duty. If she goes back up to the front in Italy, or sits here waiting for the invasion, either way she'll be given men and women to train and teach and coddle. She will be Sergeant Cole. She will be Dain Sticklin.

I'll be Mackie! she thinks, recalling her first sergeant,

all the way back at the beginning. In her memory Sergeant Mackie has become an almost mythic figure. "I have no business being sergeant," Rio says.

"Neither do I," Frangie says, but grins as she adds, "but if it comes to it I'll take the extra pay."

"Nah, I can't . . . ," Rio says. "I don't want that . . . that responsibility. You two don't get it. The sergeant is the . . . the . . . ." She shrugs helplessly.

"The one who leads his people into the valley of the shadow of death," Frangie says, earning a snort from Rio.

The car runs along the base of the cliffs, white chalk rising abruptly to their left, the English Channel on their right.

"Driver?" Rainy says suddenly. "Can you pull over? I want to look."

They climb out, breath steaming in the cold. They stand side by side, looking out across the water, three young soldiers in their best uniforms, newly adorned with the Silver Star.

"France is over there about twenty miles or so," Rainy says. "In a few weeks or months a very large number of GIs are going to land on some beach over there."

They stare some more, and Rio lights a cigarette. She's landed on beaches in North Africa, in Sicily, and on the mainland of Italy. This time will be worse. This time the Germans will know the Allies are coming in earnest. This time it will be to the death.

Rainy says, "Some of those GIs will get hurt, and they'll need a medic."

Frangie nods. "Too few medics, too many hurt boys."

"Well, they'll have one with a Silver Star," Rainy says, and claps a hand on Frangie's shoulder.

"I guess they will," Frangie says with a sigh.

"But will they have sergeants?" Rainy moves to stand right in front of Rio. "When they found me, when I finally figured out that I was safe, you know what kept going through my head, Richlin?"

Rio shakes her head.

"I am not some wild-eyed patriot," Rainy says softly. "When I started out I trusted in orders. I trusted my superiors. Well, I don't trust so much anymore, but even . . . before . . . even before, I don't think anyone would ever have mistaken me as a sentimental person or an uncritical person."

That earns a wry smile from both Rio and Frangie.

"But what went through my head, again and again, as I . . ." She fights through the tightening of her throat. "As I lay there in my own piss and blood, what I thought was, thank God for the US Army." Then in a whisper, "Thank God for the US fugged-up-beyond-all-recognition Army."

"Dammit," Rio says, and wipes angrily at a tear.

"And you know what, *Sergeant* Richlin? There's a

whole bunch of people, millions of them, right over there, right across that water, who are praying for the US Army. And a bunch of green kids from Alabama and Nebraska are going to jump out of planes and go running out of boats trying to *be* that army. Half of them won't know which end of a rifle to point at the Krauts. You know what those green kids will need? You know what all those GIs and all those millions of people over there will need?"

Rio grits her teeth, willing herself not to be swayed, not to be influenced by high-flown words.

"They'll need people who know how to fight and how to keep guys from getting killed," Rainy says. "What do we call those people, Richlin? What do we call those people, Rio Richlin from Cow Paddy or Bugtussle or wherever the hell you're from?"

Rio shakes her head from side to side, negation but . . . but also acceptance. Yes, she is swayed by Rainy's words, but wasn't it always inevitable? Was she ever really going to run away and sell war bonds?

Rainy takes Rio's shoulders in her hands and says, "Honey, I hate to tell you, but they call those people sergeants."

Rio gazes out across the steel-gray water, out across the whitecaps, past the gray navy ships patrolling. She sees her father, warning her not to play hero, to keep her head down. She sees her mother, crying that she can't lose another daughter, not again.

She gazes into a future of sunshine and fresh-baked muffins and the happy children she will have with Strand. Maybe.

And then she sees Geer and Pang, Cat and Beebee. She sees Stick and Jack. And Jenou. She even sees that green fool from the pub and a million like him, ignorant, lost, blustering, clueless idiots who will probably not last five minutes once the shooting starts.

And she sees Cassel.

And Suarez.

And Magraff.

"So," Rio says at last. "Just what is the pay for sergeants?"

We did not take Monte Cassino, Gentle Reader. It took three more tries before Polish troops finally climbed the last bloody feet.

By then the bombers had come and obliterated the monastery. That was a pity, I suppose, especially since it didn't really help. But that's war, I guess. If you don't want to see your great old buildings blown to hell, don't start wars.

General Mark Clark finally got his big moment of fame, capturing Rome. Yep. American forces took Rome on June 4, 1944. The world had two days to give a damn and then, well, you know what happened on June 6, 1944.

I call it justice: the great glory hound general had his glory dimmed. Too bad he left so many thousands of good men and women dead on the way. And they're still fighting in Italy, even with the Russkies closing in on Berlin and the Americans racing to the Wolf's Lair. I don't know what history will have to say about the battles for Italy, but from where I sit it looks like a huge damned waste.

But that's the word for all war, isn't it? Waste. Villages and towns and great cities turned to rubble; civilians homeless, wandering the fields trying to find a blade of grass to eat, waiting for sons and husbands who aren't ever coming home.

In Italy we had Brits, Canadians, Aussies, Kiwis—who came damned close to taking Cassino when it was their turn—men from every end of the French or British empire, those crazy-brave Poles, and us Americans. And yeah, Eye-ties and Krauts too, though don't expect me to shed a tear for them, those fools who followed madmen and now sit hungry and cold in the destruction they unleashed.

Waste. A waste of staggering proportions.

Oh well, forget I said that. It's all glory, kids, nothing but glory. After all, Gentle Reader, they'll need you or your kids ready to fight the next war, right? We wouldn't want you to get the idea that your war will be a waste, right?

Anyway.

Yeah, anyway.

Put it all in a box, Sergeant Cole used to say. Put it all

away and lock it up and don't open that box until . . . until you're a wounded soldier sitting in a hospital with a typewriter.

See, the thing is, it scares me, all that stuff I've put away. I thought maybe writing about it would let me get a handle on it. Well, fug it all, it's not working. Too much. Just getting this far it's too much, and we haven't gotten to France yet, or Belgium or Germany.

I warned you there would be hate. I warned you. And by the time we were all done with our time in sunny, delightful Italy, we'd started to feel it. It's hard to kill a person you don't hate. A vicious cycle, hate and killing, killing and hate.

What a wonderful world.

And more to come. Because next I will tell you about France and Belgium and Germany. I will take you to a beach named for a city in Nebraska.

Omaha Beach, Gentle Reader. And the forest. And the Bulge.

And hell itself, which the Krauts called Buchenwald.

AUTHOR'S NOTE

There will be those who think my depiction of racism in the wartime American military and the country at large is overly harsh. Sadly, this is nonsense. The reality was worse than I have the opportunity to show in this necessarily limited narrative.

It is all but impossible to convey the depth and virulence of racism against African Americans and Japanese Americans that was common in that generation. I've used the word *Nigra* throughout, a term I learned when I lived in the Florida Panhandle in the sixties. It was how the better class of racist referred to black people, especially when talking to a Yankee like me, a slight masking of a more overtly vile word. I've used that masking throughout this series because I thought it necessary to avoid the book being rejected out of hand by libraries. But it weighs on me. I don't like masking. We all know what the Frangie Marrs of this world were called in 1942 and

1943 and 1944 and beyond.

It is useful though painful to remember that at times white defense workers would go on strike, stop making the sinews of war, simply to resist working alongside blacks. The Ku Klux Klan remained active even as black soldiers died fighting against the white supremacist Nazis. German prisoners of war shipped to the US were often given preferential treatment over black civilians and returning black veterans. And the best available data reveals that during the war years, twelve black men were lynched.

Japanese Americans were allowed to join all-Nisei battalions and limited to the European theater since it was feared they would switch sides and join the Japanese if they were sent to the Pacific. The all-Nisei battalions fought with awe-inspiring bravery in Italy, becoming some of the most decorated units in the war. The parents of those soldiers read their children's letters, and all too often their death notices, under bare bulbs in remote desert detention camps.

While many people were doing all they could to avoid the fight, African American and Japanese American leaders were fighting for the right to fight—fighting for the right to die for a country that despised them. I don't know of a more moving example of patriotism.

I have taken some liberties with history in service to narrative. I've moved black soldiers into earlier battles.

I've invented a mission for Rainy that, to the best of my knowledge, did not take place, though US intelligence did in fact reach out to elements of the Mafia. And of course, the central premise of women in combat did not occur in the US Forces at that time, though many brave women fought in Russia and in captive lands. American women, denied full equality, joined the WACs (Women's Army Corps) and the Navy and Coast Guard equivalents, the WAVES and the SPARS. Four hundred thousand women. They worked in support jobs, ferried planes, and worked as nurses. Four army nurses earned the Silver Star. And at least two hundred died.

Some readers may roll their eyes at my use of a young British princess by the name of Elizabeth Windsor. But the royal family refused to be evacuated from London, even during the worst of the Blitz, and young Elizabeth—now referred to as Her Majesty Queen Elizabeth II—did in fact hold the rank of second subaltern, and did in fact drive a truck. The Silver Star ceremony that ends this book is fictional, but I don't think it's too much of a stretch to believe that Second Subaltern Windsor would have been there, had the opportunity arisen.

—Michael Grant

B-17 Flying Fortress—American four-engine heavy bomber. The Germans called it "the Flying Porcupine" for its bristling guns. Their American crews called them Queen of the Skies.

Brass—The brass, also known as brass hats and various less G-rated terms, refers to officers, especially high-up officers such as majors, colonels, and generals.

C-47—The Douglas C-47 Skytrain was an amazingly versatile twin-engine plane used for carrying high-value freight, officers, paratroopers, and more.

C-47

Deuce-and-a-Half—The GMC CCKW was the work-horse truck of the US Army. The name refers to the fact that the truck could carry two and a half tons of men or supplies, despite the relatively pitiful ninety-one-horse-power engine.

DUKW (Duck)—The Duck was a modified deuce-and-a-half, designed to be a boat in the water and a truck on dry land.

DUKW—Duck

Focke-Wulf 190—Single-engine German Luftwaffe (air force) fighter. They were superior to early versions of the British Spitfire.

Focke-Wulf 190

Half-track—Half-tracks are trucks with wheels at the front and treads at the rear, enabling them to steer as easily as a wheeled vehicle, but cope with mud like a tank. The idea was American, and the Germans liked it so much they made their own version.

German half-track

Jerry can—A simple but extremely useful five-gallon can used to haul fuel or water. It was initially designed by the Germans, hence the name. An interesting feature is that it cannot be filled completely, meaning it will always have some air space and hence be able to float.

LST—Landing Ship Tank. At 347 feet long, 55 feet wide, they were shallow-draft vehicles with a hinged door at the front through which tanks could drive directly out onto the beach.

M1 Garand—Perhaps the best rifle carried by any army in World War II. General Patton called it "the greatest battle implement ever devised." Powerful, accurate, and durable.

Me 109—The Messerschmitt 109 was the most ubiquitous of German single-engine fighters.

Mess—Mess halls (or mess decks on ships); the mess was where meals were served and soldiers socialized.

NCO—Noncommissioned officer. NCOs are the sergeants whose job it is to carry out an officer's orders. NCOs were often more experienced than junior officers, and were (and still are) the backbone of the US Army.

Pinup—Pinups were risqué pictures of beautiful women, often in bathing suits. The most famous model was Betty Grable, whose "million-dollar legs" adorned many a barracks wall.

Betty Grable

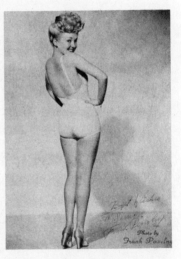

SS (and Waffen SS)—The *Schutzstaffel* were Germany's elite troops. The Waffen SS were SS troops organized into combat units. The SS were brutal, sadistic, fanatically loyal to Hitler, and as vile an organization as the human race has ever known.

Shelter half—Each was half of a two-man pup tent. The two sections would be buttoned or snapped together.

Spitfire—If it is possible for a machine to be a hero, the Supermarine Spitfire definitely qualifies. This is the British single-engine fighter that saved England.

Supermarine Spitfire

Stuka—The fearsome but slow German dive-bomber. They were often equipped with air sirens so as they dove on their targets they would make a terrifying whine.

Vichy—After the Germans overwhelmed the French defenses, they occupied the northern two-thirds of the country (Occupied France) and established a puppet government of French collaborators in the southern third. Vichy controlled French colonies abroad.

BIBLIOGRAPHY

Blackwell, Ian. *Battle for Sicily: Stepping Stone to Victory.* South Yorkshire, UK: Pen and Sword Military, 2008.

Blumenson, Martin. *Salerno to Cassino: United States Army in World War II: Mediterranean Theater of Operations, 50th Anniversary Commemorative Edition.* Center of Military History, United States Army, 1993.

Caddick-Adams, Peter. *Monte Cassino: Ten Armies in Hell.* Oxford, UK: Oxford University Press, 2012.

Cowdry, Albert E. *Fighting for Life: American Military Medicine in World War II.* New York: The Free Press, 1994.

Deane, Theresa M., and Joseph E. Schaps. *500 Days of Front Line Combat: The WWII Memoir of Ralph B. Schaps.* Lincoln, NE: iUniverse, 2003.

D'Este, Carlo. *Bitter Victory: The Battle for Sicily, 1943.* New York: Harper Perennial, 1991.

————. *Fatal Decision: Anzio and the Battle for Rome.* New York: Harper Perennial, 1991.

Follain, John. *Mussolini's Island.* London: Hodder and Stoughton, 2005.

Ford, Ken. *Cassino 1944: Breaking the Gustav Line.* Oxford, UK: Osprey Publishing, 2004.

Forty, George. *Battle for Monte Cassino.* Shepperton, UK: Ian Allan Publishing, 2004.

Hapgood, David, and David Richardson. *Monte Cassino: The Story of the Most Controversial Battle of World War II.* Cambridge, MA: Da Capo Press, 2002.

Israel, David L. *The Day the Thunderbird Cried: Untold Stories of World War II.* Medford, OR: Emek Press, 2005.

Kemp, Paul J. *The T-Class Submarine.* Annapolis, MD: Naval Institute Press, 1990.

Konstam, Angus. *Salerno 1943: The Allies Invade Southern Italy.* Oxford, UK: Osprey Publishing, 2013.

Linklater, Eric. *The Campaign in Italy.* London: Her Majesty's Stationery Office, 1977.

Mitcham, Samuel W., and Friedrich von Stauffenberg. *The Battle for Sicily: How the Allies Lost Their Chance for Total Victory.* Mechanicsburg, PA: Stackpole Books, 2007.

Murphy, Audie. *To Hell and Back.* New York: Henry Holt, 1949.

Newark, Tim. *Mafia Allies: The True Story of America's Secret Alliance with the Mob in World War II*. Minneapolis, MN: Zenith Press, 2007.

Parker, Matthew. *Monte Cassino: The Hardest-Fought Battle of World War II*. New York: Anchor Books, 2004.

Pyle, Ernie. *Brave Men*. Mattituck, NY: Aeonian Press, 1943.

Romeiser, John B. *Combat Reporter: Don Whitehead's World War II Diary and Memoirs*. Bronx, NY: Fordham University Press, 2006.

Roscoe, Theodore. *Submarine Operations in World War II*. Annapolis, MD: Naval Institute Press, 1949.

Rottman, Gordon L. *World War II Infantry Assault Tactics*. Oxford, UK: Osprey Publishing, 2008.

PURPLE HEARTS,

THE CONCLUSION TO *NEW YORK TIMES* BESTSELLING AUTHOR
MICHAEL GRANT'S EPIC ALTERNATE HISTORY SERIES.

LUPÉ CAMACHO—CAMP WORTHING (SOUTH), HAMPSHIRE, UK

"Camacho comma Gooda . . . Goo-ada . . . Gooa-loopy?"
Sergeant Fred "Bonemaker" Bonner does not speak
Spanish.

Camacho comma Guadalupé, age nineteen, cringes
and glances left and right down the line of soldiers as if
one of them can tell her whether or not to attempt to correct the sergeant.

But there are no answers in the blank faces staring forward.

"It's Guadalupé, Sergeant!" she blurts suddenly. "But
you can . . ."

She had been about say that he can call her Lupé. As

in *Loo-pay*. And then it occurred to her that old, gray-haired, fat, bent, red-nosed sergeants with many stripes on their uniform sleeves do not always want to chat about nicknames with privates.

The Bonemaker turns his weary eyes on her and says, "This here is the American army, not the *Messican* army, honey. If I say it's Gooa-loopy, it's Gooa-loopy. Now, whatever the hell your name is, get on the truck and get the hell out of here."

Guadalupé starts to go, but Bonemaker yells, "Take your paperwork. I didn't fill these forms out for nothing!"

Lupé takes the papers—there are several carbon sheets stapled together—and rushes to the truck. Or at least rushes as fast as she can with her duffel over one shoulder, her rucksack on her back with the straps cutting into her shoulders, a webbing belt festooned with canteen and ammo pouches, and her M1 Garand rifle.

She heaves her gear over the tailgate of an open deuce-and-a-half truck and struggles to get up and over the side herself until one of the half-dozen soldiers already aboard offers her a hand.

She slumps heavily onto one of the two inward-facing benches. She nods politely and is met with faces that are not so much hostile as they are preoccupied by nervousness and uncertainty. That she understands perfectly.

She is only five foot five, tall enough, she figures. She

has black hair cut very short, the sort of dark eyes that seem always to be squinting to look into the distance, a broad face that no one would describe as pretty, and dark, suntanned hands and forearms marked with lighter-toned old scars from barbed wire, branding irons, horse bites, and even a pair of tiny punctures from an irritable rattlesnake.

Guadalupé has had a mere thirteen weeks of basic training from an Arizonan sergeant who had precisely zero affection for "wetbacks," and who, as far as Lupé could tell, had no direct experience of anything war-related. Just the same, she was not a standout at basic, and to Lupé that was a victory. Lupé does not want to be here at this replacement depot, or in any other army facility, especially not in England getting ready for the invasion everyone says is finally coming.

Her only outstanding quality at basic had been her endurance. She had grown up on a ranch in southern Utah, a family-worked ranch. She started riding horses at age three, learned to accurately throw a lasso by age five, and by age twelve was doing about 90 percent of a full-grown ranch hand's work. Plus showing up for school most, if not all, of the time.

But Lupé has another talent that did not come out during training. She'd shot an eight-point mule deer buck right through the heart when she was nine at a distance of three hundred yards. She'd killed a cougar with a shot her father advised her not to take because it was near impossible.

Guadalupé Camacho could shoot.

In fact, she shot well enough to consistently fail to qualify with the M1 Garand rifle and the M1 carbine while making it look as if she were trying her best. She failed because she did not wish to go to war and shoot anyone, and she was worried that had she shown any ability she would be shipped off to the war. So on the firing range she amused herself by terrifying instructors with near-misses and general but carefully played incompetence.

It turned out not to matter. The pressure was on to move as many recruits as possible to the war in Europe, so Lupé was marked qualified with the M1 Garand, the M1 carbine, the Thompson submachine gun, and the Browning Automatic Rifle—the light machine gun known as the BAR. She had in fact never even fired the Thompson, and with the BAR she legitimately could not hit much of anything—it was nothing like a hunting rifle—but various sergeants stamped various documents and thus she was qualified.

Stamp, stamp, staple, staple, and it was off to war for Guadalupé Camacho, private, US Army.

Lupé had been drafted very much against her will. She was not a coward, nor lacking in patriotism, but she was needed at home. She had already missed the spring roundup, and if she didn't get out of the army and back to Utah she would miss the drive up to the Ogden rail-head. It was to be an old-fashioned cattle drive this year—trucks, truck tires, truck spare parts, and most of all truck fuel were hard to come by. You could buy everything on the black market, but Lupé's father simply did not do things like that. Besides, Lupé knew, he'd been pining for the days of his youth, when cowboys still occa-sionally ran cattle the old-fashioned way. So her father, looking younger than he had in twenty years, had decided to do it with horses and ropes and camping out under the stars, bringing some extra hands up from below the border—Mexican citizens not being subject to the rapa-cious needs of the US military.

Lupé felt she was missing the opportunity of a lifetime.

She looks around her now, trying not to be obvious, sizing up the others in the truck. Five men, one woman. The woman draws her eye: she is an elegant-looking white woman with blond hair and high cheekbones and an expression like a blank brick wall. Closed off. Shut up tight.

The only one who returns her gaze is a cheerful-look-ing man, or boy really, with red hair and a complexion that would have doomed him out under the pitiless sun of the prairie. He is gangly, with knees so knobby they look like softballs stuffed into his trousers. He has long, delicate fingers unmarked by scars or callouses.

Not the sort of man she's been raised around. The men she knows are Mexican or colored or Indian for the most part, compact, quiet, leathery men who can go days without speaking more than six words. Cowboys. Men whose list of personal possessions started with a well-worn saddle and ended with a sweat-stained hat. Some also owned a Bible and/or a Book of Mormon, because Guadalupé's father was a Latter-Day Saint, and he tended to hire fellow Mormons on the theory that they were less likely to get rip-roaring drunk. They were also less likely to get ideas about his young daughter.

Guadalupé's mother had died of the fever shortly after her birth. Her father, Pedro, who everyone called either Pete or Boss or (behind his back) One-Eyed Pete, was determined to raise his daughter to be a proper lady.

A proper lady who could rope, throw, and tie a two-hundred-pound calf in thirteen seconds. Not exactly rodeo time, but quick just the same. A proper lady who could cook beans and rice for twenty men and laugh along as they farted. A proper lady who could string wire, castrate a bull calf, cut a horn, or lay on a branding iron.

Now instead of putting her skills and talents to work, Lupé sits in the back of a truck beneath a threatening

British sky being eyeballed by a city boy with red hair and a happy grin.

The truck lurches off, rattling through the hectic camp, weaving through disorganized gaggles of soldiers and daredevil jeeps before heading out into the English countryside.

"Hey," the redhead says.

"Me?"

"What are you, some kind of Injun?"

Lupé blinks. "No."

"What are you then?"

"My folks come from Mexico. I come from Utah."

"Utah, huh? Well, that beats all," he says, and shakes his head. Then he leans forward and extends his hand. "Hank Hobart, from St. Paul, Minnesota. Pleased to meet you."

She's been expecting hostility—there are a lot of Texans in the army, and few of them are ready to be civil to Mexicans. So she is nonplussed by his open expression and the outstretched hand. She takes it and feels a softness she's never felt before in any hand, male or female.

"What do you do, Loopy?"

"Guadalupé," she corrects. Then, "Or Lupé."

"Loopy. That's what I said, isn't it?" He seems sincere, as though he hears no difference between his pronunciation and hers, which is more loo-*pay* than his loo-*pee*.

"Okay, Hank. I live on a cattle ranch."

His blue eyes go wide and his pale eyebrows rise to comic heights. "You're a cowgirl?"

"I guess so," she says, feeling uncomfortable since that title is generally earned by many long years of work. Where she comes from, *cowboy* means a whole lot more than *major* or *captain*.

"Guess what I do?" Hank asks. He's tall, lanky, and so pale he's practically translucent, and he owns an almost comically large nose that belongs on a statue of some noble Roman.

Lupé shakes her head. "No idea."

"I play trombone in an orchestra." He mimes moving a trombone slide.

This is so far from anything Lupé might have guessed that for a moment she can only frown and stare.

"You like jazz?" Hobart asks.

Lupé shrugs. "Like Tommy Dorsey?" It's a lucky guess. There is no radio on the ranch, and what she knows of music is restricted to cowboy tunes and church hymns. But some of her school friends have radios, and she's heard a few of the big names.

He nods. "Best trombone player around, I guess. Man, if I ever got that good . . . If ever 'I'm Getting Sentimental Over You' comes on the radio, sit down and open your ears. Man, that is one cool T-bone." He has a look on his face that Lupé associates with religious ecstasy. Then he snaps back to reality. "So, where you figure we're going?"

Lupé shrugs. This is more conversation than she's had in a long time.

"Reckon we're going to France," Hank says. He looks concerned by the idea.

Lupé nods. "Reckon so."

"Hell, yes, we're going to France," another male GI, a big slab of beef with an incongruous baby face, sandy hair, and tiny blue eyes, interjects. "We're going to finish off the Krauts. They won't know what's hit 'em." He bounces his legs a bit, with either nervousness or anticipation.

Neither Hank nor Lupé is excited at this prospect, and conversation dies out. They ride for an hour on roads choked with trucks and jeeps, ammo wagons and half-tracks, 155 Long Tom artillery pieces towed behind trucks, and even Sherman tanks. All of it, everything, is heading southeast.

At last the truck pulls into a new camp with well-ordered tents in endless rows. It looks remarkably like the last camp, and the one before that. The army, Lupé notes, owns a lot of tents.

"Last stop! Everyone off," the driver yells.

They are met by a woman corporal who appears to be in a permanent state of irritation, rather like Sergeant

Bonemaker. The corporal snatches paperwork, glances, and says, "All right, you three are going to Fifth Platoon. Report to Sergeant Sticklin." In response to their blank, sheepish stares the corporal points and says, "Go that way till you come to the company road, turn right. You know your rights from your lefts, don't you? Go right till you see a tent with a sign that says Fifth Platoon. Got it? Good. Now get lost."

The three detailed to Fifth Platoon are Lupé, Hank, and the eager fellow with the baby face who is named Rudy J. Chester. He makes a point of the "J." He's from Main Line Philadelphia, and he says that as if it's supposed to mean something special.

They find the company road, and after some questioning of busy noncoms they find the right tent. Sitting in a camp chair outside the tent are a male staff sergeant with a prominent widow's peak, pale skin, and intelligent eyes. And a woman buck sergeant with her mud-caked boots up on an empty C ration crate and a tin canteen cup of steaming coffee in her hand.

"Here they are," the staff sergeant says, at once weary and amused.

"Those are mine?" the woman buck sergeant asks. There is no attempt to disguise a critical, dubious look. "These are what I get in exchange for Cat Preeling?"

"Look at it this way, it's three for one."

"Except Cat can handle a BAR and won't wet herself the first time she hears an 88." The woman sergeant stands up, and now Lupé sees that she has a long, curved knife strapped to her thigh—definitely not army issue.

"Line up," the woman sergeant says. "No, not at attention, do I look like an officer? Is this a parade ground? I'm Sergeant Richlin. You can call me Sarge or you can call me Sergeant Richlin."

Lupé looks closely and sees that amazingly the sergeant is quite young, probably no older than she is herself. Sergeant Richlin is a bit taller than Lupé, paled by weeks living with British weather, dark hair chopped man-short, blue eyes alert and probing.

"How about I call you sweetheart?"

This from the big boy from Philadelphia, Rudy J. Chester. He's grinning, and for a moment Lupé is convinced that Sergeant Richlin will let it go. Then she sees the way Sticklin draws a sharp breath, starts to grin, looks down to hide it, shakes his head slowly side to side, and in a loud stage whisper says, "The replacements are here."

There's the sound of cots being overturned and a rush of feet. A pretty blond corporal bursts through the tent flap, blinking at the gray light as if she's just woken up, glances around, and says, "Uh-oh." And then, "Geer! Beebee! Get out here. I believe one of the replacements just back-talked Richlin."

There's a second flurry of movement, and a young man with shrewd eyes and a big galoot with an impressive forehead come piling out, faces alight with anticipation.

"What's your name?" Sergeant Richlin asks.

"Rudy J. Chester, sweetheart." He grins left, grins right, sees faces that are either appalled or giddy with expectation, and then slowly, slowly seems to guess that maybe, just maybe, he's said the wrong thing.

Rio Richlin steps up close to him, her face inches from his. He is at least four inches taller and outweighs her by better than fifty pounds. Which is why it's so surprising that in less time than it takes to blink twice, he is on the ground, facedown, with his right wrist in Richlin's grip, his arm stretched backward and twisted, and Richlin's weight on her knee pressed against his back-bent elbow.

"Oh, come on, Richlin!" the big galoot says. "Should of used the knife!"

The pretty blond shakes her head in mock disgust. "She's gone soft, Geer. It's all this high living."

Richlin lets Rudy J. Chester writhe and struggle for a few seconds before explaining, "The average human elbow can be broken with just fourteen pounds of pressure, Private Sweetheart. How many pounds of pressure would you guess I can apply against your elbow?"

Chester struggles a bit more before finally saying, "More than fourteen pounds, I guess."

"More than fourteen pounds, I guess, *Sergeant Richlin*." She gives his arm a twist that threatens to pop his shoulder out of its socket.

"More than fourteen pounds, I guess, Sergeant Richlin!"

Rio releases him. The blond corporal mimes applause. The big corporal named Geer goes back under cover. Beebee shakes his head and mutters, "I missed the first part. Can we do it over?"

Private Rudy J. Chester gets to his feet.

"Now listen to me, the three of you," Richlin says. "This is Second Squad, Fifth Platoon, Able Company, 119th Division. This is a veteran division, a veteran platoon. Everyone in this squad has been in combat. You have not. Therefore everyone in this squad outranks you. Are we clear on that?"

Three voices say, "Yes, Sergeant."

"Okay." Now Richlin allows her voice to soften. "We have a few days, at best a week, to get you ready for the real thing. The real thing will be like nothing you learned at basic. Whatever ideas you have, get them out of your head, because you know nothing."

Three heads nod. Lupé thinks, *I should have mouthed off and maybe she'd break my arm and send me home.*

At the same time, she thinks she's never before met any woman who could convincingly threaten to break a man's arm. Let alone a freckle-faced *gringa* who can't weigh more than a hundred and twenty pounds.

"This is Sergeant Sticklin, the platoon sergeant," Richlin goes on, explaining in a tone that suggests she's talking to the slow-witted. "Here's the way it goes: Franklin Delano Roosevelt gives an order to General Marshall, who gives an order to General Eisenhower, who gives an order to General O'Callaghan, who gives an order to Colonel Brace, who gives an order to Captain Passey, who gives an order to Lieutenant Horne, who gives an order to Stick—Sergeant Sticklin—and then Sergeant Sticklin and I try to figure out how to carry out that order without getting you people killed. Is that about right, Stick?"

"It is," he allows, mock-solemn.

It might be funny, but it doesn't feel that way to Lupé. There's something specific in the way she says *killed*. It's not a word to Richlin, it's a *memory*.

"Keeping you from getting killed is the main job of a sergeant. When I was a green fool of a private fresh out of basic, I had Sergeant Jedron Cole to keep me from getting killed. He kept me and Stick both from getting killed in Tunisia, and in Sicily and in Italy."

"Many times," Stick agrees.

"Now it's our job to do the same for you. Maybe you don't care about staying alive to get home again someday, but I suspect you'd prefer to stay alive, so here's how you do that: you listen to Sergeant Sticklin. You listen to me. You listen to Corporal Geer there." She crooks a thumb toward the big galoot who has already disappeared back into the tent. "Corporal Geer is my ASL, my assistant squad leader. He and I are going to train the living sh—stuffing out of you in whatever time we have in hopes that you can stay alive long enough to carry Corporal Castain's extra gear."

Still not funny, Lupé thinks. Even Rudy J. Chester looks solemn. Hank Hobart looks positively petrified.

"Now get over to Company HQ to process in," Rio says. "When you're done, grab some chow and get back here and Corporal Castain will get you settled. And about eight seconds after that, Geer is going to march you over to the rifle range and make sure you know which end to point at the Krauts."

The three recruits turn and flee, not even bothering to ask where the company HQ tent is.

But as they walk away, Lupé, who is in the rear, overhears Corporal Castain saying, "That was very good, Rio. Very Sergeant Mackie, if I may say."

And she hears a low chuckle from Dain Sticklin.

From the *New York Times* bestselling author of the Gone series

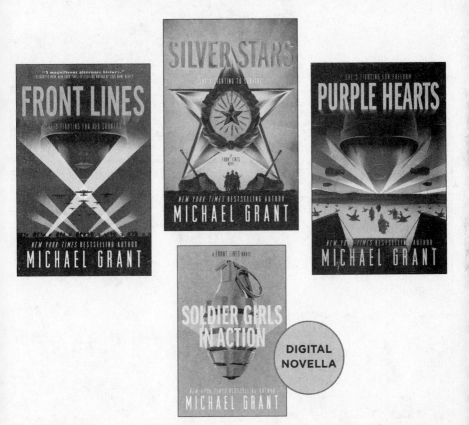

 KATHERINE TEGEN BOOKS
An Imprint of HarperCollins Publishers

www.epicreads.com

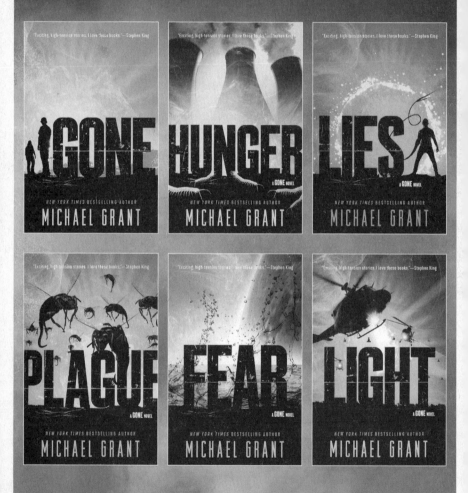

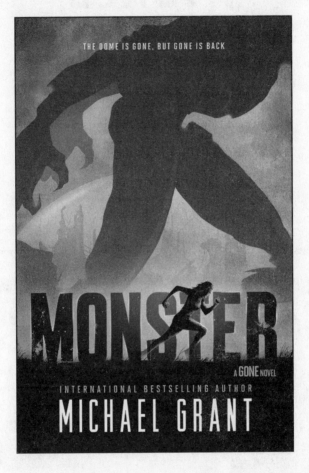